KU-434-965

Tuesday Nights in 1980

MOLLY PRENTISS

PENGUIN BOOKS

PENGUIN BOOKS

UK | USA | Canada | Ireland | Australia
India | New Zealand | South Africa

Penguin Books is part of the Penguin Random House group of companies
whose addresses can be found at global.penguinrandomhouse.com

Penguin
Random House
UK

First published in the United States of America by Scout Press,
an imprint of Simon & Schuster, Inc. 2016
First published in Great Britain by Hamish Hamilton 2016
Published in Penguin Books 2017
001

Copyright © Molly Prentiss, 2016

The moral right of the author has been asserted

Printed in Great Britain by Clays Ltd, St Ives plc

A CIP catalogue record for this book is available from the British Library

ISBN: 978–0–241–97449–0

www.greenpenguin.co.uk

MIX
Paper from
responsible sources
FSC® C018179

Penguin Random House is committed to a
sustainable future for our business, our readers
and our planet. This book is made from Forest
Stewardship Council® certified paper.

PENGUIN BOOKS

Tuesday Nights in 1980

Molly Prentiss grew up in a commune in Santa Cruz, California. She has a MFA in Creative Writing from the California College of the Arts, was a Writer in Residence at Workspace at the Lower Manhattan Cultural Council and at the Blue Mountain Center, and was chosen as an Emerging Writer Fellow by the Aspen Writers' Foundation. She is also a contributor to various literary publications. Molly Prentiss lives in Brooklyn, New York.

WITHDRAWN FROM
SANDWELL

12790203

FOR FRANCA.
AND FOR MY FAMILIES, ALL OF THEM,
YOU KNOW WHO YOU ARE.

CONTENTS

Prologue: Eating Cake Underground 1

PART ONE

    Our Year 13

    Already Famous 45

    A Girl in New York Is a Terrible Thing 77

PART TWO

    Abnormal Circumstances 107

    Painting Is Dead! 121

    No More Midnight Coca-Cola 133

PART THREE

    The Artist Leaps into the Void 147

    The Show Must Go On 163

    Lucy's Yellow 175

PART FOUR

    The Rising Sun 191

    The Missing Boy and the Lost Girl 209

    It Isn't Enough to Be Beautiful 223

PART FIVE

Fuck Sunsets 245

There's Nothing to Be Done About the Love 265

PART SIX

Minus Any God 271

Fun 283

Epilogue: One Hundred Pictures Every Night 305

Acknowledgments 319

A man's work is nothing but the slow trek to rediscover, through the detours of art, those two or three great and simple images in whose presence his heart first opened.

—ALBERT CAMUS

What is a work of art if not the gaze of another person?

—KARL OVE KNAUSGAARD

PROLOGUE

EATING CAKE UNDERGROUND

Buenos Aires, Argentina
September 1980

The meetings happen on Tuesdays, in the basement of Café Crocodile. They're at six o'clock sharp. To get there in time, Franca Engales Morales has to close up the bakery early. She has just under an hour to finish up the last cake, mop the floors, pull the grate. She's hurrying, tossing the cake's thick yellow batter with her big wooden spoon, blowing her bangs from her eyes. She swipes a finger in, licks it, decides to add poppy seeds, dumps in a generous sprinkle. Pulls her favorite Bundt pan—the red one with the scalloped edges—works a slab of butter up the sides with her fingers. Then she pours in a layer of the yellow mix, which settles like mud. A layer of brown sugar and cinnamon, and then another layer of batter. Thirty-five minutes for the cake to bake, then she'll tuck a sheet of foil around its plate. She'll step out into what's left of the winter and there will be a pang in her chest as she clicks closed the oversize lock on the grate. She'll lose customers from closing early, she knows. And she can't afford to, she knows. But what are a few customers against the rest of it? Against what will be lost if she doesn't go to the meetings at all?

What Franca does is bake cakes, and how she does it is well. She bakes quickly and efficiently, and she makes sure the cakes taste good. But here is the thing that is difficult about baking cakes: it doesn't mean much, in the grand scheme of things. Franca has grappled with this since she began working at the bakery, when she was only seventeen— the year her parents died and she and her brother had been forced to get jobs. Now she is thirty-two and she runs the place and she still can't help thinking that making cakes for people with extra money to spend on cakes is not necessarily the life that she was meant for. She can't help thinking she was meant to think just a little bit more.

Here is the thing that is difficult about thinking: this is Buenos Aires, and right now Buenos Aires does not care too much for thinking. In fact, it is as if there is a ban on thinking altogether; if you think too much you might very well never think again. You watch what you think, and you watch what you say out loud. You even watch what you wear and how you walk. When you want to think, you do it in your bed at night, lying there and watching the ceiling fan, hoping no one can hear your thoughts through the thin white curtains that separate you from the perils of the outside world.

"You're quite an idiot," is what Franca's friend Ines told her when she found out about the Tuesday meetings. "If something happens to you? Dear god I *pray* for Julian."

But Ines is the kind of friend Franca cannot let herself listen to. If Franca had listened to Ines, she never would have had Julian in the first place. "Who would want to bring a kid into *this* shit hole?" Ines had said before she knew Franca was pregnant—almost seven years ago now. Ines had already had three children, but she'd had them under Perón. "A whole different time," Ines promised. "And now? Chaos."

Yes, it had been chaotic then—Perón, during his second, tumultuous term, had just kicked the bucket and left his incompetent second wife in charge; rumors of a coup had surfaced and spread. Franca's personal life had felt similarly precarious: her brother, whom she had lived with in her parents' house since they died more than fifteen years ago, openly detested the man she had chosen to bring into the house and marry, and had finally owned up to his threat, cashing in on his American passport—just another of the things he possessed that she didn't—and abandoning her for New York City. He claimed he was leaving to pursue painting, but she knew the truth because she felt it, too: he couldn't stand to share their dead parents' house with Pascal, or even to be in the house at all; it had become three stories of sadness. He had dragged something sharp through her heart when he went; Raul's presence was like electricity, lighting up her world when it flicked on for her, darkening everything when it was shut off. It was dark when he left, and she was alone in that dark with Pascal.

She had loved Pascal, she *had*. With his straight back and his curved lip and his solemn promise that he would take care of her (for an orphan this was the *only* promise). He was a good man, and by all logical accounts he had seemed like the right choice. But it was when her brother left that she realized that Pascal's love—easy, dependable, just-fine love—was not enough. Her whole being yearned for Raul: her brother who filled the house with turpentine smell and covered the walls with his paintings; her brother who could look at her eyes and know exactly what was in her heart. She craved the closeness, the almost *too*-closeness, of *real family*, a comforting, suffocating closeness that could not be replaced. The paintings he'd left up on the walls only reminded her of his absence, and so she took them down, shoving them under beds or rolling them up to lean in corners. She began to have fantasies about packing a bag and taking Pascal's stash of cash from the pantry to buy a ticket to New York. But she didn't have a passport, and it was nearly impossible to get one these days, and the walls were lonely and closing in on her, and so she developed a new fantasy: a tiny baby, a little boy, a companion who sat and drank pear juice with her in the sun. The week after Raul left, Franca crept toward her husband in the middle of the night, and through his bleary state of half sleep, with the moon coming in, with her on top like a madwoman, Franca made herself pregnant. (That was how she thought of it, *her* making *herself* pregnant; Pascal, in true Pascal form, was rather passive in the act.)

After Julian was born, the distance between Franca and Pascal only grew wider. Franca spent her days lost in the little human she'd made, gazing into his wide, curious eyes, petting his swish of dark hair, feeding him from her breast, which felt simultaneously painful and satisfying. She was happy only when the baby was in her arms; the baby *understood* her; the baby reminded her, incredibly, of her brother. The thought of Pascal sitting in his big chair in the living room—his whiskers sticking themselves out of his face, his face sticking itself out of its collar, his hand sticking itself down his pants to itch—began to disgust Franca, and she avoided him altogether, resisted his every touch. They moved into separate rooms. When they spoke, they yelled. And then one morning in April, Franca woke up, breathed in, and understood before she got up from bed that Pascal was not in the house. That he had left her and Julian and would not come back. It was that very day that she'd gone to Café Crocodile for the first time. She'd needed to feel surrounded. She'd needed to feel smaller than something.

So no, she would not listen to Ines, who warned her with a furrowed brow that these meetings were gonna get her scooped up—the term people were using for the mysterious kidnappings that had been happening daily, all over the city, since the coup. Because the meetings remind her every time that she is not the only one who has lost something, that this is a city full of losses, a world full. And because the people at the meetings—young Lara, funny Mateo, serious Sergio, brave Wafa—are, aside from six-year-old Julian, the only family she has.

Franca pushes her way through the wind, down the six blocks to the café. Whenever she feels the familiar pang of nervousness she reminds herself that she looks harmless in her friendly blue coat, carrying the cake she's made for her friends. She remembers what Raul used to tell her: *You'd make the perfect radical, Franca. Because you look so fucking nice.* The part of her heart that belongs to her brother pulses: if only he could see her now. She quickly wonders what would have happened if he had stayed, but stops herself. Raul never responded to her letter—she could bring herself to try writing only once—and has never called the house. And so her brother will never know about these meetings, about Pascal's leaving, or about Julian, her greatest—perhaps her only—accomplishment. Her brother will never even care. Still, she knows, she's here at Café Crocodile for Raul.

Inside, Franca nods to El Jefe, the boss of the place and Lara's father. El Jefe doesn't smile with his mouth but from somewhere in his forehead. Franca remembers his forehead from all the mornings they came here when she was small, when El Jefe's hair was still black. She remembers running toward the counter with Raul, jumping on the stools and begging El Jefe for lemonades.

"They're downstairs," says El Jefe, his voice as distinguished as a butler's.

The code: knock three times, cough once. The basement door will open just a crack, which is when you must say: *Jacobo,* the password. Usually: the whole lot of them smile at her silently, mime pulling zippers over their mouths while the door is open. Usually: she sits in the orange chair closest to the door, pulls out her notes, gets started with the transcripts. But now: Something is different. Something is wrong.

No one is sitting and no one is smiling. The basement is all movement. Sergio is shoving a mess of papers into his old leather briefcase. Mateo, usually the calm one, full of jokes and immaculate impersonations of the generals, is jamming piles of books under the bed, the still-burning chunks from his cigarette falling onto the carpet, glowing orange and then dying. Lara, with her pretty, ash-colored braid, is ripping pages from the binder where they keep track of all the names—the names of the people who have gone missing, which they've been recording since the very first meeting: there are thousands now. And Wafa, who is sitting on the couch with her head in her hands, is weeping.

Mateo, panting from the weight of the bed he is lifting, says without turning toward Franca: "Remo's gone."

Franca feels a swift rush of blood through her body. She knows exactly what this means. Remo is Wafa's husband, and if they know where Remo lives, they know where Wafa lives. This means they might very well know where Wafa is right now, that Wafa is here, which means they might have followed Wafa, six men in plainclothes, driving very slowly down Calle Defensa, watching Wafa's skirt sway as she stepped inside the café. And they might still be waiting just outside, the windows of their Ford Falcons rolled down, the sunlight reflecting off their mirrored sunglasses, their cigarettes burning the minutes away, the minutes before they barge through Café Crocodile's big glass doors, hold a gun to El Jefe's head until he tells them where those fucking radicals are hiding, sparing El Jefe because the ones they want are downstairs, down the spiral staircase and through the locked basement door, which they can easily knock through with their rifles, which they will use to dig into the backs of these fucking radicals as they drag them to their low, fat, black, heavy cars.

Julian appears in Franca's mind so vividly it is as if he is in the room. Wide eyes, small hands. Too smart for a six-year-old, overly wise, since birth. Just yesterday he'd asked her in his tiny voice: *Mama, when the government gets fixed, can we visit the Brother, first thing?* Smart enough to know the country was broken, hopeful enough to think it could be fixed, astute enough to intuit his mother's secret wish: to leave for America; to find Raul. *It's not likely,* she'd said, so as not to get his hopes up. Or were they hers, these hopes?

She tries to remind herself that she's made a plan for this. Julian is at a friend's this evening, Lars's house; she has specifically set it up this way. The fact that Lars's parents, Sofie and Johan, are Danish, and are free to come and go from Argentina at their own will, is no accident.

The stack of American dollars she's stashed in Julian's backpack is no accident. But the fact that there is a plan at all is the very reason she's worried. She thinks of Sofie and Johan: blond, strict, too formal. She thinks of how scared Julian will be if she does not come to pick him up, how he will not like it if he has to spend the night in their house, which is so cold and full of angles. She suddenly longs for Pascal. If only she had been better to him. Raul was wrong about him, she knows, but she had let his opinion overshadow everything, like she always had, like she was doing still, here in this basement full of radicals: each a ticking time bomb. Look where listening to Raul has gotten her: her only son is alone in a strange house; her only husband is gone. And Raul? He's gone, too. He's the most gone of anyone.

Franca attempts to speak, to ask some question or give some answer, but finds that she cannot; her whole nervous system has gathered in her mouth. Her claustrophobia intensifies, a slow pinching of the room. When she looks up it is as if the basement has shifted slightly, as if the walls are now at a diagonal. She has the sensation she gets when she visits somewhere she has been before and the layout of things seems changed, but she can still remember the way she inhabited the space before: an unfaithful déjà vu.

Wafa lets out a low moan. "What about Simon?" she suddenly blurts, as if just remembering. Franca imagines Wafa's small son, Simon: just a year older than Julian. Suddenly everything goes wavy. The smoke from Mateo's cigarette is burning her eyes. Franca's hands slacken; the cake falls to the carpeted floor with a thud. Everyone— Sergio, Mateo, Lara, Wafa—stops what they are doing to look at her, letting a silence as dense as the cake fill the room. Their eyes are frosted over with panic. Then Sergio, suddenly possessed, does something so odd that Franca wonders if it's a hallucination. He takes the binder from Lara and rips out one of the pages, crumples it, and kneels next to Franca's fallen plate. Then he rips off the sheet of foil, stuffs the paper into a piece of the soft, still-warm cake, and shoves the slice into his mouth. Lara kneels, too, grabs a list of names, stuffs them into the cake, starts to chew. Then Mateo comes, then Wafa. They swallow the names of the people who are missing. They swallow what could get them killed.

Franca feels a sudden surge of pride in the cake. A cake that's worth something, that's pulling its weight. But this feeling leaves as swiftly as it comes, because just as Mateo is finishing his slice of cake, digging in for another, she is filled with two distinct regrets. She's left the oven at the bakery turned on. She's left her little boy with no one. And all she can do now is sit here on her knees, swallow, wait for the banging on the basement door.

PART
ONE

PORTRAIT OF MANHATTAN BY A YOUNG MAN

BODY: A tight torso, flexing with a million muscle groups. Neighborhoods connected by taxi blood. Hefty, hard shoulders of Harlem, strong pectorals of the Upper East and West Sides, the spine of Central Park and the messy lungs of Midtown. Go farther down and find the pancreatic sack, surrounded by bile, just below Union Square, and even farther are the bowels and bladders of downtown, filled with beggars, booze, little pockets of bright. And what of the parasites that have eaten up these lower guts? Who have eaten out the insides of downtown's most wary buildings? Look harder. Ventricle streets, hydrant valves; way down here is the city's throbbing heart.

EARS: If you had to describe this song, how would you describe it? The song of setting foot onto such dirty new concrete, the song of the soaring buildings, the song of looking upward, following a bird out of the thicket of metal and through the portal of blue sky. How would you describe this song, young, unknown man? You'd need eighteen musicians, surely. You'd need expectant, vibrating buildup. You'd need a genius composer, smart enough to capture what should not be allowed to go undocumented: this frequency of pure, unfettered hope.

FEET: *It feels like running away,* says an overheard voice, pumping to the rhythm of the music at a not yet familiar nightclub. *What does?* says another voice. *Manhattan,* says the first voice, and the island's name sounds like *wheeeeeee!*

LIMBS: From above, Manhattan is just a lonely arm, squirting and bending from the big body of Brooklyn. It is not until you are inside it that you see it is the vital appendage, the hand that squeezes at the rest of the world, the muscle where everything that's anything is made.

MOUTH: Come on in, the water's fine! The water's not fine but there's always wine. There's always a taxi when you need one, except when you look like you need one. There's a shitload of everything for sale. HOT DOG, HOT DOG, COCA-COLA, PRETZEL. People are dancing in Tompkins Square Park. Watch their mouths turn into O's and their bodies turn into S's. Come on in, the water's fine! This is what the bouncer at Max's says, but only when you're on the list. If you're not on the list, go take a piss. The guys in the band wear skinny ties and combat boots. There's an art project on the sidewalk, on the fire escape, in the back bathroom. Somebody's crawling through a gallery on his hands and knees, moaning. This is a project. Somebody's talking shit about Schnabel. This is a project. Somebody's mouthing the words to that song everybody's listening to: *You're just a poor girl in a rich man's house, ooh, ooh, ooh, ooh, ooh!* This, too, is a project. *Come on in,* mouths the bouncer's sour mouth. Someone's making a scene tonight, and you're about to be a part of it.

FACE: No one recognizes you here. Immediately, you want them to.

OUR YEAR

Winona George's apartment was exotic in a way that only a New Yorker would understand. A downtown New Yorker. In 1979. This is what James Bennett professed to his wife, in a spousal whisper, as they embarked on a night within the apartment's confines: Winona George's annual New Year's Eve party, their first time in attendance. Was it an old schoolhouse? Marge wanted to know. A *convent*, James said. The sleeping floor of a city convent that retained none of its convently attributes, namely humbleness, sparseness, or quiet. Winona had, in the way of so many wealthy downtowners, transformed the nontraditional space completely, both blasting it with bohemianism (rugs from Fez, lanterns, shells full of candle wax), and cutting it with classic luxury (there was a chandelier in every room). It was something old made new, made old again, which then made it new again. The effect was charming when it was not confusing.

James and Marge had gotten there quite late, and there was only an hour or so before it became 1980. It was the sort of party they usually avoided, Marge because she didn't think they *belonged*—due to such factors as gross household income and gross (as in the other kind of gross) household wardrobe options. (James's white suit, Marge had not failed to remind him before they left, still had that black stain on the back, from when he had accidentally sat on a spot of Lawrence Weiner's paint while watching him stencil onto a white wall: LEARN TO READ ART.) James agreed, but for other reasons, the primary being inevitable overstimulation. It would have been overstimulating for anyone, James guessed, as places with excessive wealth and excessive art and excessive alcohol usually were, but it was *especially* overstimulating for James, whose mind flashed with nearly psychotic colors and sounds immediately upon entering.

First and foremost there was the purple, which was the color of money—not one-dollar bills and loose-change money, but *big* money, and the people who had it. Mansions were purple, and expensive cars, and the towers made of glass that reflected the sun off the Hudson. Certain haircuts were purple, and certain names. Yvonne. Chip. Anything preceding Kennedy. Winona George herself was in the lavender family; her personal art collection included a Gaudí spire that had mysteriously been procured from the actual Sagrada Familia, and not one but *two* de Koonings.

James could sense Winona's presence almost immediately; he saw her at practically every art opening he went to, knew her color and smell by heart, though he'd rarely had to deal with her face-to-face; she always seemed so busy. Now she flew around the mahogany room like a loon in her black silk dress, coating everything and everyone with flirtatious art babble and lilac laughter. The babble itself— overwrought with intellectual tropes, heavy with important names, dripping with references that only a crowd like this one would understand (*Fluxus, metarealism, installation*)—affected James in a bodily way, with the physical feeling that he was being sprayed in the face with a garden hose. The paintings and sculptures that filled Winona's house, each with its own intense flavor or smell, flew at him from all directions; a comforting but powerful red color was being emitted by his wife; and then there was the matter of the grating chorus of violins: teeth pulling hors d'oeuvres from tiny toothpicks.

It was indeed overwhelming, but tonight James was choosing to indulge in it. Today he had received dual pieces of good news: that he had been invited to give an important lecture—at his alma mater, Columbia, on the importance of metaphor in art writing—and that, tucked under his wife's burgundy dress and stretched skin like a ripening fruit, there was a real, live human with a real, beating heart. Both of these things—recognition from the institution that had given shape to his life, along with the confirmation via a sixteen-week sonogram that he was really and truly about to give shape to *another* life—were causes to celebrate. They were finally past that precarious point of not being able to tell anyone about the baby, so why not? Why not go tell the world, and celebrate with them? There was no way to know then that it would be the last celebrating they did for a very long time, that those hours, suspended like a sack of happiness just before that happiness would dissolve, would mark that night with an *X* for years afterward: the night just before the morning when everything would change.

But for now, in Winona George's Moroccan-rugged and morosely lit convent living room, James and Marge were happy. And when Winona herself approached them, instead of recoiling as he might have on another, less buoyant evening, James was armed with confidence and charisma.

"Meet my wife!" he shouted proudly to Winona, a little too loudly he knew, for he always had trouble gauging the appropriate decimal at which to speak at parties. "And our kid!" He said while stroking Marge's barely noticeable stomach through her dress. "Meet our kid! We're just telling people."

"Oh how *lovely*," said Winona, with pursed purple lips. She had the kind of hair that was popular that year, a curtain revealing only the first act of her face: a queenly nose, confusingly colored eyes (were they *violet*?), cheekbones for days. "And how far along are you?"

"Sixteen weeks today," Marge said. And James loved the way she said it—already living with a new mother's understanding of time, where weeks were the only measurement of time that counted—with red beams coming out of her eyes like pretty lasers.

"Well congratulations to you two," Winona said. "You're very lucky, and your child will be, too! From what I can tell—and I *am* the littlest bit clairvoyant, you know—you're going to make wonderful parents. And do we think we'll get an artist?"

"I won't wish it on him," Marge said with a laugh. "Well, him or her."

Winona laughed falsely and touched Marge's shoulder. "Oh!" she exclaimed. "I almost forgot. The tradition is that I tell you the scoop on whatever artwork you're standing in front of, and then that's your painting for the year. Well not *your* painting—I'm not going to *give* it to you!—but sort of like your *spirit* painting, do you know what I mean? You hold it with you through the year. You darlings have the Frank Stella. And you see, Stella did everything backward. He started abstract when no one was being abstract! And then once everyone started going abstract, he got lush and moody and majestic. So there's your token of Winona wisdom for 1980: Be backward! Go against the tide! Do things the wrong way!" She laughed like a pretty horse.

"Won't be hard for me," James said with an awkward chuckle. He thought of how he had gotten here or anywhere: he had only ever done anything wrong, and it was only by chance that it turned into anything right.

"Oh, you shut your mouth now!" Winona practically screamed. "Your name is on the very edge of everyone's lips! Your articles are on the very first page of the arts section! Your brain is, well, I don't know what the hell your brain is, but it sure is something. And your collection! Lord knows I've wanted to get *my* paws on that since I was covered in placenta! You're *on fire*, James. And you know it."

James and Marge laughed for Winona until she got pulled away by a woman in a very puffy white dress. "It's almost time for the count-down!" the woman squealed. Winona looked back toward James and Marge and said over her shoulder: "Get ready for the first Tuesday of the year!" And then to her puffy friend: "I've always found Tuesdays so *charming*, haven't you? I do everything on Tuesdays"—her voice trailing away—"I take my shower on Tuesdays; I have my shows on Tuesdays . . . how *fortuitous* that the first day of the decade will fall . . ." Her monologue was out of range now, and she ducked back under the surface of the party as if it were a lake. In the relative quiet of her wake, James found a little bracket of time to delve into his Running List of Worries.

On James's Running List of Worries: baby food, and would it smell bad?; the Claes Oldenburg in Winona's fireplace (Was it being given enough space to breathe? Because it was making his throat close up a little bit); the wrinkle, shaped like a witch's nose, on the cuff of his pant leg, despite Marge's diligent ironing; his suit itself (Was white *out*?); would his child, if she were a girl, shove a man against the library stacks and kiss him like Marge had done to him, and at such a young age?; would his child, if he were a boy, have a small penis?; did *he* have a small penis?; and what had Winona just said a moment ago? *You're on fire, James.* But what would happen if his fire burned out?

It was true, he knew, that his brain—a brain in which a word was transformed into a color, where an image was manufactured into a bodily sensation, where applesauce tasted like sadness and winter was the color blue—was the reason he was on any front page of anything, on anyone's lips, at any party like this one. His *synesthesia*, as they had finally diagnosed it when he was sixteen—too old for it to have not fucked up his childhood—had unlocked a key to a world of art he would never have been invited into otherwise. But the way Winona had said it gave him pause, and through his happy mood he felt the Running List of Worries gather enough speed to hop the fence onto the Existential Track, where the profoundest worries— worries that came all the way from the past—ran a relay of sorts, passing the baton through the race of James's life, landing him, of all places, *here*.

SEVEN STEPS TO SYNESTHESIA

ONE: MOTHER/ORANGE

James was born *different*. Or at least that's what they called it, the doctors and the nurses, when he came out floppy and smaller than average, on November 17, 1946, in a low-ceilinged hospital in Scranton, Pennsylvania, on a morning marked only by an ambivalent drizzle. A certain anxiety had been bred into him—he screamed more than any other baby in the maternity ward, as if he already had something to say. His parents, a shifty banker (James Senior, who slept with his eyes open) and a lazy housewife (Sandy Bennett, formerly Sandy Woods, who hailed from the South, loved piña coladas, and specialized in making her son feel as different as they said he was, and not in a good way), misunderstood him from the start. His early childhood characteristics—seriousness, tenacity, anxiety surrounding food, a squeaky yet sincere laugh—made it so everyone else did, too. He didn't talk until age four, and when he did, it was in full, existential sentences.

"How old are we when we die?" was the first question he asked his mother, who swatted at him with a peach-colored flyswatter, looked at him incredulously, and said, "Are you fucking kidding me?"

"No," James said, already computing his next question in his mind, which was, "Why was I born?"

James was shorter than average, large-eared, eager to be at the center of a play group, quick to ditch the play group to study something more interesting than other humans: a caterpillar, a melting ice cube, a book. When he was eight years old he discovered his secret powers; he caught his finger in a screen door and yelled the word *Mother*, and he distinctly smelled oranges. His mother was busy painting her toenails the same pink as her pillbox, and so he sat on the front steps of his house all afternoon, saying *Mother, Mother, Mother* and breathing in deeply through his nose in between, awaiting the flash aroma of citrus.

TWO: BEIGE/DOOM

Soon after came the realization that his secret powers—the smells he smelled, the colors he saw—were not "normal." This realization came to him not as a sudden surprise but rather as a slow, steady amassing of minor incidents that made him feel crazy: Georgie called him a dumb-ass when he answered a math equation with the word *beige*; Miss Moose, his overly optimistic third-grade teacher, made notes on the margins of his homework that said things like *Inventive! But still incorrect!*; his mother began forcing him to drink a chalky powder that she mixed into glasses of water, which the pediatrician had told her would *keep her son regular*. At the young age of ten, James sensed that he was not regular even a little bit, not even at all.

Parents and teachers saw James's condition as an oddity or a lie; he was pegged with having a "vivid imagination" or a "tendency toward exaggeration," and was twice made to see school psychologists because of something he wrote in a paper or said in class.

"Your boy says he is seeing colors," he overheard a teacher tell his parents when they picked him up one day. "And . . . today he said he felt fireworks behind his eyes."

Was it a problem with his vision? Was he seeking attention? Whatever it was, Mr. and Mrs. Bennett were not pleased about it.

"No more of this crap," his father had said on the car ride home. James just looked out the window, away from the angry gray of his father's words. He would get a spanking tonight, he knew, a series of very hard spankings, probably, but he couldn't help what he had felt that day in class. The numbers had made him feel sick—the way Miss Ryder had colored them had been all wrong. Nines were blue! Tens were dark blue! And she had assigned them pinks and reds. Miss Ryder, his father, all the booger-nosed kids in his classes—everyone, including him, knew that he was doomed.

THREE: BLUE/GRACE

High school was the beginning of his blue period. James was all acne, ears, and quadratic equations. Once he stepped through the doors of

Old Forge High, his whole scope of vision was taken up by a pale, grisly blue. The green chalkboards were blue; the hair of the other kids was blue; the grass where the cheerleaders practiced was blue. This made him incredibly depressed and difficult to relate to; the other kids, he knew, saw high school as a new and exciting rainbow. When, out of nowhere, Rachel Renolds, the generously endowed junior prom queen, singled him out in the hall to see if he wanted to join the Literary Lowlifes, the club she was starting so she could have something to put on her college applications, and James, stunned, nodded enthusiastically, the following conversation went something like this:

> Rachel: "Hahahahahahaha!"
>
> James: "What?"
>
> Rachel: "You think there's *actually* a club called the Literary Lowlifes?"
>
> James: "I don't see why there couldn't be."
>
> Rachel: "Hahahahaha! That's the *point*. You *are* a lowlife, so of *course* you'd think it's real."
>
> James: "Your hair."
>
> Rachel: "What *about* my hair?"
>
> James: "It's glaucous."
>
> Rachel: "What on *earth* are you taking about, you freak?"
>
> James: "It's a kind of blue."
>
> Rachel: "You're simply the *Worst. Nerd. In. The. School.*"

The saving grace? Grace. A girl with long, silky dark hair, who, overhearing this terrible conversation, pulled James away and hid him behind the shield of her locker door.

"Rachel's a vacuous cunt," she said, surprising James to the point of breathlessness with each of those words. *Vacuous* meant she had a brain, and *cunt* meant she had an edge, two things that James coveted immediately. Even though she was popular, Grace ate lunch with him in the glasses-and-suspenders section of the quad that day, and for the rest of the year, and they maintained the kind of coed friendship where the male's unrequited romantic interest in the female was both blatant and unimportant; all that mattered was that they were *around each other*. And because Grace's father was a college professor, and because she asked him to come along when her father let her sit in on one of his night classes (Intro to Composition at U Penn), James discovered college.

Even more than the subject matter (they were doing a lesson on visual analysis, during which the professor asked the class to "have an intellectual argument with an image"), it was the *sensation* of that class that captivated James—the burgundy, regal feeling of the room, the round globes outside the windows that lit the pathways to the dormitories, the books the students spread dutifully on the desks. Driving home that night in the backseat of Grace's father's smooth, black car, James felt a new hope.

"I loved it," he whispered to Grace in the back of the car.

"I know," she whispered back, and she kissed the tip of his nose.

There was a place for him on this earth, he knew then. A place where learning was paramount and strange viewpoints were encouraged; a place where one's worth was measured by their ideas rather than height (or ear size); a place where parents didn't putter and pout and drink until one of them hit the other one, where showers and meals were communal, where brunette women wore their hair short, where good boys were made into great men, where golden lights lit pathways to the truth, and where acceptance happened before you even arrived . . . and that place was college.

FOUR: SEX/GENIUS

In college, James discovered art and sex. His first semester at Columbia, while in line for overcooked pasta at the student cafeteria, he spotted a girl whose red hair made his bladder tingle the way Grace's green eyes had, and whose face—perhaps due to the tense wrinkle in her forehead—looked like the most intelligent face he'd ever seen. Too embarrassed to talk to her while eating soggy noodles, he waited until they finished lunch and followed her out into the quad, and then across the quad, and then into a dark lecture hall.

The room was filled with students of a different breed than he had in *his* classes, as he was a history major, and this—he found out as a vibrant slide show erupted from a projector onto the front wall of the room—was an *art* class. A *graduate* art class, he discovered from the header on the leaflet that was handed out, titled *Marc Chagall's Nostalgia*. As the angular, colorful, *nostalgic* images flashed across the back wall, James felt the same tingling in his groin he had felt in the spaghetti line; Chagall had literally given him a hard-on. The redhead, who he had stupidly chosen to sit next to, giggled when she looked over at his bulging pants when the lights came on. But then, to his great surprise, she grabbed his hand and led him back through the evening air to her dorm room, where she pulled down his pants and finished him off. It was not until after this glorious, completely novel experience that James noticed that her roommate was in attendance, listening to James's first gasp of female-induced pleasure when he finally came.

He never saw the redheaded graduate student again, but he did see Chagall, in the art classes he signed up for every semester thereafter. Eventually his counselor told him he'd have to switch majors if he wanted to keep avoiding his history requirements, so he did—to art history—and never looked back. In a course titled *Paradox: Embracing the Postmodern Paradigm* he discovered Duchamp toilets, mysterious "happenings," and art as essence rather than object. In John Cage's four minutes and thirty-three seconds of silence, played during the seminar by an animated professor with Einsteinian hair, James saw the exact same speckled light he saw when listening to classical music, and tasted, quite distinctly, black pepper, which even made him sneeze. Here it was, he thought while sitting in the bright, silent room, the collisions that happened in his own brain, bursting out before him like explosions.

He called Grace from his dorm room.

"I found out what I need to do!" he blurted, unable to contain his excitement.

"And what's that, dear James?" Grace said. She had taken on a motherly quality since they'd parted after high school, and was prone to using words like *dear* and *darling*.

"I need to make *art*," James said, his mind flying.

Grace was smiling on the other end of the phone. James could hear it.

He explained to Grace what he had discovered in Painting 2B, that Kandinsky had synesthesia, and, as he had found out in English 1A, so did Nabokov—he could see colors in letters just as James did!— and they were geniuses of metaphor and color and ideas!

"You'll be great," Grace said, and James thought: *Grace is never wrong*.

So invigorated by the possibility of being or becoming a genius, James then plunged into art like it was the blue lake of the letter *O*, hardly ever rising for air.

FIVE: BAD ART/GOOD KISS

Despite fervent passion and excessive diligence, James couldn't make good art. He couldn't seem to re-create what was happening in his mind with his hands; his paintings were muddy, his sculptures made no sense, and his teachers cocked their heads during his critiques in a way that suggested confusion as to why he was here in the first place. But James didn't need their opinions to know: the art was not inside him. He loved *looking* at art. He loved *thinking about* art. But this love didn't come out of his hands—it came out of his mind.

It was confusing, this love of thinking, and James didn't know quite what to do with it. He came from a family where thinking had been considered basically unnecessary: his father had once smacked him when he had asked a question about *The Red Badge of Courage* at the dinner table, and his mother's only conversations took place with the characters she watched on television—*Don't marry him, Marcy! Don't do it!*—and in this setting, the idea of thought for thought's sake was hard to think about. He kept epic journals, pouring his thoughts onto the small square pages, but it felt like it was disappearing into an abyss—he deeply wanted someone to understand him, to communicate what he felt and saw with *another person*. With a lot of other people, maybe. With the world, even, that screamed out to him with all its colors and feelings and pain.

It wasn't until junior year, when he scribbled a rant about a student show by a woman whose drawings he quite disliked (the pictures were as rigid as wood, he argued, but weak enough to karate chop in half), and the review was somehow found (okay, he left it in the editor's mailbox) and published in the *Columbia Daily Spectator* under the clever headline "Board-Stiff," that James discovered he could write, and write well enough to be offered a position at the school paper. And it was only after Marge Hollister, the artist whose work he had criticized so ruthlessly, approached him in the quad, shoved him up against a lonely tree, and gave him a violent kiss because he had "made her rethink *everything* about *everything*," that James realized he might have found his calling, and switched majors again, this time to journalism.

"You're an odd writer," his first journalism teacher told him. "But there's influence in oddity."

Just after they met, Marge Hollister began making an entirely new kind of art (cutting up advertisements from women's magazines and drawing on top of them), disapproved of by her professors but ringing much truer to James, and he realized his professor could be right, that perhaps he could influence the way art was thought about and developed, the making of things, with mere *words*. And when he finally fucked Marge Hollister in the stacks of the library (the third sexual encounter of his life, if you counted the time Grace had brushed over his *area* in the back of her father's car) and then fell in love with Marge Hollister harder than he had ever fallen in love with anyone before (how could he *not* have, when her red was so wonderful?!), James realized his life was not on paper what it had been in his mind, and that it would never be. He thought of Flaubert's depressing yet relevant quote: "One becomes a critic when one cannot be an artist, just as a man becomes a stool pigeon when he cannot be a soldier." Perhaps he *was* a stool pigeon. Fine! He was born to be a critic, not an artist. He was born to be with Marge Hollister, maker of odd collages and impulsive love. He was born to turn the things that he actually wanted into things he wanted only after having them, just as he was born to feel one thing when he looked at another.

SIX: WILD STRAWBERRY/LOVE

At first he had been nervous to tell Marge about his condition, scared he might ruin the whole thing, that he might never get the opportunity to do what they had done in the musty Eastern Religions section of the library again if he did. He had once been stupid enough to confess to Susie Lovett, whom he had loved from afar through high school, that she smelled like buttery popcorn, and though he tried to explain to her that she didn't *actually smell like buttery popcorn*, she just *felt* like how buttery popcorn smelled, which was a *good thing,* she refused to speak to him after that and began wearing too much of her mother's perfume, which almost, if not totally, diminished the butteriness he so coveted. But the dirty hem of Marge's long skirt and the easy way she laughed had made him think that she might be different. That she might get it. And if she didn't *get it,* she still might *like it,* when he told her that having sex with her was just like eating a wild strawberry. That she was red, juicy, full of little seeds, and that when he was finished, he could still taste her sweetness for hours.

"Having sex with you is just like eating a wild strawberry," he had confessed, as they walked across campus to the building where she had

Intro to Art History and he, a course called Introduction to Connoisseurship, in which they were currently addressing "questions of relative quality" in modern art. And, perhaps because wild strawberries were a less savory and more sensual metaphor for love than buttered popcorn had been, or maybe because she really *did* get it, Marge had embraced the strange comment with her hoarse, pretty laugh, which was just as red, juicy, and sweet as the sex had been.

"You felt like a banana," she said, with another big laugh.

This exchange had prompted James to lose his breath, gasp for it again, and then trip on a ledge of uneven sidewalk. And because she laughed off his clumsiness and kissed him when they parted for class, her redness stayed all through Connoisseurship, making him feel, for once, like a connoisseur of *women*. And when the professor, a wool-vested spaz who wore a gold wedding ring shaped like an ear (his wife's ear, he later divulged to the class at a bourbon-laced mixer), lectured on the ways to tell an original work of art from a fake, James felt red and sturdy himself, knowing he had found an original, that his Marge possessed all the qualities of the real thing, and that what he was experiencing was the authentic and persistent blooming of *real love*.

That first summer, James and Marge did that thing that new lovers did: sequestered themselves from society in order to revel in each other's eyeballs, earlobes, lower regions, arm hairs, armpit smells, toes, kneecaps, and lips. Because neither of them had any income to speak of and both their leases were up, they moved into a tiny studio apartment that cost practically nothing—way, way uptown—with a sink that was also a bathtub. They had more sex than James had dreamed was possible. They talked for hours every night, sipping beer or puffing on a joint Marge had rolled or sometimes just reading side by side, then repeating whatever they had read to the other person, so they would both know the very same things.

He often explained to Marge the sensations he felt or the colors he saw at any given moment.

"You know Gordon? From Philosophy 2? Just looking at him makes me taste sweat."

"Sweat?" Marge said, laughing. "Like, human sweat?"

"Human sweat," James said.

"And how, my love, might you know what human sweat tastes like?"

"Because I taste it whenever I look at Professor Gordon."

Marge cackled. "You're officially nuts," she said. "Now tell me another one."

James went on to tell her how their apartment, being inside of it with her, felt like a slippery oyster in his throat, and how Marge's friend Delilah, with whom they ate lentils once a week at the communal brownstone she lived in on the other side of campus, put him in the mind of the word *fawn*. Whether she understood or not, Marge listened easily and with interest, saying always: *Another one. Tell me more.*

Marge, in turn, told James winding tales about the all-girls boarding school she had gone to up in Connecticut, where she was always getting into trouble. She waxed poetic about the cigarettes she had sneaked, the adult books she had bought from the back room of the local bookstore and circulated around the dorms, the time they snuck out to the all-boys school five miles away and got caught on their way back, close to 4:00 A.M. As her punishment, she was made to recite Shakespeare for three hours without stopping, but when she was finished with her three hours she had kept going, just to spite the teachers. "Much ado about nothing," she had said lightly when she finally gave it up, and had sauntered back to her dormitory, unscathed.

The dichotomy between her spirit of rebellion and deep-seated bourgeois traditionalism was perhaps what made James interested in Marge so totally, if only because his own nurture-versus-nature conflict had been so much the opposite. Marge came from the kind of family who played tennis and stuck signs on their lawn for whichever Republican candidate was up for election, but she had managed to

divorce herself from their more terrible philosophies during boarding
school and had become liberal in all the senses, taking up her father's
passion for the arts but certainly not his politics; her mother's affin-
ity for bed skirts but not for bras (in those days, Marge often went
sans lingerie). James, who had been raised on stroganoff and soup that
somehow came from a box, was endeared and intrigued by the subtle
ways in which Marge's Connecticut childhood blurted out of her at certain moments: when a game was on, she cheered louder than anyone;
or at the grocery store, where she wouldn't buy certain, tackier brands,
and favored rich, French foods—salade Niçoise, coq au vin—that one
might find on the menu at a country club.

"People who won't use butter depress me," she'd say. Or: "I don't
want to *think* about pâté, but I want to *eat* pâté, constantly."

She had a boarding school diligence; she often studied until four or
five in the morning, but then later he'd go with her to a party on campus
where she'd lay back in a whicker chair, puff on a marijuana cigarette,
and say, *James, this is how it should be. Just like this, and always*.

Back then, neither of them had any problem with being poor. They
lived on fried eggs, cans of baked beans, and, because they thought it
romantic to gorge on the thing that symbolized their new love, wild
strawberries. They'd walk a mile to the water, where they'd fill baskets from a bush that only they knew about, tucked between the river
and the Cross Bronx Expressway. The time of day was light orange,
the air was diesel and geranium, and she was red, always red, beside
him. Her hair, that first summer, was in a braid so long it hit the small
of her back when she walked.

On those walks, for the first time in his life, James felt real acceptance. His whole life he had been waiting for it, this perfect, cadmium-
color feeling of affirmation. After a lifetime of being misunderstood,
here he finally was, at the forefront of someone's world. Marge's eyes
spoke of infinity. She was plain and brunette. She was red and sturdy.

He'd give her a pink rose, a Popsicle, he'd draw her a picture and leave it on the kitchen table. When you spelled her name out, the colors were *M* (fuchsia), *A* (pure red), *R* (orange), *G* (forest green) and *E* (the brightest yellow). When they said good night, it did not mean good-bye. When he woke up next to her, said her name, he brightened.

"Why on earth would you pick me?" James often asked her as they lay in bed. "Out of all the men in the world?"

"Because you're a weirdo," she'd always say, putting her finger onto his chin or lip. "And I love a good weirdo."

The summer turned to fall and the strawberries stopped; they settled for a fruit man across the street who wore gloves and sold only small, easy-to-peel tangerines. They had just a year of school left, and each of them already knew it would not be enough; they wanted to stay in their bubble of art and learning and each other for as long as possible. And plus, neither of them knew what they might possibly do afterward; reality seemed surreal and daunting, something they'd stave off until they absolutely had to succumb to it.

"Maybe just a little longer?" Marge would say.

"What are a few more loans?" James agreed.

So together they applied for graduate programs—Marge in fine arts and James in critical and curatorial studies—and together they were accepted. Marge began making beautiful, odd drawings using a mixture of tree clippings and magazine clippings; she called them her Natural Selection series. James became enamored with a course on exiled artists from the late 1700s, specifically with the art of Francisco de Goya. James immediately associated Goya with Picasso's blue paintings—not for their content but for the color that was at their core, and for their sound, which was in both cases a bold, steady drum. His paper comparing the two painters, which only Marge could have convinced him (with a series of kisses that went from his neck to his pelvis) was valid and perfect and ready to submit, was published in the relatively-new-yet-already-important magazine *Art Forum*, an un-expected achievement that got James a whopping twenty-five dollars and a flash of orange confidence so strong that it made him want to do something outrageous.

SEVEN: THE VILLAGE/VOICE

If not quite outrageous, the proposal was at least spontaneous. James hadn't remotely thought it through. It had only occurred to him in that very moment in the middle of the street on that very warm night in the summer of 1970, on their way home from a college bar where he had uncharacteristically taken shots of tequila with some artist friends of Marge's, that Marge might have any interest in marrying him. Or that he might have any interest in marrying her, for that matter—the whole thing seemed generally archaic and conservative, and on an intellectual level, not for them. But what was intellectual about loving someone? And here was this woman, red and enormously beautiful, walking beside him with all her rosy flesh and interesting thoughts and brain he wanted to live inside, and here he was, so much sillier than her, probably undeserving, walking like a goofball, and yet she loved him, she wanted him, and he was a little drunk, and the moon was out. And there was no other way than this, nothing quite as big as this, to show her how completely he loved her, how *gardenia* this night felt, how *wild strawberry* he wanted to make her feel. There was nothing else that seemed so ultimate and right in this very moment. And so he kneeled down in front of her, into a pool of lamplight.

"What are you doing, James?" Marge said with a nervous laugh.

James wavered. He felt drunk on his happiness and the tequila, dizzy from both, and his vision was a hive of swarming red. Suddenly he couldn't imagine what he would say; his heart cinched and stopped.

"James?"

"Marge!" he managed.

"Jammmeess . . ." she said.

"I have something I want to ask you!" he practically yelled. His knee was getting wet from the damp concrete. He might throw up.

"Yes?" she said.

"I was wondering if you'd . . ." Back-of-throat dryness. Back-of-head dizziness. *Be normal. Ask her to marry you like a normal person.*

"Yes, James?"

"Be like this forever," he huffed, thinking the worst was over. He got off his knee and hugged her, falling into her a little.

"You're drunk," she said.

"On your color!" he said, putting his hand on her face. "I'm drunk on your color because you are the color of pink wine!"

She held him up with her firm shoulder. "You know when I worked at Canary's they'd have us mix the red and the white together if someone ordered blush?" she said.

"Marry me," James said quietly.

Marge's cheeks sunk.

They searched each other's faces under the lights of the buildings and the shade of the trees and the lights of the stars and the shade of the night.

James grabbed Marge's face with both hands.

"Come on," he said, desperate now.

Marge let a smile enter her shocked, wide face.

"Marry me!" James yelled, shaking her shoulders. "Come on!"

Marge's eyes welled with tears and she let out another huge throaty laugh. "Are you . . . are you kidding?" she said.

"Do you see me laughing?" he said.

Marge laughed more, and started to cry, too. "You are laughing, James."

"That's because it's funny! I'm asking you to marry me! Me! Asking you! To marry me! It's absurd! I'm absurd! I'm absurd and you're wonderful! And here I am asking you—"

"Yes," she interrupted, kissing him with her salty mouth. "I say yes, you weirdo."

. . . .

This yes was a promise. A midnight promise. A middle-of-the-road-at-midnight promise. Another of James's wild sensations, crashing around the New York night, landing in his brain like a wonderful dream. But it was also a different kind of promise. A promise that, because the world had agreed collectively to formally acknowledge such promises, was to society. It was a promise to adulthood, a promise that James was a man, a promise that he would become the man he thought of when he thought of a *husband*: someone capable, reliable, strong-willed, good. Yes, they were young. Yes, James was inexperienced when it came to what he and Marge kept referring to as "real life"—life outside of an academic setting, where more counted than pages written per night or the grade you got on your term paper. Yes, there would be tough times, big fights, months where they didn't have enough money, doubts and fears. But all of this was eclipsed by the *symbolic* yes: things were going to be different when they were married. When they put those rings on each other, they were going to grow up.

After the wedding—an expensive affair hosted by Marge's family in Connecticut—they moved from their tiny Columbia apartment into a little wooden house in the Village. Marge got a job as an art director at an advertising agency called—absurdly, James thought—*Agency*, having applied solely based on the fact that the job had *art* in its title. She seamlessly fell into a nine-to-five routine, slicking her hair back in new ways, coming home with beautiful groceries, talking about her coworkers with equal parts resentment and enjoyment. James, though, had had a rockier transition into reality. If you didn't count writing articles for the *Spectator*, which hadn't paid, James had never in his life held a job, and by certain definitions was practically unemployable. The jobs he did land that first year were of the odd sort—James was a movie-ticket ripper and a lightbulb screwer-inner and a travel agent's assistant and a typist for a writer of astrology books. None of it worked out, and whether it was because of James's odd mannerisms (wandering mind, poor sense of time and responsibility, constant references to things other people did not know or could not see) or his own boredom (typing did not hold his attention), he could not say. He understood that he was intelligent, but it was an odd sort of intelligence that others could not quite see, and he could not seem to figure out how that translated to a job, a real job in the real world.

But simultaneously, he was discovering a whole new world, the world of downtown New York, which had only one requirement for acceptance: *interest*. And James had that in spades. Immediately upon moving to the Village, by sheer proximity to so much art—its makers and its dealers and its lovers—James's mind erupted with a cacophony of ideas, colors, sensations, and images. He could hardly control himself: he wanted to taste the art, to feel it, to hold it, to *have it*. The right sculpture could still give him a hard-on (occasionally trips to the Met got embarrassing) and he continued to discover colors that were actually *new*, that he had *never seen before*.

"It was like a bruised peach," he'd try to explain to Marge, whose infatuation with his mental metaphors was waning very slightly, a fact that he did not care to admit to himself. "But if you mixed some honey in."

He stalked galleries in the daytime when no one else was there, standing for long stretches in front of pieces that made him hear beautiful music. He took photographs of the pieces and made them into slides that he could flip through in his study at night, keeping them in big brown leather binders, organized in an associative language that only James could understand. (LIGHT, read the spine of one binder. LIGHT BLUE, read another.) And though he was not big on crowds or schmoozing or hand shaking—in fact he was awkward and claustrophobic, often saying the exact wrong thing to the exact wrong person—he went to an opening almost every night; he simply could not get enough of what they opened for him.

Every kind of everything was going on downtown in those years, and he'd see any of it, whether it was at the pristine Midtown museums or the shitty new spaces in SoHo. Cindy Sherman's slick, sick realism; Robert Barry's conceptual, whimsical way with words; Jenny Holzer's very true Truisms ("A SENSE OF TIMING IS THE MARK OF GENIUS"; "AT TIMES YOUR UNCONSCIOUS IS TRUER THAN YOUR CONSCIOUS MIND"; "A LOT OF PROFESSIONALS ARE CRACKPOTS"), which were not displayed in a gallery but around the city on white broadsheets, exposing the city to its injustices and realities, to its face.

James loved it all: art as object and art as action, stiff irony and loving expressionism, nonsensical tape recordings and super-self-conscious poetry performances; he loved the appropriators and the activists and everyone in between. Still, though, the largest part of his heart belonged to the painters. Paintings, though the stodgiest and definitely the flattest form, always gave James the most pleasure. He could do cerebral for only so long before he gravitated back toward the paintings, in whose faces he could see the most real passion. It seemed honest in a way that no other form, not even photography, did. It was closest, James thought, to his own practice: an individual's perception of the universe, a map of a mind. When James read about a painting show in the *Times*, he often got to the gallery before the doors opened, stayed until they closed. For the hours in between he let the two-dimensional works turn on the many dimensions of his brain.

When he looked at art or wrote about it, it was as if James's brain were on fire: suddenly the entire universe seemed available and clear. He saw giant perspectives and tiny details. He felt gushes of wind and crawling ants, tasted burnt sugar and gazed at skies' worth of stars. He forgot about all the parts of life that were not worthy of his thoughts: dirty laundry and dirty bathrooms, small favors for Marge and small talk with colleagues, phone calls to his mother and phone bills due last month. Everything disappeared except what mattered: the potent, powerful stuff of life, the heart explosions, the color, the *truth*.

In his notebook, he jotted down the sensations he felt while looking at the work, no matter how nonsensical they might seem—*Louise Fishman=strong smell of shampoo; Bill Rice=nocturnal mood, headache.* When he got back to the house, with Marge already asleep, he would view the slides and type down his notes on his typewriter—version after version until it made some sort of sense as an art review. Every Friday he would seal one of the pieces into a manila envelope and walk it over to the New York Times building, where he dropped it in the arts editor's mailbox. Upon releasing the envelope he always felt the same combination of convictions: that the editor would never read it and it would never see the light of day, and that it was bound to be read by someone, and that when that someone did read it, it would captivate them so completely they could not deny its publication.

"I honestly can't understand if what I'm writing is good or total shit," he told Marge. "Which is ironic, isn't it, considering that I'm trying to forge a career out of understanding what is good and what is total shit."

"It's good," Marge assured him over and over, though in her voice there was a tinge of *How long can this go on for?* "The best things can take the longest to discover, right? Don't they?"

"Let's just hope this isn't a Van Gogh situation," James said. "Let's just hope I'm not dead before I can afford to be alive."

Finally, after five years of odd jobs and rejections, James got a call from Seth, the *New York Times* arts editor's squeaky assistant, who told him his article on the painter Mary Heilmann—whose Crayola-colored works made "this reviewer's heart feel like it was drinking water"—was going to print tomorrow.

"Without any edits?"

"There were no edits necessary, Mr. Bennett," squeaked the assistant. "The editor said it was fresh."

James had hung up the phone and jumped in the air. Then he sat on the floor. Then he leaped up again and ran outside, looked up and down the street, realized he had gone out there for no reason at all and turned back around to go inside, and sat down at his desk to smile until he couldn't anymore because his face hurt.

He and Marge celebrated by going out to dinner at a medium-expensive place that had been recommended by "everyone"—meaning everyone at the Agency office, the sort of crowd that knew what frisée was, how to pronounce *haricot vert*—where Marge paid. Then they had sex twice.

"You proud of me?" he said as they lay in bed.

"Extremely," she said, nuzzling her face into his chest.

And that was enough for him. He could have died that day and had no regrets, with Marge's *extremely* lingering in his ear.

After the article ran, James received a check in the mail and alongside it a medium-size package. The check was for a thousand dollars and the package was a Mary Heilmann painting, one of the pink-and-black ones, with a note from Heilmann herself, reading, *So your heart will never be thirsty. XO, MH.* James spent the thousand immediately, on a drawing by the artist and poet Joe Brainard that he had seen at a makeshift gallery in the East Village the week before—a sketch of a box of cigarettes, which made James's eyes haze over with a moony, adventurous blue. He hung the two pieces next to each other in his study—small emblems of his small success, reminding him daily that there was beauty in the world, and that he could feel that beauty in his body, and that he could put that beauty onto a page for others to experience. This was how he was meant to engage with society, he thought: from the little ship of his study, through the magnificent portal of the *New York* fucking *Times*.

Over the next years, as the seventies wore on and James and Marge pushed into their late twenties and then, as if it happened overnight, their *thirties*, people began to notice the articles, and respond to them. They called it a sixth sense—James's surreal ability to pick out the exact thing that made a work of art good or not, and in extrapolation the ability to hone in on that goodness from far away: years in advance or across a crowded room. James would look at a sculpture and find the exact arc where it became interesting (the arc that felt like an airport and blinked a whitish gray), the precise point on the map of a painting to stick his figurative pin, the mark that made the whole thing worth making at all. He wrote everything he saw behind his eyes when he looked at art—*Brice Marden preoccupies me like a shoe that has stepped in gum*, or *Schnabel, not to be funny, has too many plates in the air*—and people told him it was genius, that he was changing the very nature of art critique, that they wanted to take him out for a drink sometime, pick his brain, get his opinion on the new Sol LeWitt.

All of this led to a sort of trust: the readers trusted him to tell them whether they should spend their Saturday at a show; the artists trusted him to write about them with intelligence and fairness—even if the reviews weren't always positive, they always reflected something important and intrinsic to the work.

"I appreciate you, you know that?" a painter named Audrey Flack told James at a gallery after-party. James, the week before, had written that Audrey's hyperrealistic painting of a handful of wrapped candy was *as stale as those sorts of candies get: the kinds that have been sitting too long in a grandmother's foyer.* James had been avoiding Audrey, but here she was, being nice.

"You thought about it," she said. "You thought about it, and you got it exactly right. The feminism is embodied in that precise staleness you wrote about—that *stuffy, indoor feeling*—and you *got it.*"

This conversation led to a studio visit, where James ended up doing a complete 180 on Flack's work, and leaving with one of her paintings—it depicted a shrine of sorts, incorporating Marilyn Monroe's picture, a set of ripe pears, a burning candle, and a goblet full of silvery pearls. The painting, tucked under James's arm, smelled of all of the chickens his mother had never roasted.

Slowly at first and then exponentially, James's bodies of work had started growing: both this collection of art and his writings. Like Heilmann, the artists often gifted him paintings. Any extra money he had went to buying pieces from artists he especially admired, who he felt deserved it more than he did. They were the geniuses, he always thought. He was just a genius finder.

In direct correlation to his opinion mattering, the works of art he coveted and collected began mattering more, too. Around town, James's personal collection became a topic of envy and desire. How had he procured all these works? Where did his impeccable taste come from? Who was his dealer? And why did he not sell? Dealers knocked on James's door for a quick peek; calls came in from collectors and auction houses.

"I heard you had a Ruth Kligman over there," said one scary-sounding caller. "Mind if I come over and take a look?"

"Oh, I don't sell art," James said shyly. "I'm sorry to have wasted your time."

"Damn right I wasted my time," said the voice, and the phone hung up loudly on the other end.

When it came to the collection, James operated under a strict and self-imposed ethical code, which stated that artworks were meant to provide pleasure, not income, and art was not about fame but about feeling. His modus operandi was simple: buy pieces he loved and could (at least sort of) afford. Nothing more. If they appreciated in value (and many of them had, or would), that was fine. But the not-selling part was crucial—James took to his collection as if it were a work of art itself; selling a piece could mean ruining the whole composition. He did not want to be known as a man who simply *reviewed* art or *owned* art, but as a man who *understood* it. Who *breathed* it, even.

He always felt a bit wobbly about the attention; he wasn't in this to be noticed, he was in it to be true to himself and to the artists he loved, and to fulfill his oblique yearning to leave an impression on the world. He had discovered early on that there was a smarmy nature to much of the New York art scene—the dealers who just wanted their cut; the tastemakers who wanted to shape culture into capital; the friends of the artists who followed the artists around, trying in vain to bask in their celebrity, or at least their free champagne. But there was an element of the whole thing that James secretly took pleasure in: it felt good to be noticed, to be understood. For the first time in his life, he was not the strange bird, the odd duck, the loopy man in the corner, staring at a painting until the gallery closed. Instead, inadvertently, he was becoming part of an in-crowd. *He* was one of the tastemakers. *He*, James Bennett, had actual power of influence, which he knew had to do with the very thing that used to make him *un*cool growing up: his *affliction*. What had once been his handicap was now what allowed him to communicate with art in the way he did, to see things in a way that others couldn't, to choose the right paintings for his house and to write about them in a way no one else could.

Not to mention, he saw out of the corner of his eye, the pleasure *Marge* got out of even the most moderate of his successes.

"James has a piece coming out today!" he overheard her telling her mother on the phone. This was novel, considering that for years she had avoided uttering his name to her mother, who only worried about when that son-in-law of hers was going to get a real job.

"Front page!" Marge bragged. "Keep an eye out, okay, Mom?"

Marge didn't seem to mind that she had to pick up most of the slack moneywise (art writing paid enough but never more than that, and what James earned was more than likely spent on buying more art). She believed in him, she said, and she knew doing the thing he loved would pay off eventually. In a special moment of pride (and perhaps a better understanding of personal presentation) Marge bought him a white suit at Bloomingdale's, for more formal events or openings. He began to wear it quite often, despite that looking at it in the mirror made him smell ammonia and too-strong cologne.

But occasionally, when rent was due, for example, Marge was forced to plead with him about his art habit.

"We're sort of going broke, James," she'd say. "Do you see that we are sort of going broke?"

"I know, Marge, I know. It's just, isn't it stunning?"

That particular "it" could be anything from a miniature sketch by Richard Diebenkorn that James had ordered from California, or a mammoth spray-painted piece of cardboard by a young street artist that covered much of the living room's east wall, which James had insisted on paying the kid a thousand dollars for.

"Of course it's stunning," Marge said. "But we have to live, you know? What good is art if we can't live to enjoy it?"

"But what good is life without art?" James said, bringing her in for a hug.

"I just get worried," she said, letting him kiss her head. "We're in our thirties."

"So?"

"So we're in our thirties!"

"Tell me what being in our thirties means," James said. "Considering it is almost 1980 and we live in New York City; I don't think the suburban time line need apply to us."

"James!" Marge said, hitting him playfully. "I want a teeny baby!"

"I'll give you a teeny baby," he said, but in a way that referred more to their joke and less to real life.

Marge leaned back and looked at him. "I'm being serious, James. Can you tell from my eyes?"

James put his finger on her chin and squinted.

"Let me check," he said.

. . . .

And here was their biggest real-life endeavor: Marge was now carrying four months' worth of teeny baby inside of her—the size of an avocado, according to the woman who'd administered the sonogram that morning. To Winona's party Marge had worn a burgundy dress, of the sort that hugged her shape rather than hiding it, and James, as if he were a kid again, found himself mentally aroused when he looked at her for too long. Marge's stomach was soft and low, like a pile of sloping sand. Her breasts had grown in size and confidence, seeming to dictate to the lowly citizens (her feet, her back, her butt cheeks) how to stand and how to move. Her face had widened slightly, and paled. Layers of darkness had amassed under her eyes, and the result was something . . . well, *pomegranate*. Where she had felt *strawberry* to James before—wild and small and individual—she now felt *pomegranate*: she was holding a million seeds of new, red life.

The whole pregnancy thing had felt abstract to James until just today. He had been unable to immerse himself in the pure joy of it, and had even had the private urge to *not think about it*, since when he did he only seemed to worry. He worried that he would be a bad father, or worse, that he would not feel for his son or daughter the way he should, which was totally in love and in awe. He also selfishly wondered if a baby would transform his life into something he never signed up for, that his existence would shift completely to diaper duty and stroller rolling, and that he would not have time for or the urge to write. If he were to be completely honest, though of course with Marge he was not, he might go as far to admit that he was counting down his months and days of freedom, mentally cringing as they lapsed.

But today, when the technician had showed them the grainy sonogram, James had actually cried with happiness. It was the first ultrasound that had actually revealed something that made sense to

James—a hand, a nose, a beating heart—and it had physically made his own heart ache. It was visually stunning: a white smudgy bean in the deep cone of black, like a negative of a photograph. The black cone made him hear his father's mean voice, but the white bean made him taste salt, as if he had just run a marathon and was licking his lips of his own sweat. It was attachment to nature and commitment to the future. It was *real*. The baby was *real life*. And it was a miracle. And it was precisely this intersection of reality and miracle that kept James in awe of this life: a life that was indeed built with equal parts biology and beauty.

"Should we?" Marge said now, nudging her head toward Winona's fogging glass door. Her voice was sticky and soft.

"We should," he said.

Though it was freezing out, Winona's guests were gathering outside, on the convent's balcony, which was adorned with perilous-looking wrought-iron sculptures. James could spot the artists from a mile away: there was David Salle in his Picasso-inspired striped shirt, images of bodies projected on top of and above him, just like in his paintings. There was Baldessari, big and white-haired, who did not know how to dress for the cold; James could feel the California air radiating through his T-shirt, even from behind the glass. There was Keith Haring, whose mouse-ish size did not affect the bigness of his presence; when James looked at him, he saw entire cosmos.

What would happen to them all this year? How would 1980 change them, morph them, dictate their fates? Sometimes James worried for them, the artists he so loved and admired. The world, especially the art world, was changing; he could feel it. The city was handing out promises, dangling fame in front of even the most radical artists' noses; in turn, a sharpness was being dulled. The brilliant bohemia he'd discovered when he'd moved to the Village had been ratcheted up a notch; pop had paved the way for commercialism and plastic and shine; there was a new air of possibility and a new wave of capital coming in, which gave the scene a new edge. There was the notion, now, that one could *make it*; James had watched the luckier artists get snatched from the rubble and lifted into the cloud of success. The successful left behind them a residue of opportunity: the surreal, toxic cloud of fame and fortune that both motivated and toppled the rest of them. Even the number 8 of 1980 felt glossy and airy and shiny in his mind, like an unpoppable balloon, nothing like its bony predecessor, 7. The year ahead would either ooze with brightness or deflate with emptiness, or perhaps both. Only time—specifically *midnight*—would tell.

James followed Marge to the coatroom—Winona had dedicated a whole nun's quarters to other people's coats—and grabbed his own. It only occurred to him after Marge had already wrenched her first arm in to help her with hers; he pulled it over her other shoulder. As they headed toward the door they passed a blue-walled room, and something caught James's eye. A white firework, the smell of smoke. The audible, wonderful flapping of *butterfly wings*. James got the quickest glimpse of a young man, standing in the blue room behind a large mahogany desk, a black mole jutting from his face and his eyes glossing with what looked to be tears, before Marge tugged on James's sleeve and pulled him toward the door to the balcony.

Outside, someone yelled, "Four minutes!" which was followed by a giddy buzz of chatter. A man in a ruler-wide red tie circled with a bottle of Veuve Clicquot, topping off people's skinny glasses. Marge looked up at James. She was shivering and smiling. James felt the chill of the night on his cheeks, felt Marge's soft body leaning in against his.

"Our year," Marge said.

"Our year," James echoed, but his mind was back inside. Who was that man? And how could James make his way back into Winona's convent to find out? He'd bathroom-break himself away from Marge, through the crowd, the glass doors. He'd slither up to the blue room, peek his head inside. No one would be there, but the residue would have lingered: like when you close your eyes against the glare but the shape of the sun is still there. The man would be gone, but James would find him again. He would scour the party and the city until he did. But not before he kissed his beautiful wife, just as the clock moved the world into a new decade. Not before, somewhere in the distance, a ball was dropped.

ALREADY FAMOUS

Just hours before midnight, at the squat on East Seventh Street, Raul Engales was in the corner of the Big Room, being touched on the biceps by two barely dressed women. Some people called him a ladies' man, which he didn't mind because it was true. His looks alone—warm skin, squinted umber eyes, restless eyebrows, and a swell of jet-black hair—gave women the impression that he was as sensitive as he was serious, that his passion would outweigh his pitfalls, and that he would transport them, by way of the thick, chugging train of his shorter-than-average-but-somehow-still-dominating body, to some exotic locale that they'd never even heard of. He knew this, just as he knew the power of the mole on the right side of his face, that pointless piece of black flesh that he had once hated but had come to cherish; it seemed to have some sort of planetary pull. He kept the women who gravitated toward it in his orbit only long enough to enjoy the pleasure of them; anything beyond pleasure was not worth his time. *Women are like painting,* he had been known to say if he was drunk enough. *You want to live inside them while you are doing them. Then maybe you never want to look at them again.*

It was New Year's Eve, the squat's annual blowout party. Hardly necessary to nominate it as such, Engales thought, since every night at the squat was a party, blowout or otherwise. He was here not because he especially wanted to be but because he was always here. The squat, with its seven to twelve rotating residents, had become a sort of second home for Engales. Its core inhabitants: nonmonogamous conceptual artists Toby and Regina, performance artist and chain-smoker Horatio Caldas, sculptor and throat singer and professional grower of her own hair Selma Saint Regis, Swedish twins named Mans and Hans who had immaculate bodies and a propensity for lighting things on fire, three flamboyant parrots who squawked not-your-average obsceni-ties at newcomers (*Baby's balls sack! Mongoose! Rug muncher! Failed artist!*) . . . this was who he surrounded himself with. They were a family of misfits, and he was what they referred to as an "orphan": one of the myriad artists whom they had agreed to take in, get drunk, talk about and make art with, but who didn't live on the premises. This was the case not only because he had been gifted a rent-free apartment by a friend-of-a-friend Frenchman, but also because he didn't believe in shitting where he ate. As with his women, he sought pleasure, not headache, and with any commitment to anyone else, such as living in a cement-floored, windowpane-less ex-factory with ten other people, headache was inevitable.

Now, though it was hardly nine, Engales could already feel an energetic fuss in the room: the frenetic vibrations of people trying to place themselves in proximity to the right lips before midnight, so that when the time came to enter into the future they would not have to do it alone. But lips did not concern him just now; he had his pick of two pairs, and neither was appealing. The two women, whose sentences were all spoken like questions, were not holding his atten-tion. He scanned the crowded room for something that might, and though many things were attention-*grabbing*—Selma painting her nipples with glow-in-the-dark paint, one of the Swedes lighting a clear liquid on fire in a small glass—none of it was attention-*holding*. Raul itched for something novel, something *revelatory*. It didn't have to be a woman. It was the brink of a New Year, and he longed to cross over into it a new man. A man people knew about, paid attention to. Not only a *ladies'* man, but a *people's* man. Someone who mattered. A real artist.

At the edge of the room, just near the door, he saw the top of a hedge of hair, floating into the crowd. He recognized the hair: huge and effervescent, dominating. It was Rumi Gibraltar, who he had met outside a party last summer; she had been lounging on the stoop outside the building as if it were a daybed, in a shirt that looked to have been made from lacy napkins. Rumi, the curator who had promised him she'd come to his studio to see his paintings. Rumi, who had not kept that promise. Rumi, whose lips he would put himself in proximity to sometime before midnight, if not for pleasure then for business: he needed her to get him a show.

The woman on his right reached her face up toward his, lips first. He ignored her and shed both of the women as if they were clothing, making his way toward Rumi. She was taller than him and regal. Her hair was a masterpiece.

"Well hello, Ms. No-Show," he said when her eyes found his.

"Well hello, Mr. Delaroche," she said. She was referencing the night when they had met, when Engales had professed to her that he was a painter, and she had said to him flatly, "Don't you know that painting is dead?"

When he appeared confused she had gone on: Didn't he know Delaroche? No? Well he should look him up, because painting has been dead since 1839! When Engales had looked it up, in an encyclopedia at the NYU library the following week, he had found that Paul Delaroche had declared the whole form of painting obsolete after the invention of an early form of photography.

"I found his old ass in the encyclopedia," Engales said now.

"A studious one," she said.

"His argument doesn't hold up."

"Doesn't it?"

"There are two kinds of painters. The painter who paints to decorate, and the painter who paints to paint. Photography would only make any sort of problem for the first kind of painter."

"A studious and *actually smart* one. Good combination."

"Why haven't you come to see me?"

"I am a very busy woman," she said, her eyes leveling into him, filled with what looked like lusty promise.

"I like busy women," he said.

"Me, too," she said.

"I have a good idea," Engales said impulsively.

"Artists always think they have good ideas."

"Come see my paintings now. Come to my studio."

"It's New Year's Eve," she said.

"An observant one," he said.

"We're at a party," she said.

"Don't you know that parties are dead?" he said.

Rumi smiled with one half of her mouth: her first concession.

Before she could protest, Engales grabbed her thin arm, took her out into the icy night. Rats pitched from their path as they made their way across town on East Seventh. The cops were out in packs, scanning arrogantly, braced for the worst after what had happened last year: mobs in Times Square, a few murders, even. A woman on Broadway called to a man she was separating from regretfully, "Midnight! The Eagle! Find me! You promise?" Up Broadway to Washington Place, where it crossed with Mercer, through the locked door and up the dark stairwell to the studio Engales had come to call his own.

Engales had learned of the NYU studios from a woman he'd slept with on his third day in New York, an art student with a thick pout and a set of inappropriate pigtails, whom he had met at the Laundromat That Never Sleeps. The concept of the Laundromat had eluded him, and he had fumbled with the quarters, the locks on the washers, the darks, the lights, the little packets of soap they sold in vending machines.

"Why are you so bad at laundry?" the girl had asked, while folding a shirt that looked to belong to a baby.

"Laundry is boring," Engales had replied, knowing immediately upon looking her over—lanky limbs, a miniature skirt, the long dark pigtails framing her long young face—that they would sleep together.

"Everything's boring," she had said with a tone that showed she might mean it. When you were as young as she was—probably eighteen or nineteen, he guessed, when time seemed endless and unbreakable and empty—you still had the potential to be so bored. Though he was only twenty-three himself at that point, the girl made Engales feel old. He had perhaps become old, in spirit at least, much earlier: when your parents die, so does the idea of infinite time on the planet. Instead, you are forced into becoming weirdly wise, gaining too soon the knowledge that life is both precious and perfectly meaningless, neither philosophy leaving much room for boredom.

"Not everything," he had said, pressing her up against a spinning dryer. They left their laundry in the moldy baskets meant for transporting it from washer to dryer and went upstairs to his hotel room. The walls were papered with roses and the air was musty, and from the next room, as they had the hasty sort of sex you have with people you don't respect, they could hear the occasional scream.

"So what's it like being a rich kid?" he had asked the girl after they had finished.

"What do you mean?" she had said.

"Well, you go to that fancy university, you wear these, what do you call them?" He flopped one of her pigtails with his fingers.

"Pigtails," she said quietly.

"Pigtails!" He laughed. "Jesus."

"I don't even know why my parents pay for it," she said then, with a sort of shy defiance, propping herself up on the bed and tugging the rubber bands out of her hair. "I mean they hardly teach you anything. If my parents weren't such assholes I'd just teach myself the same stuff. Just walk into NYU and teach *myself* how to draw."

Engales's eyes were distant, looking at the roses on the wall, on whose two-dimensional petals two mosquitoes were courting each other spastically. He pushed the girl away—she was attempting to fondle his earlobe—and stood up. He suddenly very much disliked this person whom he was currently lying in bed with, but could she be on to something? He had no money at all to buy any paint or supplies. He had nothing, and nothing to lose. He looked at the girl's breasts, which were large and falling down to one side, like a pair of mating walruses; he wanted to paint the walruses, give them mustaches. Could he just walk into a school full of rich kids and act like he went there? Set up shop? When the pigtailed girl went to the bathroom, he nabbed the key from her pant pocket whose brass face read STUDIO. He might as well try.

The next day he had shaved his scruffy face and stolen a backpack from a sporting goods shop on Broadway, then walked confidently past a very fat security guard who was busy studying his own stomach. After some wandering—through poorly lit corridors that smelled like aging books and empty rooms lined with green metal cabinets—he found the painting studio, unlocked and filled with sunlight. Only two harmless-looking students were working, and he staked out the prime real estate: a corner easel with the most light, which poured onto the easel from two large windows.

Engales was in awe of his discovery: this place was his idea of heaven. He had never had an easel before; he had never even painted on canvas. All of his painting back home had taken place inside of sticky notebooks or on butcher paper, tacked to the walls of his dead parents' bedroom. This place had canvas you could just *take,* on a huge roll in the corner, and big rolls of good paper, too, and cans of turpentine, and scissors and paper cutters and wooden models of human bodies and hands whose digits moved into whatever position you wanted them to. He looked to one of the students, who was quietly painting in her own corner, for confirmation that this was indeed real, or to see if she might be as excited about all of this as he was, but she was busy getting very close to her canvas and fogging her glasses with her own breath, the same breath he would smell when he took her to bed later that week. As for the Pigtail girl, he saw her only once on campus after that; she glared at him in a way that suggested she hated him for never calling her back, then twitched her mouth in a way that suggested she'd never tell his imposter's secret to a soul.

Now Engales used the Pigtail Key to let Rumi, curator extraordinaire and very rare beauty, into the studio, at close to eleven on New Year's Eve. Of course, Engales was planning on a private experience—a little tour of his work, a little taking off of clothes. But to his surprise, the lights were on and he could hear Arlene's hippie music drifting from her back corner.

"*You're* here?" he yelled back to her.

"Where the fuck else would I be?" Arlene said in the way that Arlene said everything, with unapologetic crassness. He loved Arlene's way of speaking, which he had come to know was a distinctly *New York* accent: complaining vowels, absent R's, words emerging sideways from somewhere in her bottom jaw.

"At a party? Being a normal person? It's New Year's!"

"It's a real shame that I'm not a normal person," she said, tossing her fat brush into a tin canister. "A serious fucking shame."

Engales had met Arlene on his second day in the studio, and they had become fast, if unexpected, friends. He had guessed that she was in her late forties, from the single gray streak in her red hair and the shallow lines forking out around her eyes, and he had worried that she was the boss of the studio, ready to kick him out of his newfound art mecca.

"The boss?" Arlene had yelled. "Oh fuck no! Excuse my French. Are you French? No you couldn't be French, too rough around the edges. But no, I'm not the boss. Name's Arlene. I'm a painter."

She had said this with a proud extension of her arms and a glance down to her paint-covered dress, which was shaped like a tent and emblazoned with squiggly lines and abstract fish. The dress swung out into a circle when she wheeled around to examine the canvas that Engales had been working on.

"Well I can see that," Engales had said. "But aren't you a little . . . old? I mean, to be a student here?"

"Old? Go fuck yourself," she had said, thrusting a shoulder toward him. Then, with a little lift of her nose: "I'm what they call a *visiting artist*. Which is really quite hilarious, since technically I've been *visiting* for thirteen years. They'd never kick me out. I'm like those ugly sculptures in parks that you know were important once but are now just eyesores. Anyway, they've learned to ignore me."

Engales raised his eyebrows and gave her a nod of approval. "So you're working the system," he said.

"Well that makes two of us, doesn't it?" she said. She gave him a maternal wink, which he didn't know whether to return or ignore.

"They invited me back when I mattered," she continued. "I was one of those blips on the radar, you know? Famous for ten seconds? Now they're stuck with me. Their gain, if you ask me! Ha! Oh. And by the way? Just so you know: that painting you're working on is a piece of shit."

Then she shoved a book into Engales's chest, earmarked at a Lucian Freud painting.

"Study it," she said. "That's how you paint a fucking face."

No one had ever cared enough to tell Engales that something he was making was a piece of shit before, and he coveted it. He had protested for show, but then had studied the Freud painting deliberately, running his finger over the smooth page, noting the way the unfinished background eclipsed the face itself, and how the shadows hung so haphazardly on the skin. It was unclear whether the painting was even finished, but Engales felt that it was the white negative space that made the painting wonderful. It was the world threatening to obliterate the painting's subject, the universe licking at the subject's face, about to swallow him whole. An understanding swept through Engales, and not unhappily: he was not yet great, but greatness was out there; it was available. He had then thrown his own canvas—the first real *canvas* he had ever painted on—into the studio's big trash bin and started over. From across the room he had heard Arlene say, "Atta boy."

After that, Arlene quickly became the sort of friend one needed in New York: the friend who told you things how they were, not how you wanted them to be, but only did so because she actually respected you—otherwise, it wouldn't have been worth her time. (In New York, Engales soon learned, time was a currency potentially more valuable than actual money; everybody claimed they needed more of it.) Arlene informed him of all the times when the studio was not being used for classes ("'Cause Lord knows you don't wanna get tangled up with that whole gang of little shits," she said). She swore a lot: she swore at her canvases and swore at Engales and swore she'd never paint again. But she was always back the next day, toting ham sandwiches for the both of them, so they'd never have to stop working. They painted alongside each other for insanely long stretches, sometimes until the edges of the morning.

It was Arlene who had found him the free apartment; her friend François, a French essayist who had headed back to the old country for an indefinite number of months, agreed to entrust Engales with his place because he had a *je ne sais quoi . . . energie positif.* It was Arlene who had showed him the graffiti in the subway tunnels and the Egyptian wing of the Met, where "the hieroglyphics would blow his fucking brains out," and the best place to get pesto pizza at 4:00 A.M. ("Pesto is a *thing,* right now," she had said), and the way to call for free from a pay phone using a secret 800 number ("Look for the little blue box. It means the phreaks have hacked it"). She had taught him how to make *real* skin color (add the tiniest spot of blue), and how to "keep painting even when you hated it more than your uncle Booth." ("Who's Uncle Booth?" Engales had asked, and she had just said, "Never mind, but you'd hate him.") They went to poetry readings at A's—a loft space started by the Other Arleen, as she called her prolific artist friend, who wrote poems made of sounds and made videos on an 8mm camera and performed at MoMA, which made Arlene Number One "cringe and hoorah at the same time." They frequented Eileen's Reno Bar, where men dressed as ladies and the drinks were as stiff as the bulges in the ladies' underwear; he'd paint the man-ladies the next day, their hairy thighs and their beautiful red lips, sucking down their fiery gin martinis. It was Arlene who had taken him to the place that would for the next seven years define him and his experience: the cereal factory turned abandoned building turned party destination turned living quarters, lovingly referred to by its dwellers as simply *the squat*.

PORTRAIT OF THE SQUAT BY AN ORPHAN

EYES: The windows, busted out, are unable to close their lids. Hence: blue tarps and duct tape, till someone sells a piece and they can buy a sheet of glass. Electricity rigged by Tehching, another of the squat's resident nonresidents, who clipped the wires from across the street, ran them over: minimal sparking, no fires. Cheers to Tehching: a party, with lights(!), in his honor. Tehching, whose projects each lasted a year: live inside a wooden cell for a year, live outside for a year, and now: take a photograph of himself every hour of every day for this year, while he punches a time clock. Tehching, whose hair will grow out as the pictures progress, showing the passage of the year in just minutes. Who will eventually renounce art in his life, since his life had disappeared into art itself: that blurred horizon each and every artist hoped to reach, that only the luckiest or truest of them would.

NOSE: Resin, glue, paint, booze, day-old spaghetti sauce, and stale smoke. Smells that live in the building like its residents do: with the staunch conviction that they shall stay. No one can tell the smells of the squat to leave. They are as intrinsic to the space as the artists are, who stay up all night to make banners to hang outside that read THIS LAND IS OURS.

MOUTH: Laurie Anderson's mouth glows red when she sings. *Ah ah ah ah ah ah ah.* Laurie Anderson's mouth glows red when she sings. She taps out her own rhythm on the stick of her microphone. *Ah ah ah ah ah.* Her voice is being processed by some sort of computer machine: it is both music and nonmusic, sound and mood. *Whoooooop. Doooooooah.* The abandoned building moves its abandoned limbs to the sound that comes from that mouth, the sound that moves through that computer machine and out into the bones of the humans the abandoned building holds. The bodies no longer belong to their owners anymore, but instead to Laurie Anderson's glowing mouth.

HAIR: Selma Saint Regis cuts hers off in the squat's bathroom, frames it, leaves it on Mary Boone's doorstep, never to hear from it again.

BODY: A projection, on the west wall of the squat's biggest room, of a man dancing in a party hat. He's naked, his flabby body slapping at itself. The artist herself, who comes into the frame from time to time to dance with the man, refuses to be named or acknowledged. Her face is never visible. The man is vulnerable and aggressive in his movements. The artist is guarded and careful in relation to the camera, but provocative in relation to the man: jutting out her hips. The video ends when she takes a wad of cash from the man, who looks up at her longingly from the edge of the bed, his face suddenly sweet, sad, and guilty, all at once. Then there's a close-up of her hands, scrawling something on a matchbook. *Shake it baby, oh, shake it,* she writes, her hands shaking.

LIMBS: *I'll draw on yours if you draw on mine.* This from Jean-Michel Basquiat, who holds out his smooth arm to Raul Engales during one of the squat's better parties. The two painters square off, level into each other with their eyes. Jealousy fights with desire fights with schoolboy giddiness: they are each looking into a mirror. The arm of a man whose name has been floating through all of downtown's rougher spots, but hasn't yet been shouted to the world. The arm of a man whose presence made both women and men squirm toward him, as if he were radiating some sort of heat, whose brushstrokes, Engales had seen, *yelled at the top of their lungs.* An arm that Engales has the feeling will one day be worth millions. He has the same feeling about his own.

A new New York had emerged once Engales entered the world of the squat, spinning around him like a fabulous tornado, sucking him up and into it. The squat became more than a physical space—it was an *idea,* a *movement,* a group of people who traveled like a set of tentacles around the city, sucking the art and life out of every place they landed. Engales danced to the B-52s at Studio 54, made out with models at Max's, bummed cocaine from a performance artist with a silver-painted body, crashed maximalist parties at minimalist lofts. He hung out hungover on velour couches in illegal events spaces in what was soon to be called SoHo but was then just the nameless hellhole where the streets went rebelliously against the grid. He shook hands with old men in sweat-ringed polyester whose lawn chairs might never touch a lawn. He witnessed the quintessential fire-hydrant sprayings of the summer months, when little children screamed from the pressure of the water. He smoked cigarettes with women who weren't wearing shirts because why would they?; never went to bed before 4:00 A.M. because why would they?; never ventured above Fourteenth Street because why would they?; and generally vibrated with the artistic adrenaline that the gorgeous downtown grime produced.

It was the grime that was glamorous, he came to realize. The importance of destruction and decay that sidelined gain and growth, the way the artists gravitated toward the most destitute of places and therefore gravitated to one another—that made them all feel rich. In reality they were mostly undiscovered, and very poor, but somehow being poor in New York was not dire or scary like it was back in Argentina, where the electricity would shut off for weeks or he and his sister might not have enough food. This new life, even after the newness had sunken in, seemed like a surreal and inconsequential *portrayal* of real life. It was almost like a *painting* of a life. He often felt as if he wasn't in his own body, as if things weren't actually happening to him, and if they did they didn't count. Simultaneously he felt everything more strongly: joy, excitement, claustrophobia, anger, pleasure, inspiration. He was more inspired to make art here than he had been in his life. Where he had began painting as a way out—out of his real life, which had become almost impossible to endure—he now painted as a way *into* life; he wanted to go as deep as he could into life. All the way.

He had never before felt any influence from any other artist, but here it was impossible not to. He wanted Keith Haring's lines, Clemente's expression, Warhol's bravado, Donald Sultan's shapes. He took a sketchbook with him everywhere and often found himself in the corners of galleries, sketching something he'd been moved by. He took what he wanted and incorporated it into his own work. He morphed with the city's mood. He grabbed faces from the streets, stole hues from the stoplights. What emerged was a chaotic chorus: paintings that rang with the sounds of New York City, paintings that, despite their influences, felt and looked and sounded like nothing he'd ever felt or seen or heard.

Arlene noted how much progress he had made since she had met him.

"It's fucking crazy, really," she said late one night, over studio beers. "How someone your age can understand anything at all about anything. Too bad you smell so fucking bad, or I'd ask you to marry me."

"You think I'd marry you?" He laughed.

"No question," she said very seriously, with a fish scale's flash in her eye.

He kept painting. He kept improving. He felt it in his body, in his hands: new abilities, a new ease. The parts that had at one point been difficult—composition, certain shadows, hands—began to come easily: he created hundreds of paintings in those first years, carrying them across town to François's apartment when he finished them, stacking them against walls and under the bed. He dedicated himself to his craft, putting in the time and the hard work, telling himself that it would pay off one day, that someone would recognize him. But aside from the artists at the squat, who, by proximity had to recognize everyone who came among them, no one did. Raul Engales was making the best work he had ever made in his life, better than much of the stuff he saw at the galleries, he knew, but no one was paying attention.

Until now, when an actual gallerist was standing like a beacon of potential in his co-opted studio space.

"This is Rumi," Engales said to Arlene now. "I told you she would come."

"It only took six months!" Arlene spat. "Hello, Rumi. Nice to meet you. Don't fuck with Engales. I mean, you know what I mean."

"I don't plan on it," Rumi said coolly. "In any sense of the phrase."

"You guys are no fun," Engales said, now tugging Rumi over to his corner, where a group of his paintings leaned against the wall in angular stacks. Engales pulled them out from behind one another and stood back, motioning toward them.

"Voilà," he said. "My dead paintings."

"I see them," Rumi said, studying the canvases, which were covered in chaotic compositions filled with the stuff of Raul Engales's life: highly detailed portraits of people he had met on the street and whose faces he had memorized, the faces usually twisted up in some odd expression of pain or euphoria—and then cigarette packages, insects, dream sequences, heat waves, sunflowers, a woman's ugly foot, a woman's bare breast, a woman's reddened nipple, newspaper headlines, Spanish sayings, love poems, candy wrappers. But even though he had abandoned the straightforward portraits he had done as a teenager, it was the people—the faces and the bodies that made the impact in every painting—that were truly captivating. Looking at all of them together made even his own head spin: the people he had seen or known or liked or hated. His heart held itself from beating until Rumi spoke again.

"Not only are they *paintings*," Rumi finally said, "which I told you are *dead*, but they are *portraits*."

"So?"

"So portraits are *really* dead. People think they're dated, boring— you know we're well past *people* these days. We're onto *identities*. We're off the realism and on to the metarealism. We're off the maximalism— dare I venture to inform you that that's what we have here in front of us?—and we're even off the minimalism! We're on to *nothing as something*. Idea as product. We don't care about the something. We especially don't care about the some*one*!"

Engales's shoulders fell as his ego deflated. He felt annoyed at himself for not pushing himself harder—why had he not gone *beyond* painting like everyone else had? He thought of David Salle, whose show he had just seen at the Mary Boone Gallery with Selma, who had yet to pull her hair stunt and was wearing it long and untethered. *Smart motherfucker,* Selma had said upon seeing the work. Salle's paintings were almost collage-like, carrying and juxtaposing multiple *ideas*; the paintings *reeked* of ideas, *were* ideas; Engales had wondered to himself how it was done, how Salle had managed to convey that behind his aesthetic product was an intelligent brain, one that could fuse the very paint on the canvas with deep thoughts about the essence of humans, society, art itself. Everything that the spotlight touched these days was somehow intellectualized: a deconstruction, a deliberation, a test. Engales wasn't sure quite yet what his own *idea* even was; he only understood that to paint was to *live,* and for that reason he painted. Apparently everything he'd imagined he knew about art was all wrong.

"But fuck 'em," Rumi said suddenly. "I *love them.*"

She picked up a painting of a young girl in an embroidered tunic, whose eyes looked sad and who was holding an egg in each of her hands. Behind the girl was a cow's skull, shattering in midair, the shards of the bone so immaculately rendered that they looked as if they might cut you if you touched the canvas.

"This one here. It's wonderful. I'll take it. I'll put it in Times Square."

"What's in Times Square?" he said.

"Wait," she said, squinting at the floor full of paintings. "I'll take three. We'll do the whole little room for you."

"What's the little room? What's Times Square?" he said again.

"It's a show that I'm helping with," she said absently, lost in the paintings. "It's small and weird and the room I'm curating is in a former massage parlor—it will be a bunch of punk kids and people no one's ever heard of, and it will take your career absolutely nowhere. So don't get your panties in a bunch."

"I don't wear underwear," he said. His whole body was grinning. Times Square! A show! His own little room! In a massage parlor! And this woman! This woman with a little room and a huge mound of hair and a big, wide beautiful mouth! His heart was soaring well above the studio with the city's night birds.

"You two are fucking disgusting," Arlene yelled across the studio. Engales laughed. He then looked back to Rumi and tried to create a moment where they looked into each other's eyes, and even though he couldn't catch her eyes he thought he might catch her lips, and he leaned in . . . but Rumi held out her arm (and her arms were *long*), and told him, to his disbelief, that she was in fact a *lesbian*, and she had a girlfriend named Susan, who was an *architect*.

"Well that makes me like her a *little* bit better," Engales heard Arlene say from her corner.

Engales pulled away and scrunched up his nose. "Well, what am I supposed to do now?" he said. "It's practically midnight and I'm not about to kiss *Arlene*."

"Oh, don't you wish!" Arlene said.

"Tell you what," said Rumi. "Why don't I take you out? We'll have a night. Or part of a night, since you seem to have co-opted most of it for this little studio tour."

"Does this night include meeting someone I can kiss in exactly thirty-two minutes?" Engales looked at his hairy wrist, on which he did not wear any watch.

Rumi looked Engales up and down dramatically, lingering for longer than she needed to on his big, smooth lips. "I'm sure we can find something." She winked with both her eyes.

"Is Arlene invited?"

"Of course Arlene's invited."

"Arlene is busy!" Arlene yelled.

"Oh come *on*," Engales yelled back. "Let's go get you laid."

Arlene let out a laugh and threw her brush into a coffee can. "Oh, fuck it," she said. "Where are we going?"

"I was thinking of crashing a rich-person party," Rumi said. She had a subversive stroke of light in her tigery eyes, which Engales still found enticing, though he was no longer allowed to be enticed.

"I hate rich people!" Arlene said. "I'm in."

"I'm in," Engales said with a shrug.

"Follow me," Rumi said, her eyes flashing with promising flecks of gold.

The rich people were all standing out on the rich-person balcony by the time they arrived, so Rumi, Arlene, and Engales had the rest of the wild, expansive set of rooms to themselves. First Rumi gave them a through-the-glass-door debriefing of who was in attendance—there's Federico Rossi, owns half of the permanent collection at MoMA; there's James Bennett, writes for the *Times*, if you're lucky you'll get a review but you never know with Bennett, kind of an odd duck that one; and there is John Baldessari—looks like he has no idea how to dress for a New York winter, huh? Engales gazed out at the rich people. He wanted to paint each and every one of them: a woman in a burgundy dress and open gray peacoat, whose stomach held an odd shape: a sort of sloped triangle, barely noticeable, wonderfully strange; a tiny man in suspenders whose wave of hair was about to crash. And then there was the man who Rumi said wrote for the *Times*—the *Times*!—the back of his balding head poking up out of his natty overcoat: a head that Engales both wanted to render (a white stroke, for its sheen), and to get inside of (what would a writer for the *New York Times* see in his paintings?). *Someday*, he vowed right then. Mentally he tucked a snapshot of James Bennett's shiny head into a pocket of his brain, for someday.

"Bup bup," said Rumi, pulling Engales toward the rich-person fridge, which they ransacked, finishing a bottle of champagne in a matter of minutes, clanking their glasses and becoming louder as they drank. Then they wandered around the maze of dimly lit, insanely decorated, art-filled rooms, gushing over the de Koonings in the dining room, sniffing at the Stella behind the sofa in the living room, ogling a Claes Oldenburg sculpture of an ice-cream cone that sat sweetly and snugly in the fireplace, its melted parts seemingly made specifically for the little brick hole. The whole labyrinth of the place invited exploration and sleuthing, with its dim lights and zebra-skinned chairs and mahogany doors, and what were those? Pews? From a church? Eventually the three of them split up, each entering different rooms off the long hallway, toting their glasses of champagne like drunken detectives.

Engales found himself in a den-like room, with a writing desk lit by a low lawyer's lamp. Unlike the other rooms, there was no art on the walls; they were empty and painted a deep royal blue. There was only the writing table, the lamp, and a circle of light that haloed a tape recorder. Engales made his way around the desk and sat in the big leather chair behind it. On the tape recorder was a small white card that read: *Milan Knížák: Broken Music Composition, 1979*. Engales knew the name; Arlene had talked about Knížák, a Czech performance artist who was famous for his happenings and social art in Prague. Curious, Engales pressed the play button on the recorder. A rough, scratchy music emerged, halting and starting as if a record were being pulled back and then released. But the original song still retained some of its shape: a deep, old tune with slices of singing that made Engales's stomach flutter.

The music—in its brokenness and its sadness and its beauty—reminded him distinctly of home, of something his father would have put on, some scratched-up record he had bought on a trip to Italy, that he had probably found in the back of some hundred-year-old shop, or else a Beatles record he had bought in London or New York from a street vendor, not caring that it was a used, decrepit copy.

"Listen to this!" his father would have told him and his sister, Franca. "Listen to this beautiful thing that a human made!"

"But it's *scratched*," Engales or his sister would have said.

"But that's the *point*," his father would have said back. "The imperfections, the time that's passed, the hiccups . . . that's the wear of the *world* on it. That's the *life*."

Engales was surprised at how moved he felt now, listening to the ruptured music in this rich person's blue room. The sound felt religious and powerful, sincere and vulnerable. It was like a discovery, of some part inside his body that released both deep pleasure and profound ache, a tugging of that part. It was a moment he would remember later for what it did to him: think about home, but *really* think about home, for the first time since he had fled it.

His sister, Franca, had betrayed him: she had gotten married. To a spineless man named Pascal Morales, at San Pedro González Telmo church, on a rainy morning in July of 1973. She hadn't told Engales she'd done it because she'd known he'd disapprove. She'd only come home one afternoon with a gold ring on her finger and a guilty look on her face, gone straight to the kitchen and begun to make one of her cakes. It was only later that Engales would realize that his sister had been making her own wedding cake, a round, sugary thing that would sit on their kitchen counter for weeks, that no one would eat but that no one could bring themselves to throw away.

He wouldn't have admitted why he was so angry that morning, and all the mornings afterward, but both he and Franca knew. Franca was *his*, and her marriage to Pascal was a distinct threat to their siblinghood. Since their parents' death, she had been the only one who cared at all about him, and, being that he was prone to staying out late and drinking himself into oblivion, her caring was the only thing that defined them as any sort of family. She was the one who waited up when Engales came home at three in the morning, reeking of smoke. She was the one who asked him too often what he was doing and what he wanted to eat, when the answer to both of these things was always *nothing*. She was the one who listened through the walls when he brought women home, knew what lusty crimes he had committed, when he had stolen a girl's virginity or been cold to her and made her cry. He resented Franca massively, sometimes wanting to scream at her that she was *not his fucking mother*, but he knew, too, how easily he could undo her, undo *them*.

He knew that in order to survive, Franca and Engales had to maintain the precise balance of silence and understanding that could only be held by siblings who had shared as great a loss as they had. Franca saw everything, all his dark spots, all his faults, all his points of pain. Because she was the only one who had those same dark spots, different but similar faults, different but similar pain. Sometimes he could hardly look her in the eyes for fear he would witness his own despair. He would avoid her, go to another room in the house, the house too big for just the two of them, where they circled around each other like moths or cats or ghosts. At the same time he knew she was there; he could feel her care through the walls, and this is what mattered. There was someone else in the world who was witness to his sadness, and part of it.

Their parents, Eva and Braulio Engales, had died in October 1965 when Braulio, drunk, crashed their Di Tella Magnette into a tree on the way home from a weekend at Mar del Plata. Raul was fourteen years old, Franca seventeen. It was the same day that ten Argentine explorers made it to the South Pole. Operation 90, it was called, because the South Pole was at ninety degrees south. Franca and Engales sat on the stiff floral couch in the living room with the television on, watching the explorers salute the flag in their orange uniforms. The guy who had come by the house just a few hours earlier—blue suit, clean-shaven face, hands that looked like a woman's—had told them their parents had died on impact, on the highway just outside of Miramar. Impact: like a bird hitting a glass window. But Raul and Franca would carry a different vision of their death around with them, a death that they would refer to for the rest of their time together as Operation 90.

A slow thaw, a South Pole freeze, their parents laying at ninety degrees south, holding each other's hands under the Argentine flag.

To an outsider, Eva and Braulio might have struck you as the type of people who *would* die young, if only because they were in a constant state of motion that was nearly reckless. They flung themselves onto airplanes and trains, jetting to Brussels on a whim, or up to Córdoba for a meeting, then drove, as they had that fateful night, down to the beach for a weekend of cocktails and communism talk with their somehow never busy bohemian friends. What they did remained vague to Raul and Franca: something to do with international politics and, as they dubbed it, *the slow fight toward social justice.* If nothing else, their constant travels had left their children with the ability to care for themselves for long stretches (something that would come in handy when they never returned), and a vague residue of radicalism (*Never trust anyone who wants to be in charge*, his father had often said). Also, a US passport for Raul; they had had him during a six-month stint in New York City, a story they loved to tell—*our American boy*, they'd say in English at parties—and a fact that linked him to the continent above, kept Raul studying English through his teenage years, just in case he ever wanted to go north. Franca, three years old at the time, had been given only a temporary visa.

The first years after their parents' death, Raul kept expecting them to come home, to whirl through the house in their new, foreign clothes, his mother's long skirts and belled sleeves swishing over tabletops as she arranged the trinkets they had picked up: a set of brightly colored nesting dolls, an engraved wooden box lined with purple velvet, a giant cow's skull, which would hang above the fireplace until Raul, two years after they died, would stand on a chair, pull it down, and break it into pieces over his knee.

After he began to take their absence more seriously, to stop waking up expecting them to have come back, he started to feel the loss in his body. It was like a dark, lethargic mass, a blob of anger and pain that would sometimes have him drinking straight from whiskey bottles, sometimes stealing from grocery stores, and sometimes paralyzed, utterly unable to get out of bed. It was the ache that kept him from attending most of his classes at school, in favor of smoking cigarettes in the alley on the side of the building. The first time Franca discovered his hiding spot he was not surprised—she somehow always knew where he was, as if she had a sixth sense. But he was surprised when she squatted down next to him in her navy uniform and, instead of scolding him or telling him to go back to class, took the cigarette from his hand and breathed in a slow, silent drag. She looked up at the sky, which had two puffy clouds floating in it.

"Looks like tits," Franca said.

And he had busted up laughing, and she had, too, the kind of ridiculous, necessary laughter that only siblings shared. They laughed until their stomachs hurt, and when they stopped, Engales had felt terrified. He remembered thinking, in that moment, that this would be the only time he ever laughed. That the laughter was just a small break in more endless aching, which was almost worse than having never felt relief.

In order to make enough money to afford to stay in their parents' house, both Franca and Raul had to take jobs. Raul painted houses for rich people—mostly military families—in Palermo and Recoleta; Franca worked at the bakery, which she would later take over. They created necessary habits: taking baths together—with their backs toward each other—so as to have enough warm water; lighting candles instead of turning on lights, telling each other stories alternately, so the other could fall asleep. They existed this way—parentless, but together—for eight long years, before Pascal Morales came around and cracked their delicate balance right down the middle.

Pascal had been selling magazine subscriptions door-to-door, and when he'd knocked on theirs and seen Franca, he'd told her she was more beautiful than the woman on the cover of the magazines he was carrying, who happened to be Brigitte Bardot. "Nobody's more beautiful than Brigitte Bardot," Franca had said in her shy way, but Pascal had already sold her—on both the compliment and the subscription—and she went out to dinner with him that very night.

"You bought a fucking magazine subscription from that asshole?" Engales yelled at her when she got home from the date.

"He's not so bad," Franca had said. "He took me to that new place, Tia Andino. Raul, he can afford Tia Andino!"

"Well, we cannot afford magazine subscriptions!" Raul yelled.

"But we could if he helped us!" Franca pleaded. "What if he could take care of us?"

Raul just looked at her and shook his head. What she was really saying was that he, Engales, could *not* take care of them. That he was not enough. What hurt the most is that he knew he wasn't. That he wasn't a strong enough man to take care of his own sister, or even himself.

Quickly, though, he saw that Pascal was not up for the task, either. The man had a sneaky, weaselly quality to him, and something told Engales that if the house were to suddenly catch fire, Pascal would sprint out the door to save himself without a thought cast back to Franca. Engales performed a series of miniature tests—break the hinge on the back door and see if Pascal will even try to fix it (he didn't); voice a disgustingly conservative political opinion (something pro-Perón, who had essentially turned into a fascist) over dinner to see if Pascal would object (he didn't)—which told him that Pascal was not only unworthy of dating his sister but unworthy of setting foot in their house at all.

"He's a pansy, Franca," he tried to tell his sister, after they'd been dating a few months (already much too long, in Engales's opinion). "A conservative pansy. He's not for you!"

"It's too bad you feel that way," said Franca. "Because I've asked him to move in."

In the hottest part of January in 1973, Pascal brought over a truckload of furniture that, in its attempt to look modern, only appeared hideously cheap and clashed in an upsetting way with their mother's antique glass tables and ornate, beautiful couch cushions. He installed a giant brown square of a chair in the living room and installed himself atop it, a spot which he would come to think he *owned,* and where he would sit for long, seemingly endless stretches, watching the most conservative of the news stations, his knotty feet propped up on their mother's glass table as if it were not a precious memento of their dead parents but a disposable ottoman, built just for him and his bony heels.

Pascal's presence drove Engales to practically live at El Federal, the bar around the corner, where he could go to drink and be silent and where he didn't have to smell Morales's thick breath or hear Morales's farting in the night or see Morales's hair in the drain of the tub. All of the habits with his sister were interrupted—Pascal paid to have the lights turned back on; he slept in the bed with Franca, and Raul slept back in his childhood bedroom, in his old, creaky twin bed. There was scarcely enough hot water for the three of them, and Engales's baths were almost always freezing. The thought of his sister sleeping with Pascal nearly drove him mad, and this he blamed on her.

"He's not going to save you," he shouted at her one night when they had both been unable to sleep, and had wandered, as they had done in their youth, to the dark kitchen. "He's not going to bring back Mom and Dad!"

He had made Franca cry that night, as he would many times before he left.

"You have to let me live my life, Raul," she said. "You're going to leave one day and then where will I be? I need someone."

"Well, he's not the right someone!" he yelled at her.

She had clamped her hot hand on his shoulder, given him the look she gave that meant *don't*.

Buenos Aires, for Raul Engales, was becoming a series of *don't*s, he saw then. *Don't* come between your sister and her sleazy new boyfriend. *Don't* feel comfortable or welcome in your own house. *Don't* sleep with women who hang out too late at El Federal, looking to escape their own husbands (their husbands will find you, chase you down Calle Defensa, and force you to hide in the dark behind the Dumpster). *Don't* gain any recognition for your paintings, which are at this point only a pathetic hobby, not worth anyone's time (not that anyone cared about art right now in Buenos Aires, where things were becoming too fucked up to care about such frivolous endeavors). And *don't*, when your sister tells you she has married Pascal Morales at the San Pedro Gonzáles Telmo church yesterday morning, try for one more second to disguise your abhorrence of him, of *them*, because Pascal Morales is here to stay, in this enormous old house your parents saddled you with, that even with its four bedrooms is not big enough for three.

Do pull your American passport from your father's old writing desk, run your palm over its gold emboss, and remember your father saying, *It's a city of pure poetry, I'm telling you, kids.*

You are ready for poetry. You are through with the suffocating text that has become your life in this old house.

In the end Franca had begged him not to go. In the earliest part of the morning, on Saturday, June 29, of 1974, just two days before Perón's death would rock the country and one day before Raul turned twenty-three, as he walked away from the house with his backpack, he heard Franca yell from their front stoop: *Don't leave, Raul! Please don't leave!*

He could not look back at her. If he looked back he would never be able to look forward. He would see her holding her silly cake, which she had baked for his birthday in one final plea to make him stay, in her old blue coat that used to be their mother's. He was terrified to leave her: the only person who cared about him and the only home he'd ever known. He did.

The door to the blue room opened and Engales, startled, knocked over his champagne glass. Thankfully it was empty, or he would have spilled all over *Broken Music Composition, 1979*. At the door was a woman—not beautiful, but important-looking—sporting a black silk dress and a fountain of graying black hair.

"You've found the Knížák," she said in a rich-person voice: the kind of voice that was so nonchalant, so languid, that it ended up sounding uptight.

"I'm sorry," Engales said, picking up the glass. "I was just listening."

"Listen all you want," she said, entering the room and extending a polished hand. "That's what it's here for. I'm Winona."

"Hello, Winona."

"It's beautiful, isn't it? Completely new. Completely odd."

"Yes, very," Engales said. For some reason the woman was making him feel nervous, and he didn't know whether he should get up from the leather chair or stay where he was. He looked into the warped tunnel of his champagne glass.

"You know, I saw him in Prague," she said casually, as if Prague were a neighborhood in New York that she frequented. "Doing his *Demonstration for All the Senses*? Wasn't it remarkable? All these funny actions, absurd actions, really. At one point the participants had to sit in a room where perfume had been spilled for five whole minutes. Ha! Can you *imagine*?"

Engales smiled but didn't respond. He got the feeling she was one of those people who liked to talk, and that she was important, and that this was her house, and so he should let her.

She moved closer to him, putting her hand on his bicep.

"What are you, thirty?" She said.

"Twenty-nine," he said with a gulp; he was rounding up.

"Too young to be alone at midnight," she said. "And too handsome." But just when Engales thought she might pet his face, she grabbed it instead, and used the grip to pull him to standing, then toward the door.

"You've got to find yourself a woman to smooch then," she said coolly. "There are only a few moments left!"

"I guess so," Engales said.

"Oh, but wait!" Winona said, her rich eyes brightening. "I forgot to give you your fortune. Everyone gets a fortune, based on the piece of art they've ended up with. You got *Broken Music*." Then she paused, her face becoming white and serious.

"I don't want to be *grave*," she said slowly, her eyes narrowing. "But this piece has a sinister quality. You'll have to do what Milan Knížák did. You'll have to lose everything—the whole song you've memorized and thought you loved—in order to make something truly beautiful."

Engales was quiet; Winona's face had taken on a crazy-lady quality; he only wanted to leave and go back to his night of drinking with Arlene and Rumi.

"You're an artist, am I right?" Winona said.

"How did you know?"

"I have a way of knowing these sorts of things," she said, nodding at Engales's hand with her eyes. Engales looked down at his fingernails, which were lined with blue paint.

"Ahh."

He stared at his hands and thought of the very first moment he knew he wanted to make art: in Señor Romano's class, when he had seen a slide of Yves Klein jumping from a building to what looked to be his death. It had occurred to him then and it occurred to him now that art was about making yourself visible and making yourself disappear all at once. Visible because you were leaving your mark; invisible because it was so much bigger than you that it swallowed you. You were just this tiny thing, and the art was huge. The art was a big void that you could jump into, try to fill, and swim in forever. When he looked up again, Winona was gone. The clock in the corner informed him that so was 1979.

When Engales emerged outside, the crowd was engaged in post-midnight hoopla: extra kisses, extra champagne, extra confetti, just for good measure. He saw that Arlene had found a beau of sorts: a short man with a prominent mustache, who had led her to a corner of the balcony and was feeding her grapes on a stick. When she saw Engales she pointed at the grapes and mouthed: *Means good luck in Spain!*

Engales gave her a thumbs-up and a raised-eyebrow face. Rumi had gone missing, and he was once again unsatisfied with his surroundings—all there was was the drone of high-end chatter, a sea of old men in tuxes, a few younger women who did not interest him in the least, in designer clothes whose price tags were meant to stand in for style. He scanned for the writer, but he must have already left, which for some reason saddened him. *Someday.* In general, Engales could feel the night taking its inevitable turn for the worse: the memory of the music, or the memory of the memories that the music had conjured, played in his head, alongside Winona's odd psychic reading. The party began to feel both surreal and unimportant. What was he doing here? So far away from home, with all these rich people he didn't know, drunk on champagne?

He had managed in the past few years to avoid such thoughts. The city had consumed him so, he had refused to think about Franca hardly at all, had only sent her one postcard saying he had arrived, to which she had responded with a lengthy, overly sentimental letter that ended with a cryptic: *I've got big news, Raul. But I'd rather tell you over the phone. If you might call? Yours. Yours always. F.* He hadn't written back, and he hadn't called. Her letter had felt like looking her in the eyes: there was just too much there. The letter reeked of home, and he didn't want to think about home. This was his home now, and Franca's big news—surely it was something domestic, they'd bought a new house, sold the bakery, or else Franca had gotten pregnant with Pascal's child—could wait.

But now, with the New Year upon him and the music still in his mind, he couldn't help it. He wondered what Franca was doing. If she was drinking champagne, unless the military had banned that, too, or maybe she was asleep. But then again, he didn't have to wonder. He knew. He always knew. Franca was sitting by the window with a glass of water, looking out and up at the moon. She was wondering where her brother was, what he was doing right now. But then again, she didn't have to wonder. She knew. She always knew. Her brother was on a balcony with a bunch of rich people, looking out and up at the moon, thinking of her.

Cigarette.

Engales escaped back through the glass doors and through the maze of rooms and down a dark stairwell and back out to the street. There he found Rumi, just as he had the first night he met her, sitting on the stoop next door as if she had appeared by magic lamp. At the sight of her, a trophy of the future, all thoughts of Franca fell away again. Here was his life, right here on this stoop, living inside of Rumi's beautiful mound of hair.

"Well, if it isn't the painter," Rumi said.

"Well, if it isn't the lesbian," he said, sitting next to her on the cold step, starting his immaculate cigarette-rolling process.

"Why'd you leave?" she said. "You were getting on so famously with Winona."

"You saw that?"

"Yes, I saw that. And I'll tell you exactly what is going to happen from here. Winona will find you. You've captured her interest, and once Winona George's interest is captured, she follows. She's like an art hawk."

"What do you mean?" He coughed a bit of smoke out into the cold air; it looked like a flower.

"Just wait," Rumi said. "Soon you'll get a call. A call will turn into a dinner, which will turn into a studio visit. You'll become her pet for a while. You'll get a show at one of her galleries. She's pals with a few of the best critics, including Bennett; you'll get a review before you know it. It's done. Your fate is sealed. You're already famous, Raul."

Engales laughed. "I don't think so. She didn't even get my name."

"Just wait," Rumi said. "You'll never give a shit about Times Square after what she does to you. But at least I can say I knew you when." She winked.

"So what do we do now?" Engales said, bringing Rumi's plastic watch up to his nose.

"We go to the best bar in New York City and we toast preemptively to your success," said Rumi. She pushed herself up from the stoop with what looked to be a last breath of effort. "Maybe we can even find someone for you to kiss."

They got up to go, pausing for just a moment to watch Keith, who was painting an enormous heart on a temporary barricade across the street; inside of it he wrote in his bulbous script: *1980*. When he turned around and saw them across the street, he gave them a juicy grin. *You guys headed to the squat later, or what?*

A GIRL IN NEW YORK IS
A TERRIBLE THING

I t was just after midnight on New Year's Eve, in the first hours of the
bubbly new decade, when Lucy Marie Olliason fell in love at first
sight. She had been making a round of Manhattans for a mob of
mannequin-like models, inwardly lamenting the anticlimactic climax
of the night, when the Love that she First Sighted came into the bar
and quickly, with the tossing of his black hair and the awkward yet
charming grin he gave her, made her realize that the night had actually just begun. He forced himself to the front of the bar, through
two big men she had been serving Long Island iced teas, and put his
forearms on the bar like he was about to eat a plate of spaghetti. The
mole on the side of his face said: *Spot.*

"What?" she said. Had he said something? Or had she hallucinated?
She could feel her provincial stupidity shining through her and she
longed for the excellent coolness of a real local, even a dash of it. But
there was no acquiring that in the amount of time she had, which was
seconds, nanoseconds even, before this man said what he'd said again.

"*Spot!* I'm naming you that. I've just given you that name, right
now."

Her heart leaped. This was the sort of thing she had believed in
then, during her first winter in New York. She believed in a handsome
man walking into her bar, a sort of downtown knight, a savior. She

believed in the intimacy of nicknames. She believed in good luck and good looks. (And this man's looks—hair that was dark enough to be exotic but wavy enough to be familiar, lips that bow-tied at the cleft and smiled easily, and triangular, almost sinister eyebrows—were *definitely* good.) She believed in this man's eyes (warm as redwood bark) and in this man's mole (a rubbery knob that wagged when he spoke), and she believed she could love that mole, that beautiful mole, that bounded out of his face and toward her, when he touched her earlobe over the bar. She believed in fate and destiny, and that she had stumbled upon hers, when he told her, leaning over the bar and whispering into her ear, that he was a painter. Finally, after the months that had felt like years in the Big City, in the first moments of the new decade, she had met her first artist. One of the men in her stolen library book. One of the men whose lives she had so badly wanted to know.

Lucy had arrived in New York City just five months earlier, in July 1979, during the peak of a massive heat wave that had rendered even the rats lethargic. She was twenty-one years old. She had pulled the trigger on the move—from Ketchum, Idaho, to what people in Ketchum, Idaho, called the "Big City" or the "Big Apple" or sometimes even the "Capital of the World"—because of a book and a postcard, which she believed to be signs.

The book she had found in the art section of the Ketchum Library, a black glossy volume called simply *Downtown*. It was full of photographs of paintings and sculptures. Huge, looming sculptures, bigger than bodies, and paintings whose compositions made, to Lucy, no sense at all. She loved the feeling that she didn't understand something, that there were things out in the world that she might be in awe of, that could elude her. But even more than the objects it was the artists themselves who interested her: the black-and-white pictures of these men—yes, they were mostly men—whose eyes shone alongside their artworks with ideas and city intelligence. She wanted to know everything about them: what they ate for dinner; who their wives were; how they thought up their odd creations. Was what moved these men the same thing that moved her? The unbearable feeling that if you didn't *do* something, if you didn't *fill up the entire world with your longings*, then you would explode? Lucy checked the book out many times in a row, until the librarian told her she needed to leave a week in between checkouts, and she grew embarrassed, thinking that the librarian knew what she was doing with it, which was staring at the photographs of men, dreaming of them, and occasionally reaching down over the crotch of her jeans and pressing her hand there, while she looked into a particularly beautiful artist's eyes.

The postcard she had found while she was driving her father's pickup to her friend Karly's house—a white flash, caught in the grass on the side of the road—that she had for some reason felt the need to pull over and examine. It was a faded picture of the New York skyline on a black night, in all its jagged, sparkly glory. The back said: *See you soon, girlywog.* Her heart actually stopped when she read it. *Girlywog.* The same absurd noun that her mother had bestowed upon her as a term of endearment: *Sleep tight, girlywog.* Though she had no idea who would send a postcard like this, or whose dashboard it had flown off in order to land on this particular patch of weeds, or who the real girlywog was, she knew that it was meant for her. She had turned the truck around and gone back to her parents' house, walked into the kitchen where they were preparing dinner, and told their backs: she was moving to New York and that was final.

"You know you don't have to go," her mother had said the night before she left. She was sitting on the edge of Lucy's bed, watching her pack the rest of her clothes into an enormous black void of a suitcase that she had bought for five bucks at the Ketchum Goodwill. "You've got your whole life! Nobody's making you go, you know."

"If someone was making me go," Lucy said with sarcasm left over from her teenage years, "I wouldn't be going."

She had been stuck in Ketchum since high school, along with a whole crew of creepy townies who had not felt the need to apply for college, working at Mason & Mick's, the hardware store where she had actually been *born*. No one was making her go; she was going because she physically had to.

"I know, I know," her mother said, in a voice that Lucy wanted to recoil from and already missed. "It's your decision. I'm just saying. Just putting it out there. Options."

Lucy's mother knew her better than anyone, because the truth was they were made of the same stuff: unfulfilled desires, pale Norwegian skin, warring impulses to be comfortable or to be courageous, sweet or sour. The difference was that her mother's wars had already been fought, her desires already mostly squashed or else fulfilled, and she had ended up here, in a house in the middle of what some might call nowhere. The light in the bedroom was dim, the way all light becomes in rooms made entirely of unfinished wood. The wood sucked up the light into its grain, and turned what it did not consume a burnt orange color. The whole house was like this, a barnish place on a twelve-acre patch of land, flanked by two emerald hills and nestled in a grove of grand firs; there was never a time of day without shadows.

Her mother played with a tassel of one of the blankets, kneading it between her thumb and forefinger.

"Randall could figure something out for you here," she said. "And not just the elementary stuff. Lord knows you can write. He'd be having you write whole briefs for him, would be my guess."

Her mother had done that night what everyone in town had been doing for weeks: tried to convince her that the wooded borders of Ketchum, Idaho, were where the world ended. Everything you needed was right here, they all said. But her book and her postcard and something else inside her told her otherwise. She believed that the world was wide and available and filled with the potential for feeling and subversion and art and wonder. She secretly took pleasure in the fact that all of Ketchum, including her own mother, thought she was crazy. She was smart enough to know that crazy also meant brave.

"But you'll land on something there, too," her mother said that night. "You've always been so pretty. And they do have all the big modeling agencies there."

From her mother, this was a backhanded compliment, and they both knew it. Lucy knew that her mother meant that she would probably *not* land on something, not unless that something was as unsubstantial as *modeling*. Apparently the Lord knew she could write briefs for a subpar lawyer in Ketchum, but in the Capital of the World? Not a chance. Her mother also understood that it made Lucy uncomfortable when people talked of her beauty, which was as much a fact as her suitcase, black and too big, sitting there in the room with them. It was the kind of beauty that model scouts saw in fourteen-year-olds at the mall—and that might have happened to her if there was any mall for her to wander around in—undeniable, accessible, wholesome, and yet vaguely sad. Her hair had been white-blond when she was little, and now it was the tawny, vulnerable brown of towheads after puberty everywhere, and its lackluster color only enhanced the very noticeable smoothness, the very particular rosiness, the very recognizable symmetry of her face.

"Models don't eat, Mom," she said, tossing a pair of sneakers into the suitcase. "I, on the other hand, am constantly starving."

"I'm just worried," her mother said, shifting her motherly weight onto her hand. "You know how I get."

"I do know how you get, and it's ridiculous," said Lucy. "I'm an adult, Mom. I'll figure it out."

She knew it was unconvincing, because she was unconvinced herself. Was she an adult? Would she figure it out? She had no idea what she would do in New York; she only knew that she was going. She imagined an office on an eleventh floor. She imagined a skirt with pleats, something she did not have yet because you could only find it there. And then she imagined darker things, in vague spurts that excited her immensely: a nightclub with a strobe light, a man's arm with a tattoo on it, a fiery night of smashed windows and stealing; she had seen footage of the blackout on the news.

"Well you've always been different, haven't you?" her mother said. "You've always had . . . what is it? Zest. You've had zest." Her blue eyes were clouding and Lucy didn't want it to come, though she knew it would: the story of how she was born.

"I still remember when you were born," her mother said. Here it was. Lucy didn't want to hear the story because there was no story, and she had heard it too many times. The story about the hardware store—where she had been employed for the last six years, organizing bolts and washers and wire—on the thirteenth of October, just after the storm that had blanketed all of Idaho in a thick white that would stay for months on end. Winter had come early, and so had Lucy, apparently, pushing her way out of her mother three whole weeks before her due date, right there in the aisle of Mason & Mick's, between the lightbulbs and the light sockets. Mick, of Mason & Mick's, had cut the cord with a pair of garden shears.

Lucy didn't want to have only one story. She wanted a whole life made out of stories: momentum, propulsion, characters, change. In a small town like this there were only so many ways to feel moved by change, and they were too subtle to be interesting—a snowstorm like the one on the night she was born; a litter of puppies born in town; a boy's hand on her breast in the cab of his musty truck; the married art teacher, telling her in his soft teacher voice that he just couldn't do this anymore. Though she always tried to provoke something into happening—calling the teacher's house in the middle of the night, getting drunk on the bottle of Johnnie Walker her parents had in the cabinet, going to loud concerts and drunken bonfires in the middle of snowy fields—the stories always ended up the same. There were only, after the bonfires or fiery moments of passion were over, more wet drives to friends' houses, pale afternoons filled with rivers and waiting, gas station parking lots, excuses. Time in Ketchum moved like the shadows that cloaked her house—so slowly you couldn't see it.

"Good story, Mom," she said with that same sarcasm, although she couldn't help but smile. She took a deep breath and scanned the dim bedroom, as if to breathe in the gymnastics trophies from the days when a cartwheel earned you your own personal statue, the framed photographs of friends making peace signs, the posters of rock bands that had never passed through Ketchum but whose records she found in free bins at the thrift stores downtown. These were all the things she would leave behind. She scanned the hundreds of faces, animals, mouths, and eyes that lived in the grain of the wooden walls. Though she had grown up in this house, knew all its creaks and cracks between planks, she had still allowed it to frighten her: the two-dimensional wood-grain animals, the vulnerability of its being in the middle of nowhere, ready to be ravaged by fire or lightning bolt, the sounds the house made, which her mother assured her was "settling": the house getting more comfortable in itself, while she was growing less so. What she wanted was people. Potential saviors, all at arm's reach from her, so that if the animal in the wood grain jumped out of the wood she could scream, and someone would hear.

"It's almost time to leave, girlywog," her mother said. She smelled like Lubriderm lotion and damp soil.

"I'm ready," she had said, feeling only remotely guilty as she set *Downtown* into her suitcase, so shiny and satisfying in its library plastic.

When she looked back on it later, she would think of her arrival and the weeks that followed as some of the most benevolent she could remember, when heartbreak belonged to the city itself—beggars on Bond Street, fearless rats, a hand hanging out the window of the subway at the West Fourth Street station, holding a knife. Her arrival: the red-eye flight, the heavy suitcases, the air thick with that lethargic summer hope. The taxicab that smelled of urine, candy, and leather: the *taxicab*, a thing that so epitomized the New York of her mind, that made her feel adult and modern and that raced toward the skyline almost as fast as her heart. Then the street—Wooster, that was the wonky, exciting name of the street where the taxi had dropped her—that smelled like garbage, smoke, and something sweet, which she would later find out were the delicious sticky buns at R & K, a bakery around the corner on Prince, whose walls were tiled in yellow bricks, sticky with sugar and grime. But that first day, with the scarily hot sun beating down on the crowded street, she hadn't known about R & K, just as she hadn't known about anything that lay in front of her. Especially not where to go right then, toting her heavy suitcase, people swarming around her as she stood paralyzed on the street corner, looking up into the sky as if it might give her an answer.

But, as if by telepathic magic, it did. The sky produced, on a small yet significant gust of hot wind, a flying piece of paper. The flying piece of paper read *Room for rent. Girls only. Call Jamie.* Under the handwritten message was a lipstick mark, pink and puckered— someone had actually *kissed* the paper—and then a phone number made up of mostly ones and twos. She couldn't help but link the word *girl* to *girlywog,* and to the postcard, and to the paper trail of fate that had brought her here. She found herself fascinated by the kiss, wanting, oddly, to kiss it back. The paper had a phone number on it, which she called from a pay phone, with one of the quarters her mother had made her keep in her pocket, for emergencies. What emergency could be handled with a quarter, Lucy hadn't been sure, but as the coin clanked into its silver slot she silently thanked her mother, closed her eyes tightly as the phone made its first loud ring.

A raspy yet youngish voice answered—"Oh, thank *gawd* someone is fucking *calling,* I need to rent this shithole ASAP"—and told Lucy to come over right away, not that she *guaranteed* anything, they had to get acquainted before she signed on to *living* with someone she didn't even *know*.

"Okay," Lucy said. "Can you tell me how to get there?"

"You know the Chinese laundry place with the big cat in the window?"

Lucy said she did not know.

"Right off Tompkins Square Park, the place with the cat? Still no? Jesus, what are you, *new here*?"

"Yes," Lucy said shyly. Yes she was.

"Tell you what," the voice said. "Just get to Avenue B and Seventh Street, I'll come down."

Despite the ridiculous heat and the difficulty of the suitcases, the walk to Jamie's was thrilling. There was the feeling that a school bell had just been rung and everyone had rushed out of their classes and into the streets, and they were now out to partake in whatever the world could offer them. There were incredibly short-shorts and there was incredibly large hair. One woman's torso was entirely exposed aside from one band of her unitard that covered each nipple; she also wore a large black hat. There was UNIQUE CLOTHING and COMING SOON EAST VILLAGE VIDEO and BEST PORN IN TOWN XXX. Everything—walls, telephone booths, sidewalks—was painted on or marked, in unfamiliar, intriguing scribbles that said cryptic things like DESTROY or LOVERS WANTED. She passed a place called the Aztec Lounge, where a sign read: REFRESHING! ECLECTIC! SOOTHING COCKTAILS! ANCIENT AMULET KEEPS OUT DEMONS! This both frightened and excited her, and she wondered what demons lived here that would require an ancient amulet to keep out.

Lucy wove among the new streets, unnoticed. The feeling of it— of not being recognized or watched—made her giddy and terrified. She could do whatever she pleased. She could take any turn. She could write on a wall herself, if she wanted; who was there to see her besides all these people who didn't care? There was no Mick telling her to sweep the floors and no mother asking when she would be home.

She could answer an ad she found blowing in the wind. Everything awaited her. The buildings soared. Kids played in the streets in their underwear. She was arriving. This was her arrival.

Jamie, who was standing on the corner in what looked to be lingerie, was smoking the longest and thinnest cigarette Lucy had ever seen. Though it was only 10:00 A.M. and she was still in her sleep clothes, Jamie's lips were already painted a bright red, the same red as the paper kiss. Lucy had lugged her suitcase what seemed like a hundred blocks, and the sweat trickling from her armpits was making its way down to the waistband of her jeans, which, faced with Jamie, seemed highly unfashionable. Jamie was all legs and lipstick, wearing an intimidating musk perfume, and Lucy wondered if her trail of fate had failed her, if she should follow this woman at all. But then again, she did need a place. And a hotel would be expensive; she had only her mother's quarters, a book of checks linked to a new bank account she had started with the money she'd made at Mason & Mick's: twelve hundred and fourteen dollars, which seemed like a lot until you began to calculate how long it would actually last. She smiled tentatively and followed smoking Jamie upstairs, watching her black, skimpy chemise work its way up the stairs and up her thin thighs.

The stairwell smelled of urine, paint, and cigarettes: the New York stairwell smell. *Not* the Idaho stairwell smell (old wood, mud, pine). Then she thought: but Idaho doesn't even have stairwells! Had she ever been in a stairwell? This thrilled her: a new physicality; a new layout for her life. "Hope you're in the market for a walk-up," Jamie called back to her. Lucy smiled. *Walk-up*. This was her new language. These stairs were her new portal.

"Welcome to Kleindeutschland," Jamie said breathlessly when they got upstairs, to a dismal, white-walled apartment furnished with nothing but an old orange couch, whose material reminded Lucy of a clown's suit.

"Thank you," Lucy said nervously, not understanding Jamie's reference, but not wanting to seem stupid by asking about it.

"Little Germany," Jamie clarified. "This street? Used to be the German Broadway. The storefront downstairs? Used to be a cobbler. Now, of course, it's a porn shop. Personally I like to imagine the Germans phasing in to the new biz. You know, cobbling dicks for a living."

Jamie laughed roughly as she inhaled on her cigarette. Lucy forced herself to laugh a little bit, too. She pulled her suitcase into the tiny room—closet-size, with no closet of its own—looked up at the ceilings, which were, oddly she thought, made of tin, indented with a flowery pattern. A crack ran from the central light fixture down to the bedroom's door, where it was dead-ended by a loose piece of finishing. The crack made Lucy feel nervous, and then, as she followed it down to the floor, where a glinting black bug scurried around the baseboard, she was pushed into full-blown panic. She looked to Jamie for some sort of explanation, but her new roommate was unfazed.

"The love shack," Jamie said dryly. "Space for a bed, and hey, that's all ya really need, right?"

Love shack? Dick cobbling? Enormous, foreign insects? Lucy felt the blood drain from her face. She felt as white as the paint on the walls. Cracked as the paint on the walls. Hair as bright as the moon out the window of the plane that got her here. That one window to open. She did, impressing herself with her decisive action, how easily the glass shot upward. Hot air flooded in. Wood floors covered in splatters of paint. She stood in her new home.

Jamie pulled a cigarette from her blue-and-white pack and held it out for Lucy. She took it, slowly, and put it in her mouth. She had never smoked a cigarette before, and had never wanted to. But now, with no one watching her, it felt exciting and novel and right. The flame of Jaime's match moved toward her; she could feel the heat on her face. Jaime lit the bright white end of the cigarette and Lucy inhaled.

"So tell me everything," said Jamie. Her voice had changed almost entirely, from intimidating to intimate, nearly sexy, her face so close to Lucy's as she blew out the match. Lucy felt the panic again—what could she possibly tell this woman, this woman wearing practically nothing but lipstick, who had most likely heard every story ever told, seen everything there was to see? But Jamie smiled suddenly, and there was a gap in her teeth, and the gap told Lucy things were going to be okay.

"What do you want to know?" Lucy said, taking another drag.

"Just everything," Jamie said. "Everything you've got."

This is how New York began. A willingness, and then a pause. An attitude, a confidence, and then this: cracked walls and huge bugs, your first cigarette, the taste of your own fear. Fear not for what might be in store but for what might *not* be, that your bravery, which looked so big in your hometown, would not amount to anything, that New York City would not deliver on its promise, for something grand and glamorous, unknown and unknowable. Suddenly it was as if everything you knew about space before (the V-shape of a highway that went on forever, expansive wooden decks, backyards that never ended, the shapes between the leaves where the sun filtered through and made stars) has been discarded, put in a box that you cannot unlock until you go back.

But how can you go back? You have only just gotten here.

Now, as Lucy toured the dismal bathroom (a ring of mold circumnavigating the toilet), the two-burner stove ("Busted since May," said Jamie), the bars on the windows (*But why, when they were so many flights up?*), her throat got caught in itself. What had she imagined? A picturesque painter's loft with huge squares of light coming in? A shiny mug of coffee on a white desk? A professional pleated skirt? A set of high heels in the corner of a huge room, sitting pretty beside a stack of very interesting books? No, that was not her New York. Her New York was one hundred square feet of hell and dust.

She suddenly felt the deep urge to create a feeling of *okay* for herself.

"Jamie?"

"Yes, Idaho?"

"Where can I get some paint?"

The paint store: in Ketchum she would have had to drive there. Here: right down the busy block. Six or ten guys working. New Yorkers to the bone, but Lucy didn't know about them yet.

"What can we get fo' yah, sweethawt?" one said, his buzz cut buzzing.

"Yellow," she said. "I'm looking for yellow."

"We've got Sunshine and we've got Scotch," the paint man said. "And those ah the best."

She studied the charming swatches. In Ketchum she would have chosen Sunshine. But Scotch, she decided (a decision whose equivalent she would make again and again in her new New York life), pointing to the darker yellow, the one that almost looked orange. She'd be here for only a year or so, anyway; the color didn't have to matter.

"Absahlootly, no problem; absahlootly, no problem," said the paint man as he rallied a paint mixer into its dramatic whir. "No problem at ahl."

No problem. She could do this. Paint the walls and feel brighter. Buy coffee from the deli downstairs. Listen to Jamie's loud, chaotic music through the walls, let her heart boom with its energy. She would make a tiny orange sun of a room and she would be fine. The painting would fill her day. The sun would fall. She would get through her very first day in the Big City without any problems . . . until she was so exhausted that her eyelids were falling and realized—she'd laugh about this to herself later, but right then it was tragic—that she had no bed.

The tip of Jamie's cigarette appeared in the doorway just as she had this thought.

"Come on, Ida," Jamie said. "We're going out."

"I'm sort of exhausted," Lucy said. She looked down at herself: white shirt and bad jeans, all flecked with scotch-colored paint.

"This is New York. Everyone's exhausted," Jamie said. "Come on, put some shoes on. We're going to the Paradise."

Reluctantly Lucy got up, unzipped and flopped open her suitcase.

"I don't really have anything to . . . ," she said, looking back at Jamie.

"Oh, Jesus," Jamie said, blowing smoke. "Now I have to dress you? Come on."

Jamie outfitted Lucy in a tight, cropped shirt with plastic geometric shapes sewn onto the fabric and a pair of faded black jeans whose waist reached well above her belly button. The outfit seemed absurd to Lucy, but she figured it was what people wore to Paradise, and so she went with it, accepting as well a smear of cotton-candy-colored lipstick— another of Jamie's signature hues. Jamie threw a lot of exotically wom- anly items—more lipsticks; hard, red candies; condoms; cigarettes— into a little sparkly white bag that made an extra-satisfying click when it closed, and Lucy wondered if she should have a little bag like this, too, but she did not, so she stuffed a few five-dollar bills in her pocket and followed Jamie down the stairs and out the door and all the way across the city—which was crackling with the noises of a young, hot night—to the Paradise Garage; the sign boasted a neon muscle man.

This is a girl on her first night in New York. A girl in someone else's clothes. A girl who can feel the slice of her stomach showing, between someone else's shirt and someone else's jeans. A girl who is being handed a drink involving gin, that tastes like poison and sunshine at once. A girl in a room full of other girls just like her, who have come here to tunnel down into their own dark parts and find the light. A girl who is being swept out into the middle of a crash of dancing bodies, who lets her own body writhe among them, who lets the fire of the gin heat her already hot stomach, who begins to wiggle her extremities,

who lets two beautiful boys who are dancing together pull her between them, who laughs while they gyrate against her, who lets the
beautiful red and purple lights spin around and inside of her, thinking:
This is it, this is it, this is it.

Lucy woke up the next morning, in Jamie's bed, to a feeling of extreme hollowness. Where was she? What had last night meant? Where
had that feeling—the energy of newness, the blissful tug of communal
movement, the *absence of any worry*—gone, and how could she get it
back? Now she was all headache and smeared makeup and fear. Jamie's
slender back was turned to her: the back of someone she did not know
at all, on the other side of an unfamiliar bed. A witchy tapestry hung
above them; on it sperm-like shapes spawned and multiplied around
some Indian goddess. There was a torn Blondie poster on the wall to her
left, and a line of nails strung with Jamie's bounteous necklaces. A tube
of deodorant on the dresser. A box of Tampax and a lipstick kiss on the
mirror. These things comforted her only slightly: this was the stuff of
girls everywhere. But the panic returned when she thought about what
she would do now, awake and alone in the city that was supposed to be
her home. She thought she might wait for Jamie to wake up—maybe
they would make breakfast?—but she also had the feeling that it might
be hours before Jamie woke up, and that someone like Jamie probably
didn't make or eat breakfast at all. Plus, the broken stove.

She quietly slid out of the bed, gathered herself, splashed water on
her face from the pink, rusty sink. Before she went downstairs and out
into the world, she crept back into Jamie's room to grab her little white
purse from the night before. She emptied it and filled it with her own
things: her stupid green wallet and her cherry ChapStick and then, for
good measure, one of Jamie's cigarettes, which she pulled from the
pack on the dresser: a tiny, precious scroll. Just borrowing, she told
herself. Borrowing from her new friend.

. . . .

Outside, New York was being New York. The hot asphalt was steam-
ing, the little dogs were being toted or followed by their eccentrically
dressed masters, the clothes were bright and skimpy, the smell was
sewer and candied nuts, the newspapers were cracking open at the
café tables, the sunglasses were enormous, the scrawls on the walls
seemed to vibrate. Lucy wandered down the avenue, in search of
nothing and everything.

What she found: fire escapes zigzagging like lightning bolts on the
sides of every building, painted over so many times that their surfaces
resembled blistering human skin; a group of men in the park wearing
orange and white singing the same low song, over and over; a burp-
ing black suitcase on Avenue A, revealing a bright red bra; a car radio
blasting Mexican horns, its owner flicking his tongue out to reveal
gold-covered teeth; sidewalk grates opening and slamming like the
lids of boxes, offering glimpses of a whole other dark world below this
whole dark world; a spiky, spray-painted crown on a red wall; an abandoned lot, home to a rusted tricycle, a large bird, a sleeping man wearing a ripped plaid jumpsuit, and miraculously, a swatch of morning
glories that had just now yawned open.

Lucy had no reference point for this landscape. It was entirely new
to her, and so she could not place it within herself. It moved upward
instead of out. It moved outward instead of in. It was only the middle
of the morning and already it was a circus of catcalls and coffee smells
and crazy sounds. Was she frightened by it? Disgusted? Terrified?
Intrigued? All of these things. She wanted nothing more than to call
her mother. She wanted anything but to call her mother. She was both
desperate and open. Her mind filled and emptied; she didn't know it,
but she was already bracing herself, becoming immune. Through her
flat shoes, she felt the city's hot concrete. Her hot concrete. She could
walk everywhere. She did.

There were problems with living in New York that were not problems anywhere else in the world. Lucy had only thought of her move here as a singular large-scale risk, an enormous leap of trust that required the bravery everyone back home had questioned. Lucy had never considered the wicked guilt of doing nothing in a city constructed around always doing *something*, or the ordeal of subway tokens, or the carrying of many, many plastic bags that dug into your hands like blades, or the clothes one had to buy in order to feel even remotely comfortable existing among the real New Yorkers, who seemed to know exactly what to wear at all times—when to bring an umbrella, when you were supposed to switch to boots. The skirt she had imagined did not exist, she found, and even if it had it wouldn't be *right*. The right skirt, in New York City in 1979, would not be pleated or formal. In fact it probably wouldn't be a skirt at all but some version of the tight leggings she saw Jamie and the other girls wearing, tight leggings with large shirts, almost to the knees. She would need much more than new clothes to become a New Yorker anyway, she saw during those first days and weeks in the city. She would need to change entirely, and not in any of the ways she had expected.

She let Jamie bleach her hair in the sink. "*Hot, Idaho,*" Jamie said.

At a stall on St. Mark's Place, she had a man with big round pieces of wood in his earlobes pierce her nose with a silver hoop. "*Even hotter.*"

Based on an advertisement where an attractive, wholesome-looking girl held a glass of whiskey under the text: SINCE WHEN DO YOU DRINK JIM BEAM? SINCE I DISCOVERED IT'S SO MIXABLE, Lucy began ordering Jim Beam on the rocks, both wanting to be the wholesome girl who mixed it with something and wanting nothing to do with her.

. . . .

She kept her eyes open for the artists in her book, but it seemed Jamie did not frequent the same locales that they would; she met, instead, a series of male suitors who were cleanly dressed and messily drunk, who were looking for a blonde like her to take their minds off their work. Jamie explained that she hated these assholes, too, but they were just another necessary evil in a place that ran on necessary evils. "*Plus*," Jamie whispered, "*I find their blandness excessively interesting.*" Lucy got drinks bought for her—raspberry martinis were a thing—but always skirted out of the chunky, sweaty grasps of the men, often opting to go outside and look up and out at the buildings, to smoke one of her new cigarettes on a stoop and watch the city twinkle itself toward morning.

It wasn't long before she had spent all the money she'd saved, and she was ashamed to call her parents for more, not that they had any to send her. She ate hardly anything—bread and butter, candy bars, an apple—but even with her meager ways she could not afford the rent Jamie was asking for: $206, on the fifteenth of the month.

Although she had known she would need a job, she had not given thought to how she would get one, and, she began to see after a number of discouraging interviews, a job was not going to fall out of the sky like Jamie's apartment listing had. Each day during those first few weeks, as she climbed from the sweltering underground of the subway stations or taped up a blister she had gotten from walking around the city aimlessly, or felt like a fool in her silly-looking sneakers, slashed with neon yellow strips of plastic, which had seemed so advanced in Ketchum but horribly wrong now, she questioned her decision to come here. Each day she had countless moments where she thought she just couldn't hack it, where she longed for the wooden walls of her bedroom, Ketchum's clean air, an afternoon with nothing around her and nothing to do. On multiple occasions she found herself in tears in a phone booth or on a stoop, sometimes even in the dressing room of a clothing store whose clothes she couldn't afford, always with other people's hungry eyes on her, filled with a voyeurism linked to the deep need to see reflections of themselves in similar situations at other times; everyone knew there was nowhere to cry in New York.

It was in the middle of one of these lacrimal instances, in a midtown subway station, on her way home from a botched interview (at an independent bookstore, where apparently you had to know the authors and titles of every classic ever written, on command), dressed probably inappropriately in one of Jamie's shorter skirts, that Lucy saw her first New York City artist.

On the other side of the tracks, between the rusting pillars, a man crouched, then erupted like a star, then crouched again. A red stream of paint followed his hand wherever it moved, like magic. The man was small; whatever he was drawing was big. What he was drawing was still unclear; she moved closer to the tracks so she could see. A figure of sorts, an arm, a leg. The most confident lines in the world, rushing from his body like a song. Lucy wanted to watch him forever, this small, magical artist, but she felt the pressure-wind of her train coming to obscure her view and whisk her away. *But wait. This was it.* Yellow intrusion of train light. *But wait!* The man was just finishing. The train screeched and flashed in front of her. She jumped in, scurried to the window on the opposite side. The man was gone, just like that. What was left on the wall was a giant penis, a penis with arms and legs and a penis of his own, which was being sucked by another penis. Lucy made one enormous sound like a laugh. *A penis being sucked by another penis?!* She was the only one in the subway car, which she was grateful for, because she could let herself feel the heat from what she just saw: heat that ran from her heart to her stomach, whether for the artist or his vulgar image, she didn't need to know.

When she broke the bad news about the interview to Jamie— "Didn't go well, Jame. Should have paid better attention in English"— Jamie only scoffed.

"It's terrible, isn't it?" she said, while mixing a very dirty-looking martini in a mason jar. "Being a girl in New York? It's just the fucking worst."

But Lucy wasn't sure yet. She wasn't sure if it was the worst or the very, very best.

During her fourth week in the apartment, in the armpit nightmare that was early August in the city, Jamie invited people over: a crew of guys whose names all started with R. Immediately Lucy wondered if any of them were artists; immediately she found out that they were not. Ryan, whom Jamie had been sleeping with even though she confessed to Lucy that she thought he was "missing some brain cells," had big arm muscles and a crooked nose. ("Not the only part of him that's crooked," Jamie told her later.) He was talking about a movie he had gone to the night before, something about sharks that he'd seen while significantly high; he couldn't get the theme song out of his head. Rob, who was more beautiful than the rest when it came to his face, but who stood and was depressingly short, rolled his eyes in Ryan's direction as he talked, then gave Lucy a high five. Randy, a too-nice guy with a long ponytail and an army coat, said very slowly, between hits from a joint that was almost burning out, "Hey, Lucy, we heard you were looking for a job."

Lucy smiled.

"Can I get a hit of that?" she said. She realized it was the first time since getting here that she felt confident enough to ask for something, not to wait for it to befall her, and as she sucked the smoke into her lungs she felt good, and alive, and she said to Randy, "What's the job?"

He told her it was at a bar. A bartender job.

Lucy looked, glassy-eyed, over at Jamie, who gave her a sad smile.

"Don't be an asshole, Ida," Jamie said. "This city is built off of people doing things they don't wanna do."

Jamie, Lucy had found out, worked as a massage therapist in the financial district. "The men get really tense," she had said. "All that money, all that trading." She had said the words *money* and *trading* as if she were running out of breath, and Lucy understood that Jamie's massages sometimes, if not always, ended up being more than just massages. Jamie also tended to work overtime, from her "home office," and Lucy often heard the exchanges taking place: the *trading*, she assumed, then the *money*.

Lucy gulped. She felt simultaneously depressed and excited. She imagined herself in high heels, serving fancy people fancy cocktails. It would just be temporary. She could do it for a while—work on her feet until she got on her feet, so to speak. She pushed away an impulsive thought of her mother, what her mother might say about her working at a bar, which went something like: *You move all the way out there, so far from your mother, to . . .*

Randy sighed. "Jamie, why you gotta knock my place of employment like that? It's an upstanding place. Right, Rob? Rob's there every night. Right, Rob?"

"I'll take it," Lucy said quickly, sipping from a beer Jamie had handed her. "I mean, if Rob's there every night . . ." She winked at Rob in a way she figured was cute.

"There's a place where you can buy live snakes down on Canal," Randy said, out of nowhere. "I was thinking about getting one."

They all laughed, which made Lucy feel okay about things. Thinking about being part of a group of people sitting together and laughing. She imagined Randy with a snake around his neck, serving someone a raspberry martini.

And so Random Randy, as Jamie and Lucy would start to call him because of his propensity to bring up totally irrelevant subjects at odd times, took her to the Eagle, an underground (both figuratively and literally) bar in the West Village. It was a kitschy, divey place, where the walls were made of fake stones, and there was the vague sense that the bar itself was tucked inside of a log cabin. Randy bent over a plug and a string of red chili pepper lights went on around the windows, though in the daylight you couldn't really see that they were on. The chili pepper lights made Lucy want to get back on a plane to Idaho, where she would be working for Randall, the lawyer, not Randy, the bartender. She agreed with her mother's imaginary critique: she did not move to New York City to work in a *bar*. But then again, what did she move to New York City to do? And what else was there? Randy intercepted her with an arm thrown around her waist, guiding her back behind the bar for what he called the "grand tour."

"This is the ice," he said. "And here are the wells. And the glasses rack up like so. And you want to be sure not to use the Coke button here. 'Cause Sprite comes out."

Lucy took the soda gun in her hand. She tested the sprayer tentatively, coaxing a foam of Coke from its mouth, which landed in a stainless-steel sink.

"And here are Jamie's matchbooks," Randy said, pulling one of the white squares from a candy jar and tossing it to Lucy. She carefully fingered the little booklet, and when Randy told her to, opened it. On the inside was a message: *DON'T BE CRAZY. BE WILD.*

Lucy laughed once but then didn't know if she should be laughing, so she stopped. "What are these?"

"One of Jamie's projects," Randy said. "She writes down the things that the guys say to her, the guys she sleeps with. She's one of those creative types, you know? Not like me. I'm just . . . regular."

"Oh, you're not regular, Randy."

"It's fine," Randy said. "I don't mind. I don't need to be an artist. There are enough of those in this city, I'll tell you that."

"So Jamie is an artist?"

"Let's just say she's not sleeping with those guys for the money.

Although there's that, too, I guess. I'm not one to explain it, but it's all part of some big art project. She tapes them. Sets up a camera. Then she sort of leads them into things. Put on my lingerie, do a dance, cry like a baby. She's got these miserable Wall Street guys on tape, acting like fools."

"Isn't that sort of . . . fucked up?"

"Isn't life sort of fucked up?"

Lucy smiled down at her matchbook, then tucked it into her pocket. So Jamie was an artist. She lived with an artist. The thought made her heart quicken.

"But don't bring it up with her," Randy said, now sounding tentative, rubbing the part between his nose and his mouth. "She's not into talking about it. I guess you could say she's not really into the whole artist *thing*, you know? She's more of a lone wolf. Says she wants someone to find the tapes when she dies."

Lucy was quiet; she watched Randy suck in a batch of stale air and raise his arms to stretch.

"That's about it for the tour, really!" Randy said. "If you don't know what's in a drink? Ask your customer. Your customer always knows."

But there were no customers yet, at four in the afternoon, and Lucy stood behind the sink wondering if this was indeed her fate: an empty bar with dust shimmering in the sunlight, an empty life.

But quickly the empty life began to fill with bar regulars (Sandy the shoe-repair guy and Pat the failed writer and Gabby the hickey-boasting hooker), and Jamie's crew of men friends, and bits of toxic white powder and slices of the moon, spotted in the valleys between the buildings after her shifts, close to 4:00 A.M. She began to know the streets (Sullivan, Delancey, Mott) and the subways (*screech, ding, swoosh, spark*) and the outfits (big boots, big shirts, small pants or small boots, small shirts, big pants). And with her post at the Eagle came extraordinarily easy access to one of the things New York had in as much abundance as pretzels: *men*.

....

Bret with one *t*. Large loft, small penis, too many candles, who cared, she liked him. Small penis or not, he didn't like her enough not to move to California three days after their meeting, for a job at a computer company that had been started in someone's garage.

Tom with no shirt on, offered to help her carry a mattress up to her apartment. Fell onto the mattress and fucked; when Lucy woke up, he had migrated to Jamie's bed.

A woodworker whose name she didn't know who took her to pancakes at Pearl Diner and kissed her in the subway, who when she asked him his name at the end of the night said: *married*.

And on and on; the men adored and then disposed of her. With each of them she felt briefly and tightly tethered, hopeful that they would deliver her to that place that she craved: the deep dark cavern of love and lust, the place where longing stopped. But none of them did, and in between her encounters with them, and usually even during, she felt deeply alone. And besides, when she thought about it hard enough, from the part of her that craved something beyond just a body in the bed, she knew they did not interest her. She briefly tried to turn her experiences with them into a project, like Jamie had, but she knew it wasn't hers. What *was* hers? She didn't know. For now it was the twelve-foot expanse of mahogany that she wiped a hundred times a night, behind which she had started to feel almost, if not totally, at home; by December the smell of the old limes didn't bother her anymore.

As the months grew colder (cold was something that she *knew*, from the endless, deep winters in Ketchum) she actually began to feel a tinge of comfort in the chaos that was her new life—the street fights and the snow trudging and the late nights—and to take a sort of young-person solace in her loneliness, floating nicely in her melancholy, which was reminiscent of her teenage years in Idaho, the sad mountains, the ease of getting caught up in her own plight. This was part of the waiting, she knew. She knew if she waited long enough it would happen. The big bang, the cosmic crash, the delightful disturbance that would determine her true city fate.

Of course that was back when Lucy still believed in fate at all. When she still held superstitions—if she said things out loud, she felt they wouldn't come true, and if she wished for things hard enough, she thought they might. First stars, worry dolls, lucky pennies, matchbooks—she had alternately believed in these as things that might alter her entire course in the world. That postcard on the side of the road was one of these things. Jamie's red lipstick was one of these things. And Randy, who randomly invited her to be a bartender at the Eagle on Bleecker Street, he was one, too. She let herself believe that all of this—coming to this city, taking this job—was all a part of a cosmic plan for something big to happen in her very small life. She just had to wait. She had to wait until she had mixed a million drinks. Until the matchbook she pulled from the jar read: *KISS ME HARDER.* Until time tipped past midnight and it was technically Tuesday and officially 1980. She just had to wait until the crowd died down and parted and the noise around her silenced and the red chili pepper lights were the only lights left in the world—for something, or someone, to change her life.

Should old acquaintance be forgot, and never brought to mind? The song was still playing in Lucy's head when the black mole—which stood like a monument paying homage to the idea of beauty—began its journey toward her face. In this suspended moment lived all of the questions: Would he be like all the others? Would he kiss her over the bar and then disappear off the planet? Or would he, like her deep stomach was telling her he would, *love her?*

His lips! His lips! His lips! Due to his lips, she knew that this would *not* be like all the others. Due to his lips, she knew that he was darker, deeper: that thing she had been looking for. Due to his lips, her old acquaintances would be forgot forever, and there would be only him.

When he pulled away she reached into her pocket for one of Jamie's matchbooks that she'd nabbed earlier that day, slid it across the bar to the man. *KISS ME HARDER*, it read. He did.

He stayed with her while she closed down the bar, following her like an eager dog while she scrubbed the counters, kissing her incrementally while she counted the tips. Then he carried her, literally on his back, across town to the squat, as he called it, where the latest part of a huge party was still going on. He introduced her to everyone— Boss the African jazzman and Horatio—*Horatio, get low!* Engales yelled to him—in his white underwear, held high with yellow suspenders. And Selma, with her newly cropped, exotically spiky head of hair, a voice like a cocoon—*ohhhhhh, Saint Selma*—and her small saggy breasts, which were displayed in plaster casts all over the room. ("See those?" Selma said, pointing to one of the sculptures. "Those are my titties. Take one home if you want.") *So this was where they were,* Lucy thought. All the artists she had been searching for, who, unlike Jamie, were not cloaking their projects but parading them around in this insane, deteriorating, divine palace of messy, outrageous *art.*

Lucy spotted a small man painting himself, literally, into one of the corners of the room. Her heart leaped. She knew that man! It was the man from the subway station! Those were his lines—so sure, so graphic, so magical; she pulled at Engales's hand.

"I know him!" she said giddily.

"You know Keith?" Engales said.

"Yes!" Lucy said, bouncing. "I saw him painting in the subway. He was painting a penis."

She felt embarrassed right after she said it, both for the word *penis* and for the fact that she had claimed to know someone from having seen him across the subway tracks. But Engales found it charming, apparently, and smiled, kissed her on the forehead.

"You are very adorable, Spot, do you know that?" he said. He then led her down a darkened hallway and into an empty, cement-floored room where he pressed her up against the drywall, looked into her eyes with a crazy, almost capitalistic determination, and said: "*Spot, you are the American dream.*" And all she could do was laugh the very particular laugh of a girl in love. Tilt of chin. Sparkle of half-closed eyes. Half smile, no teeth. Then—here it was—eyes all the way open, pupils floating to the top when she looked up, *I'm yours*, they said, she knew it, *I'm yours*.

As the squat's party faded, he tugged her out into the street and up the five black blocks to his apartment, which was filled with nothing but his reckless, wonderful paintings. He set her down on the bed and told her to: "Hold still, I'm going to paint you."

There was this: him reaching like a madman for paint and brushes, a long spell of sitting still when her body was aching for more of him, the scratchy collar of her sequined shirt, the resulting picture—herself as a giant, mystical thing, a beautiful monster.

And then there was this: him leaving the painting and climbing onto the bed with her and grabbing her head with his two hands.

They devoured each other. And surely (his tongue in her ear), most definitely (his sticky body on top of hers), undeniably (his eyes like he loved her), he would change her fate. She woke up the next morning to see the still-wet picture of herself, knowing forever had started, if forever were what forever felt like, which was a year in New York City when you were in love.

PART
TWO

ABNORMAL CIRCUMSTANCES

Under normal circumstances, James and Marge would not be uptown on a Tuesday night. They would especially not be at Sotheby's auction house, a place where James had personally vowed never to set foot. But James was not operating under normal circumstances tonight. He was operating under the circumstances of the worst day of his life, if he had to cast a judgment, a day within a series of days, encased within a series of months, during which he saw no color besides the color that was *actually* there, heard no sound besides the annoying racket of reality. And so the night was not yellow, as it should have been, and Marge was not red, as she should have been, and Marge was not holding a small baby, as she should have been, but was instead holding her arms around her waist, as depressed as he was to be here. They were here to sell James's beloved Richard Estes painting, the one of the storefront window on Thirty-fourth Street, a favorite in his personal collection that he had promised himself he'd never sell.

The auction room was vast, filled with the tinkling sound of hypothesis and worry and excitement. *Who would buy what?* The black curtains scalloped like a tide. *How much would it sell for?* Someone's dress caught the light. *Who would surprise them tonight, and how would they do it?* The room handled the murmur expertly, parsing it and folding it into the very architecture of the space, into the cuffs of the men's shirtsleeves, the soft curls of women's hair; into the chandeliers, which tentacled around the ceiling like crystal-studded octopi, working flecks of anxious light around the room.

James waited impatiently for the larger quiet to settle in, the quiet he imagined expressed the essence of an event like this, a quiet that spoke of refinery and nervous patience. In the meantime he scanned the room, wondering who might purchase the Estes. A woman with a beak for a nose. A man with a choke-making bow tie. He doubted anyone would find in his painting what he once did: the smell of doughnuts; the taste of rain; the color of his wife's nylons.

What he had once found. What he had seen and felt, and smelled, and *lived by* his whole adult life. It had gone missing in what felt like the flash of a camera: one white bulb breaks, and a life is captured and frozen in however it existed in that moment.

That moment: midnight on Winona George's balcony, a cold sea of hair and diamonds. A collective chanting of the countdown—*five, four, three*—and snow begins to fall, and then the old year breaks into the new one and the sky breaks open with confetti, and there is sloppy kissing and loud *hurrahs!* And James and Marge are kissing and the world is spinning with all its spangled bravado. A drunken man with a mustache and his drunken redheaded companion make their merry rounds, tangoing across the balcony. Glitter falls. The redheaded companion in her off-base bohemian dress falls, clutched in the mustache's besuited arms. And they fall right into and on top of Marge. *Holy fuck!* says the bohemian girlfriend with a laugh, too old to be a girlfriend, James now sees, and *Oopsy daisy!* yells her suited suitor. And this is the moment—Marge on the ground saying, *I'm okay, I'm okay,* trying to laugh, James saying frantically, *It's just that she's . . . pregnant*—when everything breaks.

Marge, though she said she was fine when they got home, woke in the early morning to a circle of blood leaking from her and out onto the bed, spreading quickly, like a red frost.

James had panicked then. He had felt as if he couldn't breathe. He had carried Marge down the stairs and the blood had gotten everywhere. His lungs hurt and tears came. Through his wet eyes he somehow found them a cab and somehow told the driver to take them to a hospital, and he somehow listened as the doctor told them patronizingly what they mostly already knew—this doesn't happen very often in the second trimester, it is a very small percentage, but it *can* happen, and it happened to you. Neither of them thought to tell the doctor about the fall on the balcony, either because they were caught up in their panic or because they did not want to admit it had happened—as if it would have been admitting that in some way the miscarriage had been *their* fault . . . if they had only stayed home from that party . . . if they had only acted like responsible, with-child adults!

James saw behind the doctor's words a black circle, slowly moving toward him. He felt an aching in his joints, especially in his feet. The hospital, to him, smelled of fire and smoke. He felt a surreal haze forming around him as they made their way back to the apartment, thinking: How could they be on their way back to their apartment? How would they enter the living room? How would they go to sleep? Not when so much had been lost.

But they did sleep, they slept in scary depth, the kind of sleep people sleep when they do not want to face waking life. They slept through the mean light of morning that pierced through the crack in the curtains. They slept through the middle of the day. When one of them stirred, the other held them still. Not now, they said with their arms. Not yet.

When James finally did let his lids open, though, for long enough to let in the light fully, he felt immediately that something was different. Where he usually woke to a mixture of Marge's red and the season's signature—light green (spring), static blue (winter), navy-blue-almost-black (fall), or warm buttery yellow (summer)—this morning he saw nothing. Nothing, that is, aside from the light that was *actually* gliding through the windows and onto his sleeping wife, a light that held none of the colors usually so active in the prism of his mind. Stupidly he walked over to Marge's side of the bed and ran his hand through the slice of light that fell on her, as if by touching it it would change color. It didn't. Just white, bright, normal January light, falling onto his wife's pale face. He saw nothing. Felt nothing. Nothing at all.

He rushed into the bathroom and stared at himself in the mirror, slapped his face, threw water onto it. He opened and closed his eyes frantically, thinking if he blinked them hard enough he might spark the colors back into action. But whereas the mirror usually tinted a greenish color (James himself was the color of split-pea soup), he saw only his pale, unshaven face, puffy with tiredness, long but somehow still pudgy, sliding back into his balding forehead. No split pea: just blotchy skin. He smacked at his forehead with the heel of his hand. Nothing. He pricked his skin between a pair of tweezers: pain was usually marked by the sound of crashing waves and that black spot between his eyes. Nothing.

The final test: James brought himself to look at the Ruth Kligman painting near the mirror, the one he had bought for Marge when they were first married and that made him see bright, flashy orange snakes behind his eyes—it looked muddy and empty. *How could the Ruth Kligman look empty?!* He felt his breath suck into him, the pain of tears about to come. He crumpled onto the toilet and put his face in his hands. Clear, invisible, empty tears fell—they were as meaningless as his reflection in the mirror. But they poured from him in a steady, loud stream. The blood on the stairs. The sheets. The balcony. The emptiness in his mind. He cried so hard that Marge, even in her debilitated state, hobbled from her bed into the bathroom. She saw him hunched and rocking like a madman on the toilet, crying his eyes out, and came to hug and pet him.

"It's okay," she whispered down into his large ear. "We can try again, James. Even the doctor said, we can try again."

But Marge began crying with him, and their two chests heaved together like the heartbeat of a broken heart.

From there things only got worse. James tried with spastic urgency to retrieve his sensibilities—he went to countless art shows, read poems that usually made his colors go wild (O'Hara's line "how terrible orange is, and life" had once made him roller-coaster dizzy), exposed himself to extreme temperatures and odd foods—but nothing worked. O'Hara didn't work. Rutabaga didn't work. The Metropolitan Museum of fucking Art didn't work.

He soon found that writing didn't work, either, not without his sensations. He stared at blank pages and cursed his blank brain. For the immediate future, this was okay; he had enough almost-finished articles—which only needed editing and not added ideas—to keep the *Times* column going for a couple months. After that, he offered to curate a selection of guest columnists, to bide his time. But by April this was tired, and there was nothing left, and he began to miss his deadlines completely.

He asked for two weeks off from his column, then three. When he finally brought himself to cobble together a review, of Jeff Koons's window installation at the New Museum, it was immediately rejected, on grounds of being, as the Arts editor's squeaky assistant Seth had put it, *vacuous.*

"Well, it *should* be vacuous!" James yelled at Seth. "The installation is a bunch of vacuums! Form as content, Seth! Didn't they teach you anything in journalism school?"

Seth just stuttered a half-assed apology, hung up on James.

This was only the first of many rejections that followed, from the paper that had so confidently published him for years, given him his own little corner of newsprint in which to spill his every whimsical thought. Each rejection came with a new qualifier from Seth: *impersonal, unrealistic, lacking oomph.* When Marge flicked through the Sunday paper to the Arts section, like she always did, James made the excuse that he was working on a more research-based piece that was taking him longer than most, and that he'd be in next week's, don't worry. He couldn't bring himself to tell her about the rejections; he still wanted to prove the *Times*, and himself, wrong. He needed to keep trying.

But another month passed without a bite from the newspaper. And then two. And then finally, in June, they gave away the column completely. To someone, according to Seth, "whose interests were more in line with the publication's." Seth added tentatively: "Oh, and Mr. Bennett? He asked me to tell you not to send any more submissions through."

"Excuse me?" James said.

"He says your time at the *Times* is done," Seth said. "Okay?"

Not okay. In the lead on James's List of Running Worries: that losing his invisible powers had rendered him completely invisible. Close behind: that he was a terrible human being for not telling any of this to Marge. But he didn't want to worry her; and how she worried! He of all people knew how unproductive and paralyzing worrying could be, and he did not want to weigh on her, like he always seemed to.

So he didn't tell her; he couldn't. Not in June, when Marge's grandfather had a stroke; not in July, when he died in his sleep and she took three weeks off of work to be with her family in Connecticut; not in August, when their apartment got so hot that the slightest disturbance would surely lead to a screaming match; this was divorce weather. It wasn't until September, when he was meant to give his metaphor lecture at Columbia, and then, fearing he would have no metaphors to talk about and would have to stand in silence in front of all those eager faces, called the program director and canceled, that he knew the problem was too big to hide. Not to mention the fact of their joint savings account, which was dipping into the red zone in a way it hadn't before, pulling James's confidence and heart down with it. He'd have to tell her. That he was not an upstanding American citizen / valid human / real man, and that he had been keeping this fact from her for the better part of the year.

He took her to a diner on Sixth Avenue, where they went when they wanted to feel like real New Yorkers. At the tail end of a mostly quiet breakfast, he pressed one of his hands over the smooth part of his head, inhaled as much air as was available in the stuffy, bacon-aired room.

"If I tell you something," he said, wishing with all his might that it wasn't fall, that so much time had not passed, "will you promise not to be angry?"

"Why would I be angry?" Marge said.

Next to Marge at the diner counter was an elderly woman with a pearl ring and puffy curls, and when Marge said this the woman chuckled, seeming to impart that *of course* she was going to be angry, a woman was always angry at her husband for one thing or another. For a second James imagined it was Marge as an old woman, and he was an old man, and they were sitting here under these diner lights as old people who had spent their entire lives together, living inside the bubble of all the unspoken things that being old together entailed. Suddenly James felt that there was no more time left on the planet.

"They took away my column," he blurted.

"What do you mean? Why?"

He watched Marge's hand press into the speckled Formica counter. The knuckles raised like a small, knotty hill. This was Marge when matters concerning real life were on the line: *all knuckles*.

"But it's because," he went on, seeing that she was unclear on how to react. "It's because . . . well, don't think I'm insane, but . . . the strawberries are gone."

He looked from the hand and into his wife's face. The face had gone pale.

"*My* strawberries?" she said. Her face retracted, as if she had been slapped.

"Yes," he said. "And everything else, too."

"And that's why they scrapped your column?"

"I've tried. So hard. I'm trying *so hard*. I've sent in fifteen articles now. Maybe twenty. None stuck. Nothing is sticking. It's like my brain was switched off or something. It's just . . . *blank*."

The old woman got up abruptly to go to the bathroom, patting her cloud of hair with her hands. James was thankful and embarrassed.

"James, I don't even know what to say."

"Say it will come back."

"How could I say that? How would I know that? I'm just hearing this, James. My first time hearing this. You told me you were doing something that needed research."

"I didn't mean to not tell you, or to lie, or . . . anything. I just didn't want to make you upset. I didn't want to be the disappointing man that I always am. The burden that I always am."

"You're not disappointing."

"I am."

"You're not disappointing, James. But you cannot lie to me. That's part of the deal. It's part of the real-life deal. I don't care if you aren't making money. But I need to know about it."

"I know that, but I just . . . I didn't want to give up. I still don't want to give up."

"Do you think you should, though?" she said. She said it quietly, and even kindly, but she said it.

"What?"

"I'm sorry," she said. "It's just that I feel like—for both of our sakes—maybe you need to think about what's going to work for you. For us. You're a part of a relationship, we're an *us*, remember?

Something bad happened, we lost our baby, and I get it. I feel it, too. I want to go into a hole and never come out. But that was nine months ago, James, and now you have to move on. You have to be a real human in the world just like the rest of us. You have to help me. You have to work. Especially if we want to try again, with another baby."

James felt a dull ache in his chest: an ache he had expected but that still ached. On his Running List of Worries: that another baby was an impossibility due to the fact that his sperm were lame, near invisible little tadpoles that couldn't navigate the treacherous terrain of his wife's insides. Though they were taking all the necessary steps—taking Marge's temperature religiously, keeping a journal that tracked her ovulation, having sex in the kitchen, if her timer happened to go off when they were in the middle of dinner—there was something off about the whole thing, and both of them knew it. And that something, they both also knew, was James. It was as if Marge's eggs could sense in James's sperm the just-not-himself-ness of their creator. Before, when he had had his colors, he had seen his sperm as a brilliant fireworks show, a whole Fourth of July celebration complete with the national anthem and hot dogs and fun barbecue smoke, taking off into his wife. Now: lame tadpoles.

"You're right," James said with a suck of his breath. "You're totally, one hundred percent right. I'll pick one. Tonight, I'll pick one."

When they got home from the diner they would stand in the living room together and look around, and silently he would choose one of his artworks, which in lieu of months of paychecks he would sell. As he surveyed the walls full of paintings he would note with sadness that they no longer looked like they once had, like they were alive in the world, and could change it. But it did not make it hurt less to let go of one, which also meant letting go of his pride.

"The Estes," he would say, with little conviction. "Worth the most." But he would really choose the Estes for Marge. He knew she didn't like the painting very much, for its cold perfection. She preferred the Kligman, whose strokes reminded her of her own internal sensibility: warm and abstract, yet pristine in its choices, deliberate and smart. She would blink up at him, twist her mouth as if to say she was sorry. And yet within the face also lay one glint of satisfaction, as if one corner of Marge's mouth were saying: *This is what you get*. He would swallow hard, mount a step stool. Together they would take the painting down from the wall, set it gently by the door.

Now here he was at Sotheby's, officially selling out. The lights in the auction house dimmed and the voices followed, the collective murmur fading into a hush: the conversations of all the rich people being grabbed up by the nets of the chandeliers. James braced himself. Felt Marge's soft hand on his thigh, which should have felt comforting but didn't. He wasn't allowed to resent her for this, he knew, but, even if it was very subtle, he could feel it. The tingly yet almost unfeelable sensation of resenting the person you loved most in the world. A warm hand on a stiff thigh.

"Welcome to Sotheby's," a slick-haired woman said robotically, in an English accent—one of the voices you heard in an airport, telling you which terminal you were in. "You'll find the titles and estimates of each work of art in your program. There will be no need to speak your bid; a hand will do."

Marge mumbled something about the whole thing being pretentious. He could tell she was trying to lighten things, to make the night feel like something other than what it was, which was a symbol of his general failure. James barely heard her anyway, because his mind was running through his list. Worry about seeing his painting on the chopping block of the stage. Worry that it would sell. Worry that it *wouldn't* sell. Worry that it would sell for less than what it was worth. Worry that either way it didn't matter—that nothing much mattered anymore.

The paintings that entered and exited the auction stage now felt and tasted and smelled like nothing. The first few works were straightforward and pristine: in line with the photorealist aspect of his Estes. They disappeared into the hands of big collector so-and-so, and then big collector so-and-so's friend—a network of so-and-sos that James understood were the most influential buyers in the city, or perhaps in the world. The momentum was meant to build as the auction progressed, the paintings becoming more valuable and more powerful as the evening went on, each scrolling across the stage with its worth floating above it like a kite. The auction helpers, dressed in their white-and-black auction-helper outfits, brought out paintings by Chuck Close, Frank Stella, Andy Warhol. Usually James would balk at a Warhol: the colors would smack of stage fright and sickness. Now? He felt nothing of the hospital-sadness they usually evoked.

The paintings brought a tight, hushed energy to the room as they were revealed on the stage; everyone had seen the program, they knew what was coming, but the physical presence of the work still cast its grandeur over the audience, created the kinetic jolt of proximity— like being in a room with someone you were in love with. Or was that the money, the vision of the money, the floating price tag that moved the people in this room? James couldn't tell. Things were selling for hundreds of thousands, seven hundred thousand, into the millions(!); James could feel Marge bristling beside him each time the gavel came down, with either excitement or nerves he couldn't tell, as a pile of invisible money left someone's hands. James grabbed for Marge's hand. His Estes was only three paintings away, at the precipice of the crescendo of silence, the tiptop of the hush. He bit his lip, tasting skin, and only skin.

James would wonder later if it was fate that brought him to that auction house that night, the night that, after running through the standard big-name paintings, Sotheby's had decided to do something unprecedented: they hosted a small auction for works they had acquired by donation from an anonymous collector—paintings by promising lesser-known artists who were not even in the program. The auctioneer announced this departure from routine with a sort of subversive coolness. Didn't it have to be fate that the first of these works, a huge painting by an artist that James had never heard of, rolled onto the stage at precisely the moment when James was about to leave? And that, when he saw it, even from his perch near the back of the auction house, he saw bright, frantic, unbelievable, joyous, terrible, uncontrollable, perfect yellow flashes behind his eyes? The *same exact* bright, frantic, unbelievable, joyous, terrible, uncontrollable, perfect yellow flashes—those *butterfly wings*!—that he had seen on New Year's Eve, coming from the man in the blue room? Could it have been fate that made his heart leap upward in his chest, his brain flood with song—a symphony of sorts, complete with all the violins of the Village, all the songs of New York, the falsetto voices of every piece of art he had ever loved—the corner of his eyes wet with tears, and his right hand shoot up into the air to bid?

Marge whipped a glance in his direction; he could feel the sting of her eyes.

"What are you doing?" she whispered. "James!"

He was aware of the silent faces turning toward him like animated flowers, cheery, blissed-out Warhol flowers, electric poppies, all focused on his hand, which was rising up and up as if he had no control over it, as if it were not his hand at all.

"What are you doing!" Marge spat again, still through her teeth but louder this time, yanking at his arm.

"Shhh," was all he said. The room held its breath. The velvet curtains creaked.

James was experiencing a color so pleasant he felt he might melt into the chair. The painting was a giant canvas boasting a larger-than-life blond woman, whose shirt sparkled like a fresh ocean, whose eyes were fishhooks, whose feet, and their largeness, made him smell the metallic grit of old pennies. His mind sparked and flashed. Zigzagged and flew. There were sprigs of fresh mint, a rebellious cigarette he had smoked when he was twenty, a night under the stars with a girl who had only wanted to be his friend. He slumped into a backseat at an all-night drive-in; he blushed; he wept.

And then it was done; a collective exhale as the gavel hit its mark. He had just *bought* a painting—he didn't even know who the artist was!—and Marge was reeling, furious, sweating; she stormed out of the auction room, scooting her backside over the knees of the New York elite, without even an angry glance back toward James.

James sat there in his chair, dumbfounded, convincing himself he had just done the right thing. It had to be a coincidence that the painting by the artist no one had ever heard of ended up costing him just over what he had made on the Estes painting moments ago, due to the fact that, from somewhere in the back, Winona George had circulated a rumor about this artist's bright future in her hands. It had to be, *certainly had to be,* fate that he had gotten the same sensations tonight as he had on New Year's, the last good sensations he'd felt before he lost them entirely. This painting would be a key, he knew. The key back into the house of his own mind.

Of course, fate was not an excuse when it came to explaining all this to Marge later. Marge, who had lost her baby. Marge, who had done so much to support him. Marge, the woman who had worked her way up from assistant art director to actual art director while he worked himself down from writer to nonwriter. Marge who had been paying all the bills since they lost the baby back in January, *nine months* ago now, and who only wanted him to be a little bit sensible, to share her dreams of even a remote amount of stability. To not do something insanely stupid like buy an absurdly expensive painting, when they could hardly afford to pay their rent.

She had left the auction house in a rage: all dark hair and snarled lips, the cleft in her chin flooding with red anger—he had been able to see the red again! Just after looking at the painting, he could see Marge's bright red again! She would not talk to him for days afterward, maybe weeks. She was going to *kill* him. But he couldn't be bothered to think about that for long. His mind, as he walked slowly home, down the wide sleeve of Eighth Avenue and under the shaded collar of the Village, was still fixated on the painting. So fixated, in fact, that he could have sworn, at one point, that he was *inside* of it. That the girl who was its central figure was floating down the sidewalk across the street from him, emitting that same yellow light from somewhere near her abdomen.

It couldn't possibly be her. He watched the light swish coolly in front of her. Not possible. A siren sang a city lullaby. But what crazy fate, if it was! A wheel made a mess out of a whiskey bottle. Should he cross the street to find out? No, he'd leave it like this: a wonderful, fateful night. A cat decided: *west*. The girl who could have been in his painting sang a name that could have been his own into the night.

PAINTING IS DEAD!

The day of Raul Engales's accident started with a dream. His sister was reading him a list from her childhood notebook: a list of all the things he had done wrong in his life. *Broke Daisy Montez's heart. Stole cigarettes from the blind guy with the tobacco cart. Broke off Tina Camada's engagement by fucking Tina Camada in the dressing room of the clothing store she worked in and getting caught by the manager, who was cousins with Tina Camada's fiancé. Flunked school. Smoked too much. Killed a cat.* The list went on. In the dream, Engales shook his sister by the shoulders to make her stop. He shook her so hard her eyes rolled back in her head and she stopped breathing. Then he ran away, sprinting down the avenues and alleyways of Buenos Aires like a fugitive on the loose, knowing his sister was dead and that he had killed her.

The dream eventually shocked him awake. He had managed not to think of Franca at all since New Year's, after which there was Lucy, who had sufficed—by extravagant use of her tongue, nipples, voice, toes, and hands—to pull him away from his thoughts of *then* and into pure actions of *now*. She had led him through the spring and summer with the ever-present feeling that *now* was the only thing there was; with Lucy there was no Argentina, there was no Franca or Pascal, there was no black smudge of pain at the memory of the big, empty house. And so it was all the more unnerving to have seen his sister so vividly in his sleep, and to see her disappear.

With the idea that pleasure might help in erasing the dream's eerie residue, he reached an arm out and pulled Lucy toward him. He closed his eyes to the bright September light, which was coming in flat and fierce through the window, and rubbed himself against her. Soon she was awake and panting beneath him, her little body reacting to the push and pull of his. *Well aren't you feisty today?* she said after they finished, but Engales was already up and putting on his shoes.

The sex had worked, he told himself, as he pushed his way out onto Avenue A. He would not let the day be tainted by the dream. But outside, there were more disturbances: the frowning woman on the stoop of his apartment, her leg wrapped in gauze and her teeth missing, telling him, *Mister, it's painful. Mister, please.* The bird that had crashed into a glass window and lay splayed in the middle of the crosswalk on Second, barely breathing and with an injured wing. The mentally handicapped crossing guard, who held a big red stop sign for almost five whole minutes, looking into Engales's eyes as if he were daring him to cross without his blessing. On Mercer, just near the studio, the man with a blond beard who thrust a flier into Engales's hand: a boy had gone missing that morning, on his way to the bus.

Some might have taken these spectral instances to be signs, but Engales didn't believe in signs. Signs were for the superstitious, just as luck, the whole idea of it, was for the lucky. If he had thought for one second that the morning's odd composition was anything other than the average urban reminder that life was gross and strange, he would not have gone to the studio that day. But he did what any real New Yorker would: ignore the gross and strange, because in a city like this, it was the only thing there was. Plus, there was no time for signs, he thought, as he folded the missing-boy flier and stuck it in his shirt pocket. For the first time in his life, he owed something to the world.

The world meaning Winona George. As Rumi had predicted, Winona had found him. After five months of silence after New Year's, Engales had mostly given up on her, but then she showed up at the Times Square show in June (which, contrary to Rumi's predictions, had been *hugely* attended, and apparently by all the right people). *The Village Voice*, the next week, called it the "First Radical Art Show of the '80s," and it seemed it was all anyone could talk about afterward. The next morning, Winona George called him in a tizzy.

"Pick me, Raul!" she'd said, in a voice as simultaneously regal and flighty as her hair: the sonic equivalent of commercial promise. "Everyone will be asking, but don't listen to them because they don't matter. Pick me for your gallerist; I will take you to the top, you'll see, you little young prize."

And he had. And she had. Or she was about to: since that call there had been a buzz in the air and the buzz was about him. Overnight, thanks to Winona, his name had started to mean something, at least if you were at the right party in the right loft with the right people in the right part of town. And now he was beholden to an opening date for his first *real* show—September 23, just a week from today—a show that, Winona had revealed, would be reviewed in the *New York Times*. "Bennett has a little thing for you, it seems," she'd said over the phone. "And I can't say I blame him." James Bennett from the balcony. James Bennett from the *Times*. True, he hadn't seen Bennett's name in the paper for some months now, but he trusted there was a reason for that; perhaps Bennett hadn't seen anything that impressed him lately. Perhaps Engales's show would be the thing that *did*, making it all the more exciting for them both when he wrote about it. But the date of the show was descending on him with the speed of a falling brick, and Engales still had four more paintings to finish. His throat clenched at the thought.

. . . .

He'd attempted to finish the work at the apartment, where he'd been
doing most of his work of late. François's apartment, since Lucy had
moved in, had become a den of art and sex, each fueling the other,
improving the other, depending on the other to reach its maximum
potential. Mouth on neck, brush to canvas, hands on breasts, color on
paper—the summer had been one of the most productive, painting-
wise, that he'd ever had. Lucy sat in the bedroom with him while he
sketched and smoked. She sometimes sketched, too, in a notebook he
had gotten her at Pearl Paint. Sometimes she just sat in the corner with
a green Popsicle, watching him, which he surprisingly didn't mind at
all. Usually someone watching him would annoy him, but it was as if
her love of the paintings, the way she looked at them and studied them
and talked about them, brought them to life. With her eyes on them,
the paintings suddenly became real. No longer were they something
that existed only in his mind or heart, but in the mind and heart of
someone he loved.

Yes, *loved*; Engales had transformed rather quickly from a ladies'
man into a man in love. Unlike any other woman he'd dealt with,
Lucy didn't detract from his art, she added. She was not separate from
the painting, but a part of it. That there was someone in existence who
could inspire him to be better at what he loved, and to love it even
more, was perhaps one of the most stellar of the many stellar reasons
to be around the bright creature of Lucy every day and all the time.
On a stoop with a cigarette, on an overturned tire with a beer, on
Bleecker Street at midnight, kissing in a darkened doorway. She came
with him to shows—she'd boldly told Jeff Koons she didn't understand the point of his vacuums, to which Koons had replied lightly:
Are you bored? Yes? Then you understand—and she came with him to
the squat, where she wove herself into the tapestry of artists quite
gracefully, asking intelligent questions about Toby's latest project

(blindfolding himself for a week, in an exploration of total darkness, about which Lucy had queried, *How will you present something so intangible to the public?*). She'd get as drunk and delightful as any of them, and was game for joining in on whatever performance or experiment they were getting up to that night, be it a sing-along to one of Selma's melancholy guitar melodies or a work session where they improved on sections of the building with stolen hammers and borrowed saws and recycled nails. Occasionally Engales felt like Lucy's teacher, explaining why a conceptual artist had chosen to cut holes in the floor of abandoned buildings, or rejigger a typewriter as a critique on the media, but at other times he felt like her student. Lucy was not burdened by the scene yet, the hype or the desire for fame or the jaded conversations or the endless critical dialogue. Whatever innocence she had (if easily stolen) was matched with intelligence (if naive), and she often saw things in a nuanced, surprising, and, in Engales's mind, brilliant way. She'd stand in front of a sculpture and tweak her head and pout her mouth and say something like, *It's ugly, but that's why it's good.*

Lucy gave everything new energy, a new perspective. The sour-smelling herbs of Chinatown, the sweat on the subway, the sirens at night: the grossest of sensations became appealing to him, with her there to give them meaning. The all-night excursions to the Mudd Club or Max's became rife with stolen moments of pleasure; they'd find each other in a crowd and somehow it would feel new each time, like they'd just met right then. (*I found a blade of grass tacked to the bathroom wall,* she'd say. *It was so beautiful.*) They'd escape together back to his apartment, where she'd lie in bed and watch an enormous moth in the upper corner of the room—they'd named him Max, after the venue where they had just spent the night gawking over at Andy Warhol's table, then not caring about Andy Warhol because they had each other. And then he'd start painting. It could be midnight or morning when they got home, but he'd always start painting. *You're a maniac,* she'd say. *You're a mouse,* he'd say with a grin. The paintings piled up around them, their own little fort.

Something *would* happen with the paintings, this much was clear. Both of them could feel it: the pressure that the paintings built, the inevitability of their success; it was only a matter of when. The idea of fame hovered over him. Lucy stroked that idea, cradled it and kissed it; her belief in him was total. And when Winona George called, the idea of fame consolidating into a mass and then landing, they leaped around the apartment like children, their hands wrapped around each other's forearms, their blood so bubbly they felt drunk.

But as the show grew nearer, Engales had become frazzled and undone, and Lucy's presence, her eyes on the paintings and her body in the room, became a reminder that her love for the paintings was possibly not enough. There was a whole world in which he could fail, and if he did, she would be witness to that failure. He imagined this James Bennett person reviewing the show, what he might say. If he panned it, could Engales handle it? And if he glorified it, could he handle that, either? Painting had been his salvation through everything, and now it was going to be judged, potentially wrecked, by a public he didn't necessarily trust. The apartment had become full of these humming doubts. Flies buzzed around and got caught in mounds of paint. Lucy buzzed around, too, annoying him now. Suddenly, under the stress of the world outside their bubble, Lucy's presence had become a liability.

"I'll miss you too much," she'd said before he'd left for the studio this morning, still lying naked in the bed, draped in the sheet of early fall light.

"Don't," he'd said.

The studio smelled like it always did, turpentine and cleaning fluid, plus Arlene: her signature combination of body odor, Egyptian musk, and yerba maté, which, inspired by Engales's Argentineanism, she had started drinking out of a gourd. Arlene had been acting different since New Year's, unsettled and easily annoyed, and she had developed a new antagonism toward Engales that he was pretty sure had to do with Lucy. He was spending too much time with that *girl*, she'd said more than once. And not enough time in the studio.

"I'm painting more than ever," he told her calmly each time, but she shook her head.

"I'm just saying nothing great ever came from being in love," she'd said.

Engales had given her a skeptical look and she had yelled, "It's true! Name one genius thing that came out of someone fucking their way into oblivion!"

"Human life?" he had said, with as much actual annoyance as humor.

"Human life is crap," she had said, and then she had mumbled something under her breath, and Engales could have sworn it had the tone of a confession, though he couldn't be sure.

Now Arlene stood wide-legged on her wobbly ladder, holding her gourd in one hand and her brush in the other. Her underarm hair spurted out in a shock of orange, and Engales imagined painting that hair—a spiky orange scribble with a dry-bristled brush. He felt a softness for her even as he ignored her; he probably always would. He pulled a painting of a limp-faced Chinese woman, holding a head of bok choy like a trophy, from the back of his unfinished stack.

He had seen the Chinese woman on his first week in New York City, and though that was years ago now, he still remembered her face almost perfectly. One part of the face was drooping, as if the skin that covered it had lost all elasticity, and the fat of the cheek had migrated down into the hammock of loose skin. He had stared at her for probably too long, until she looked up from her bok choy and directly at him. He saw in her eyes the sort of pain that he guessed was reserved for the deformed; the eyes seemed to say, *This is how it is, how it will always be, and there's nothing I can do about it except keep living.* He pitied her. He remembered the pity just as well as he remembered the face. He also remembered how he had felt the urge to smile at her because of this pity, but had then forced himself to revoke the pity and the smile, which seemed to satisfy her: she had toasted him with her leafy greens. It was then, on his very first day, that he knew he had found his place in New York, a place for the deranged and wrecked and bold, a place where pity couldn't exist if it wanted to because there would have to be too much of it. The woman had wobbled away with her cloth bags, and as she did, he thought he heard her begin to sing.

These were the kinds of moments that popped up again and again in Engales's artwork; these were the kinds of people who populated his life with their flaws. He loved the flaws; they were invariably the most interesting parts of people's faces and bodies, the parts that held the strangest lines, the most beautiful shadows. Wounds and deformities and cracks and boils and stomachs: this was the stuff that moved Engales. Usually while he detailed a broken nose or sketched a lumpy body he felt as if he was zeroing in on what it meant to be alive. He could hear his father saying: *The scratches are what makes a life*.

He had started painting portraits the year his parents died, thanks to an obese and kind art teacher named Señor Romano. Aside from English, art was the only class he never skipped, much because Romano had taken a special liking to him that was beyond the pity that the other teachers doled out—the same pity that he hated to feel in any form now. If Romano pitied him, it had never shown; he seemed to understand that what Raul wanted was to be treated like a human, not a child who had lost his parents. In class, they did boring drawing projects and elementary color wheels, but when Señor Romano saw the way Raul engaged with the materials—his sketches of fruit became deranged faces, he cut up his color wheels and collaged them together to make an entirely new rainbow—he sent Raul home with a wooden briefcase full of half-squeezed bottles of oil paint and used brushes. "This doesn't come out with water," Señor Romano had told him, his only piece of instruction. He also gave him a tin of turpentine and a new name; he'd call him by his last name, Engales. That would be his artist's name.

Engales had begged paper off Maurizio, the butcher down the block. Maurizio, like everyone else in the neighborhood, would give Raul or Franca most anything they wanted; he and his sister only had to blink their eyes like the orphans they were. They got free steak from Maurizio; gross, free candies from the grocer; free bread from the bakery where Franca worked. When Raul got home he taped a sheet of the butcher paper to the wall of his bedroom and squirted some of the paints onto one of his mother's china plates. Here was one perk of having dead parents: you could paint with the china, and use the walls as your easel. The first thing that came to his mind to paint was Señor Romano himself: his tomato cheeks, his puffy eyelids, his big body, which filled the huge piece of butcher paper. He started with Romano's edges, and then he found himself zooming in on small areas he had noticed: the deep lines around Romano's eyes, the handsome lips, the tie that slung down over his huge stomach and was covered in a paisley pattern that Engales remembered almost photographically. It felt so completely natural to him it was as if he wasn't even in control of his own hand, as if the hand were re-creating Romano all on its own. He could see Romano there in the room with him, and he could feel him. For the first time since his parents had died, he did not feel entirely alone.

The painting then became obsessive. He painted after school and into the night. He asked Romano for more supplies, and with his own money, Romano bought him an entire stock of brand-new paints and brushes to add to the wooden box. Engales populated his bedroom with figures: the lady in the red hat who he passed on the street on his way to school; the old man who made them lemonades at Café Crocodile, whom they called El Jefe; Maurizio, whose face was shaped like a laugh; the girl he thought was beautiful in his English class, whose top lip looked like a half-moon. He painted tens and perhaps hundreds of portraits of his sister, who was the only one who would actually sit for him: Franca in a party hat; Franca wearing their father's suit; Franca with a flower in her mouth like a tango dancer; Franca frowning, because that was how he knew her face the best. When his bedroom walls became too small to hold all the large sheets of paper, he began to store them under his bed in big stacks. One morning he woke up to see that Franca had found his stash, and that the paintings had been pinned up on every empty wall throughout the house. He found Franca herself standing in the hallway outside their parents' bedroom, touching a rendition of her own face.

The painting also did something else: it pointed toward escape. Just a month before he died, Engales's father had spent a week in New York City and had returned with an infectious enthusiasm for the place. "It's swarming with artists and musicians and writers," Braulio had reported over dinner. "I mean, just *listen* to this!" Engales's father then put on a flamboyant jazz record that bipped and bopped and hiccupped and screeched on the player through the rest of Braulio's exotic descriptions of the far-off city: underground poetry rooms, fantastic fashion, smoke that rose like breath from the holes in the street. Taken by his father's excitement, fourteen-year-old Raul asked bluntly, "When can I go?" Braulio chuckled, leaned back, wiped steak sauce from his big face. "Whenever you want, son. Thanks to your fetal impatience, you can go to America whenever you see properly fit." Raul had been born a month before his due date, at the tail end of his parents' stay there, and it had become one of their little family jokes: Raul was born for New York City.

And now here he was: a part of that world his father had described, or at least about to be a part of it, if he could bring himself to finish this Chinese woman's bulbous cheek. He paid special attention to the cheek, painstakingly adding wrinkles, highlighting it just right. But then he had been working on it for hours and it wasn't just right. It wasn't the woman who he remembered. The face did not feel like her face. Instead of acknowledging the viewer with forgiveness, she held a look of mistrust. Where was it coming from? Her eyes? The creases around her mouth? The cheek itself?

He stood back to take a look. The flaw didn't feel like a flaw, it felt planned.

The Winona George complex, Arlene had named the uneasiness he felt now, the whirlpool of doubt that had begun to circulate in the studio and in his head. He had always wanted exactly what he had now: to be able to paint for a reason. But now that he had one, he felt that the reason was arbitrary, which made the painting seem that way.

A panic swept through him, and he felt his confidence sliding down the epic slope of almost-failure toward failure itself. Quickly the panic mixed with the fear he had felt in his dream that morning, creating a spiral of things to add to Franca's list. *Left his sister with a stupid, spineless husband in a country that was practically self-destructing. Left without turning around to look at her, without saying good-bye. Never returning her letter, never finding out her big news.* Why was he thinking about her now?

From across the room, he heard Arlene yell: *"Do something else, Raul."*

This was code for one of Arlene's earliest studio lessons: when you start doubting, you stop painting. You eat a sandwich, walk around the block, do jumping jacks, make sketches. Anything to circumnavigate the doubt, change its course. Doubt was the fucking enemy, Arlene said. Of all good art.

Though Engales was not in the mood to listen to Arlene, he knew she was right; the doubt was feeding off the strange morning, filling him quickly, sinking him. But he couldn't take a walk—he had so much to do. He had to make the sketches for his four new paintings, so he decided to cut paper. They had only bulk paper at the studio, which came in enormous sheets, which he would rip, then rip again, then stack, then cut all at once, until he had a bunch of rough-edged squares. When he had ripped the whole roll, he inserted his book-size stack into the guillotine, a paper cutter meant to cut entire volumes, in the darker corner of the studio. He slid the paper to the back edge of the cutter with his hand.

....

There was a flash. It was silver and slick: a mirror breaking; a window slamming shut. Franca's body went limp in his arms. His heart stopped. His sister's heart stopped. Broken music played from somewhere outside. When he looked up, his hand was lying on the counter behind the blade of the guillotine, completely severed from the rest of his body.

For an entire minute, he glares at it. The thick, silver blade, separating one part of him from the other. The wall of the metal up against the hair and skin of his arm. Arlene's red hair is flying toward him like a fire. Her long skirt with the elephants on it. A scream from one of the students cracks through the heavy air. On the windows, fog spreads and shrinks with the collective breath of the room. His arm, cut just under the elbow, is a cross section of red and white, now bleeding out over the counter and onto the floor.

Arlene wraps the stump of his wrist in a paint rag, her mouth open with frenzied, frantic questions, but Engales cannot hear or see her. Instead, he sees Franca's face in her face: strewn with sadness because she has dropped a carton of eggs. The rag turns orange rapidly, the stain of blood blooming out to its edges. Franca watches the orange yolk bleed into the sidewalk's veins. Everything goes white, then red, then white. Engales walks on ahead of her. *Hurry up, egghead. They're just eggs.* He vomits, greenish, into the stainless-steel sink.

Arlene knots the hand itself into another rag and places the bundle into a tin canister used for paintbrushes. His dead fingers blacken in the turpentine. He opens his mouth to scream, but nothing comes out. There is his painting hand in a can full of paintbrushes. There is the gaping hole of his mouth.

NO MORE MIDNIGHT
COCA-COLA

t is a dream. This was what Lucy told herself when she showed up at St. Vincent's hospital, coatless, still slightly high from a bump of cocaine Random Randy had given her at the bar just before she'd taken Arlene's call. The cocaine had felt necessary at the time, a little bump to lift her just a little bit above her circumstance: the front end of her regular Tuesday-night shift, where she was dealing with the 4:00 P.M.–ers, those downtrodden enough to seek afternoon refuge in whiskey and Lucy's tits. But now the drugs only contributed to the sense that the scene she was living in could not be real. It was only dreams that rooms turned into other rooms so quickly and without transition, that the log cabin of the Eagle could transform into the stark, bright hall of St. Vincent's hospital in what felt like one seamless instant. It was only in dreams that thin, bruised men, flanked by turquoise curtains and dingy bedside lamps, looked out on you from their rooms as if their diseases were your fault: the sad, almost-ghosts of an epidemic you knew close to nothing about. And it was only in dreams—or perhaps only nightmares—when you saw something like what Lucy saw in the papery bed of room 1313: her lover, sleeping beside the bandaged stump of his own arm, its tip bright red with tenacious blood.

"Finally," said a voice. Arlene's New Yorker voice, always adding O's in where they didn't belong. *F-O-inally.* Lucy gulped. That Arlene did not like Lucy was as much a fact as the bloody stump, which Lucy could not take her eyes off of as she approached.

"I came as fast as I could," she said to Arlene, as if it mattered what she said to Arlene. "I ran here."

From the foot of the bed, Lucy looked up its lumpy landscape to her lover's face: so peaceful in sleep, his deep pores filled with paint or dirt, that mouth that she had so recently kissed so carelessly, the way you kissed when you assumed there were endless kisses, a lifetime of them even. Her eyes welled and sprung with tears, which she attempted unsuccessfully to swat away with her sleeve.

"Oh, Jesus," Arlene said from her chair by the bed. Lucy did her best to ignore Arlene, but Arlene was right. Oh, Jesus. *Oh, Jesus* was right.

A very tragic reaction to tragedy is to think about what a short time it's been since things were *not tragic*. How *just last week* you were eating tangerines on an abandoned church pew parked outside the squat, throwing the peels onto the heap of uncollected garbage that, in the latest strike, had grown taller than you were. How *just last month* you were pulling your Goodwill suitcase, full of all your T-shirts and bras and dreams, up the stairs of your lover's apartment, its ridiculous weight less exhausting than exhilarating: a symbol of sharing a life with the man you loved. How *just a few months ago* you had basked in the neon PEEP-O-RAMAs and LIVE NUDE REVUEs and XXX's of Times Square as if they were Idaho moonlight, walked through the maze of rooms and hallways of TIMES SQUARE: ART OF THE FUTURE on the arm of your painter, an arm that felt as sturdy as the branch of a fir. How just after that you were listening to Captain Beefheart and His Magic Band (*They really are magic!* your painter had yelled to you), and watching him dance in the way he danced: defying everything that already existed, making something entirely new with his body. *Somewhere in his movements: the tango. Somewhere in his movements: the nothing to lose.*

How he'd stopped like he stopped, when something caught his attention and he couldn't *not* move toward it. It was a man in the corner, his head holding up a nest of dreadlocks, his face boyish and his grin beautiful. Your painter had pulled a permanent pen from the pocket of his dirty jeans. The dreadlocked man had taken the pen, pushed up your painter's sleeve, and written on his arm. *SAMO says: Never quit*, he had written. Then he drew a cigarette after the words, with the smoke reaching down onto your painter's right hand. *That's Jean-Michel*, your painter had purred afterward, the foreign name sparkling in his mouth. A charge, almost electric, had radiated off the arm afterward, a *magic*.

That moment had been as heavy as a fruit. It was a moment that *meant* something, you could tell, the kind of moment people would talk about later, when the moment itself was long since gone.

But the moment had passed, and no one was talking about it. The new moment was a severed arm, a hospital room, turquoise curtains, memories of sweet times that now felt sour. Lucy moved around to the side of the bed and crouched in front of Arlene.

"What happened?" she asked Arlene in a little whisper, though she didn't know if she wanted to know, or if she wanted Arlene to speak.

"A tragedy," Arlene said dryly. "A fucking tragedy is what happened."

Lucy gulped; she wished desperately that Arlene wasn't there. She wanted to be alone with Engales when he woke up, for him to see her face and find solace in it; she wanted to kiss the pain out of him. She reached up to touch the arm, which was moist and hot, like it got when he danced for too long and too hard, or when they kissed for too long and too hard. . . .

Arlene stood up from her chair. "I have to go home now," she stated, more to the room than to Lucy. "Or else I'll drive myself mad."

But then she surprised Lucy: she clasped her thin arms around her, nuzzled her musky red hair into her neck. She squeezed, and Lucy felt the calming sensation of being held still by another person's tight grasp.

"Honest to fucking god," Arlene whispered into Lucy's neck. "Honest to fucking god I'll drive myself mad."

Engales slept for hours, or what felt like hours. Lucy took over Arlene's post in the plastic-covered chair next to the bed, which squeaked like a dying animal when she moved at all. The hospital room shifted and spun. Nurses hovered, moth-like, but when Lucy asked them questions—*When will he wake up? Can it be fixed? What's the next step?*—they flew away. Time was passing—it should have been very late by now—but it all felt like one suspended second, the time before a clock's hand gathers enough momentum to tick forward. Lucy stood up, sat down, stood up, sat down again. Kissed her lover's forehead, which was as sticky and warm as an overripe fruit. As hours passed, a singular worry solidified and grew heavy: *What would he be like when he woke up?* She suddenly longed for Arlene to come back, if only to be a buffer if he were terribly angry.

Lucy had seen Engales angry once since she'd known him, and she never wanted to see it again. It had been an especially wild night at the squat, and they had stayed late, as they often did; they knew that the after-hours were the best hours, when everyone who didn't matter left, when Chinese food was ordered from Kim's Lucky Good Food on First Avenue, when a joint materialized from someone's breast pocket and was lit, when the Dobro guitar with the Hawaiian scene painted on it was picked up and played, when the conversations took on a wavy, fluid, often existential quality. That night, Toby had gotten onto one of his favorite subjects of late, *the commercialization of art*, or, as he liked to call it, *the butt-raping of the creative class*. He had stated alternately (and quite drunkenly) that said butt-raping was the artist's fault—they should not give it up so easily by selling to those rich-prick galleries at the drop of a hat—and that it was said rich pricks' fault—their own lack of taste meant that they needed to preen the artists for theirs.

"They'll stick their dick somewhere interesting for once," he'd ranted. "Just to see what it feels like. And when it feels good, better than anything they've ever felt because their lives are boring as hell, they'll buy it, because they *can*."

Lucy had known that this would be a sensitive topic for Engales; he had just signed on with Winona, and had been defending the decision, which he knew would be considered *selling out* to the artists at the squat, to her and to himself, though no one had voiced any judgment. Until right then, when Toby said: "Well, why don't we just ask Mr. Golden Boy over here? What does it feel like, Mr. Golden Boy, to have sold your artistic integrity to a woman with a poodle for hair?"

Engales had started off calmly. "In what world"—he had countered, smoke rising from his cigarette like a scarf being tugged out of a magician's sleeve—"should someone be blamed for taking money for something they make? And likewise, why should someone be blamed for wanting to *spend* their money on something that someone else made? This is our *work*, Toby. This is the thing we do instead of sitting in a desk chair. Shouldn't it allow us to survive?"

"We *are surviving*," Toby said. "And on our own terms!"

"Are we, though? You live in an empty factory where you freeze your ass off every night and that you could get kicked out of at any moment. I haven't eaten anything but beef jerky sticks today. Personally I want to sell the *shit* out of my paintings. I want a fucking steak and a side salad. With that kind of fancy lettuce that tastes like air."

"Oh come *on*," Toby had said flamboyantly. "That Winona woman's got your dick on a string! But what she's telling you? That you're going to be some star now? It's all a load of crap. Nobody's going to remember you, just like they won't remember the next Joe Schmo who sells a million-dollar painting to a rich dude. They'll remember us for the way we live, for how we stayed true to ourselves. That's what they'll remember. Not how we sold out to make a buck."

Engales had gotten the coldest look in his eyes then, one that Lucy had never seen. "*The reason people come to America is to sell out, you privileged piece of shit. That's what America is for.*"

"Well America can suck my cock," Toby said as he got up to fetch one of his art projects (a rug he had woven out of parking tickets he'd gotten on his VW van) and held a lighter to its corner. It ignited instantly, creating a glow that made his face look like a cartoon devil. Then the Swedes joined in—when there was fire involved, they couldn't *not*—committing a series of pyrotechnic crimes that included burning one of Selma's booby sculptures ("Not one of my *busts*!" Selma cried, but with a laugh). When Toby took the match to one of Engales's drawings, which he had made that summer with Lucy watching on, Engales threw himself on top of him, pinning his shoulders to the cement floor.

"*That's not yours*," he said in a voice that Lucy had not heard before, and that terrified her. The terror was not so much because she thought Engales would hurt her, or hurt anyone, but because she couldn't see him. Right then she had had the distinct feeling that she didn't know the man she loved at all. And even after Engales had gotten off Toby, and calmed down fairly quickly by way of a Budweiser and half of the communal joint, remnants of the feeling remained; Raul Engales had an unknowable shadow inside of him.

She felt the same way now, as she waited for Engales's eyes to open; she couldn't see him, and she didn't know what he'd do when he woke up. If he had been so angry when one of his drawings was destroyed, how would he feel when his whole practice, the whole thing of making art was taken from him? She simultaneously wanted to be close to him when he woke and to be far away: Idaho far, in her mother's arms. Searching for anything familiar, she grabbed for his plaid shirt on the back of the chair, brought it to her face to smell it, at which point she realized it was covered in the stiff crust of brown blood. As she threw it down she noticed a piece of paper in its pocket, pulled it out. But just as she was about to open it, she felt his eyes on her.

His eyes on her in the back of a cab as they flew through the city at 5:00 A.M.: filled with adoration. His eyes on her as they danced at Eileen's Reno Bar: filled with lust. His eyes on her as he painted her: filled with curiosity. His eyes on her now: filled with hate.

Pure, unfettered hate, coming from the eyes of the man in whose apartment her suitcase lived now, in whose bed she slept now, in whose life she lived now.

"What the fuck are you doing here?" he said, his voice made of gravel, those eyes—shining metallic with morphine—slicing into her. "Where's Arlene?"

Lucy's heart clenched like a fist; he wanted Arlene, not her.

"Arlene called me," she said, but everything was a dream again, and in a dream one's own voice did not matter, and she choked on the words.

"I want you to leave," he said, suddenly turning his head to face the dirty hospital wall. "And I don't want you to come back. I don't want to see you again."

Just last week he'd said: *My favorite thing about you is when you look at yourself in the mirror like a teenager.* She'd said: *My favorite thing about you is your hands.*

Just last month: holding each other's shoulders, jumping around in a circle, like crazy monkeys, around the apartment. His very own show! His very own show!

Now: *I don't want to see you again.*

In dreams people repeat the worst things over and over, as if on a loop. *I don't want to see you again. Again again again. Never again.* In a dream you can cry endlessly and not even know you're crying. You can cry so loudly and not even know you're crying. You can shake your hands like insane fans and a dreamy, mothy nurse will escort you into a hallway. She will hold down your arms and hug you so tightly that you will be forced to stop shaking, like Arlene had. Perhaps this is the only possible thing that could comfort you: being forced to be still. Eventually, after she has held you long enough, she will guide you down the dream hallway, deposit you out onto the street.

There will be no giant parking lot with a car for you to get into, no green hedges or row of pine trees, no mother. Nothing physical to separate the sick from the city, the end of the world from the rest of it. This is trauma in a city: a layering of one tragic space onto another, one surreal picture jutting right up into the next. It has been only however long it had been, and yet you can already tell, as you step out into the night, that everything in the city has completely changed.

It was late. Lucy didn't know how late, but she knew that it was late. She had learned to read the telltale signs of lateness from her almost-morning walks home from the Eagle: shut grates and alley cats; circles of glowing eyes in the parks, the eyes of people who had spent all day sleeping and would spend all night getting high. Garbage trucks—those nocturnal, mechanical armadillos—roamed, creaked, and banged. Homeless men lurched from their concrete beds. Sirens flew down the streets and then up into the colander of the sky, through the holes of the stars. The moon was somewhere, but she wasn't sure where.

You were supposed to be scared in these streets, at this hour, but Lucy never had been. The things that scared her—oblivion, wildfires, aloneness—were not hazards here like they were out in the woods, and she had the general feeling that if anything bad happened to her, someone would save her from it. The city, with its million arms and million lights, would scoop her up, absorb her, rock her to sleep in its

madness. But now she felt scared for a new reason: the world of the
night did not have Raul Engales in it.

How could it be late if he was not here with her? He *was* lateness;
everything late belonged to him. The doorway on Bleecker he'd
shoved her into for a kiss, only to hear a homeless man growl underneath them. The vending machine he had kicked because he felt like
it, only to have a Coke fall out: another of the universe's many gifts,
meant just for him. *Midnight Coca-Cola!* he had yelled. *Coca-Cola
Midnight!* The drawing of a chicken with a human's head he had done
with his fat permanent marker on the wooden barricade on Prince
Street: still there now. R & K Bakery, where they found each other on
that July evening, when someone had been murdered on the roof of
the Met, where they had hugged, pressed their bodies together, then
fed each other cinnamon rolls until morning, when they emerged into
the sticky city with sticky fingers.

As she moved through the lateness, bleary-eyed and rejected and
hopeless, she noticed something strange. Cones of white light, shifting in half-moons over the ground and around the corners of buildings. She saw when she got closer that the lights were emerging from
hunched, phantasmal forms that scooted and floated through the dark
streets. They were sparse at first, and then as she turned onto Prince,
they were many.

When she was close enough for the lights to illuminate their faces, she
realized that the zombie-like forms were women, in loose-fitting pants
or housedresses, their hair in knots on top of their heads, or down and
long, thinning at the ends. When she had studied enough of them, she
saw that their eyes were like her own mother's eyes: deep with knowing,
maternally frantic, heavy, and alert. They were calling a name.

Jacob! They yelled in husky night-mother voices. *Jacob! Jacob! Jacob!*

The name rang through the dream of the night as if the dream
were a valley, ricocheting off its sky-scraping mountains.

On the corner of Prince and Broadway, one of the women came toward her. Lucy tried to avoid her eyes but then found herself caught in their motherly net. The woman, wearing an outfit made entirely of peach linen, dug a flashlight out of a huge straw bag, handed it gently to Lucy.

"Someone's lost," she said, with more than a little desperation. "We thank you for your help."

She handed Lucy a stack of white fliers and a plastic box of pushpins. When she disappeared down Broome, Lucy wanted desperately to call her back. Those lines forking from her eyes. Those linen clothes; that good face. She needed her. She needed a mother, any mother, more than anything else in the world.

She thought of her own mother on the edge of the bed, reading to her from a chapter book. Her mother who always stopped reading the story at the best part, telling her it was time for bed. She would scream and kick. She wanted to see how it would end! She wanted to know the fate of the main character, who was a girl, just like her. She couldn't wait, and yet she had to. In vain, she'd stay up all night, trying to teach herself to read the big words on the page. But she was too small. And the world of the book was too big.

MISSING CHILD, the flier read, in large block letters. *JACOB REY. Last seen at Broadway and Lafayette at 8:00 A.M. Male. Hispanic. Six years old. 40 inches. Dark hair, brown eyes. Wearing a red shirt and his pilot's cap, blue sneakers with fluorescent stripes, carrying a blue cloth backpack with dinosaurs imprinted. Persons having any information, please call 212-555-4545. $10,000 Reward.*

The picture above the text was of a small dark boy with wobbly eyes and a tentative half smile. A bowl of messy hair and a softly rounded nose: both handsome and silly-looking at the same time, like someone who had never given a thought to danger.

She imagined the young boy, unable to defend himself against the huge world, wandering the streets that could seem so cruel if you did not know your place in them. She thought of Engales's mean eyes. Of his rocky voice, telling her never to come back. She thought of the bloody bandage of his arm and his bloody shirt. Then she remembered the folded paper she had taken from that shirt, stuffed in her own pocket. She pulled it from her pocket now, opened it.

It was him. It was Jacob Rey. Raul had been carrying around a picture of this very same lost boy.

Lucy felt her heart roar in the way it only could in dreams. Fate was at work here, she could feel it. The loss of the boy and the loss of the hand would now be sewn up together into the same chunk of her mind and her heart, linked by the fact of their tragedies and by the dream that encompassed them. Linked by a shirt pocket and a Tuesday in September: the fates of the boy and the man, her own fate right in between, colored by the moon's scary glare.

She began to sense that the air had changed. It held the manic buzz of tragedy, as if its particles were being rung like alarms. It was the same buzz from the night of the Met murder. The same buzz she had felt through the screen of her parents' TV when she had watched the footage from the '77 blackout. It was both eerie and exciting, frenzied and more alive than ever. It was during a tragedy, Lucy thought right then, that a woman who hated you hugged you around the neck. That a group of people who didn't know one another searched together all through the night. That mothers roamed the streets in packs, swooshing their warm lights. It was during a tragedy, she tried to tell herself, that fate would intervene in the form of love. Something would save her. And she would save something.

Impulsively she flicked on the flashlight. She yelled Jacob's name into the night. She had no way of knowing then what she'd do if she actually found a lost boy, how her heart would pound, if her blood would go cold, if she could save him or help him at all. She'd have to wait a few weeks for that, until one showed up at her door.

PART
THREE

THE ARTIST LEAPS
INTO THE VOID

Raul Engales was released from the hospital on the Tuesday that should have been the Winona George show, with an extra roll of gauze and a bottle of painkillers. They had kept him for a week, due to an infection in the stitches that held together the leaves of skin that had been stretched over the stump of his arm. Stitches that railroaded over its foreign peninsula, then halted abruptly, tied off with brackets of wire where everything—the wound and the arm—dead-ended. The infection made the surrounding skin turn black, then red, then yellow. The yellow leaked down his forearm, shored off at his elbow. The whole thing a torch of pain and uselessness.

The irony that his release from the hospital coincided with his would-have-been release into the art world was not lost on Engales. It cut through him like a new knife. It was only two short months ago that Winona George had been popping open what he assumed to be an absurdly priced bottle of champagne in his meager living room, glugging it into mason jars—his only glasses—for him and for Lucy, while Winona rambled a list of incomprehensible attributes of Raul Engales's that would make the art world swoon.

"You've got the I-don't-know-whats," she had said. "You've got the I-was-born-with-its and the self-taughts and the something-somethings.

You're an insider outsider, do you know what I mean? Do you two pretty young things have any idea what I'm saying?"

Engales had *not* had any idea what she was saying—Winona had a way of making the English language, which he took pride in being fluent in, completely unintelligible—and he also didn't care. All he knew was that the most-talked-about gallerist in New York City, the one who had singlehandedly brought up some of the most revered (and now moneyed) artists, who had spoon-fed the art world digestible yet hearty helpings of neo-Expressionism, and who had reminded the world at large that art was and should be *valuable*, sometimes insanely so, was standing in his poorly lit living room serving him champagne, offering him a solo show that she claimed would *drop him like an anvil into the center of everything*. He couldn't help but hate this memory now, as he was swiveled out of the hospital by a set of revolving doors that thwacked to a *you're on your own now* stop when he stepped outside. And he couldn't help but curse Winona George for dropping her anvil in exactly the wrong place.

Though they had technically told him he could leave that morning, he had not been able to bring himself to go out into the world in such bright daylight—for people to see him in *such bright daylight*—and so he had sat in a corner of the waiting room, pretending to read a magazine, until he was sure it was dark. Now, outside, a stiff wind had started. Wind was the worst of all forms of weather, in Engales's opinion, its only purpose to knock leaves from trees and create tears in people's eyes. The wind moved up through the sleeve of his jacket and knocked on the ball of gauze the doctors had wrapped, mummy-style, around his arm, asking to be let in. *Oh, of course,* the gauze must have said to the wind, opening its little holes just wide enough for the cold to lick at his stitches. *Be my guest at the freak show.*

That's what he was now, he knew. A freak. A cripple. One of the people who other people looked at and thought: *Poor man*. The eyes of everyone he came in contact with this past week—doctors, nurses, sick patients who passed in the hall—all registered that least favorite emotion of his: *pity*. He already knew these eyes, and too well. These were the eyes of the adults in San Telmo, who gave him and Franca free groceries, who tilted their heads with the weight of their half-baked sorrow. The difference now was that his loss was visible. You wore dead parents inside your body. You wore a dead hand like a badge, a badge that alerted people that it was time to position their heads, eyebrows, eyes, and mouths in pity position. *Tilt everything. Try not to wince.*

Lucy's eyes—when she showed up at the hospital that first night, high on cocaine, he could tell from the way her jaw was moving—were the worst of all the eyes. He had understood this immediately upon seeing her, crouching over him in fear, her mascara smeared like Japanese ink. In Lucy's eyes was the worst kind of pity: pity mixed with love. It was impossible to love someone—or love someone in the way she had loved him before, which was with deep reverence, as if he were *king of something*—and also pity him. Pity canceled out belief; you could not believe in someone you pitied. *Oh, my love,* she had said when he had opened his eyes. The pity had sounded in the word *oh,* and it made him want to hit something. *Leave,* he had told her. *I don't want to see you. So leave.*

She had left, but she had come back the next day, and the one after that. Ripped tights, messy hair, a face that had been up all night or crying or both. A face that he had painted and kissed so many times that he knew it by heart: eyes you could see the reflection of a room in, pupils like black universes, a nose that turned up ever so slightly, and that always reminded him of his sister's fingernails, which, instead of curving over like an old woman's, lifted away from her hands like concave potato chips. But all the things he had found beautiful about Lucy changed when he saw her in that hospital room. Her eyes reflected only the disgusting image of himself, lying under a blanket that looked to be made for a child, illustrated with *flying pigs*. Her red nose pointed up at the spongy ceiling, or toward the television, on which played the same show over and over, whose main subject seemed to be shoulder pads. When Lucy tried to press one of her stupid matchbooks in his palm—one of those things she did to be cute or relevant or intimate, and that he had once believed to be all of those things—he threw the matchbook against the hospital wall. But he had to throw it with his left hand, and it bounced awkwardly from the arm of the chair Lucy was sitting in, and this only enraged him more. For Lucy to see him like this was a complete disaster. To keep himself from crying he had set out to make her cry (he had always been the sort of person who knew how to make another person cry), by saying: *Those matchbooks aren't even your project, Lucy. You don't have a project. You aren't an artist, so please stop fucking trying.*

It had been cruel, he knew, but then again, so was life. Life was one huge cutting remark, one blade that cut you all the way down. Life was waking up every morning for the rest of your life to ten bright seconds when you thought you had two hands, only to face the tingling, empty terror that was losing one of them, over and over and over, every single time you opened your eyes. Life was the wind licking at your wound through the sleeve of your coat as you stepped onto Greenwich Street and vomited a week's worth of morphine into an open manhole. Life was trying to decide, as you wiped your mouth with your floppy sleeve, where the hell you would go from here.

The only places Engales could think to go, the places that had been the map of his life for the last six years, sounded awful if not absurd to him now. The squat would be not only freezing and loud but rich in the currency that he could no longer deal in: art and the artists, paint and glue and wire, ideas that could be turned into realities and dreams that hung on shoestrings, like the bare lightbulbs from the wood beams. The idea of seeing Toby or Selma or Regina, of relaying the dirty story of the guillotine and the morphine drip and his timely release— *just when he was about to make it*—made him sick to his stomach, and right then he vowed he would not go back to the squat ever again.

There was Arlene's place on Sullivan, filled with hundreds of plants and the smell of incense and Egyptian musk, her six cats rustling in the leaves, some African or French or Sicilian song playing on the record player. Engales had always loved Arlene's place—it was homey in its eccentricities and always warm, and he knew Arlene would invite him in, make him yerba maté, and hold his head against her breast, sing him to sleep with some New Yorker voodoo song. But it would not be comforting; it would only make things worse. Someone who knew you as well as Arlene knew him could only reflect his pain, magnify it.

And of course he wouldn't dare go back to his own apartment, the place where his unfinished paintings lay in stacks and where Lucy would surely be, pouting on the bed in one of her big T-shirts, waiting for him. *Stop fucking waiting for me,* he wanted to yell to her from across town, just as he had wanted to yell across the Americas to Franca so many times. *Everyone stop waiting for me.*

Cigarette.

It was four avenues to Telemondo's, but tobacco was a dollar cheaper there than anywhere else and what did he care about time? Time was the only thing he had. He walked and time passed or didn't pass, how could he know. He walked and his body moved or didn't move, how could he know. He couldn't know because he was no longer in his own body; he was above himself, watching, and what he saw was a freak on the loose, in a city that was no longer his home.

At Broadway and Eighth: TELEMONDO'S / BEER / CIGARETTE / MAGAZINE / EGG CREAM SODA / ON SALE NOW. Bright lights and the Telemondo guy, who always said the same thing: *That will be one hundred and twenty-two pennies.* Engales counted on him saying the stupid penny joke; it would mean things were in some way how they had always been. But the Telemondo guy didn't say anything. He handed

Engales the pouch of tobacco sullenly, and when Engales tried to pay, he waved away the money.

Engales stormed back out into the night, once again incensed. Was this how it would be from now on? More handouts? Free cigarettes? No jokes? The only thing that could infuriate him more was what happened next, which was that he tried to roll a cigarette and found out that, with one hand, he couldn't. Tobacco fell like snow to the ground; the paper crinkled and stuck. He had to go back into Telemondo's, tell the guy he wanted to exchange for prerolled cigarettes, whose taste he didn't like. "Those ones cost more," the Telemondo guy said. Engales glared at him, as if challenging him to ask for money from a cripple, and took the pack without paying him a cent.

Cigarette.

Its bad taste made him feel only very slightly better. He smoked with his left hand (which canceled out the slightly better), and kept walking toward nowhere. It was fully dark now, the sort of early dark that haunted the fall months, a thin blanket thrown over the city's head. Pink neon buzzed above him, and then the rustle of pigeon wings, and then the rude rumble of a garbage truck, on its Tuesday-night crawl. How could one man be shoving garbage into the claws of a garbage truck and another man be showing paintings in the Winona George Gallery? Another man who had just happened to get lucky; a slot had opened up just for him, when the slotted artist lost his hand. Engales watched as the garbage man leaped from the side of the truck and grabbed four huge black bags at once. He shot Engales a toothy, genuine grin.

One man would be grinning while the art lovers toasted in his name. Another man would never paint again.

Without painting, transformation was not possible. Without painting, the real world was only the real world: an impossible place to exist.

And so why did he have to exist at all? he thought, as he headed south now, down the black river of Broadway, toward a sign in the distance that read: GET BAILED OUT! When existence, from here on out, would just be one long ugly moment? Could the blade not have killed him? Could Arlene not have done what a real friend would do and snapped his neck? Could she have seen, as he did, as they careened out into the street, negotiating the streams of sewer water and arm blood, the street sign, once *Mercer,* which had mysteriously morphed to *Mercy*? And that begged her, or someone, to deliver one last morsel of that mercy? To bail him out? Could he not have bled out into the studio until he could bleed no more, so that he would not have to be existing now, on the way to nowhere, on the slow track to dying a nobody?

At Bond Street he found himself stopping at the sight of the street sign.

Bond Street: printed in sparse Helvetica on the postcards he'd sent out a few weeks ago, the invitations to his first real opening.

Bond Street: where some of the best painters of the decade had shown their work, and where he was meant to have shown his work tonight.

Bond Street: where the Winona George Gallery sat primly halfway down the block, a little beacon of white light in a tunnel of industrial dark.

He had not meant to walk this way. He meant to walk no way, to nowhere. But then, he had. And now he could not help but be curious. Curiosity about the man who had taken his spot in the spotlight, whose paintings hung where his should have, whose beautiful girlfriend or wife was lifting her face up to his in a congratulatory kiss. And if curiosity would kill him, he would take it. He would die of curiosity right here, right now. He would step, despite himself, onto the wonky cobblestones of Bond Street. He would gravitate, despite himself, toward the voices, coming from the crescent of light that streamed from the gallery's door. *Get in here, you hussy! One hell of a show. I could give a shit about your mother's diet, Selma. Did you live the dream down there or what? You're just another one of those Basel bitches now, aren't you? Don't lie.*

Despite himself, he became moth-like, moving toward the light, thinking it was the sun. Despite himself he began to believe that the light was the only way up, no matter that the light itself would singe him.

PORTRAIT OF AN ART SHOW BY THE ARTIST WHO IS NOT PRESENT

EYES: A show that's been hung by a blind man. A man who doesn't know shape from shape, dark from light; composition eludes him. The paintings are all wrong. They're the wrong ones and in the wrong places. What blind man had gone to Raul Engales's apartment and fetched the wrong fucking paintings and hung them in the wrong fucking way? It is this sight—his own heinous paintings, some still unfinished, that were never meant to see the light of day, at least not like this—that makes him wish that instead of losing a hand he could have lost his eyes.

HEART: His own. *Thwup thwap*. Paintings. *Thwup thwap*. Hanging. *Thwup thwap*. Here. *Thwup thwap*. Without. *Thwup thwap*. Him.

HEADS: Bemused nodding when they're chatting, thoughtful tilting when they gaze at the walls, crazy backward thrusting when they open their happy mouths to laugh. The heads in the gallery move with the nonchalance that comes with being empty. The heads in the gallery move with the nonchalance that comes with being whole.

HANDS: Selma's on Toby's back. Toby's on his own hips. Regina's over her mouth when she eats the hummus dip that no one ever eats. Horatio's around a plastic cup of red wine. Winona's in the air, gesticulating flippantly toward the walls. *Oh, darlings*, she's saying, probably, like a cartoon of someone who cares about art.

MOUTH: *Cigarette*.

BODY: A slow dissolve of his own flesh, as he watches the room of his old life breathe and laugh without him. Soon his body will be gone completely, like the smoke he exhales and like the shadows he stands in, which will disappear come morning.

HEART: Maurizio, the butcher from Calle Brasil, holds a lamb's heart in his hands. He isn't supposed to be here at all—Maurizio is from another time, another part of his life and another series of paintings—and yet Engales sees a little red dot below him, the mark that means he's been sold. The heart he holds drips blood onto the nodding head of someone blond.

HEAD: The someone blond is the only someone blond. The head is *Lucy's head*, translucent in its brightness, unmistakable in its brightness, terrible in its brightness. Lucy's head is a siren and a scream and a stupid ball that Engales wants to throw. *What the fuck is she doing here?* She is talking to Winona George, whose own hair spouts from her head like a graying palm tree. Winona George and someone else. Winona George and a man whose face Engales cannot see. A man in a very ugly and somewhat familiar white suit jacket.

NOSE: Engales presses his to the bottom corner of the gallery window. Through the fog of his breath he watches a transformation occur before him. He watches Lucy's face morph from disinterested to interested (this he sees in her forehead, which creases between the brows when she wants something). He watches Winona retreat from the conversation and become absorbed into another (Winona is like a sponge, wringing herself out onto someone and then moving on to soak in someone else). He watches the man in the white suit jacket put his hand on Lucy's shoulder. He watches *a man* put his *hand on Lucy's shoulder*. And then he sees, unmistakably, *this*:

Tilt of chin. Sparkle of half-closed eye. Half smile, no teeth. And finally— here it is—eyes all the way open, pupils floating to the top when she looks up, I'm yours, *they say,* she knows it, *I'm yours.*

Engales remembered the look on Lucy's face from that first night at the Eagle: the look that meant she loved him, and that he would love her. He remembered, also, how when she laughed and the laugh sparkled like her shirt did, that he hadn't *wanted* to love her. Love, like luck, was for the lucky. Love was for the people who could afford to lose it, for those who had room in their lives for loss, whose quota of losses had not already been filled. "Orphans shouldn't fall in love," Raul remembered telling Franca once, in one of their debates about the legitimacy of her relationship with Pascal Morales. Franca had glared at him. "You're wrong," she had said shakily. "Orphans *have* to fall in love."

Apparently his sister had been right. Because though Engales had tried to avoid falling in love with Lucy, though he'd tried to sleep with other women in the beginning of their time together, and tried to avoid calling her his girlfriend for a number of months, it was as if there had been no choice. He was him and she was her. She was her, with her very own set of intriguing contradictions, her specific combination of deviousness and delusion and delight, of half-formed wit and fully formed wonder, with the matchbooks she left in his pocket, the hot air she breathed when she slept, her innocence and her desire to destroy that innocence. She was her and he was him. And they were them and this was love.

But he regretted ever having met her now, ever having fallen for her trick flame, as he watched her betray him so easily. She had come here, to this show, when she knew what had happened to him. For all he knew she had even helped to orchestrate it; no one else had the key to François's place, where all his paintings were. She had worn that same sparkling shirt. And she had tilted her head in her very special way for another man, another man who she was now following through the crowd, through the door, and out into the same night shadows Engales was hiding in.

He ducked back into his corner. His skin grew hot and his head slammed with barbaric thoughts: run after her; smack her with the stump of his arm; find a knife somehow, put it in the back of the white suit. But instead, he followed them. In the shadows, like a creepy, crippled spy. They were walking in synch and talking and *laughing*. The man—Engales had still not seen his face—was telling some sort of story, gesticulating with his pale hands. On the back of the white suit jacket, Engales noted a black stain, as if the man had sat in paint. *Slob*, Engales thought. And to take the judgment a step further: *Nobody wears a white suit anymore*. They were on Second Avenue now. And they were at East Tenth now. And then they were in front of Engales's own apartment now. And then they were BOTH. GOING. INSIDE.

As the heavy door of his own apartment building slammed behind them, Engales heaved out of his shadow and made a noise with his mouth that to anyone watching would have been called a roar, but to him felt like the only thing available, the last noise left in the world. He tried to conjure what he had felt in the hospital: *He did not want her. He did not want her. He did not want her.* And yet it didn't feel that way. He suddenly wanted her desperately, hatefully, stupidly, entirely. He wanted to feel how he had felt with her before this all happened: invincible, like a comet that could only move forward and would never burn out. He wanted to dance with her at Eileen's and have breakfast with her at Binibon, and he wanted to touch her skin with both of his hands, wrapping them around her little body with complete, satisfying control. He wanted to walk across the Williamsburg Bridge with her, like they had done only a few weeks ago, up the slow, red hill of it and into a sea of men with black hats and curls dangling from their heads like springs, men he would paint later that night. He wanted to be in the middle of the bridge again, telling her about his dream. *He would rise to the top*, he had said in the middle of the bridge, just as the late summer breeze had picked up. *Like a piece of gold in a pan full of sand*. It was something he had never said out loud before, to anyone, but she made him want to say it. He would rise to the top, he said again, this time out into the East River, to the five boroughs, to the skyline, to the sky. *Like a piece of gold in a pan full of sand*.

But that was not his fate, was it? And did it take something like this—a total and complete ruining—to begin to acknowledge that fate existed at all, and that a terrible one had befallen him? An image of Lucy's armpit flashed into his head. That little hollow space: a gray, intimate shadow. He imagined her lifting her shirt. Tilting her head. Sucking a cock. He flung his hand, hard, into the building's brick wall. He felt a rush of blood seep from his stitches, not to be contained by the world's most pointless wad of gauze.

LIFE IS CONFUSING AT THIS POINT—SAMO

This, flanked by I LOVE MAXINE and CALL YOUR MOTHER, on the wall of the phone booth you find yourself in moments later, while attempting to end your own life, on the corner of Tenth Street and Avenue A.

There are ten bright seconds when you forget there was an accident. When you think you can respond to SAMO's scrawl like you always do, a tradition you've kept up for years now: a battle—or was it a sort of courting dance?—of scrawls on walls and on arms.

You'd write: LUCY OLLIASON IS A WHORE.

And yet you have no hand to write with: your ten bright seconds are gone. There are only these four dirty walls, this phone with no one on the other end, these pills.

The pill bottle is one of the many things in the world that is made with the idea that the person who will open it will have two hands. One to hold its little orange body, one to press down on and tear off its head. You smash its head into the silver box of the telephone until the cap breaks off and the pills fly like little white marbles to the floor of the telephone booth.

You pick them up one by one. You swallow them.

Your throat is lined with sand.

When the wavy feeling of the pills brushes at your cheek, you notice something. A little blue box—perched like some mechanical tumor on the top of the phone. It is the little blue box that Arlene had told you about so long ago. You hear her muscley voice: *It means the phreaks have hacked it. Once you have the secret number, you can call anyone you fucking want for free.*

You can call anyone you fucking want for free, and your heart squirms, and your mind is only a smooth wave.

Your heart squirms and there is a dial tone and then the rattle of a real ring, and you are there with your sister, under the kitchen table, tying your parents' shoes together.

Answer. Please answer.

You are there with her. She is whispering a secret recipe into your ear. A recipe that makes kids into adults and adults into kids.

Cigarette.

Please answer.

You are there with her, and she is pretending to be asleep. You are pretending to be asleep, too. Each of you knows you are doing the other a favor. Pretending to be asleep but not actually being asleep. If you were actually asleep, it would be considered a betrayal.

Please answer. You are the only thing that's left.

When she picks up she will gasp, even before she hears your voice. She will know it's you because she always knows it's you. You will both be silent at first and then it will be sudden, the way she returns to you,

you'll be children in matching corduroy pants, with parents, dinner, the light coming in, black-and-white cartoons, forts made of bed sheets, the stories your mother tells, hours of Loba de Menos, small shoes, city flowers, trinkets brought home from Italy or Russia, your father's Beatles record on the record player, your mother dancing in her bell-sleeved dress—somewhere in there, the tango, somewhere in there, the *nothing to lose*—your even breathing as you pretend to be asleep for each other, the flicking of your toes, which promises you are not.

But there is only ringing, and you curse the little blue box, which doesn't seem to be working properly, does it? And you rip the little phreak box from the top of the phone and throw it to the ground and yell, to no one, *motherfucker!*

And why would she talk to you if she had picked up? After you had abandoned her for so long? Why would you expect her to show up for your tragedy when you had never shown up for her, not even to hear her big news? And why had you called her anyway? When nothing meant anything? When everything meant nothing? Why had you turned to her when the world was ending if the world was already ending, whether you got a hold of your sister or not?

The coins bang back into their clanky chamber at the bottom of the phone. The white shape of that man's suit jacket blazes under your eyelids. There are exactly six more pills—there had been twenty-five to start with—and you take them all in one swallow, slumping onto the wet floor of the phone booth on Tenth Street until your sister tucks you under a blanket of nothingness. *Go ahead, Raul,* she whispers. *Disappear off the face of the earth.*

You are there with her, crouching over her crate of broken eggs, the remnants of the terrible accident.

You are there with her, shoving a piece of her good cake in your mouth, resenting her, thanking god for her.

But you hadn't said thank you. You hadn't ever said thank you.

You have to call her back, but the phreak box is on the floor now, a pile of blue and red wires.

It's okay, she says, stroking your cheek with her potato chip fingernails. *You're okay, you're okay, you're okay.*

White suit, moon glow, smooth wave. Take her to see what you've made. Prove to her that you have made something. Show her why you left her, show her how it was worth it.

Exit the phone booth, lumber back down Second Avenue, your eyes heavy as loaves of bread. On Bond Street again, toward the well-lit room where everyone is saying your name. Show her the heads of the people who are saying your name. Show her how they move so easily on the necks of the people who are saying your name.

Show her your slide show, Señor Romano's big belly shadow in the way of the projector.

Slide one: all blue. That wonderful, original void.

Let your body dissolve into millions of particles, let them hover together in a fog, then dissipate.

A blue square. A hard stoop. Let your eyes close all the way.

Change slides: black, then white, then black.

Change slides: Yves jumping from the eaves.

You're okay. You're okay. You're okay. Just fall asleep now, to the sound of the sirens and the dogs and the trucks on the cobblestones, their metal roofs clanging.

How can one man be dragging garbage while another man . . .

You're okay.

Sprinkle yourself among the sounds of the city, like a dust with a finite place to fall.

Change slides: the artist falls toward the pavement below, toward death in the name of art.

THE SHOW MUST GO ON

Everyone who was anyone: that was the phrase certain people, probably the people who were *not* anyone, might have used to describe the attendees of the Raul Engales show at the Winona George Gallery. Lucy had watched them file in from her perch in the corner: the collectors and the critics and the never-ending stream of Winona's personal friends, who managed to cover Winona's powdered face in lipstick marks before the wine was even uncorked. Rumi was there, her big hair expanding to fit the space, and some of the same people from the Times Square show—Lucy recognized a couple who only dressed in head-to-toe red, and a lanky man in a baseball hat that read, in blue embroidery, ART IS MY HELL.

All of their friends from the squat were there, too—Toby and Regina circulated like a two-headed insect, wearing one long scarf that was tied around both of their necks; Horatio and Selma trailed them, Horatio in checkerboard pants he'd spray-painted himself and Selma in a shirt that looked to be made of cellophane, revealing the shape and shadows of her small, ubiquitous breasts. But though Lucy had spent the summer reveling in their grimy genius, emulating their curiosity and their conversation, she knew now that they were not her real friends; they belonged to Engales. Engales would not want her to tell any of them about his accident, she knew, and so the terror of it would be hers alone to bear, while she attempted to avoid the artists, clinging to the periphery of the party with the paintings, her back toward the room as she studied her lover's subjects.

But it wasn't long before they spotted and approached her, with questions about Engales's whereabouts. "We haven't seen him around," said Toby. "And he's *always around*," said Regina. Lucy shrugged and changed the subject to the problem of commercial galleries, which she knew would distract Toby, at least long enough to figure out another tactic of evasion. When he got to the part where he compared the gallery artists to factory laborers, she snuck away into the crowd, where she began to see that the rumor of Engales's absence had officially started to circle. *A family emergency maybe*, one large woman with an alligator head on her purse said. *I heard no one's seen him in a week*, someone else countered. Soon, after enough time had passed and enough wine had been consumed, Raul Engales's absence began to gain even more dramatic traction. *I hope he didn't disappear like that boy*, an old woman with an emerald broach said with passion. *Isn't that just the most tragic thing?* Horatio stopped Lucy next to a painting of a Chinese woman with a deformed cheek, holding a wad of bok choy. Lucy noticed only now a blank spot in the woman's sweater: a spot that had not been finished. She thought of the floor of the studio where she'd picked up the painting a few days earlier—stained with blackish blood.

"When do you think he'll show up?" Horatio said in his blocky accent.

"Probably soon!" Lucy said, trying to be cheery, though her eyes were still on the blank spot and her stomach was hot with fear that she had done every single wrong thing.

She knew Engales wouldn't show up soon, or ever. And if he did— if by some stroke of magic they had let him out of the hospital and he happened to find out that the show had not been canceled—he would only be furious with her, even more than he already was. He would know or find out that it was her who had made this whole thing happen. That it was her who had called the number Winona had left on the message machine, set up a meeting. Who had gotten Random Randy from the bar to come over with the truck and help her haul the paintings to the gallery. He'd find out that it was her who had signed the papers agreeing to the terms of sale, whose fault it would be when all of his paintings were gone, and all that was left was a wad of cash. She thought, desperately now as she watched Winona stick a red dot on the bok choy painting: *Why on earth did I do this?*

She did it because of cereal. More specifically, she did it because of milk. She hadn't eaten anything for two whole days after seeing the bloody gauze wrapped around Engales's arm, and, while trying to buy cigarettes and beer with the vague idea that she needed some sort of sustenance, the Telemondo guy noticed the shape she was in.

"You look no good," he said to her, and she just shook her head, put the blue package of cigarettes on the counter.

"*You* look no good," she said back.

He ignored her and pulled a box of cereal from a shelf and a carton of milk from the fridge behind him.

"No charge," he said, his brown eyes steady on hers. She slowly, tentatively, pulled the meager groceries from the counter, seeming to sense from the Telemondo guy's eyes that she should take them, or else. *Or else what?* she wanted to say, but instead she just left, walking like a zombie through the East Village with the cereal in one hand and the milk in the other.

It was because of these groceries that she went into the kitchen, a skinny arm of a room that she seldom entered; she wasn't much for cooking, and lately, not eating, either. And it was because she went into the kitchen and set down her miserable fare and stood there wondering if she should eat some of the cereal or not that she noticed two things. One: on the back of the milk carton was Jacob Rey's face. Two: on the bulky black answering machine was a blinking red light.

These things were surprising not only in their juxtaposition but in their novelty: Jacob Rey's face belonged on telephone poles and bulletin boards, out in the grave wide world, not here in her domestic realm. Never before had Lucy seen a missing person advertised on a household product, and Jacob Rey's face, a mascot for that terrible night, seemed to have been placed here just for her, as if his ghost had followed her into Engales's kitchen. His image both haunted and intrigued her: a family's private loss made into a public image, then sent by way of a common dairy product into people's private homes. Involuntarily she imagined her own face on the milk carton, but it was while she was doing this that she noticed the message machine—a relic of the previous tenant's, Engales had told her, that still had François's outgoing message: *Bonjour. It's François. Who are you?*—blinking for her attention like the eyes of a hopeful puppy waiting to be pet. Lucy pushed the button.

First the machine spoke in the way machines speak: a human's voice turned into a robot's, unable to make the curves of words and so piecing them together at the angles, like numbers on a digital clock.

TOOSDAY, SEPT-EM-BHER SIX-TEENTH. THREE OH FIVE PEE EM.

Last Tuesday. *The same day as the accident.*

Then, in stark contrast to the robot, a husky woman's voice.

Raul. Sorry to call so late. But I have wonderful news. Sotheby's went swimmingly. More than swimmingly—you're practically rich already and we haven't even had the show! And you won't believe who bought it. Let's just say it's someone with fantastic taste. Call me back, Raul. Five five nine, oh nine four seven. It's Winona, by the way, Raul. Oh and get your ass over here with the rest of the paintings, my little star. We're about to show you off to the world.

Lucy had understood right then that the message was meant for her, just like Jacob Rey's face on the back of her milk. Just as she had been asked by the mother on Broadway to help her search for Jacob, she was being asked now, by Winona, to make sure Raul Engales's show went up next week. Her logic was perhaps skewed, she knew. But in the blur of the moment, so rife with messages, she reasoned that it was her *duty* to share Raul Engales's paintings with the world. She even went so far as to convince herself that the show, if it went as *swimmingly* as the auction, might turn Engales back toward himself, that he would witness his own success and visualize a future of possibility and prospects, rather than one of hopelessness. If Engales could see that the world loved his paintings, she thought, perhaps he could love himself again. And maybe even love her.

So she had called Winona back. And as for the milk carton, she had dumped out its contents into the sink—forgoing cereal altogether—and set it on the windowsill above Raul Engales's bed: a talisman, or an offering to no one.

Now, at the gallery, as she deflected questions dizzily, Lucy realized she had been an idiot to think this was a good idea; it wasn't her place. If Engales were to see her now, in her sparkly shirt drinking sparkling wine, he would hate her. He would hate her more than he already seemed to hate her. (*It isn't your project,* she imagined him saying, over and over in her head.) And now all she wanted to do was leave. But Winona—who was in a tizzy, Lucy could tell by her hair: usually a pristine fountain, now teased into a Pomeranian-like pouf—would not have that. She found Lucy in the corner, by the wine, and put one of her pointy-nailed hands on Lucy's shoulder.

"So what's the deal, Miss Lucy?" she said. "Where's our guy?"

Lucy couldn't answer at first, and took large swallows of her wine.

"I mean seriously," Winona went on. "You don't just miss this. You don't *miss* your *debut*. Not in this city. Not with Winona George."

Did he have *stage fright?* she wanted to know. *Was he scared of all the people who are going to fall in complete love with him? Had he skipped town? Was he ill?*

"I couldn't tell you," Lucy said, avoiding Winona's eyes. But Lucy was a bad liar, and Winona was a bad person to lie to: like a predatory bird, she would peck the flesh until she hit the bone.

"An accident," Lucy finally divulged after the pecking began to hurt, the word pushing like something spiky in her mouth. "There's been an accident."

"What *kind* of accident?" Winona flared. "Is everything *all right?*"

"Not really," Lucy said.

Winona George, who Lucy had imagined would be very angry with her for pulling the wool over her eyes this whole week, was instead visibly *excited*. The mystery of the artist's whereabouts would simply make everything more interesting. Tragedy was what art was *about*, Lucy could imagine Winona saying, in her high-brow, low-pitched voice. It took tragedy to be an artist in the first place, or at least a tragic heart, and anything on top of that was just a Van Gogh–style bonus, a chip off the old ear, and then eventually, when they *died*, a posthumous cash cow.

"If he *died*, though," Winona actually did have the nerve to say, "I'll need to know. Because there's a whole other thing that goes on with that. We'll need to do the finances differently. And I'll need to know."

"He didn't die," Lucy said softly, looking down at her heavy black boots, which had at one point seemed so important—she had bought them because she had seen Regina from the squat wearing similarly aggressive footwear—and now felt like a burden.

"Then *what?*" Winona was saying. "What happened? Lucy, you *do* need to tell me. You know that, don't you?"

Just then a man walked up between them, his long nose inserting himself like a blinder between Winona and Lucy, blocking Winona's interrogation. Lucy saw Winona's face change, from frantic to cool, and then to mildly uncomfortable.

"Well if it isn't James Bennett," she said. "I'm so *thrilled* you're here. And what do you think? Isn't he fabulous? Can I show you around? I am happy to give you some sound bites for your piece. . . . This one here is called *Chinatown*, you'll notice the juxtaposition of the physical and metaphysical, this deformed cheek and the unfinished piece here, this hole in the work. . . ."

The man ignored Winona and looked straight, hard, direct at Lucy. His gaze was awful and invasive, and Lucy looked away, toward the wall beside her, the way you were supposed to when a man looked at you like that.

"It's you," the man said, still looking at her. His eyes were a clear, chaotic blue: eyes you could see through, the kind Lucy had never trusted, though she was aware that they were a direct reflection of her own.

"Ha! James!" Winona said quite loudly. "Always the odd duck, aren't you, James?" She inserted her own nose between James's and Lucy's now, a little game of noses.

"It's you!" he said again, his smile broadening to reveal a set of stained, amiable teeth. "You're the girl in my painting!"

A strange feeling rushed up into Lucy at being recognized like this. It was a double recognition, first by this man (who had called her a *girl*, that delicious little word that tinkled from the mouth, half of the word from the postcard that had brought her here), and then by Engales, who seemed so far away from her now. She thought of that first night he had painted her, how strange and exciting it had felt to have someone look at her for that long. The itchy collar of her sequin shirt, the same one she wore now. His eyes moving up and down, up and down again, as he studied her lines and her colors. Lucy now looked up at this man, this man she didn't know but who knew her, who was living with that very portrait.

"How do you have that painting?" Lucy asked, though right when she asked it she knew the answer. *And you won't believe who bought it. Let's just say it's someone with fantastic taste.*

"Well because of *me*!" Winona breathed. "It was a Sotheby's situation. Absurd, really, how much of a cut those people take. If I had known how much James was going to spend on that thing I would have sold it directly to him myself!"

But Winona's voice began to dissolve into the noise of the room as the two of them, Lucy and James, looked at each other. And in that looking Lucy felt something shift inside her, though she couldn't pinpoint quite what it was.

"You know I thought I saw you one night, before," said the man with apparently fantastic taste, his voice drifting. "In the park."

"In the park?" she said.

"Yes, in the park."

"Oh," she said. "I don't remember being in the park."

Something was definitely happening: a moment was happening. Winona, seeming to recognize it, held up her two hands, said *Jesus Christ*, and sunk away from them. But what was it? What was happening? It wasn't attraction, surely, since this James person was not handsome in any way she could define or understand. And it was not recognition, not in the sense that she knew him, because she had never laid eyes on this man before. But there was recognition of the feeling itself, it was familiar to her, the sense that the whole landscape of her life was about to change, and that she could be the one to change it.

She could steal her mother's turquoise beads from her dresser— the ones she had admired for so long and imagined swallowing like little candies or wearing them in the bath like a mermaid—and her mother would never know because she would bury them behind the house, cover them with a pile of pine needles.

She could find her high school art teacher—the one whose eyes looked right into her heart in class—at the school dance, in the bright hallway outside the bathroom. She could take him inside that bathroom, pull down his pants.

She could move to New York City, pierce her nose, bleach her hair, sleep with a painter. By sleeping with him, she could make him love her.

She could actively, *viciously, if necessary*, follow her heart, and in doing so, affect the hearts of others.

She could allow her stomach to grow hot, as this James Bennett's eyes reached into some special, dark spot inside her.

"I didn't approach you, well, because I wasn't sure it was you!" James said then. "And also because it would have been odd."

"And this isn't?" she said, surprised to hear herself laugh quickly after she said it. She had not laughed in a week, since the accident.

"You're right," James said. "This is odd. I'm sorry. I don't mean to be odd. I just am. I *am* odd. That's what I've been trying to tell people my whole life. I *just am* odd."

Lucy laughed again. Why was she laughing? Who was this guy, whose hair was thin and getting thinner, whose ears were translucent and large, whose suit was dated and wrinkled and *white*? And why was he making her laugh, on a night when no one should be laughing, because a man, the man she *loved*, had gotten *hurt*, and would never do the thing he lived for again, and here they all were, celebrating in spite of that. All of it was a bad idea. She should really go, she thought, scanning the room for a clear path to the door. But then James Bennett said something, and she found herself tangled in it, unable to move her feet.

"If I tell you something," he said. "Do you promise to maintain that I am just *odd*, and not totally crazy?"

"Okay," she found herself saying. *Tell me*, she found her eyes saying, with their flitting lashes. This was something she knew how to do, flit her lashes to say *tell me*.

"You are very yellow," he said. He had a bald spot, Lucy saw. A shiny, ugly bald spot.

"I'm *yellow*?" she said, and she noticed that her voice was becoming playful in a way she was not intending. "I'm yellow. Hm. I think I'll have to go with crazy on this one."

"Understood," James said, smiling lightly. "I just thought I'd tell you anyway, though. It's very rare, at least lately, that I see such a bright color."

Lucy found herself struggling to point her thoughts back to Engales: she was sad, remember? And yet they kept wandering back into the present moment, back to the present person, back to James. Her ache was being quickly transformed into a longing, and the lower parts of her body felt hot and tingly, against her deepest will.

"I don't like being here," she said suddenly.

"Why's that?" James asked. "Because a crazy man is telling you that you are the color of a zucchini flower? It's that exact color—of a zucchini flower!"

"It makes me sad," she said, ignoring James's odd joke, if it could have been called a joke. "To be around all these paintings."

"Are you going to leave, then?" James said, with surprising seriousness.

"Are you going to come with me, then?" she said, with surprising seriousness.

It was too fast, this back-and-forth, and Lucy regretted it as soon as she said it. She watched James's face fall with indecision.

"Oh," he said, playing with his hands.

"Oh, you don't have to," she said. "Never mind. I mean. I just meant walking me home. That's all I meant. Because I'm going to leave. But you don't have to. I mean I don't even know you."

"Oh, um, sure!" He brightened, thankful for her gift of a way out. "A walk sounds great. It's so cold."

For some reason both of them laughed at this, and again, Lucy wondered why she was laughing when no joke had been told. Was she laughing *at* him? Was she laughing *at* this man, in his funny outfit, with his bumbling manner? Or at *herself*, for feeling intrigued by him, for talking to him at all?

But no, she knew as they wove through the crowd and emerged into the street, and then walked down it easily and silently, leaving everyone who was anyone behind, not caring or remembering that the people from the squat might see them leave together (and maybe, in that scary, off-limits part of herself, even wanting them to). She wanted to laugh again, so she did. She wanted to toss her arm through the triangle of James Bennett's arm, so she did. There was nothing funny and there was nothing fun about any of it, about anything. But she was just *laughing*. Like a person does. Because she *had to*. She had to be swept up, carried away. She had to disappear. She had to be alive in this moment. A moment and a mood that *just felt right*, and then, as they neared Raul Engales's apartment on the alley off Avenue A, just wrong enough to light it on fire.

LUCY'S YELLOW

H*e had only meant to walk her home.*

He had only meant to walk her home.

He had only meant to walk her, the girl in his painting, home. Because it was late at night and girls like her—young girls, blond, beautiful girls, girls who have paintings made in their likeness—should not be walking through the dangerous streets of downtown New York alone.

Right?

Right?

He had only meant to walk her home. Instead, he was entering his own home with the colors of another woman all over him, the colors that had changed everything. Under the influence of the colors—which had pounced on him like predatory cats when he walked into the Winona George Gallery—*meaning* itself changed almost entirely. Under the influence of his colors, *meaning* to do something meant practically nothing, just like *meaning* to make a quiet entrance when your wife was asleep upstairs didn't make the third stair up to his bedroom lose its creak.

I didn't mean to, he wanted to say to the stair. *But you did,* the stair whined back at him. *You did.* He had.

He had gone to Raul Engales's show that evening with a soaring heart; it was finally here, the evening he'd been waiting for. The show had been all he could think about for weeks, ever since he'd bought the Engales painting, stared at it for twenty-four hours straight (to Marge's confusion and chagrin), and then promptly called Winona to find out what she knew about this Raul Engales person, and how he could see more of his work.

"Oh, didn't you know?" Winona had said. "It was me who put it up for sale! Kind of a test, really, to see if he would sell well. I do that sometimes, at those little things Sotheby's does, where they bring in the hopefuls at the end there. Turns out he sold for *quite a lot,* as you *know*, James, but I wasn't expecting it to be *you*, of all people, I mean I thought you were *above* auctions!"

"I was. I mean, I am . . ."

"Anyway," Winona broke in. "He's my new guy. Fabulous. The talent. The energy. Just fabulous. I'm throwing him into the ring with a solo show. Little bastard hasn't returned any of my calls, of course, but then again I'm sure he's busy painting! *Prolific,* that one."

A solo show. The thought thrilled James. He imagined a whole gallery full of Raul Engales paintings, a whole sea of sensations. And he imagined meeting Raul Engales finally—the man who'd conjured the butterfly wings and angelic music on New Year's—and shaking his hand; he imagined a spark, literally, flying from that hand.

"Does the fact that you spent an exorbitant amount of money on his painting mean that you will review his show?" Winona said, using her manipulative/flirtatious voice.

"You can count on it," James said, beaming.

Yes, she could count on it. He could do this. After all, the man responsible for the show was the man responsible for the painting that now leaned so beautifully on his mantel and on his heart. The painting that had entered his consciousness and his spirit and was now sitting inside of him somewhere, like an extra rib. If the other work in the show was anything like the painting he now owned, he would have no trouble with the writing. His article would contain all the magic that the painting did, and that the show surely would. He marked the date of the show on Marge's kitchen calendar—on which she had not so long ago written things like *ovulating*, but where she now only wrote things like *rent*—with a large, ambiguous star. He watched the star grow closer as Marge ticked off the days with her *X*'s (ticking off days was something Marge did, as if by living through each day, deleting it from time, she had completed a task). He couldn't wait. The piece he wrote about Raul Engales would be the pièce de résistance of his career, the piece of writing that would get him back to writing.

Are you proud of me? he would ask Marge when the article came out, its stately columns of text dominating the front page of the Arts section.

Extremely, she'd say. She'd read it out loud to him over Sunday eggs, like she did.

But yesterday, the Monday before the Tuesday that was the show, James had been unexpectedly nervous. The day had gained the sweaty stench of too much anticipation; it had been given the death kiss of exaggerated buildup. His Running List began to gain momentum: What if the other paintings didn't do for him what that first one did? What if he couldn't write about them at all? What if this article was bound to fail, just as all the others he'd sent in this year had? What if the Arts editor refused to even read it? What if he failed Marge again? Would it be the last time she allowed him to?

Marge made it clear, mostly with her excessive use of the *sigh*, the official sound of spousal judgment, that he was continuing to disappoint her. First he had lied about the column, then he had bought the painting without consulting her, and now he was sitting in front of it for long stretches, doing nothing but letting his eyes bulge from his head. He knew what she was thinking when she watched him from the kitchen doorway: if this painting meant *that* much to him, as much as a year's worth of rent and his wife's trust, he should probably be writing about it.

"Get any writing done today?" she'd say at dinner, her voice higher than nature had made it.

"Gestation," James had to say. "Percolation. *Ideas*."

"Any good ones?" she'd say. She was trying, he knew, to make the passive aggression less aggressive, to cut it with something familiar, with love perhaps. But he wanted to tell her that passive aggression, by definition, was *already* a covering-up, that you couldn't get away with covering up twice. Instead, he'd stay quiet, and Marge would sigh again and put something away in the fridge. The cold air would blow from it: another sigh.

The sighing would usually make him feel like a useless piece of crap; he'd pander to Marge, apologize. But now, with the painting in the house and in his brain, he began to resent it—and the rest of Marge's attitude—and to believe it was coming from exactly the wrong place. What Marge wanted, he felt, was for him to succeed in some understandable way, some direct way that she could tell her friends and her mother about, and that she could use to make herself feel safe and normal, when what he wanted was perhaps exactly the opposite. He wanted to succeed in a way that was not necessarily understandable. How could it be, when it was *inside of him and only him*? Marge's presence began to feel restricting, inhibiting, just as he was starting to feel free again. He felt far from her, as if she was on the other side of a lake, and the water was too cold to want to get in and swim to her. Knowing she was still furious about the painting he'd spent all their money on, he didn't even tell her about his plan to write about the show. He didn't tell her about the show at all. Instead, he watched his painting from the couch, let himself fly away on its wings. He'd surprise her with his success, in one big, lovely swoop that would flip their world back to normal. Until then, he'd have to live with the sighs.

So it surprised him when Marge interrupted his couch paralysis that morning with a shocking proposal.

"Fuck me," she whispered, landing, front-ways, on his lap. They hadn't "tried," in the baby-making sense, since the auction, so the proposal felt even more out of left field than it might have otherwise; Marge was not the kind of woman who used the word *fuck* when speaking about *lovemaking*.

"Are you ovulating?" he had said, stupidly, trying to wrestle the newspaper he had been pretending to read out from between their bodies. It stuck.

"I don't care," she said, her eyes like steel traps.

"Okay," James said. "Sorry, it just hasn't seemed like you've wanted to lately. I thought you were mad at me."

"I *am* mad at you, James. You're an idiot. But I still want to have your baby. Or *a* baby." She smiled with one tiny corner of her mouth.

James laughed, with effort. "Very funny," he said. He put his hands around her backside, which felt somehow novel in this position: a new fruit. She kissed his neck and he felt a rush of blood move through his body. With the painting behind her, she glowed red. He moved inside of her and kissed her wild-strawberry face. His worries melted; he suddenly felt sublimely happy. The thought of the Raul Engales show—where he'd arrive tomorrow night at six; he'd wear his white suit—made him pant with pleasure. Then his eyes landed on the eyes of the girl in the painting, on their little white sparkles of light on the black olives of her pupils, and—*holy shit that felt good*—he ejaculated into Marge without any warning at all. Marge sighed and rolled off him, her face seeming to say, *Can't you do anything right?*

The answer was no. No, he could not do anything right, not one thing. He had proven that to himself time and again, and then in a grand way tonight, at the Winona George Gallery. At the gallery, full of Engales's immaculate, outrageous portraits, James had experienced all the bright flashes, the water splashes, the music that nearly brought him to tears, all the sensual phenomena from the blue room, everything he'd hoped for. But it was not until he saw the girl in the corner—the girl in his painting whose gaze had brought him to completion against his will the day before—with her bowl of yellow hair and her almond-shaped, glinting eyes, that he felt the nucleus of all of the sensations, the most powerful of all the colors. The girl radiated a spectacular heat, as if her skin could have burned him to the touch, and she was the deepest, most beautiful *yellow*.

It struck him like a fist in the face: she was the girl from the night in the park, the girl who was combing the park with her circle of light. And now she was lighting up the room with her wild, open gold. He approached her. *What in the* holy hell, *James?!* He approached her. *What in the yellow, spangly hell?!* He approached her and then immediately regretted doing so. Because as soon as she spoke it was as if a fire hydrant opened up inside of him; the room around him fell away; the paintings no longer mattered; the painter himself no longer mattered (in fact, James never noticed that Raul Engales himself never showed up); it was as if this girl had swallowed him, and now he was swimming around inside of her.

Inside of her. He had only meant to walk her home, but he had found himself *inside of her*.

His plan now, upon coming home from the apartment where he had slept with her, was to erase it from his mind: her sequin shirt, torn off to reveal her small white body. He would absolutely delete the image of her hungry eyes, the tears that glistened in their corners. He planned on denying the very existence of her nipples, the unfinished faces on the canvases that surrounded the bed, the sparks and the bright snakes that had flown around the room. But this proved difficult when, on the third, creaky stair, he caught a glimpse of the giant portrait of her again, hanging like a blazing square of yellow sex above the fireplace.

He attempted avoidance. He held a hand up to his eyes as he

changed his course, went back down the stairs to the bathroom, where he'd need to shower the smell of her off of him—coconut and tar, slashed with cheap Chinatown perfume. He shielded his face again as he climbed the open staircase to the loft, where Marge was asleep on her side: a mound of white goodness. He slid into bed as quietly as he could, letting her roll instinctively onto him. They had always slept like this: James on his back, like a board, and Marge like a malleable beanbag, sinking and fitting over him. Even when she was angry with him, her mood betrayed her in her sleep; she was peaceful.

But though he could feel her body up against his own, Marge once again felt oceans and light-years and miles away. His mind reeled with the events of the night. The quiet street, the smooth walk, the feeling of Lucy's brightness, the blackness of the apartment where his penis had been inside of her body.

His penis. A stranger's body. A room as black as his heart. The yellow. *Fuck*.

Sleep eluded him. The squabbles and sirens and drunken stumblings of the world quieted. The night wore thin and the lateness began to wear on his brain. He began to feel sick and worried, and worried sick, and sick in the head. Marge's skin felt sticky and terrible and off-limits, as if he shouldn't be allowed to touch it. He wasn't the sort of guy who did this. He wasn't a guy who *slept with other women*, who even *noticed other women*, and yet, somehow, he *had*. He had betrayed Marge, who he loved more than anything, who had taken care of him and loved him despite all of his faults, for a woman he cared nothing about. He could hardly comprehend how bad this was. How awful he felt. How bad this was. How awful he felt. How bad this was. How awful he felt.

How bad this was. How awful he felt.

And then: how curious.

Curiosity, creeping in alongside his worry in that deepest part of the night. The part of the night where he had known his brain to turn on him, letting all the wrong things in. Alongside the worry blinked

some sort of sexy shame. He squirmed and tossed and was blinded by
the moon on his face, but in the agitation and anxiety there was fire
and excitement and the memory of pleasure. At the height of this feeling, when he simply could not bear Marge's weight on him any longer,
he slipped out from under her and crept back down the stairs. He
flicked on a light and sat on the couch, right in front of the painting.

Immediately the yellow appeared, humming from the corners of
his eyes and then filling them. His face involuntarily morphed into
a smile. His body tingled, and he felt splashes of divinely refreshing water on his face. He felt the blood rush to his groin, his underwear tighten. Lucy was looking at him, just as she had hours before.
She (bleach blond) was looking at *him* (painfully bald) in a way that
suggested attraction. Her eyes were narrowing and her skin looked
radioactively hot. Her shoulders were so small! Her eyes were doing a
thing! He should leave, but he was staying. In the new experience, the
one he was having while staring at Lucy's portrait in the privacy of his
own home, he felt no tremor of nerves as he had earlier: only bright,
deep color. Only bleach blond. Only sudden.

Suddenly: She dove for him. She was like a famous diver. She had
a body so *other,* so different from the body he knew, so thin, almost a
boy's. So breastless. So un-Marge. Should he try to get out from under
her? Should he push her away? But Marge had disappeared already,
now that Lucy's mouth was all over his. He could not remember his
own wife. In his arms this new woman dissolved and she pushed. She
was a lime after a shot of strong tequila. She was no sunglasses and no
sunscreen when you needed both. She was wet tar where your feet got
stuck. Her mouth was all tongue and teeth.

The sex was fierce and warm. She watermelloned and heliumed
on top of him. She was forgiving, she forgave him for everything;
she was no one, she mattered not at all, she was the lack of pressure,
a simple balloon, floating away. But she was not floating away. She
was here. She was nipple, white, pink, flesh. She was back of arm,

back of leg. She was past midnight, dreamy, nonexistent. She was the feeling after laughter, which was the same as relief, which was the same as swimming. She had a starfish tongue, a bat's body, a regal bowl of hair. She was ALL SKIN. She had NOTHING UNDERNEATH. She had never happened before. She was ALL NEW. She was a thumbtack pressing into the bottom of his foot; she was wind chimes and ripples on water, light breezes; then she was a tunnel of wind; she was roaring; she loved him; she did not love him, she was an orgasm; she died for him; she was splitting in two; she wrapped her legs like a spider; she was a venomous spider; she was a wicked snake; he exploded; he loved her; he didn't love her; he loved *Marge*; he had always loved Marge, and Marge was coming down the stairs in her T-shirt and her underwear, and he looked up at her, and her face told him that she knew, but she didn't know, how could she know? He looked up at his wife, so solid, so red, and his eyes shone, he knew, with both guilt and apology.

"It's so late," she said quietly.

"I'm sorry," he said. "I'm coming back."

But even when he comes back—slides into bed with his wife, touches her face, makes her coffee the next morning, reads to her from the paper—James will not be back. He will feel an itch in his brain, like a spider running across and into its grooves. It will tickle, and like all tickling, it will lead to unbearable laughter: the wildest and most sincere form of pleasure. It will lead him back to Lucy.

She will be lying like a blond disaster on the bed. She will pull him toward her, and down. She has been feeling the itch, too, though her itch is a different kind. It is an itch that itches the way a scab does: new skin growing over a place that has been punctured, stretching the skin around it. She understands that she is only meant to scratch around its edges, for scratching the thing itself would make healing impossible.

And yet she cannot help it. The relief of the scratch seems worth the blood of a whole new open wound.

They will have sex again, and then again. They will meet up in the mornings that whole week, and then the week after that, when Marge goes to work. Their sex will be filled with expectation. James will expect the fireworks, and in those fireworks some fundamental shift; she will be the portal back into himself, the light switch that re-illuminates the world. Lucy will expect a losing of herself, a forgetting, a reprieve from the hollowness she feels when alone. She will expect, also, the apartment door to swing open, Raul Engales to walk in on them and, in a fury, tear them apart. *Please*, she will plead while James is inside of her. *Please please please*.

They will not speak of Raul Engales: this will be an unwritten law. Saying his name would be admitting what they are doing, which is clinging to each other, when the person they meant to cling to is nowhere to be found. *This is it*, they will try to tell themselves, and each other, over and over again. They pant with enough vigor to drown out this other thought: *Where is the man I came here for?*

But no matter how hard they fuck, no matter how blue the leaves outside turn and how yellow the room becomes, no matter how naked they get and how ravenously they devour each other, they will not be able to get rid of the itch. The more they try to scratch it the worse it will get, and the door will never open, and they will never get caught, and they will be forced to keep trying, to become more hollow each time they fill each other: many times per morning, for two weeks that feel like much more than that.

In the yellow haze of these two weeks, James will lose all sight of the article he is supposed to be writing, that he'd promised to Winona George, to himself, to his wife, to the world. It's too late anyway, he knows. This isn't the kind of city that waits around. This isn't the kind of city that gives a shit about the sins you're committing in order to escape your reality. But in the yellow haze of the affair, the city itself will fall away, reality will fall away, the idea of Raul Engales will fall away, until, on a cold morning—October now, and James is walking aimlessly again—he sees Lucy unexpectedly, out in the real world, and it will all come flooding back.

When James spots her—sitting at the Binibon diner on Second Avenue, in one of the red booths, alone—he will realize, instantly, what he has done. Because when he sees her there behind the glass, no color will appear. She will just be a regular girl, awash in regular diner light. And he'll know right then: they'd met among the paintings. They'd fucked among the paintings. Lucy's yellow had enveloped him, tricked him into thinking it was all he needed to survive. But it hadn't been Lucy's yellow at all. It had been Raul Engales's.

No matter how too-late he was, no matter two whole weeks—an eternity, in art time—were lost. No matter that he'd probably gone too far down the path of Lucy to find his way out with any grace. No matter that he'd lost his way, taken the detour of this absurd, obscene affair. He would see it clearly then, while walking away from the diner and from Lucy. He should have been trying to find Raul Engales the whole time.

PART
FOUR

PORTRAIT OF THE END OF AN ERA

EYES: Toby, in a Peruvian poncho, trudges up to the squat with a giant chandelier on his back. A crystal falls from one of the chandelier's many hands, hits the pavement, tinks, rolls. *Magnificent!* says Regina, who's come outside in her nightgown to greet the chandelier. Noose it up and light the thing, till the windows of the squat twinkle like the pupils of a man in love. *I'll do anything I want to,* says the twinkle of a pupil of a man in love. *And I'll keep doing it until my heart's broken. Till someone holds a gun to my back.*

LIMBS: Two red streamers, left over from a weeks-ago party, have pushed through the sleeves of the second-floor windows. They wave at the naked lindens, the sky, the cops that have just pulled up across the street.

MOUTH: WE'VE GOT A TYPICAL SITUATION HERE, JIMBO. WHADDAWE GOT, CLEM? BUNCHA THOSE ARTISTIC TYPES. STAY CLEAR A THEIR GLUE GUNS THIS TIME, EH, JIMBO? EH? KEEP YA MOUTH OFFA THOSE GLUE GUNS?! SHOVE IT UP YOUR HAIRY ASS, CLEM. DO YOUR FUCKING JOB.

STOMACH: Rumbling as things are knocked and gathered. Emptied.

CHEST: *Those are my tits!* yells Selma, from behind the thick, un-openable window of the police car, at a cop who's exited the building with a plaster statue of a pair of breasts. *You can't take that! Those are my fucking tits!* The cop studies the sculpture, then sets it on top of a rusty garbage can. He has sausagey fingers, which he uses to grab the breasts, then squeeze. *Oh, really?* the cop says. *Oh, really?*

BODY: *It's just plywood and brick. It's just brick and mortar. It's just nails and sheetrock. It's just concrete and metal.* Tell yourself these things, like little prayers. Whisper them in hushed tones that sound like the round brushes on the bottoms of trucks that clean the streets at night. *We can get more plywood. There is always more brick. Mortar, we hear, is in high supply. If we wanted concrete and metal, we could just go to jail.* Don't think of the street sweeper whose brush is humming over the side-walk, just steps from where you're trying to sleep. He's almost done with his shift; he'll park his truck in Queens, fumble through the city back to his apartment in Chinatown. He'll flick on and off his light, boil water for no reason, turn on a television. You, on the other hand, are homeless now, mumbling about construction materials under the eave of a depressing dental office on Seventh Street with your ten law-breaking comrades, wondering where you might go tomorrow, if you'll have to split up, thinking about how you miss the piece of plywood that was drilled above the squat's bathroom sink, where your toothbrush sat, ready to be used whenever you wanted to feel clean.

MOUTH: Though they've never done so before, Toby and Selma grab each other's faces, kiss. *When tragedy strikes*, Toby whispers into Selma's ear, which has plaster stuck in it, from a mold she's made that hasn't even begun to dry.

THE RISING SUN

When the squat got ransacked and shut down unexpect edly, on a Tuesday morning just after breakfast, Raul Engales and James Bennett saw the whole thing from the south-facing window of the Rising Sun Rehabilitation Clinic, where Raul Engales had been admitted three weeks ago after failing to die. High on the list of unfortunate things about the Rising Sun, to say nothing of its bright pink walls and lethargic nurses, was its regretful location—on East Seventh and Avenue A, right across the street from his old stomping grounds. High on the list of unfortunate things about Raul Engales's life was that he was living it.

James had brought coffee—since he'd started his daily visits a week ago, Engales hadn't had to drink the crap they served in the Rising Sun's cafeteria; a small but significant relief. The fact of them sipping the hot, delicious stuff while watching the cop cars—three of them now—pull up and then empty themselves of beefy, navy-clad law enforcers gave the scene a removed sensation, as if they were watching a movie or a television show, whose characters happened to have been the cast of Raul Engales's previous life.

"They're your friends in there?" James asked, worried. He was always worried, Engales thought. One of those people who was always worried.

"Only a matter of time, I guess."

There was the *blip blip blip* of the siren used halfway, then the sagging clangs of key rings and the thick thunks of heavy boots. They watched the cops bang with their mad hands on the squat's blue door—the door Selma had painted at 7:00 A.M. one morning because she had dreamed of a blue door and had to realize the dream immediately—then kick through it. With his left hand, Engales struggled to pop the window open; at the Rising Sun, you were only allowed a crack, lest you lose your shit and try to jump out.

"BAD DAY TO STEAL A CHANDELIER, BUDDY." Engales could hear the cop's barrely voice, perhaps genetically modified to sound like *asshole*, all the way from here. "REAL BAD DAY."

"Crap," said James Bennett. "Will they go to jail?"

"You're the type who's scared of cops, aren't you?" Engales said. The cold air slithered all over them.

"I had a feeling about today," James said. "I woke up to purple."

"When you talk like a crazy person," Engales said, eyes on the cops' backs as they filed in the door. "It's hard to be around you. It really is."

"Did you know they're putting Jean-Michel in a *movie* now?" James said, turning to look at Engales pleadingly.

"What's that got to do with anything?" Engales said. He did not particularly want to think about Jean-Michel Basquiat's cinematic debut, or his rising fame, or anything happening out in the world that did not include him.

"I'm saying that this"—James opened his hand toward the window—"is going to happen everywhere. To everything. The buildings, the artists themselves, everything is going to be stolen, or at least bought. The money's coming downtown, and it'll be this, over and over again. Everything's going to change, is what I'm saying. Just watch."

They watched. The blue tarps from the squat's second-floor windows puffed in the wind. The cops had gone inside now, and left the front door open behind them, and Engales imagined the cold air blowing into the squat's common room, the chill that outdid the space heaters and crept under sweaters, no matter how many you piled on. When it was cold like this, back when Engales spent every spare moment at the squat, they'd have the Swedes build one of their massive fires on the concrete slab in the back; outside with fire was warmer than inside without. Not that warmth had mattered much to them. They had had one another, and they had their projects, and they had this space they could make their own—these were the things that kept them from freezing.

Engales realized this bust was an opportunity for relief: finally the squat would stop taunting him from across the street. Finally he'd be able to sleep without imagining what might be happening over there, wondering what he was missing. For three weeks he'd been listening to the sounds of his old life seeping through the window's crack— Selma's cosmic howling, parties raging until the aching hours of the night, an experimental poetry reading during which everyone had yelled in unison: "VERY UNNERVING. VERY UNNERVING. VERY UNNERVING INDEED!" And now he could be free of that; if not peace of mind, there would at least be silence.

But he didn't feel relief now, as he waited for his friends to be escorted out of the place they'd spent the last years turning into a manifestation of their dreams. He felt only deep, unexpected sadness, if not for their loss than for the fact that he could not partake in it. He had helped make the squat during the time he'd spent there—the kitchen shelves, the handwoven hammock, the studio walls—and so he should be there when it got destroyed. He should be there, mouthing off to the cops with Toby, standing in front of Selma so they wouldn't cuff her. Instead, he was here, in his own private hell across the street, trapped with a bunch of drunks and lunatics and people with giant limps or missing limbs, watching his old life like a voyeur with an obsessive failed writer. How had this become *him*? How was this his *life*? Why, and how, was he *here*?

Because of Winona George.

Because of Winona George, Raul Engales had not died by way of painkiller overdose three weeks ago, on the night of the show that would have been his artistic debut. Instead, Winona had found him passed out and drooling on a stoop on Bond Street, while stiletto-stepping toward a yellow cab. She'd dragged him into the car herself and instructed the cabbie to drive with meteoric speed to St. Vincent's.

"That cabbie didn't have the slightest idea what meteoric meant," Winona relayed after Engales's stomach had been forcefully pumped at the same hospital where they had sewn up his arm. (*Practically a regular here*, one nurse tried to joke.) "But he still drove like hell," Winona went on. "And thank god for that, or you would have been a dead man."

"If only," Engales had said.

"Oh, don't say that," Winona had said. "Things got bad there for a second, I know, darling. But there's still a life to be lived. And you're in good hands now."

Whose good hands? Engales wanted to say. The hands of the handsome hospital doctors, whose capableness was a threat to Engales's very being? Winona's, whose mauve manicure made him actually nauseous? Some god's? Who had already proved himself either non-existent or evil? Good hands, Engales thought while gazing up into the hollow caves of Winona's cheekbones from the hospital bed, did not exist anymore.

But Winona had disagreed. There was hope for Raul Engales yet—more life to be lived and more fame to be had, if only he got some help. She was adamant: he would be admitted somewhere where he could recover and rehabilitate; she would foot the bill.

And so it was because of Winona George that Engales was not sent home to François's apartment but to the Rising Sun (or as the people at the squat had called it, the *Rubber Room*, both because it housed the neighborhood's crazier set and because the clinic on the first floor

gave out condoms for free). Here he was to endure the depressing aesthetic blend of homespun hospitality and medical sterility that he expected was common in New York City wellness institutions: peppy
construction paper signage (IF IT'S YELLOW LET IT MELLOW, read one,
in the communal bathroom), hospital-blue sheets, jail-thin mattresses,
glass mobiles that reflected colorful light onto his face in the morning.
He was to share a small room with an ex-alcoholic roommate named
Darcy, who sang gospel before going to bed every night and shined
his shoes after every time he wore them. He was to take orders and
pills from a fantastically bitchy nurse named Lupa, whose Mexican
Spanish was both lazy and lippy and whose nose was almost as wide as
her face. And he was to attend therapy of all kinds: talk therapy with a
man named Germond Germond, who had told Engales, absurdly, *you
can just call me Germond*; art therapy (it couldn't get more ironic) with
Carmen Rose, who never once spoke but did an incredible amount of
nodding and tempera paint mixing; and physical therapy with Debbie,
a peppy blond sports trainer who attempted to train his left hand into
a one-man show by making him turn the knobs of an Etch A Sketch.
"It's different with everyone," Debbie said sweetly when Engales
asked her how fucking long this was going to take. "We need to re-
train your mind to understand your new body. It's a process."

But Engales didn't want to understand his new body, or his new
life, or undergo any process at all. He did not want to hear the sounds
of a party at the squat while he tried to fall asleep. He did not want to
do therapy, of any kind. And he especially did not want to be cooped
up in a little room for hours with the awful images that triangled
around in his mind: the terror of the white suit jacket, leading Lucy
off into the night; his childhood house, empty on the other end of the
phreak-tapped pay phone; the silver blade of the guillotine, slamming
down onto his arm; Franca's eggs, their bleeding yolk. And so he'd
shut his eyes with force, but under the lids he'd just get a more jum-
bled version of the images that haunted him. Jacket, ringing, yolk/

blood. Germond, Germond, yolk, jacket. Lupa's nose, jacket, Etch A Sketch, blood. *Meet me at the squat, midnight at the squat, four in the morning at the squat, never again at the squat. Hallelujah,* white yolk, red yolk, THIS IS UNNERVING, Lupa's cigarette smell, ringing, ringing, ringing, gone.

But then, on the Tuesday of his second week there, the hellish rhythm of his rehabilitation was interrupted, when a man showed up toward the end of visiting hours, covered in rain. Something about him was familiar, but Engales couldn't place him at first. Around the cuffs of the man's slacks, little moats formed.

"Sorry about this," the man said, motioning at the dripping. "I lost my umbrella. Maybe I never had one? I never know with umbrellas."

Lupa tucked her head into the room. "Thees is Meester James Bennett," she said in her I'm-a-hard-ass voice. "Miss George lady sends him. Be nice."

Engales's heart flapped ever so slightly. *James Bennett.* That's why the man looked familiar: Engales flashed on the New Year's Eve party, when Rumi had listed off the important people on the balcony. He remembered Bennett's slumped silhouette, his shiny head. He thought of Winona's promise: an article in the *Times*, by the most *revered* art writer, all about his show. Engales bristled, first with the sort of hope he felt when he woke up in the morning: ten bright seconds during which a writer from the *New York Times* was here to write an article about *him*.

Engales reached for a towel that hung on the doorknob of the closet, threw it at the man. He caught it, rubbed it over his shoulders, down his legs. Then the ten bright seconds faded, as quickly as they'd arrived. James Bennett could only be here to write about one thing: the accident, the hand. He imagined headlines—"Failed Painter Lands in Loony Bin." "Crippled Artist Never to Paint Again." "Hand and

Career Severed." *Read all about it*. He then imagined Lucy picking up the paper and seeing his sob story on the front page. There would be a close-up of his wrinkled arm, the black notches of the stitches appalling and obvious, Frankensteinian. He suddenly felt violated—the same way he had felt when the Telemondo guy didn't tell his penny joke. The world would forever treat him differently, look at him differently; the hand would define him from here on out. The hand would be his only story.

"I'm not doing interviews," Engales said quickly then, averting James Bennett's gaze.

"Me neither," said James, taking off his tiny round glasses to rub the water from his face.

"Then what are you doing here?" Engales said.

"Well," James Bennett said breathlessly, as if he had just climbed many flights of stairs. "To tell you the truth, I'm trying to figure out the meaning of my life."

Just then, when James Bennett returned his glasses to his face, Engales saw it: the telltale registering of the missing hand, which was laid out on the arm of Engales's chair like a pink dick. This was the pattern: normal face, wide-eyed frightened face, rejiggered fake normal face, then sinking face. James Bennett had not known about the accident. He wasn't here to write about the accident.

Usually there was a final resting stage: the eyebrow-tilt of *pity*. But James Bennett's face didn't move into the final stage. Instead, it shifted into a wide-eyed, slack-mouthed expression of what could only be considered *awe*.

"Shit," James said.

Engales watched skeptically as James Bennett's pale face contorted into a sort of euphoric mess: all eye-bulging and nostril-flaring and cheek-scrunching.

"It's happening," James said.

"*What's* happening?" Engales asked; he was too curious not to.

"Um," James managed, screeching a chair around next to Engales's, padding his wet loafers across the linoleum, sitting, the whole time keeping his buggy eyes on Raul Engales's face. Engales could feel the tug of the stitches in his arm, like they could burst.

"It's like a crown," James said, his head tilting. "Or kind of a halo. It's sort of a golden color. It's beautiful. It's like the blue room. I knew it!"

Engales scooted his chair away a bit; the linoleum screamed. "You're officially freaking me out," he said. "So unless you tell me what the hell you're talking about, I'm going to call Lupa back in."

"Oh, I'm sorry," James said, taking off his glasses again to rub his eyes. "I'm being odd, aren't I? I can't help it. I just feel so much. You're making me feel so much."

"Lupa!" Engales yelled to the door, but Lupa didn't come.

James jumped into an explanation: He had a sort of disability, he explained. No, an *ability*. He had an ability to see things that weren't there, to hear things and to feel things and to smell things that did not exist in the real world. His wires were crossed, he explained. Like a switchboard operator who hooked the wrong two people up for conversation, and those two people ended up hitting it off.

Engales watched him, still highly skeptical. Rumi had been right on New Year's when she had called James Bennett an odd duck. And yet Engales felt something he hadn't felt in a while. He felt warm. Ever since the accident, he had been cold, as if his wound were an open window out of which all his body heat escaped. Now, in James Bennett's presence, he felt his blood heating.

Just then Lupa blasted in, flared her nose and declared that visiting hours ended at precisely one o'clock and it was now *one oh five* and Mary Spinoza was going to fry her ass like a *chicharrón* if Bennett didn't get out on the double. James stood, leaving a little puddle of rain where his ass had been, and reached out to shake Engales's hand.

"Nice try," Engales said. James Bennett looked down at his

hand—he had defaulted to his right—and was overcome with what looked to be real shame.

"Shit," James said.

"That's what you have to say?" Engales said. "Shit?" He could feel the warmth leaving him.

"I'd like to leave something here if I could," James had said, searching a bulky messenger bag Engales had not noticed before. He pulled a heavy brown leather book from the bag, dumped it onto Engales's lap.

"What the fuck is this?" Engales said.

"What used to be the meaning of my life," James Bennett said. "Let me know what you find."

When Darcy left to play poker in the common room, Engales, curious, had explored the leather binder. On its edge, on a sticker, there was a cryptic scrawl: HUNGER / SUN YELLOW / RAUL ENGALES. What kind of psychotic labeling system was this? And why was Engales's name involved? When he opened it, it was full of the tiny white squares of slides meant for projectors. Engales ran his left hand over the satisfyingly smooth plastic, then pulled one of the slides out of its little sleeve. He lifted it toward the window. In the little square he saw a face. He tilted the slide so the light worked its way into the face: it was Francis Bacon's, the portrait of him by Lucian Freud. The same portrait Arlene had showed him on that first day in the studio, as the counterpoint to his own piece of shit.

The coincidence was eerie, just like the binder itself. Just like James Bennett himself, who had showed up out of nowhere for no reason Engales could understand, said some very weird shit, then left him with a bunch of slides and no projector. Or was there a projector? He recalled that he had seen one in the physical-therapy room, which Debbie used to give her Body and Soul lectures: a picture of a lean woman on a beach, a picture of a bowl of oatmeal, a picture of all the muscles in a hand. Luckily Debbie had a little thing for Engales—the way she massaged his arm during their lessons was nothing short of erotic— and so when he asked her to borrow the projector and the room she flirtatiously agreed, with a caveat: *Only if I can stay and watch.*

"Fine," Engales said, pulling up two chairs and shutting the door of the physical-therapy room. He loaded a page of slides, and flicked on the projector. A vibrant picture appeared on the wall behind the robotic-looking shadows of the workout machines. It was another painting Engales knew: an untitled work by Francesco Clemente, of a woman flanked by two naked men. The woman had a wide red mouth and a thick braid coming down over one of her shoulders. The men stood in individual pools of blue, holding their hands over their heads, posing for her.

"I feel a ménage à trois coming on," Debbie said, as if the painting were a television show of the sort he assumed she watched, where the girls wore jean jackets and chewed gum, just like she did.

Engales ignored her and let the image sink into him. He had loved the painting the moment he first saw it, at a show at one of the bigger galleries a couple years ago; he loved it still. He loved the frank fear that inhabited the woman's face, and he loved the question the painting posed: Could one love two people? Or would so much love make them drown, as this woman's pained face suggested? He thought of Lucy, loving some other man in his apartment. A bell rang inside him: perhaps she was drowning. Perhaps, even if she did love that man in the white suit, she also still loved him. The brilliance of the painting soothed him, the fact that it was making him think in so many layers. *Two for two*.

Engales clicked through the page of slides, and when it was done, the page after that, and by the third page it became clear that things were only getting eerier. The works in James Bennett's HUNGER / SUN YELLOW / RAUL ENGALES binder were almost all works that he himself had fallen in love with at various points in his life. There were Hockney's winter trees, Jean-Michel's monstrous figures, Matisse's cutouts, and Avant's street scrawls. There was even one of Horatio's action paintings that Engales had watched him make at a midnight performance in an empty building in the Meatpacking District, one of his boxing glove pieces. Even the paintings Engales had never seen before moved him, vibrated within him, and the whole thing made the backs of his eyes tight with held-back tears.

"We could get you back there," Debbie said suddenly, when the wall went black. "You're making strides with your left flexors. The palmar interossei are what need work, but we can get there."

"Thank you, Debbie," he said, pulling himself up from his chair with some effort. He felt exhausted. "But no thank you, Debbie."

His mind, anyway, was not on his own hand or his own painting, or on Debbie, but on the slides, and on James Bennett. His heart was aflutter with the speed and love and color that the slides held. He had not felt this speed or love or color since the accident, and looking at this collection of slides only confirmed a suspicion Engales had had when James Bennett was in his room: James Bennett held a hand of cards that Engales wanted to see, and to know. Then Engales's mind went totally blank, because Debbie was at work at the button of his jeans.

"Physical therapy?" she said from below him, her lashes twittering.

James returned the next day at the same time, and again the day after that, and quickly he became the kind of visitor one needed in a rehab clinic: the kind who kept coming back. In exchange for agreeing to the Rising Sun at all, Engales had made Winona promise not to tell any of his friends—especially Lucy, he'd said with a clenched jaw—where he was. She'd eventually agreed, but had reasoned that Bennett was not Engales's friend and therefore did not count; Winona loved a good loophole. But Engales didn't begrudge her for sending James. In a place where there was nothing to look forward to except for Sunday movie night or Friday pizza night or Tuesday oatmeal bar, James's presence, if strange, was actually a welcome distraction.

On the second day James came to visit, perhaps because Engales had been moved by the paintings in the book of slides, Engales had felt open, ready to talk. And they did talk, in a way that Engales had not talked to anyone for as long as he could remember, about people they both knew (Jean-Michel, Selma Saint Regis) and artists with ego problems (Toby), and projects they'd seen that lit them up (James Turrell's light and space works) and projects that left them cold (Jeff Koons, the vacuums). Engales's staunch conviction that he was finished with art, thinking about it even, faded to the background during these conversations, as they took unexpected turns (James spoke of getting a hard-on when he saw a Matisse, for one), or went unexpectedly deep (Engales told James about his parents: *I painted people because I had no people*). They talked at length about the slides in the binder, and at special length about the Freud.

"The wonderful thing is that its unclear whether it's finished!" James had said. "That white background! You feel the entire tension of the painter's plight in that background! His whole internal drama: Should he keep going? Or should he leave it so perfectly undone? Did he stop because he doubted himself or because he loved what he had made? It's all there, the whole story and the whole big question!"

Engales nodded slightly. He remembered when Arlene had first showed him the painting, how he had had such a similar thought. James launched into a spirited little speech about Bacon and Freud, about their friendship and their days spent in the studio together, smoking, eating, talking, painting each other. Then their gambling, how they'd hock their cars or their paintings to pay their growing debts. How the gambling was the same as the painting, when you thought about it; art was always a hunch, a lead you followed into the dark, whose outcome you'd never know until it was all over, a game that you could lose.

"I always felt like the best artists knew what their outcome would be," Engales said. "That they had an idea first, and then the work came out of that idea. I don't have any ideas. I always just painted until there was a painting. I always thought I must be doing something wrong."

"Oh, no," said James spiritedly, his eyes widening. "You are underestimating the power of the associative brain! That's what an artist is! Someone whose way of looking at the world—just their gaze—is already an idea in itself!"

Engales was quiet, thinking this over. He imagined Bacon and Freud, their wrinkled faces, the smell of the turpentine, the tiny bits of blue they'd add for each other's shadows. Somehow sitting here with James Bennett, talking about two old guys and ideas and art, no matter that he could no longer make it anymore, made him feel not-so-terrible. He could feel it happening, perhaps against his own will, or perhaps because of it, so quickly and seamlessly that he couldn't have seen it coming or articulated its trajectory: James Bennett was becoming his friend. And what, right then, did he have to lose? He'd follow this hunch into the dark. He'd maybe even bet on it.

A game: Raul Engales holds a slide from the binder up to the window. James Bennett blurts out what he feels when he looks at it. "Laundry detergent!" James says when Engales holds up a Walter Robinson slide. "Astonished gray!" he says about Robert Longo's Men in the Cities. "What the fuck is *astonished gray*?" says Engales; they laugh. "My wife's neck," James says to a Ross Bleckner piece, of wavy lines that cascade down the tiny window like hair.

An Engales proclamation: "Fuck abstraction and fuck surrealism and fuck sunsets. Especially fuck sunsets. Give me nostrils, you know? Big ugly ones. With boogers."

A James question: "What happened to your hand?"
An Engales answer: "I was robbed."

A James proclamation: "It could come back. You never know. One day you could wake up and have it back. The color of the world, the beauty of it. Trust me, I *know*."
An Engales rejection: "You don't know shit."

An Engales question: "What are you doing here again?"
A James answer: "Talking to you."

"My bet's on a gallery," James Bennett said now, from his perch at the window, as they watched the cops tuck the artists into the backs of their low cop cars, one by one. "And this, ladies and gentlemen, is the great irony of capitalism. How about we kick out the artists to make room for the art?"

"There's Regina," Engales said. Regina, with her dishwater-blond hair stuck to her tear-stained face, had never before seemed vulnerable to Engales. Now she looked like a frightened fawn, her legs and lips wobbling. Behind her, the rest of them followed—Selma in her long black pirate's coat; Toby in his Peruvian poncho that seemed, in the light of the day, both culturally and visually offensive; Horatio, carrying only his paint-covered boxing gloves. Engales felt the distinct tug of exclusion again; he wanted desperately to be in that line with them. But why? Why would he wish himself into this terrible scene? Why did he suddenly want back into his old life, right when it was being upended?

A memory appeared to him with so much vividness he could have painted it, and before he could realize it he was speaking the memory out loud.

"The apartment building across from ours burned down," Engales said. The memory, when verbalized, gained physical traction; he felt the heat from the fire on his face. "When I was fifteen, the year after my parents died. We were just teenagers, alone in this giant house, just me and my sister. I woke up because it had gotten so hot, the flames were all the way across the street but the heat was blasting through our window. Bright orange flames, like they were fake, from a movie. I woke up my sister and we ran downstairs and out into the street, where the whole neighborhood was outside watching the fire eat up this building. We stood and watched it for a while, and I knew exactly what my sister was thinking, because I was thinking it, too."

"Which was?"

"We wanted to be the kids whose house had burned down," he said.

James was quiet. By the looks of it, his bodega coffee had gotten cold, its cream blanketing its surface.

"All the families from the apartment building moved into a temporary pavilion in the park, all together," Engales went on, his eyes glazing as his mind moved away from the present and into the past. "We didn't have a pavilion. We just had this huge, freezing house."

Down on the street, they saw Selma begin to scream and try to wriggle from the cop who held her: a huge, red-faced man with a blond mustache and porky lips. With seemingly little effort, he stilled her.

"We tried to go and stand with the group of people from the fire," Engales went on. "They were all crying, and we wanted to cry with them, but we couldn't. We knew it wasn't ours; it wasn't our tragedy. And suddenly we looked at each other and without even consulting each other, we took off running down the street. We had both known the other was going to run, and to where. We went to the cemetery and sat on top of our parents' graves. I was on Dad's and Franca was on Mom's. We had never been to the graves before—we were too scared to see them, or to imagine that our parents' bodies were actually in them. But we went that night. We had both known we had to go, at exactly the same time. We knew where our tragedy was, and we had to feel it right then."

Why he was telling this to James Bennett now he didn't know exactly, but Engales couldn't stop talking. It was the first time he had spoken about Franca since he had arrived in New York; he hadn't even told Lucy about her. It was as if Franca had been a caged animal inside of him, and now she was thrashing around, trying to get out.

"With Franca," he went on. "It was one of those things where we were too close. We understood too much about each other. We saw too much. It almost hurt to be around her."

"Is that why you came here?"

"It's my fault," Engales said. His voice had gotten low and dark, as black as the coffee in his hand.

"What's your fault?"

"I left her there. Even when I fucking *knew what would happen*."

"What would happen?"

"I had a dream about her on the morning of my accident. And then I saw her, right when it happened, when the blade was in my arm I saw her."

"So you don't *know* something happened. Have you called her?"

"You don't get what I'm saying, do you? You have no idea what I'm talking about. I left her alone with a man who can't take care of her. Something's happened. The country's fucked and something happened, I just know it."

"But you haven't talked to anybody yet and—"

"Just shut up," Engales said, his face suddenly enflamed. "Just stop telling me things you know nothing about. And also? So you know? I'm not going to paint again. Never a-fucking-gain. Do you hear me? Can your associative brain comprehend that? So stop trying to act like you know anything about my life. Like it's all so fucking clear to you."

"I'm sorry, I . . . I shouldn't have said anything," James said, taken aback by Engales's sudden hostile outburst. "I just get confused. Because it seems clear. When I'm around you, everything seems clear."

"Well, it's not," Engales said, his heart still trampling over his lungs in his chest. He wanted to show Franca his arm right then. She was the only one who would understand its scar.

The two men went quiet and looked back out the window, where a white plastic bag had gotten caught in the nearest tree. When the wind freed it, its message was revealed: I ♥ NEW YORK. It soared into the white sky until the sky swallowed it. Below, switches were flicked and sirens started. Then the artists were gone.

THE MISSING BOY AND
THE LOST GIRL

L ucy woke from a whiskey-soaked sleep to the unsettling sound of sirens and a loud knocking on the apartment door. A siren in the morning was like a drink before noon: it was a signal that things were getting bad. The sound of knocking, however, was a relief. *James had come back*.

She wobbled up into a sitting position, rolled her legs off the bed. Her head china-dolled to one side, too heavy for its own neck. The floor of the apartment was betraying her, tilting this way and that, and she had the distinct feeling that she couldn't place herself in time. Was it actually October? Had the last month of her life actually happened? Had Engales actually lost his hand? And disappeared? And had James Bennett actually taken his place in the bed for two whole weeks after the show, then abruptly disappeared himself, without so much as a call? Also: last night. Was she, could she possibly be, *twenty-three?*

She stumbled to the door, the idea of James's warm body under his ugly trench coat pulling her forward. She'd sink into him. She'd ask him where he'd been all week, but then she'd tell him she understood. She knew he had a life. She knew he couldn't come every day. *Still*, she'd say. *I missed you*. Which was only true within the confines of the thing they'd created together, which was, of course, a big old lie. Still:

a soothing lie. A lie she wouldn't mind right now; at least there was another human involved.

No, said the cruel, pulsing world of the worst hangover of all time. *You shan't be wrecking any homes today.* It was not James at the door. At the door, when Lucy yanked open the rusty deadbolt and pulled it open, was a tall, blond woman in a gray overcoat, holding the hand of a very small boy.

The missing boy, Lucy thought, just before she felt a hand grab her insides and twist. She ran to the bathroom, emptied herself of last night.

Last night had been a mess of lipstick and whiskey: the kind of night a girl has when the men she counts on to save her do not. It had been her twenty-third birthday, and there had been no one to celebrate with, and nothing worth celebrating. There was no Engales—she'd tried in vain to track him down, but *nothing*—and there was no James; he'd stopped showing up at the apartment a week ago, without any explanation. She spent the morning feeling sorry for herself, remembering her last birthday, when Jamie and the R boys had made her a lumpy cake and, when it proved to be inedible, took her out to the Mudd Club, where they'd spun around and around on the dance floor, spilling their drinks, just one in a million groups of friends in New York, out to feed on the city together. Now there was no together, there was no one, and when a birthday alone became too much for her to fathom, she'd finally decided to take things into her own hands; she would call James's house, ask him where he'd been, convince him to come over, kiss him until he adored her again.

This call called for the steely nerves that could only be achieved through alcohol, so she'd gone to Telemondo's for a flask. She chose Jim Beam, held the bottle to her chest like a comforting teddy bear, humble in its little brown bag. As she was leaving, she had paused to flip through a magazine on the rack near the door. It flapped open to an ad for lipstick that read: *Does any man really understand you?*

No, she had thought as she scanned the image of a busty brunette, whose lips were laced with risky iridescence. The ad was for Revlon's Cherries in the Snow, another of the lipstick colors that Jamie swore by. *Nobody really does.*

Nobody knew that she had a flat silver washer from Mason & Mick's tucked in her front pocket at all times; they probably assumed it was the presumptuous outline of an unused condom. Nobody knew what she really smelled like, which was soil and manure and honeysuckle from the garden; they knew her smell as stale cigarettes, knock-off perfume from Chinatown, cherry lip gloss, sex. Nobody knew what her mother called her: *girlywog;* here she was *Raul's chick* or *Ida* or *'Tender.* Nobody knew that as soon as it got dark she went out into the city with a flashlight to look for a missing child, or that she slept surrounded by milk cartons with that child's face on it; if they did, they'd think that it was a *project,* some foray into their artistic world, rather than what it actually was, which was girlish superstition, lonely reaching. They didn't want to talk about superstition in New York. They wanted cold, hard facts: like if you are or are not fucking a married man in your newly crippled boyfriend's bed.

Revlon understands you as you really are . . . Oh-so-warm and a little reckless.

Okay, then, Revlon. Okay, then, New York. One tube of Cherries in the Snow from the pharmacy across the street, placed slyly in the pocket of her lumberjack coat that used to be her dad's. One smear of the stuff on her cracking lips, using the pay phone's grimy silver surface as a mirror. One—no, two—swigs of the Jim Beam, for the steeling of nerves. One quick scan of the soft, flimsy pages of the pay phone's phonebook, to find one James Bennett's phone number. But look, here's something even better. James Bennett's *address.*

She could steal her mother's turquoise; she could determine her own fate; she could walk across town to 24 Jane Street and look into James Bennett's smaller-than-average window.

This was where he lived, where he *actually* lived, with his *wife*, who was standing now at the kitchen counter, working at something with a knife. Lucy stood there, wobbly with whiskey, looking in on this woman. A woman with soft brown hair and a purple shirt. A woman with a casserole pan. A woman who had probably gone to college. In other words, the very opposite of Lucy. Then there was James, who came through to the kitchen to wrap his arms around her. The arms said: *I have known how to wrap my arms around this person for my whole life.* The arms said: *You, Lucy Marie Olliason, are a terrible fucking person.*

She had burst into Jim Beam tears. *Since when do you drink Jim Beam? Since I realized it could make me burst into tears at any given moment.* James did not love her; Engales did not love her; neither of them even knew her; nobody fucking knew her. She rubbed the iridescent lipstick from her mouth with her wrist. She fled down Jane and back across town, but not before making stops at every bar she saw along the way. In each of them, she made some version of the same sloppy scene. At the Eagle, she put Blondie on the jukebox and danced alone (if you could call it dancing; it was mostly arms); Random Randy watched on sadly. At the Aztec Lounge she pulled a fat man's tie and kissed his rosy, blubbery face. At Eileen's Reno Bar, where plastic plants hung from the ceiling and the men wore blue, sparkly shadow, she pounded her fist on the bar and tried to recount to the bartender her plight.

"We were *just here*," she whined. "Me and Raul. We were dancing, and Winona had just called. He was so happy. 'Winona George *loves me*,' he said. I told him everybody loved him. 'Like who?' he said. 'Like me,' I said. It was the first time I told him. That I loved him, I mean."

The bartender didn't care about this story, or the ones she recounted after that, about his hand, about James, about James's wife in the window. No one cared. In the end, Devereux, a transvestite who was often at the squat, had walked her home, whispering, *Darling daffodil, darling rose,* over and over in her sweet, deliberately pitched voice, until Lucy threw up onto Devereux's sparkly shoes.

Male. Hispanic. *Six years old. 40 inches. Dark hair, brown eyes.*

It's *him,* Lucy thought as she splashed her face with water in the bathroom, in whose sink a water cockroach had taken up residence, not to be drowned for anything. The boy at the door had to be Jacob Rey. He met all the descriptions on the milk cartons, and hadn't he been carrying a backpack? Jacob Rey had a backpack. She thought of the night of the accident, the searching, ghostly faces of the mothers. She had known then that she had entered into the fate of the boy, and here he was. Here was the missing boy, right here at the door. Here was fate, coming for her.

No, said the cruel, pulsing world of the worst hangover of all time, when she went back out to find him at the door. *You shan't be saving any lost boys today.*

It wasn't Jacob Rey, she saw now. The eyes were different. They were not Jacob Rey's eyes, and yet they were still familiar. She knew the boy in some other way. In some other way that involved his eyes.

"Are you the wife?" the blond woman said, in halting English, before Lucy could place the boy's eyes into the library of eyes she knew.

"Excuse me?" Lucy said, reorienting herself toward the woman, whose cheeks were like two pink cherries. *Cherries in the Snow.* The thought of the lipstick made her want to vomit again. She sucked in her breath.

"Raul Engales's wife?" the woman said.

Whether it was because she wished it to be true or because she couldn't think straight, Lucy didn't know, but she nodded.

"Good then," the tall woman said. She extracted an orange envelope from her wide purse, pulled out a white sheet of paper, and pressed it into Lucy's hands. It was a letter, written in beautiful, un-smudged script. The words were written in Spanish.

"Oh, I don't read Spanish," Lucy said apologetically.

The woman tapped at the paper, to an indented section.

Raul Engales (hermano)

265 Avenue A, Apartment 6

New York, New York 10009

Lucy looked up at the woman, whose pale face held no answers. Lucy was thoroughly confused. *Hermano.* This much she knew in Spanish. But Engales had never mentioned a brother or sister. He had always said he had no family—they were all dead.

"Sorry," Lucy said, holding her own forehead, which felt hot. "I'm not understanding. Who are you?"

"I am Sofie," the blond woman said, in halting, mechanical English. "The neighbor of Raul's sister, Franca."

"I don't think Raul has a sister," she said. Lucy for some reason thought of the water cockroach she'd seen in the sink a moment ago, its sickening shiny head, gasping for air from the drain.

Another, smaller piece of paper was pulled from the envelope by Sofie and placed on top of the first. It was a postcard of the New York City skyline, in all its black-and-white jagged glory. It was strikingly similar to the postcard Lucy had found in the grass in Ketchum, and when she saw it her heart stopped. All the lines of fate were crossing, though she could not understand how, or why. When she flipped the postcard over she saw a few Spanish words in Engales's handwriting, then his big, beautiful initials, *R. E.*

"What is this?" Lucy said.

"Proof," the woman said. Her voice was like a jet plane: slick and pointed, with a whoosh of resonance trailing it.

Lucy looked at her blankly, wondering if Sofie meant this as an affront to Lucy or if something was being lost in translation; English was definitely not the woman's first language. Was her proof meant to prove Lucy wrong, show her that Engales *did* have a sister, a sister who he sent postcards to? To show her that her own husband had kept things from her? Things as substantial as siblings? Lucy felt a pang in her chest, which she took as proof that she didn't know Raul Engales as well as she thought she did. That perhaps she didn't know him at all.

"Do you have tea?" Sofie said, filling in for Lucy's silence. "We are quite cold. A cup of tea would be nice."

"Sure," Lucy said without thinking, forgetting for a second that she was not the kind of person who served tea, and that there was no tea in Raul Engales's apartment, and never had been. The lack of tea, an epic domestic failure, made her feel suddenly guilty, like she had done something absolutely wrong. She went to the kitchen anyway, put her hands on the edges of the sink, tried to breathe. The little light on the message machine did not blink. No messages.

"Sorry," said Lucy when she returned, her head shaking apologetically. "I'm sorry, but we don't have any tea here. We don't really have anything here anymore."

The word *we* felt like a lie. It comforted her.

"Shall we go out for some then?" the woman said. "Maybe Raul will be back when we're finished?"

Lucy looked down at herself, realizing only now that she had been wearing only Engales's shirt this whole time. Her husband's shirt, Sofie would think, which buoyed her. "I'll get dressed," she said. "I'll get dressed for tea."

Outside, the sky was high and gray. The windy storm that had raged the night before had vanished and left wet streets and torn branches in its wake. Lucy led the woman and the boy down Avenue A and across Seventh Street. Though she had so many questions: What, exactly, was this woman doing in New York City? Where, exactly, was the boy's mother, who was apparently Engales's sister? Why, exactly, hadn't Engales told her he had a sister? Where, exactly, should she take the woman and the boy for tea? But she couldn't bring herself to ask any of them. Instead, they walked in silence, her mind swirling with hangover and confusion. She longed for Engales, for the sureness she had seen in him when they first met. Perhaps only men could obtain that particular brand of sureness, she thought. Or perhaps only one man. Perhaps only him. She wondered if the sureness had actually been pride. And if he had lost all of it when he had lost his hand. If that was why he'd shunned her, why he hadn't come home.

The three of them walked down Second toward Binibon, the only place she could think of, where she and Engales had gone for many a late breakfast after many a long night of drinking at the squat. She went there often now, when she wanted to feel like he was with her. At Eighth they passed a man in a wheelchair wearing all yellow, with a sign that read BANANA MAN: WORLD'S OLDEST BAREFOOT WATER-SKIER. She watched as the small boy stared at Banana Man, his head turning to follow him as they passed. Banana Man held up one of his wrinkled hands and yelled: *Welcome to New York City! Where everybody gets kicked outta their homes!* In an abandoned lot on their left, a bit of chain-link fence acted as a coatrack for the homeless; Lucy watched a man's tie smack a dirty wool coat, whose owner, Lucy imagined sadly, definitely hadn't gotten the job.

At Binibon, a bell chimed as they entered, and they were greeted by a gust of warm air. The place was empty aside from two older men, holding hands at the back table, and Devereux—whose presence, a nod toward last night and a past life, made Lucy want to turn around and walk out. Luckily Devereux was not judgmental, and when she turned to see Lucy's odd threesome, she just smiled and said, *Hello, daffodil,* like nothing had happened the night before and nothing about this—a foreign lady, a small boy, a huge men's shirt over a pair of ripped black tights—was strange.

Lucy smiled at her quickly—she had always been fond of Devereux, whose emboldened sense of self outshined any strangeness in her appearance: the flatness of her chest, the stubble that grew through her face makeup. You got the sense that Devereux was just Devereux, that she was exactly on the outside as she was on the inside, and she wasn't about to change for anyone—a quality that Lucy envied. Today Devereux wore purple eye shadow with sparkles in it, and severe black boots that reached her knee. Lucy led Sofie and the boy to a booth near the window: the booth, she knew, where the red leather had the fewest cracks.

Sofie looked very confused as she looked over the menu, so Lucy attempted to explain it by simply reading the options out loud. Chicken liver mushroom omelet. Ratatouille omelet. Omelet Provençal. Steak and eggs. Sofie pointed doubtfully at Provençal for her, steak and eggs for the boy. Lucy ordered only coffee, and put her hands around the hot mug when they brought it, watching the girls behind the counter put pieces of pie on plates, chat about nothing, shake their hair from their bandannas. *Oh*, she thought. *To be one of those girls.*

Besides addressing the menu, she and Sofie had still not talked at all since they had left the apartment, and Sofie's face had become withdrawn. Lucy felt deeply worried. What would she tell this woman? That she had no idea where Engales was? That they had come all this way to see someone who could not be found? But she had already said she was his wife! Wouldn't a wife know where her husband was? She was in too deep.

In the silver napkin holder, Lucy noticed the corner of a matchbook, tucked in with the pillow of napkins. She slowly and secretively pulled the matchbook out, opened it under the table. *YOU'RE A LAMB*, it read, in Jamie's all-caps scrawl. Jamie had been here, and Lucy wished to the heavens that she'd come back right now, sweep in with her lipstick and her confidence and save Lucy from whatever this

mess was. She imagined Jamie's gross suitor, calling her a lamb. But
Jamie wasn't a lamb. Lucy was the lamb. The pathetic little sheep that
needed a shepherd. She was as much of a lamb as the little boy, whose
eyes were cast down at the marbled tabletop.

The food arrived on the arms of Maria José, the waitress Engales
had always flirted with, telling her she was his favorite waitress, but
Shhhh, don't tell your friends behind the counter. Lucy smiled tentatively
up at Maria José, whose breasts were spilling like hams out of her
shirt. She was the opposite of Lucy in every way: exotically dark, vo-
luptuous, with the sensual appeal of someone who provided food.

"Lucy," Maria José said, sweetly but with a hint of resentment, as
she lay the huge plate of steak and eggs down in front of the small boy.
"Now who do we have here?"

The table was silent. She looked at Sofie for help.

Maria José, seeming to have some lingual intuition, asked the
question in Spanish, and Sofie responded quickly: "Julian."

Not Jacob Rey. *Julian.*

Maria José and Sofie then had an entire conversation in Spanish
that Lucy couldn't understand. Maria José spoke rapidly and tenderly,
and Sofie more slowly and squarely. Maria José with her hand on her
hips, and Sofie with her hands pressed flat on the table in front of her.
At one point, Maria José's eyebrows crunched with what could only
be worry, and she made a *tsk-tsk* sound with her tongue. While they
spoke, Lucy looked at the boy. He was gazing timidly at his giant
plate of food. She saw that his steak had come out in a huge, flat slab,
and that he would have trouble eating it. Lucy leaned across the table
and began to cut the steak into small, bite-size chunks. But the boy
pulled on the sleeve of Sofie's shirt and pointed to a glass case at the
counter, filled with pastries and doughnuts.

Maria José smiled. Sofie looked guilty. "He has sweet tooth, we
found out," she said in her clunky accented English.

Lucy stopped cutting up the steak. She saw that Devereux had been eavesdropping, and now she sauntered over to their table with a platter of doughnuts she had grabbed from the case.

"Take your pick, honey child," Devereux said, leaning over the small boy. The boy looked up at Devereux's sparkling eyes and long, curly fake hair. He looked at Sofie for approval; she nodded.

"Go ahead," Devereux said in her sweetest voice. "The Binibon doughnuts? They're piping hot and coated in sugar, just like your auntie Devereux." She giggled to the table.

"Thanks, Dev," Lucy said to her. "For everything."

"Anything for a friend of a friend like you," Devereux said, prancing in her hot pants back to her stool, holding the doughnut platter like a cocktail waitress might, on the tips of her fingers, over her big shoulder. Maria José, bumping into Devereux lightly, said, "You trying to run me out of a job here, Miss Devereux?" They laughed, and Devereux said, "Girl, with as much coffee as I be drinkin', you'll *always* have a job."

The boy was busy ripping his doughnut into tiny pieces, placing them on his tongue, letting them sit there for a moment before he swallowed. His steak got cold and hard, and Lucy picked up a piece of it with her fingers, winked at the boy when she put it in her mouth. Immediately she regretted doing it, though, and looked out the window while she swallowed.

After they ate, Lucy didn't know what to do with them. She knew Engales wouldn't be home if they went back there, that he'd probably never be home, but where else was there to go? She wanted to shirk herself of the responsibility she had come into, walk down the street alone, go into any of the shops she felt like, leave the blond woman and the boy to find their own way around. She wanted to go to the record store with Engales like they used to, browse the ten-cent bins. Or to be alone with James in the apartment, letting him talk to her in his strange way about her particular taste, her smell, her singular body. But instead she was here, with this woman and this child, standing outside of the restaurant in the cold, looking at the street.

"I'm not sure Raul will be home yet," Lucy said slowly. "He said he'd be out all day." Silently Lucy prayed Sofie had not planned on staying at Engales's. There was no extra bed, no couch even. "Where are you staying?" she ventured.

"A hotel. Middle of town."

Lucy nodded, shoved her hands in the pockets of her too-thin lumberjack coat. The boy was kicking a small rock around in circles below them.

"Sofie," she said slowly, "what are you doing here? Where is Julian's mother? Can you tell me what's going on?"

Sofie's eyes shifted away from Lucy and toward the street, as if they were trying to escape. Then, suddenly, she felt Sofie's big hands on her shoulders. There was a nervous sort of force in the hands, an energy that could have been read as panic. Sofie looked at her straight in the face and her blue eyes grew big and wide.

"I am sorry to do this," she said, her beautiful, severe face becoming clay-like, morphing into anguish or regret. She pressed Julian's little red backpack into Lucy's chest, along with the orange envelope. "It's the only thing I can do," she said. "For Franca."

Then Sofie took off up Second Avenue, walking briskly in her gray overcoat, which Lucy saw now was of the sort cultured, wealthy women wore: crisp shoulders, probably lined with silk. She had already gotten a block away before Lucy grabbed the boy's hand and pulled him behind her.

"Where are you going?" she called, but Sofie didn't turn around. Lucy began to run, tugging the boy. "You can't just leave!" Lucy yelled. Her strides lengthened in desperation; the boy struggled to keep up. Sofie, just a few paces ahead of her now, stepped into the street and held her arm up at a taxi. "No!" Lucy wailed, realizing she sounded like a child. "Where are you going?! No!!"

Sofie got into the yellow car and disappeared up the avenue.

Lucy yelled after the cab. "You can't just leave me with a kid!" she said. "Raul isn't here! I'm twenty-two years old!" But her voice cracked, and the car was gone, and she'd misspoken, she wasn't twenty-two anymore, and it didn't matter anyway, because the sound of her yelling was swept up into the wind like the sound of the mothers' voices on the night of the missing boy.

IT ISN'T ENOUGH TO
BE BEAUTIFUL

James came home after his visit to the Rising Sun to the smell
of brussels sprouts and a brutally cold house. It had been a
good day, he told himself as he de-scarfed and de-jacketed
and de-loafered in the vestibule. Despite the fact that he had just witnessed the very depressing scene of ten artists being kicked out from
their makeshift home by a crew of asshole cops, today had been a day
within a series of days where things were starting to look up. Raul Engales was starting to trust him, and better still, he was starting to trust
himself. He hadn't been to see Lucy in almost a week now, and it felt
good. A corner was being turned. Around it was the calm and colorful
life that he had been meant to live. Fall was fiddling with the city with
its windy fingers, and things were going to be okay.

Marge was standing in front of the open oven when he walked into
the kitchen, holding her dress out so the hot air would come up and
under it. The light surrounding her was a wonderful, soulful, warm
red. Marge's red was back from the grave ever since he'd met Raul.

"Heater's broken again," she said to James, her back still to him.

"Again?" he said, coming up from behind her, sliding his cold
hands into her armpits. Gestures like these—the hands in the armpits, the kiss on the cheek—had been difficult for James in the past
few weeks: expressions of intimacy that were actually a bunch of little

lies. But he felt better about it now, like a smoker who had gone a week without a cigarette: he had kicked his habit, officially, and he could do this now, he could put his cold hands in his wife's warm armpits. Yes!

"I smell cabbage brains," James said.

"Ding ding," Marge said.

"Lovely," James said.

"They're good for us," Marge said. Then she turned around and grabbed his face and kissed it.

Somehow, Marge was happier with him now than she had been in a while: another, more major success. Ever since he had started visiting Raul Engales—only a week ago, but it felt like he had known him forever—everything had shifted. He had started to write again, in long, inspired spurts that lasted well into the night, and for this Marge appeared relieved, if not delighted. Perhaps her expectations had gone down now that she had seen him get so low—she did not seem worried that he had not tried to *publish* any of the work—or perhaps she was just tired of being upset. "I like to see you like this," she said one night, resting her chin on the doorframe of his studio before she went up to bed. "I like to see *you* like this," he had said back to her, in awe of her strawberry mouth. "I'm glad you're back," she said before going upstairs again, her soft familiar steps as comforting as rain on a tin roof.

He was glad, too. The writing he was doing felt good in a whole new way: aside from igniting the colors (Engales, in the flesh, was the richest Yves Klein blue), there was something about Raul Engales's essence, the way he existed in the world, that had altered James's feelings about writing as a whole, its purpose, its function, its *feeling*. Here was a man who had lost the ability to create, which had previously been his sole reason for existing. Here was a man who had been robbed of the very thing that defined him. If not because of Engales, James was writing *for* him. It didn't matter if it was terrible—and most of it was, he had narrowed it down to a few sentences that he actually liked—it just mattered that he *did it*. Because he could. He wrote about, well, anything he felt like writing about—his visits with Engales, and about trying to connect with his mother and father, and about losing the baby, and about losing his colors and finding them again in all the strangest places. He had written about Lucy, which had felt like a release of sorts, as cleansing as a church confession, amplifying the feeling that he had done the very right thing by discontinuing their affair, and he had written about Marge, how he still loved her desperately, and could not understand how he had gotten so far from her. He had written more than a hundred pages in just a week, and the way things were going, he knew he had hundreds more in him.

Yes. It was good to be back. But it was also terrifying. Because in the Venn diagram of his life, between the circles of Lucy's yellow and Engales's blue and Marge's red—the colors, even when he wasn't around Raul, had regained their strength since meeting him—there were shaded zones where the circles overlapped, shaded zones full of worries, and of lies.

YELLOW: He had not told Lucy that he knew where Engales was. Though he knew she was desperate, and that she had been searching for him, and though he had stopped seeing her himself, he could not handle the thought of them together. He'd ready himself to call her and tell her about the Rising Sun, but then he'd imagine her visiting Engales there, her lips on his, her tongue in his ear, and he would stop himself. Yes, it was jealousy, partly, but it was also fear. What if she told Engales she'd been seeing him? It would destroy everything he'd built with Engales, which at this point was his last chance.

BLUE: He had not told Engales about his affair with Lucy, for obvious reasons. He wanted to bask in him, and write about him, and drink up his color, and if Engales knew about Lucy all of that would end. He was really starting to *like* Engales, to care about him in a way that he rarely cared about anyone. If his lie were revealed he'd not only lose his colors, he'd also lose a real friend. But he couldn't stop. He kept visiting him every day at noon. He kept digging deeper. He kept growing richer with colors. Sucking them from Engales as if they were a very addictive elixir.

RED: The worst and most prominent betrayal, of course, was lying, repeatedly, to Marge. He had not told her—both because it felt too close to the realm of his affair and because Marge had developed a serious distaste for even the name *Raul Engales* due to the painting that symbolized James's fucking up—about his visits to the Rising Sun. Instead, he created an artist out of thin air from a name he'd seen on the buzzer at Lucy's apartment. *François Bellamy*. He was writing a piece on François Bellamy. That's what he was doing in his study, late into the night. And Marge bought it, because why wouldn't she? Believing in François Bellamy gave Marge a reason to believe in James.

The lies, in short, were working. And James was having his colors and eating them, too. He prayed the spheres would continue to drift from one another, like continents that would eventually break completely apart. He prayed that all of this was not going to blow up in his face. But for now the lies were working and he was okay. He was here with his red wife in their cold house, his hands tucked snugly in her armpits.

"I guess I have to close this eventually," Marge said as she pulled up the oven's door. "But I don't *want to*."

"I'll keep you warm," James said. He turned her around and hugged her tightly. As he did he had a wonderful picture in his mind: of Marge on the top of Mount Etna, on their honeymoon to Sicily, in a pair of ugly cargo shorts and a floppy hat, yelling down to him from her higher perch on the path. He had realized then that she was fundamentally better than him. She was higher on the mountain. She was real and wonderful and he didn't deserve her. And look at him now: he had been right.

"Let's have wine," Marge said, breaking free from his hug and getting a bottle from the cupboard.

"Let's," James said.

"And then let's eat," Marge said.

"Let's," James said.

"And then let's baby-make," Marge said in her baby voice that she used to talk about sex.

"Let's," said James, though the idea made him nervous; he worried Lucy's stench still clung to him. He knew that saying he didn't feel like having sex would hurt her, or mean something that it shouldn't, and they had been on such shaky ground so recently, and he had to abide by her baby clock. He couldn't ruin the night, it had been so pleasant, and so he let her undo his belt, and then unzip his zipper, praying for some cosmic interruption that would save him from sleeping with his own wife.

The cosmic interruption came, in the form of the doorbell's deep whale song. Relief washed over him.

"I'll get it!" he said, probably too readily, buttoning his pants as he headed for the door.

"Who could that possibly be?" Marge said, her voice streaked with annoyance.

"Who knows!" James called, just when he realized he *did* know, because coming through the stained glass was a cloud of yellow.

James felt like a Richard Hambleton painting he had seen on Bleecker Street a few days ago: a black shadow, frozen in midleap, shot in the chest with a red splatter of blood. How was she *here*? And how was she *yellow*? He had been so sure that he was rid of her, so proud of his discovery that he could get the same sensations—*better* sensations—simply by seeing Raul Engales every day. He didn't need her. But now she was here and she was bright and he was paralyzed. He couldn't very well open the door and let Lucy in, and he couldn't *not* open the door, and have Marge ask him who it had been. He could lie and say it was a saleslady, but did salesladies even exist anymore? And if he knew Lucy, which he felt he was starting to, he knew she was not going to give up; she was not one with much care for the world outside of herself, and she would ring the bell again.

Not knowing what else to do, he opened the door quickly, let a whoosh of cold air into the house, closed the door behind him. Nervous blood, pumping all through his veins. Lucy. Lucy with her small nose. Lucy, here even though he had renounced her for good. Lucy, standing there with a little boy.

"What are you *doing* here?" James whisper-yelled.

"I'm sorry," Lucy said. Her face was white with fear and cold, and there was snot coming from her nose, glinting in the streetlights on her upper lip. "But you were the only . . . old person that I knew."

"Old person?" James said. "Is that how you think of me? How did you find my house? I'm having dinner with my *wife*. How did you find me here?"

"There's a thing called a phone book," she said. "You're in it."

"That doesn't mean you can come here! What are you thinking?"

"I don't know what I'm thinking! How am I supposed to think?" Lucy said, too loudly, making James turn around and peer through the colored glass. "I have nowhere else to go!"

"And why do you have a child with you?!"

Lucy was shaking, wearing the kind of coat that wasn't appropriate for the deep fall. Her lips were weirdly opalescent: or was that just his mind? Part of James wanted to invite her in, make her coffee, hug her. But what was he thinking? She had to *leave*. He had to tell her to leave right this minute, before everything was ruined beyond repair. He was just getting his life back on track, just making things right with Marge, just about to have oceans between his continents of lies. And now the biggest lie was on his stoop, toting a child.

"Look," he said to her. "My wife is inside. You need to go." He looked at the boy, whose eyes were wide with fear, and whose hair was doing that thing that little boys' hair did, tossing like a whirlpool at the crown of his head.

"It's not like I *want* to be here," Lucy spat back. "I'm not asking you to fuck me."

James practically screamed *Shhhhhhhh!*

"I'm just saying I'm not trying to break up your marriage," she went on. "I'm here because I have no one else to ask. I don't know *one responsible person* in this *entire city*. And this lady . . . this lady I've never even met! Left me with this *boy*—"

"Well who is he?" James said.

"*He is Raul Engales's nephew*," Lucy whispered.

Oh, Jesus, James thought, his head now throbbing with cold. Lucy's eyes were becoming huge pits of yellow and blue; his own vision was clouding.

"Some lady dropped him off," she went on. "Flew all the way from Argentina—and I don't know what to *do*. I can't find Raul, I have no one, I don't know how to take care of a kid . . . I have nowhere to go! I went to Jamie's and she was with a guy in her room! I went to the squat and no one was there—the whole place had been cleared out, everything was gone, even the parrots! I didn't know what to do!"

Lucy began to practically hyperventilate as she relayed her plight. As she did, the young boy, as any young boy would do if his caretaker were to expose themselves as terrified and therefore untrustworthy, began to cry softly himself, and the whole scene escalated into a tizzy of tears and breath.

James stepped down to the stair above Lucy's. He put his arms around her and held her small, cold body. Her youth, every time he had met up with her in the apartment, had come forth in brash confidence and predatory sexuality. Now it exposed her fear, her need for attention.

Raul Engales's nephew. All the way from Argentina.

He thought of what Engales had talked about that morning, about his sister, worrying that she wasn't safe. It couldn't be that Engales's intuition had been right, could it? But then, here was this boy, without a mother in sight.

He had to help, but what would he tell Marge? Why had he lied to her, when he had known the only outcome was to get caught? Why did lies always breed more lies? How had that first lie turn him into a *liar?* He felt himself fading. He willed himself to fade all the way. Lucy standing there crying, not going anywhere anytime soon. The kid crying. His own body fading.

"It's okay," he said softly, absently, to himself or to Lucy, he couldn't tell. "It will be okay." He bent down to hold the boy's shoulders, to pet his head. Then he stood and hugged Lucy again. He realized as he hugged her that he had never been someone that other people asked for comfort. Now he knew why. He disappeared as he hugged her. He was not really there. He felt surprised that it seemed to be working at all, that Lucy was leaning into him, grabbing his shirt. That he could convince someone with an embrace that things would be okay, even when he did not believe that they would be. Especially not when Marge opened the door behind him to find him wrapped around a young blond woman she had never seen before.

"What's going on?" she said. She tossed her hair back, like she did. "Who is this?"

James turned around to look at her, knowing his face was betraying him, like it did.

"I'll explain," James said to her. Then he looked at Lucy, whose face was still dashed with tears. He felt, though he didn't want to, a surge of love for her, for her messy bleached hair, her hopelessness. "Um, why don't we all go inside?"

Lucy on the couch, Marge on the big chair, the boy on Lucy's lap, Lucy's portrait on the mantel. James's eyes and brain darted from one of these terrors to the next. He had ruined everything, he had gone too far; his mind was awash with all of it. Yellow whirred past him, and Marge's red like a watercolor, and the orange that ensued from their mixing was so dizzying he thought he might faint. How would he fix this?

"Does someone want to tell me what is going on?" Marge, to the rest of them. He was someone. He was the someone who should tell her what was going on. But he had become mute.

To his horror and surprise, Lucy chimed in.

"I'm Lucy," she said, her hand extending like a turtle's head from her plaid coat, out toward Marge.

Stop speaking, James wanted to hiss at her. But his voice was trapped behind the layers of sensations, which had coagulated into a glass wall around him.

To his horror and surprise, Marge chimed in.

"I'm Marge," she said. "Nice to meet you. I'm guessing I don't need to tell you that you look familiar?" Marge nodded her head back toward the painting behind her. How had he forgotten this about his own wife, that her desire for pleasantness would trump any suspicion, erase any annoyance, curb any curiosity, and she would *be polite to the woman who, a week ago, he had fucked standing up, against Raul Engales's apartment wall?* Almost all of the panic he had seen in Lucy on the stoop had evaporated, now that she was talking with his pleasant, perfect wife, and Marge's face had been suddenly stripped of annoyance, and was now motherly and open.

Lucy smiled back. *Lucy smiled back!* What was going on here?

What was this alternate universe? Was there some kind of code between women that he did not know about, where the default was being . . . *nice?* Why was this happening in his living room? Why was this happening in his life?

"And who is this?" Marge said, gesturing toward the boy.

"This is Julian. That's why I'm here. I just met him today. And I barely know your husband, I just met him at a gallery once, and he recognized me from the painting, so we chatted, and I didn't mean to come over here like this, I just didn't have anywhere to go . . . I'm brand-new in the city . . . I don't know how to take care of kids, and this lady, Sofie, left Julian with me, and so I came here, because, well . . ."

"So you're in a pickle?" Marge nodded in the way that a teacher nods to a student who hasn't passed a test: with pity and warning, but most deeply, a desire to help.

"Yes, I guess you could say that."

James was still reeling, his back pressed against the back of the couch, his hands gripping the cushions near his thighs. Suddenly he heard himself speak.

"No, she isn't in a pickle," he said rigidly. "She's ready to leave now, is what she is."

Marge looked at James, her eyes narrowing. He knew this look. It was the look she gave when he said something off base at a party, when he was accidentally rude to a dinner guest, when he failed, as he had so many times in their years together, to be a normal and upstanding man. He decided he should not speak anymore unless absolutely necessary. *Shut the fuck up, James.*

"Let's start from the beginning, though," Marge was saying to Lucy, having seemingly forgotten about James altogether now. "You were saying a woman left this boy with you."

"Yes. She was tall and blond and spoke Spanish and said she was friends with Raul's sister, but she didn't seem like she was from Argentina."

"And did she tell you where she was staying?"

"She only said 'middle of town,' so she probably meant Midtown, but then she left right after that—all of a sudden. She got into a cab and left me standing in the street with this boy, and I have no idea how to find her again."

"And was she a relative of the boy's?"

"A neighbor, was what she said."

Marge became thoughtful. James could not bear to watch her, trying calmly to solve Lucy's problem. But this was why Marge was so wonderful. This was why he loved her! She was so *in the real world* that she could look at real problems and dissect and solve them. She could be kind and gracious while she was doing it. She could be patient and forgiving.

But could she forgive this? If she knew what this *this* actually was?

"What we'll do," Marge concluded, "is go to Child Services. I'll look it up, and I'll go with you, and we can start there."

James felt the orange in the room press down on his eyes. It was as strong as a stoplight. He knew what he needed to do. He closed his eyes against the light. Squinted hard.

"No," he said with a painful wince, shaking his head. "You can't go to Child Services. Nobody is going to Child Services."

"And why is that?" Marge said, calm still, but obviously frustrated.

"Because I know who's responsible for this boy, and if he goes to Child Services he might never get out. So no. We can't really take him to Child Services. Nope."

"What?" Marge said. "What are you talking about? What do you mean you know who's responsible for him?"

James's eyes were still shut; he could not bring himself to open them to reveal what was in front of him. Marge, Lucy, the boy, the painting.

"Raul Engales is responsible for him. I have been visiting Raul Engales at a rehabilitation hospital, where he's been since his accident. He told me about his sister today. Just today, he was worried about her."

The room was quiet for a second. When James opened his eyes, he saw Marge and Lucy glaring at him: Marge's gray eyes, Lucy's blue eyes, both sets fixated on his face. Both of their pretty mouths agape. Both of their tongues.

"You know where he is?" Lucy suddenly gasped. "And you didn't tell me?"

"Since when are you visiting someone in a rehab clinic?" Marge questioned loudly.

Lucy and Marge said these things at the exact same time, and their voices, on top of each other, combined to make a double helix of roaring sound in James's ears, not unlike a siren. *Fuck*.

"Wait," Marge said, looking at James, who would not return her gaze. "James, why would you have told her?" She looked at Lucy. "Why would he have told you anything?"

Lucy looked up, her eyes as frozen as arctic lakes. James could see regret in them, but it didn't matter. He knew what he had to do now. He closed his eyes again, swam slowly into the sound.

"I could have told her when I saw her last," he said. "Which was last Tuesday, October seventh. I saw her for fifteen days in a row, and we had sex twenty-two times. I had an affair, Marge. It's over now; it's done, but it doesn't excuse it. I'm a terrible man. And I'm so sorry. I'm so, so sorry."

The screaming in his brain stopped. There was only the static hum of the orange of the two women he loved, sitting in the same room. There was only Marge's voice, tight as a balloon, saying: "So this is François Bellamy. You lying sack of shit."

James had mostly expected Marge to leave right then, to get up and march out the door and head straight to her mother's, or her friend Delilah's, or anywhere where he wasn't. But he should have known she wouldn't; she wouldn't leave for all the same reasons that she would want to, because James was a fuckup of the first degree who she could now officially refuse to trust, and without her, everything would fall apart.

Marge's least favorite thing was when things fell apart: piecrusts, finished jigsaw puzzles, lives. Where there was chaos, even of a moderate degree, she took action. She did the thing you were supposed to do, and would not abandon it simply because she felt angry, or because it was hard, or because it was messy. She was a cleaner-upper of messes, a fixer of things. She could not and would not leave James here alone with a child, because James would not know what to do. So she would stay. She would be the glue.

But not before she told Lucy to leave, with a quick and tearful lecture about what having dignity meant, especially as a beautiful woman. *It isn't enough to be beautiful,* James thought he heard her say, though with the ringing in his ears he couldn't know for sure. *Beautiful is for other people. You have to be something for* you.

But when Lucy cried then, in his living room, in front of his wife, James began to see that Marge was not actually mad at Lucy, and that Lucy was not mad at Marge. Even though they were completely different women, even though their only commonality was that they had slept with James, which should make them jealous, or suspicious, or angry with each other, they were on the same team. They were women who had been wronged, and he was the man who had wronged them. When Marge told Lucy that she needed to leave, and that she should leave Julian here with them, at least for the night, the seriousness in her voice was also gentle, as if she had been Lucy once.

When had Marge been Lucy? James could hardly imagine it now: Marge as a very young woman, new to life's rough parts, bumbling through them with her marijuana and her line drawings. He missed her. He missed every version of her, though technically all the versions were still inside of her somewhere, and she was right here in the house with him, just within his reach.

And yet she was so far. Lucy was gone now and Marge was so far.

. . . .

And then Marge was moving. Because if she were still, even for one
second, the falling apart would start. She was boiling a pot of water
and cooking a box of pasta. She was carrying the boy to the table, sitting him atop a large couch pillow, forking small bits of food for him.
She was making up a bed on the couch—right next to James, and yet
so far away from James!—with the softest blankets she could find,
ones that her mother had brought from Connecticut that they had
never used, James favoring the ratty, heavy quilts over the plush, friv-
olously fleecy blankets—tucking their edges lovingly into the cracks.
Did the boy need anything? Did he want to watch the television? He
could watch only one show, if so. The boy didn't answer, possibly not
understanding her or possibly too terrified to talk, but she went on
asking him questions, setting him up. How could she be doing all this
now? James himself was paralyzed, his hands glued to his sides. But
then again here was the difference between him and Marge: Marge
was the glue and his hands were glued to his sides. Marge did things.
He sat in one place, merely thinking them.

Before she went upstairs to bed, Marge said to James with her eyes:
You're staying down here. And: *I'm staying for the boy.*

In the middle of the night, Julian peed. James felt the hot liquid move
under his leg. He jolted, bringing his fists to his eyes with nocturnal
instinct. He flicked on the light to see the wet blanket, Julian's wet
eyes. "Ohhhh no. Julian? What happened, kiddo? Did we have an
accident?" This was what adults said to kids, right? They said "we"?
And they said "accident"?

James had a sudden and distinct memory of being four or five years
old himself, being so scared to ask his father to take him to the bathroom during church that he had wet himself. The fear of his father was

greater than the fear of warm liquid on his leg. He had had the feeling that he was stuck in a body that wasn't his, needing things he didn't want it to need, and that he was all alone in the world.

Was this how Julian felt now, looking up at him with his big, guilty, fearful eyes? Had he simply been too frightened to wake James up to ask him to use the bathroom? Or was this just something little kids did, something normal? Either way, James desperately wanted him to feel okay. But how did one make a child feel okay? Especially if the child could not understand him?

"Don't worry, kiddo," he said. He pulled Julian up by the armpits. He walked him to the bathroom, flicked on the light with his elbow, set him down on the tile, and inched off his little pants. "One leg out," he said, trying to say something that sounded like something Marge would say. "Okay, two legs out." The pants were miniature little chinos, khaki in color and now half dark with pee. James put them in a pile in the corner, along with Julian's underwear, which had green frogs on them. "Okay, arms up," James said. Julian's arms went up. He pulled off his little striped shirt. His little arms were cold and thin, and James didn't know exactly how to handle him.

Should he go get Marge? No way. This wasn't a hard thing. And he couldn't ask her for anything, not now.

"We'd better get this water running," he said, as if narrating his every move would somehow make the boy more open to it. "We'll make it the perfect temperature. Not too hot, okay? Here, Julian, you stay right here for just one more second, I'll get the water going, and we'll have a nice hot bath, okay?"

Julian's face looked as if it might crack into tears at any moment, but he held his lips tight and his face tight and he nodded. He was shivering, and James realized simultaneously how tiny and vulnerable he was and how much he looked like Raul.

When the water got warm enough James plugged the drain and lifted Julian into the bath. He felt nervous and awkward, like someone on the first day of a job. Trying to go through motions he had never gone through before with some sort of gracefulness or knowledge that he did not have. He imagined Marge watching him, like a boss, assessing his every move.

"Here we go," he said. He scrubbed Julian's body. He told him to close his eyes when he did the shampoo. He remembered how much it stung to get soap in your eyes. He remembered being at a friend's house when he was small and taking a bath and having the friend's mother tell him to close his eyes. He had never been told by anyone to close his eyes before. His mother had never told him to close his eyes. He had simply let his eyes sting, then rubbed them with his fists. He gently washed Julian's soft flop of dark hair with Marge's lavender shampoo.

James had always wondered, especially when Marge was pregnant, if he would be able to comfort a child in the way he had always wanted to be comforted. He wondered about his ability for selflessness, and he wondered about the feeling of his own touch. Would he be able to touch someone small with care and lightness? Would he be able to kiss a child's head? Would he be able to conjure these actions out of nowhere, having never received them from his own parents? Would he be able to develop the language of loving a child? Was it something you could learn?

James pulled the plug from the cooling bath, pulled Julian out by the armpits, wrapped him in a towel that Marge had just washed. In the doorway between the bedroom and the bathroom, in the little stream of light that came through the stained glass window at the door, Julian's head tilted into the little space between his shoulder and his neck, the space where Marge's head always went when they lay in bed. The spot was like a little portal for affection, a way into intimacy. It was the space on the body that best held the head of another human. He and Marge had even talked about it: *I love putting my head in your nook*, she had said when they were younger. When had she stopped saying that? Would she ever say it again? James pulled the wet sheets from the couch and covered it with a fresh towel, and they lay back down, this time with Julian's head resting on James's thigh. They were warm from the steam of the bath, and the boy was asleep almost instantly. James's eyes, in contrast, remained open, glued to the painting whose colors had shattered his life.

Marge woke at six thirty on the dot, like she did. James's eyes, which had finally closed at some ungodly hour of the morning, shot open when he heard her feet on the stairs. Look at her. Wafts of kind brown bangs. Had he not noticed this before, these bangs? Had he been so blinded by Lucy that he had not noticed that his wife's hair had changed?

He pulled Julian's head up off his leg and got up to meet Marge in the kitchen. She ignored him, went about her aggressive business of making breakfast, packing herself a lunch, then setting up Tupperware full of things for Julian to eat. James watched her carefulness carefully. Should he say something? Should he go to her?

"Did he sleep?" Marge said. Her back to him.

"Yes."

She opened a cupboard, closed it again.

"Did you sleep?" she said.

"Not much," he said.

"Good," she said.

"He went to the bathroom," James said, feeling a wave of shame pass through him.

"What do you mean?" Marge said. She was cutting the plastic off a pack of breakfast sausages; her knife paused like a backslash in the air.

"I mean he peed. In his pants. I put a towel on the couch."

Suddenly Marge let out a spurt of a laugh. It almost frightened James, it was so unexpected. The spurt became a throaty howl. Her face flew backward as the laugh grew in volume and size, a genuine, deep, hearty laugh.

"What?" James said defensively. But he saw that she was not going to stop her laughing, that she was going to keep going until her stomach hurt, and this was when he loved her most, when she was laughing until her stomach hurt, saying, *Stop making me laugh, seriously, stop making me laugh!* It was infectious, and James began to feel it, too, the hilarity of the situation, of life, and of putting towels on couches. He wanted to make sure Marge would keep laughing, that they would keep laughing together, but just when he thought he might say something else funny, he saw that Marge was collapsing over the sink, and that her laughter was no longer laughter. Marge had gone straight from laughing to crying, and now her body was heaving, her hands covering her face.

James went up to her and put his hands on her back. He willed them to be the hands Marge used to know and love, *hands that could heal her,* she used to say, but she shrugged him off.

"Why'd you do it, James?"

James just looked at her, shook his head. He was only mildly aware that his mouth was open, his lips wagging.

"No," she said. "I already know why. I know just how this goes. The woman gets older, uglier, gets pregnant and loses the baby, still has the stretch marks from it, and my hair is getting *limp,* James! My boobs are limp! And I'm a *nag!* Oh, fuck."

James was still shaking his head, harder now. "No, Marge. That's not it. None of that is it. Not at all."

She looked up at him, her gray, wet eyes as hard and shiny as marbles.

"Why do you get to be the genius?" she said.

"What?" he asked, incredulous.

"You get to live on some other genius planet," she said. "You get to operate in this completely other world. While I'm stuck here in this one, with this fucking . . . sausage! In its fucking plastic!" She waggled the Styrofoam tray she was holding; it splattered a bit.

He tried to touch her arm but again she rejected him, snapping her shoulder away from his hand.

"I'm right here with you," James tried to say. "I am. I'm here. Just like this, and always, remember?"

"You haven't been here for years," Marge said. "Even before this. Before that . . . girl. You were off looking at art while I was working in a cubicle. The place where I work? Where I am about to go right now to make money to pay our rent? It has foam walls. Did you know that? Did you know that the place where I work has foam walls? And I use things called Post-its? And there is carpet? No, because you've never been there. You've never had to go there. And I am happy and I am okay and I keep going every day because that's how it is, James. That's how we've worked this out. You write when the inspiration strikes you. You fuck a girl when the inspiration strikes you. And I go back to the foam walls and swallow it."

She began to cry with gusto now, her nose running and the back of her wrist wiping at the snot.

"You know what the real kicker is?" she said, the knife in her hand bouncing. "I gave up all the things you loved about me to keep us together—my art, my sense of adventure, all of it. I thought I could pick up all the slack, that I could save you, that I could save us. And where has it gotten me? It got me to you not loving me anymore."

"I never asked you to give up anything, Marge, and you haven't lost me, I'm right here . . ."

"But you *did*! You did ask me. You asked me with every painting you bought. You asked me with every bill you didn't pay. You boxed me out, James. There wasn't room for two of us to follow every one of our fucking whims."

"Marge, no. I still love you. I never stopped and I never will stop. You're the very best person I know." He was crying now, too. He wanted to hug her so tightly that all of the sadness would come into him, but he knew she wouldn't let him.

Then, like she was so good at doing, she pulled herself together with a few quick strokes. She pulled her hair out of its band and pulled it back up again. She pulled in her breath. She pulled down her sweater. And then she pointed to the living room with her knife.

"That boy is all alone," she said crisply.

"I know," James said.

"We can't keep him here," she said.

"We have to," he said.

"When did you get so sure?" Marge said, shaking her head.

"Just until Engales is out," James said.

"You have never been sure of anything in your entire life," Marge said, her teeth clenching. And with desperate suddenness, she turned away from him, toward her sausages. She cut the skins that bound their feet together and they landed, sighing out into the pan.

PART
FIVE

FUCK SUNSETS

Lupa Consuelo walks out of the Rising Sun just before sunset. She doesn't look back at the building; she shouldn't. She crosses the street, crosses herself. She thinks about Tia Consuelo and Baby Consuelo and Mama Consuelo: all the people who shape her life outside of that place, the people—the *women*—who make her life a living and breathing thing that means anything at all. She's on her way to buy soup supplies, then to the Laundromat to pick up Baby C from Tia C, then back home to cook for all of them. It's one of God's little gifts, she thinks, that tonight is her night to make soup: something to set her sights on. Something outside the Rising Sun. God's gift, or else Mama Consuelo's blessed order.

Lupa feels bad about it, she does. She feels bad for everybody she's leaving behind, all the sorry souls who landed themselves in that place—God help them—a place she'd never have to set foot in again but where the patients have to stay, in twin beds that she happens to know are as hard as rocks. And though it was her final straw—or what did they call it, her Achilles' heel?—she feels especially bad for what had happened with Raul Engales.

Sure, she could have seen it coming. With that too-smart-for-his-own-good Bennett and that poor crippled soul, Raul, who hadn't wanted any visitors anyway. She shouldn't have allowed it, let alone encouraged it. These were the things they taught you to watch out for, to stop before they started. But what was it that they said? Hindsight twenty-twenty? Yes, hindsight twenty-twenty. How could she have stopped it before it started? Even if she had been on duty like she should have been, instead of sneaking a cigarette in the stairwell, where she always sneaked cigarettes, three a day, max, how could she have prevented the incident? The incident that caused her supervisor, Mary Spinoza, to do what Mary Spinoza did best: fire dedicated employees of the Rising Sun—she had already canned four since she came on as manager in January—like a shotgun going off, *BAM!* Just like that and Lupa didn't have a job. *BAM!* Baby C didn't have a new school uniform. *BAM!* Raul Engales would be stuck there for another month and moved to the Floor for the Potentially Violent, where Lupa happened to know one of the patients had killed another patient with a ballpoint pen, back in '78. If anyone would have listened, Lupa could have told them that Raul Engales was as clean as a bar of soap, as violent as a fucking hummingbird, and that it was James Bennett's fault—she had liked James Bennett, she *had,* but from the information she had gotten from Darcy Phillips afterward, she knew it was *James's fault*: James had worn the wrong suit on the wrong day and messed with the wrong man.

Sometimes you wore the wrong suit on the wrong day. Sometimes you smoked your cigarette in the stairway at the wrong time. Sometimes it's fate, and whatever happens happens, and God looks down on you and smiles and says: Lupa C? You're going to be as fine as a sunny day.

Lupa disobeys herself at the last second, looks back at the easternmost window on the third floor. She thinks she sees Engales's crippled shadow, but she can't be sure. She had taken a liking to Raul Engales. She had liked his meanness mixed with his vulnerability. She had wanted to help him. She feels a tinge of guilt that she had not been able to. But she also feels free, freer than she can remember feeling in a very long time. She pulls one of her cigarettes out, crosses herself again. *Forgive me, God, I shouldn't smoke. Thank you, God, for saving me from that place full of lost souls. Thank you for soup, and for Tia Consuelo and Baby Consuelo and Mama Consuelo. Thank you, James Bennett, for wearing that God-awful—forgive me, God—white suit.*

Marge leaves work fifteen minutes early, just before sunset, though she knows Evan Aarons, the boss who tried to put his hand down her shirt at an afternoon cocktail hour last Christmas, and whom she's been simultaneously pandering to and avoiding since, doesn't like it when she leaves early. She feels guilty. She always feels guilty. But Evan Aarons—shouldn't it be Aaron Evans, anyway?—can fuck himself. Evan Aarons can shove the fifteen minutes up his ass. Evan Aarons can fire her if he wants. In fact, Evan Aarons, please do. She's got more important shit to worry about at the very moment.

She is anxious to get home to see what happened re: Julian (*re:* an office word, meant for memos, that she's embarrassingly started to use in conversation), if he's had an okay day with Delilah, Marge's friend she's asked to watch him for her first day back at work; she'd taken the previous week off to be with the boy herself. Now she is anxious to get back to him, and to get everything on her mental list checked off: Gristedes for dinner stuff—whatever looks good—plus kids' toothpaste for Julian because he refused to brush his teeth with theirs, plus toilet paper, plus tampons because there's no fucking way she's pregnant this month, plus wine from the wine shop, because she needs it tonight like she's been needing it all week: the bottle at the side of the bed where she's been sleeping alone; and who is she kidding, she hasn't been brushing her own teeth, either.

She walks hurriedly and with purpose. The weather's changed and it has officially become fall and she's got tights on and she hates tights. They dig into the parts of her that she doesn't want to be reminded of. She was wearing tights—maternity tights, with extra give in the waistband—this past New Year's. She avoids thinking about this past New Year's at all costs. She thinks about it now, because of the tights. *Fuck tights.* She manages to avoid the thoughts that generally follow: what her life would have been like now, if it weren't for last New Year's, etc., etc. She allows herself one happy specific: *she would have lost all the baby weight by now.*

At Gristedes, Marge is sucked into the vacuum of cold and lights. Everything is bright, airy, in order. Colorful packages run like rainbows on the shelf. Everything is in its place. She loves grocery stores and she loves pharmacies. There is so much potential in every aisle. Everything could fill you, make you more beautiful, fix something. Every product you buy could define you, somehow. Do you buy the more expensive jar of pickled beets? You do.

She exits, stressed with the new weight of her boon and the knowledge that it is already 6:17, and she's supposed to be home at six thirty, and can she make it? Though why would it matter if she didn't? James will have gotten home by now and told Delilah to go home. She realizes that this is what her rush is about. She does not trust James to be alone with the child. There will inevitably be a James-scale disaster if she lets that happen, which will require Marge-scale repairs. Rush, Marge. There's a wind coming up the avenue, but you can push through it.

On Bank, a man in an upstairs apartment practices for a musical performance. *You make me feel so young!* he sings. He is probably some Broadway understudy's understudy, Marge thinks disparagingly. *Bells will be rung!* The song makes her think of James when James was James, of herself when she was herself. She thinks of the golden light of their apartment up at Columbia, of both of them at the kitchen table, working on their projects across from each other. She thinks of the way the glue she used for her collages smelled: metallic and exciting, like work and play at the same time. She misses herself.

On Bethune, under the trees, Marge wonders why she feels a tinge of excitement, somewhere deep, somewhere unspoken for. It is not the singing, which is bad. It is not the memories, which ache more than inspire. It is the light. It is her favorite time of day, always has been. The moments leading up to dinner, when the workday is done, when you have a bottle of red wine in your heavy bag. Just like the drugstore, dinner is a promise. It is something steady and tangible, knowable and beautiful. And there is a boy waiting for you to feed him, and a man. And right now she doesn't let the fact that the man is one who has cheated on her and the boy is one who will be taken away from her any minute get in the way of that. The feeling is low enough in her body that no logic applies to it.

She is almost home—on Jane, just in front of the Laundromat where Mrs. Consuelo had translated and read her the letter that she found in Julian's backpack and said, so sad, *In case of death or disappearance . . .* —when a woman runs directly into her. Groceries clunk and roll all over the ground, carrot tops splay like a dead woman's hair. The woman gasps her apologies. Marge mumbles that it's fine and bends to repack the bags. The jar of expensive beets has broken and is bleeding out onto the sidewalk. "I'm so sorry, I'm so sorry," says the woman. "Let me. Let me. No let me."

They rise in tandem, find each other's eyes. The woman is a bit older than her—is she herself old enough to call herself middle-aged, she wonders? No, not really, not yet, she is not as old as this woman, *phew*. The woman has a mane of red hair. She wears a flowy dress with an outrageous pattern on it: no tights. Instead she has eccentric cowboy boots and a trench coat of sorts, with many, *many* pockets.

"Do I know you?" the woman asks, searching her.

Marge looks down quickly, as if to check if any of her groceries have been stolen in the scuffle. She feels her face flush, re: this woman. "No," she says. "No, I don't believe you do. Excuse me."

But the woman's face has given her goose bumps.

She pushes past the woman and toward her little house, the little
house where she has spent most of what she would call her adult life.
The house where she had been pregnant once. The house where James
had told her that he had been unfaithful to her and where she had
cried and told him she would never forgive him. The house where she
would forgive him. The house where she would cook these groceries
into a dinner and where she would get the boy to brush his teeth with
his new toothpaste and where she would put him to bed and kiss his
forehead. This is what she has time for, given her extra fifteen minutes. What she doesn't have time for is the woman who has twice now
knocked her down, causing her to lose her baby and her beets. What
she doesn't have time for is her husband's busted, swollen face, when
he opens the door and makes her least favorite of his expressions, the
one that looks like *oops*.

Arlene Arlene Arlene! Pull yourself together. That woman is fine,
Raul is fine, you're fine. You didn't do anything wrong. Not then, not
now. Not that day in the studio, when you put the severed hand into
that big can of turpentine. Not when you pulled the hand out again,
afraid you had ruined it, wrapped it in a rag, packed it in your purse.
They couldn't have reattached it anyway, even the doctor said; all the
tendons had been sliced beyond repair. Sliced! Turpentine didn't slice.
Turpentine *blackened*, apparently. The hand you had presented the
doctor was *black*. Jesus Christ, Arlene. Really?

Really. It had definitely been her, the woman from New Year's. She
had been wearing burgundy that night. You remember because you
always remember burgundy; it is the only color that is exactly as ugly
as it is beautiful.

That night: You had met someone named Claude and let his
Spanishnness get to you. Claude had made your shoulders go slack
with his accent, which was the thing that meant, whether you liked it

or not, that you would sleep with him. Whether your shoulders had gone slack on purpose, and whether Raul Engales's official snubbing of you earlier in the evening had had anything to do with that, was debatable. Jesus Christ hell fuck bitch. Raul was a baby! Claude was a man of ripe age, like you. Where you belong! With someone old and foreign like Claude. Claude had given you some sort of rolled cigarette, surely laced with something; who cared, what the hell? You had gotten dizzy and you had become a fucking ignoramus. You had shouted *1980, assholes!* And you had, for reasons you cannot remember, eaten grapes.

And then you had seen Raul Engales through the glass of the glass door, finding his way into a room with Winona George. That bitch! She was as old as you! What was Raul doing in a room, alone, with Winona fucking George?! You had tilted a bit, trying to get a better look: Would they kiss? Would he press her against one of the blue walls? You had tilted and then you had tilted too far and you had *fallen*. Your fall had been cushioned by a welcome ball of flesh. That woman you just saw on the street. It had been her, her flesh. Her soft stomach that you had landed into with your full weight. Her burgundy dress you had spilled champagne onto, creating continents of wet on the world of her belly. Her less-attractive-than-her husband who had said, to your terror, *It's just that she's . . . pregnant.*

The next morning, in bed with Claude, whom you suddenly hated, you had remembered the whole scene in abstract but visceral detail. The give of her stomach. Her little scream. You had thought you might have hurt the baby. You had worried about it for months. You lost sleep. You went to *therapy for this woman.* And you had just seen her on the fucking street and what had you done? Murder her beets. Kill her carrots. Knock her down and take yourself with her: the two of you clumsily grabbing for cans and cereal boxes and tampons. You still didn't know. How could you know? If you had hurt that woman's baby like you had so feared? Blackened her life like you had blackened

Engales's hand? Oh, fuck, Arlene, you've fucked so many things up in your life it's scary.

Your therapist would say, definitively: *no*. But your therapist is an asshole with a goatee, and now is your only chance. To stop wondering forever. To turn. To turn and follow the New Year's Eve lady, see which stoop she ascends. To knock on the door, act calm, cool, collected, just a regular lady in a regular cargo coat and regular cowboy boots. To let yourself feel the deep, poignant relief when you see that little boy. They already had a kid; so no matter what, you hadn't ruined their only chance. They have a little healthy kid with nice hair and cute shoes, whose eyes—holy shit—look exactly like Raul's.

Engales has been moved to a floor whose walls are not pink but a sad, clinical blue. There are no orange cups and there is no Darcy and there is no Lupa. Engales hated Lupa, she was a good old-fashioned bitch, as Darcy had so eloquently put it, but now, without her, Engales finds himself wanting her. He had heard Spinoza blowing up at her. He had heard the Spanish word for *fired*. He knows it was his fault. But there are so many regrets, and Lupa is just one of them.

From his new room, he can see directly into the abandoned squat, into the dark corridor that led to the room where he first fooled around with Lucy; the room next to it, where he had helped Selma mix her plaster; the makeshift shower made of a spigot and hose, where Mans and Hans worked out their pyrotechnics, with easy access to the only water source. He remembers one of the first nights he was at the squat with Arlene, when a brunette woman had showed up in a black leotard and begun to dance among the crowd. Eventually people made space for her, watching her graceful body scrunch and wave and bend. She had a piece of charcoal in each of her hands, and she began to mark surfaces with her gestures: huge sweeps of the arms, broad, reaching strokes. "That's Trisha," Arlene had said, but Engales hadn't much cared what the woman's name was. What he was interested in was the way she filled and used the space, like it was all hers for the taking. What he was interested in were the lines she was making: arcs like almost-full moons, hatches like ladder rungs. At the end of her performance, Trisha climbed out one of the windows and onto the street, disappearing as quickly as she had arrived. Behind her the charcoal stripes rang with her movements. She was gone, but she was also still there.

Now the blue tarps and plexiglass windows that Tehching had rigged are gone, and the wounds of the windows are black pits of nothingness, where the guts and the soul and the art of the place have been extracted by people who don't know what guts and soul and art are. Engales wonders if Trisha's marks are still on the walls and floors, though he doubts it. He imagines the sad smudging of charcoal, the way it fades if you don't lock it in with that toxic spray. In front of the building, across the street, a drunk man performs vulgar mock intercourse with a fire hydrant. Engales's left fist pulses like a blinking light with terrific, understandable pain.

The rest of the pain he feels is not understandable. The empty squat. What Lucy had done. Those things James Bennett had said. What he had done to James Bennett's face.

He had not believed James at first, when he came in last week, stuttering through a spiel about "some things Engales needed to know." He had let the facts James presented hit him like little pellets of an impossible reality, being tossed right at his head. *Your sister. Son. Safe. Sofie.* Impossible, he had thought. Franca didn't have a son. He had shaken his head. But deep inside he knew. He knew that it was Franca's big news, big news that was being delivered by James Bennett because he had been too proud to find it out for himself. But how? He remembered thinking in the little span of time before he punched James Bennett's lights out. How had James Bennett gotten Franca's big news?

That was when he saw, draped on the shoulders of the plastic chair where James Bennett sat, the white suit jacket.

The image that had been burned into his mind that night resurfaced: the white rectangle of that suit with the black stain on the back of the jacket, like a little hole, as it accompanied Lucy down the darkened avenue. He could see Lucy's flirtatious head tilt, feel the shadows he had lurked in and the press of the cold concrete. He could feel the hot rage he had felt that night, the rage that suit had conjured, seeping into him now.

It couldn't be.

It couldn't have been that *James*, the only person he had allowed himself to talk to or trust since the accident, had been the one who took Lucy home that night, who he had watched disappear into his own apartment building. It couldn't have been James—balding, ugly, annoying *James*—who had been having an affair with Lucy. And whom Lucy had gone to when Franca's big news—a *son*; Franca had *a son*—had showed up at the apartment, the apartment whose address Franca would have kept and saved in her little black book from that lone postcard he'd sent so long ago. No. It was too far-fetched. But Engales's eyes were fixed on the jacket.

"Hand that to me," Engales had said suddenly.

"Hand what to you?" James said.

"That jacket."

"What do you want with my jacket?"

"Hand me the fucking jacket."

Just as Engales was finding the black stain on the back of the jacket, the black stain that would out James Bennett as an unfaithful, heartless bastard, something fell out of the jacket's pocket that would beat the stain to it. It was a matchbook: small, white, with its little red stripe of *strike here*. Engales looked up at James, whose face was suddenly as white and stretched as a canvas. Engales had picked the matchbook up from the floor, undone its fold with the thumb of his left hand. The inside of the matchbook read: *THIS IS UNHOLY.*

Oh, yes, James. Yes it is.

Engales was on top of James faster than a single heartbeat. His good hand drilled into James Bennett's lying face. Again: James Bennett's face as Pascal Morales's face. Again: James Bennett's face as his irresponsible dead father's face, dead on impact against a highway tree. Again: James Bennett's face as the fuck who did whatever had been done to Franca. When Lupa finally intervened, Engales shoved her aside. Again. James Bennett slumped in a bloody wreck, pleading *I'm sorry*. Again. Again again again.

After it was over, Mary Spinoza herself had led Engales to a room where he could do no harm to others, where visitors weren't welcome and the walls were blue. His rights were read to him—not that they felt like rights—and his sentence delivered. For this incident: another month at the Rising Sun.

He is in that room now, a full week later and still burning with anger, and the sun is fading, turning the blue walls brown. He slouches in a hard chair, watching a woman in a third-story window across the street walk casually around her apartment, naked. Her feet flop flatly in front of her. Her body is lean and unremarkable. Her triangle of pubic hair marks her like a target. She glances out the window, as if to check who is looking in on her. She does not see Engales, who is cloaked in shadow. She sees no one, and her little show has gone unwitnessed. She pouts out into the night, pulls a shade down, disappears. Engales forgets her immediately. His mind is across town, with a boy he's never met. His hand is on the letter from his sister, that James Bennett had limply pressed against Engales's chest before he was dragged off, covered in his own nose bleed.

Raul,

*Did you know that in the long time that you and I have been brother
and sister, I've never asked you for anything? I know what you're
thinking: my sister is full of shit. But it's true. I've made a point of it.
I've never once asked you to do anything for me. Instead, I wanted to
do everything for you.*

*It backfired, I see that now. I should have asked you for something.
I should have asked you to stay. Really asked you, not just cried like
a baby on the stoop. When you left, everything went badly. Pascal
could not save me—you were right about that. I acted like a child—
you know how I can get when I'm sad, it's like I'm six again—and
eventually he left. People think it was a kidnapping—that's what's
happening here now, all over. I think he's at his mother's.*

*If you get this, it means something's gone wrong. I don't know
what's in the news up there, but things are bad here. The kidnappings
are happening to everyone, even people who aren't involved. People are
going missing, disappearing right off the streets. I'm scared, Raul. I
can't not be involved. But I need to know that Julian will be safe.*

*Yes, I know. I wanted to tell you about him, I swear. But I couldn't
send a letter; they're opening all the mail now. And I didn't know what
number to call. He's the one thing I've done right in my life, and it is
only because I owe him my entire sanity and my entire happiness that I
will now ask you for something.*

Raul, please take care of my son.

*He's five years old—probably almost six by now—born on February
16, the year after you left. He's smart—probably too smart—I think
he takes after Braulio. He likes his steak almost black, like Pascal. He
likes sweets, like me. He likes to draw, like you. Please love him for
both of us.*

Yours. Always yours.

F

. . . .

Julian Morales is sure of two things in this life: that nighttime is just daytime with an eyelid over it, and that his mother, if he does everything right, is coming to get him tonight, when the clock makes a backwards L. The first thing he knows because his mother told him so. The second thing he also knows because his mother told him so.

His mother knows everything. She knows how many cups of flour to put in and how air pushes on birds' wings to make them fly. She knows multiplication and voodoo. She knows the right stories for every situation and she knows that Tuesdays are Julian's least favorite day, since he has to go to Lars's house. She knows everything he thinks because she's telepathic, which means she can see what's happening in other people's heads. It only works with people she loves a lot, though, like Julian, and like the Brother. One time, the time she likes to talk about the most, she told the Brother (in her mind) that he needed a haircut. The Brother had gone into the bathroom right then, chopped off his thick hair himself so that it became a spiky plant. His mother had to fix it. His mother fixes everything.

Julian watches the clock, poised above Marge and James's refrigerator like an eye, like he used to watch his fish, Delmar, in its bowl. The clock chugs and bubbles and looks at him. It's too slow, just like Delmar was. Where is she? *Swim faster.* She is late, late, late. But wait, also, where is Delmar?

He prays: *Dear God, send Mom a telepathic message. Tell her I drew all the pictures in my head and baked all the cakes in my head. Tell her I would do it in real life if I could, but I'm in a house with people who talk funny. Their ovens are funny, too, and I can't find any paper. Tell her to get here fast, please. And Delmar. Remind her to feed Delmar because sometimes she forgets. Amen.*

He's sent a lot of telepathic messages lately—he'd spent many Tuesdays in a row at Lars's house, with no sight of his mother—and none of them have worked. But now things are different. He's no longer at Lars's house, where the walls were made of thick, gray cement and probably didn't let any messages through. Now he's in a house with paintings on the walls where his mother is going to meet him. Why else would Lars's mom have taken him all the way here, on an airplane and a train and in the back of a yellow car, unless this was where his mother was going to meet him? It was the only thing that made sense.

Plus, it's Tuesday, the day his mom always picks him up. He knows its Tuesday because he heard the lady at the laundry place say so, when he went there with Marge this morning. *It's only Tuesday and I'm exhausted,* the woman had said, finally in Spanish words he could understand. *Thank you, God,* he had thought. Because sure, Tuesdays were his least favorite day because his mother left him for a little while. But they were also his favorite, because when his mother came to pick him up he felt more happiness than he ever felt at any other time, the kind of happiness that made him actually jump. As if the ground couldn't handle his happiness. As if he had to give the ground a little break.

The lady who's taking care of him while James and Marge are gone is painting her fingernails with pink and then clear and it smells like poison. Julian doesn't really like her, just like he didn't really like Sofie, Lars's mom. He doesn't really like anyone who's not his mother. And why should he have to? He watches the slow clock. The sun is going down like a big ball somewhere, but Julian can't see it, only feel it. Finally he hears some keys; James is home, with a mean face on.

Julian's least favorite thing is when a face looks mean. This can be the face itself (lines in the wrong places, a mouth like a hole), or something that happened to the face (James's puffy cheeks and reddish-blackish eyes). Sometimes his father's face would look mean without anything happening to it. But only sometimes.

James tells the lady, who now has pink fingernails, something and she gets up to leave, which scares Julian because he does not want to be alone in the house with James's mean face. In his mind, he draws with his imaginary pen: *a face that doesn't look mean, a face that doesn't look mean, a face that doesn't look mean*. James says nothing, rubs Julian's head, puts a pack of peas on his eyes, bleeds from his mouth.

When Marge gets home right afterward, she has a line in the middle of her forehead like a worry. She's carrying many bags and her hair's messed up. Julian has seen his mother look like this before. He hadn't liked it then: the person who's supposed to take care of him, out of control. He doesn't like it now.

But it doesn't matter that James and Marge look mean and worried, he tells himself. Or that they are yelling at each other in the other room now, or that Marge's eyes look like almost-crying. It doesn't matter because he is leaving. His mother is coming for him. Just watch the clock and be patient like an alligator.

Be patient like an alligator. He wants to ask his mother why she always says it. Why is an alligator patient? He'll ask her when she comes. When she knocks. Three times like a *pow wow wow*. Three times like a nice face. Three times like a voodoo spell that brings mothers directly to sons, like gifts. *She's here.*

He rushes to the door. He soars like a bird with air under its wings toward the knocks.

Marge leans over him, tugs on the knob. Latches squeak and hinges sing for his mother. She's here. She's just like he remembers her: feet, legs, dress. He grasps the legs, which make a backward L with the feet. The legs laugh. It is not his mother's laugh.

He looks up.

It is not his mother's dress: his mother doesn't have a dress with fish on it.

He feels a cry like a train moving up through his body. When he opens his mouth, it comes roaring out, loud enough for his mother, wherever she is, to hear him, to come running. He gets the feeling that the cry won't stop, not ever, not until she's here. He sees James coming for him: the meanest most broken face in the world.

. . . .

On James's Running List of Worries: that his face is broken; that Raul Engales's only remaining hand is broken; that his marriage is broken; and soon, if this child's cry does not come to an end, the collective ear of the neighborhood will be broken. He wants to fix it. He wants to be the glue for once. He wants to collect the pieces of his marriage and his face and Marge's face and Raul Engales's hand and *fix it*.

Marge: scooping up Julian and rocking him to silence. Simultaneously dealing with this woman—who is she?—*Don't worry about it*, Marge says repeatedly, but the woman lingers. Should James intervene? But how might he? The space near Marge is off-limits, this she has made clear. He stands paralyzed in the living room as the redhaired woman pushes her way into their home. She stands, booted feet apart, in front of the mantel.

"No fuckin' shit!" she says, in a distinctly New York accent. "You've got one of Raul's pieces in here? Right here in the middle of all these big shots?"

"Sorry, who are you?" James says.

"Name's Arlene," she says. "I bumped into your wife. Today. But before, too. On New Year's. I always meant to check up on you, you know. Never knew where to call." Her gaze lands on Julian, her eyes engorging with the manic wideness that the childless used on children, either to seem unthreatening or to disguise that they themselves are threatened. "Well, look at *this* little adorable person. Why so sad? Huh, little adorable person? I *am* new. You gotta get used to people, right?" The lady scrunches Julian's wet, teary face in her hand.

James knocks a quick glance over at Marge, evaluates her. She's holding Julian like a baby and looking right at him, her eyes saying:

It's not worth it. It's not worth it, he agrees. He gives her what he hopes is a comforting nod.

He sees the scene from Arlene's eyes. He is a father, with his family. With his wife, her bangs, their boy. They are not rich enough for airplane trips but can rent a car and go to Maine. They have dinner out, once a week, maybe Tuesdays. They take baths, all three of them, crowded into the little city tub. They go to the park and watch the roller skaters. They find beauty in the small parts of life. They find beauty in one another. It's all they need.

He sees the life from his own eyes: a crying boy whom he did not father, a woman he loves who has revoked reciprocation, a room full of paintings he doesn't deserve. His face is swollen into what feels like one enormous lump. There are no sensations, no colors, no smells— perhaps Engales had punched them all right out of him, stealing them back as quickly as he had given them in the first place. There is just a room full of things he loves that don't want to love him back. He feels suddenly and deeply exhausted.

"I'm selling it," he says, perhaps too softly for anyone to hear.

The room goes blank and quiet. Then, at the same moment, both Marge and Arlene say: "You're *what*?"

"I'm selling it. I'm selling that painting you're looking at, Arlene, because it is a no-good piece of shit that has ruined my life. And I am selling the one next to it because a guy gave it to me for free at a garage sale even though it's worth fifteen thousand dollars and I was too much of an asshole to tell him, even though I knew precisely how badly I was ripping him off. And I'm selling that one there, the Nan Goldin picture, because even though I was the one to *discover* Nan Goldin, I found that picture in a goddamned Dumpster outside her studio. That one there I bought entirely with Marge's money, and that one I bought with what was supposed to be my share of the rent. I didn't earn any of this. I don't deserve it. I don't deserve you, Marge.

But you do deserve my help. Now if you'll excuse me," he says, feeling stirred up and dizzy now, "I'm going to call Winona."

James walks into the kitchen, where there is a red phone mounted to their white wall. A phone that, even if it doesn't fix everything, will at least free him from it. He imagines the walls with nothing on them, a clean sweep. From the living room he hears Arlene's flummoxed voice. "Does he mean *Winona George?*" He knows Marge won't answer. He knows Marge like the top of his own foot. He knows Marge like he knows his Hockney painting and his Kligman, and his Engales. She will be quiet now, letting the lie that the boy is theirs sink into her, soften, sweeten, stop . . . no, keep going. Arlene is insistent: "*Winona the rich lady? With the hair?*" James dials a number he now knows by heart.

Winona is ecstatic. Has wanted her paws on this collection for *years*. Already has it all planned: they'll do it at the new spot, the first show in the new space, in December, yes, the perfect festive nip before all the festive nips. Have Warren come down to hang it, do a few olives, a nice Chard. She'll wear her leather pants. OH FUCK YES: HER LEATHER PANTS. Phenomenal. It will be phenomenal, James, you just wait. Everyone who's anyone will be there. We'll sell every last thing, I'll bet my boob job on it. It will be gone before you can say *surrealism* three times, James. You won't have to worry about a thing.

Ooh! The sunset is insane tonight, James. Have you been outside? I'm on my roof, James. On the cordless. You heard about these things? NO CORDS. It breaks up sometimes—can you hear me, James? Yes? You can't see it? Oh, it is quite the thing. Orange and pink, smeared all over the river like a goddamned painting. I guess that's the problem with sunsets, though, right? You can't keep them.

Sigh. Maybe that's why they're beautiful, though? Are you still there, James? The cordless. Because we can't keep them?

"Fuck sunsets," James says flatly, just as Winona sees that much-coveted green flash. She knows it's a mirage—refraction, is what they call it—but she'll take it. She loves nothing more on this earth than fleeting beauty.

THERE'S NOTHING TO BE DONE ABOUT THE LOVE

November is the color of the outside of an eggplant. It smells like the inside of an old woman's jewelry box. *Get outta bed*, you'd want to tell November if you saw it. *Do something*. Winter nudges at the city with its cold shoulder. The edges of windows become shores of chill. Cashmere emerges. Wool, not yet. The month lumbers, as if half-asleep. It's waiting. It knows. November is a month that *knows*. It knows that hearts everywhere are about to break; happens this time every year.

Marge and James circle each other in their little house, like animals who haven't met. James wags for attention, panders; Marge sniffs. Their voices shake when they say certain words: *Julian, strawberry, home*. Marge could leave at any minute. She doesn't. Marge will leave when Julian is gone. Or else she won't. They kiss once, after dinner, when both of them feel like crying. They sleep separately. Julian cries nightly, like a ritual. To fix it, give Julian a pen and paper; he'll quiet down, then draw forever. James tacks Julian's drawings up on the wall like substitutes for his paintings, which have been taken down, wrapped in plastic, stacked against the wall by the door. In some ways but not all, it works.

The drawing is just one of the things they've learned about Julian from the letter they'd had translated by Mrs. Consuelo the dry cleaner. Other things: he's almost six years old, with a birthday in February. Smart for his age; no English. His mother's in trouble. Raul Engales is his only hope.

They have exactly four weeks until Engales is let out of the Rising Sun. James hadn't wanted to press charges, but Spinoza had called the cops anyway; they'd let him off the hook, with good behavior, if he stayed at the Rising Sun for another month. This knowledge has been obtained via Lupa, who has thought to call James's house from her own, where, she says almost sadly, she is cooking soup for everyone. For four weeks, though, Julian is theirs.

Movies show at 8:00 P.M. on Sundays. Engales watches romantic comedies, regular comedies, horrors. Another movie plays in his head: his sister standing above a boy. Rewind. *His sister standing above a boy*. Rewind. *His sister standing above a boy*. Back in his room, he watches the girl across the street pull off her shirt again, look directly into his eyes. She has found him. He presses his body up against the glass: his hand, his jeans, his tongue.

A group of mothers meets in a badly lit room. There is a wilting balloon in the corner that reads *Happy One-Oh*. Someone's brought coffee in a thick thermos, but no one drinks it. They hold their hands like little personal knots in front of them on the table. *We still have everywhere east of A*, the mother in the red beret says. *We've been looking for months now*, the mother in the black, large-shouldered jacket says. *What's that supposed to mean?* says the mother in the emerald terry-cloth robe. She hasn't taken off the robe since July. She won't take it off until he's found, one year and seventeen days from now, crammed into the sideboards of a SoHo basement, his backpack the most alive thing about him.

At the Museum of Natural History, Julian points up to the big blue whale. Marge holds his hand; James can see the tightness of her grip from the other side of the room. The light in the room is as blue as the whale, not because James's mind is making it so, but only because the museum's lit it that way: a false oceanic depth.

James thinks about how Leonardo da Vinci painted using aerial perspective, which was based on the idea that the atmosphere absorbed certain colors. Objects that were closer to the painter always had more blue in them. Objects that were farther away, less blue.

It doesn't matter, he thinks now, whether he's close or far from the things he loves most in the world. He's screwed. They all are. Marge has fallen in love with the boy. He can see it in the way she is using her arms. It's as obvious as the giant mammal that hangs above them. That's the thing about love, he thinks. There's nothing to be done about it.

At Part Deux, the abandoned Chinese market on Grand Street where the members of the squat have taken up residence, a line has been drawn. Literally: Selma Saint Regis has drawn a chalk line, in a circle around her body, on the gnarling floorboards. "I'll sit inside this circle until they force me out," she says. "And if Reagan wins, I'll refuse to eat." She's practically hysterical, hasn't eaten anything real in days. "*Shhh*," says Toby, who grabs her under the armpits, pulls her up, drags her out of the circle and into their makeshift bed. "It'll never last," she says to Toby. "Nothing does," says Toby. "Not this," she says. "*Us.*" Toby nods solemnly. Nothing does, nothing does.

. . . .

Lucy approaches a tall woman with a name tag that reads: SPINOZA. Spinoza wags a finger that's as big as the fake dicks in the porn shop under Jamie's house. "Na ah ah!" Spinoza says: a power tattle. "Nobody sees Raul Engales anymore. Nobody can see that man at this point in time—he's got a month left at least. The law. And to think I fired one of my best nurses 'cause of him." Spinoza smacks her jaw. Lucy drifts back out onto East Seventh Street. Across the way, the empty squat complains: *I haven't had any fun in weeks.* She knows how it feels. She goes back to Jamie's, where she's reassumed her old position as the good girl of the house. She takes a shower, runs her hands over the rusting tiles. Uses a lotion that smells like lavender. Still feels dirty. She hasn't been the good girl of the house for as long as she can remember. She touches her own hands, thinks of her mother for a long time.

"I'm pretending," says Marge, to her coffee.

"I know," says James, to his bleeding eggs. The sky outside is the color of sky.

"That it's not going to end," Marge says.

"I know," James says.

The eggs make James think of Franca, a person he has never met and never will, whose letter Marge had translated by the lady at the Laundromat, whose translation had made him cry.

The sky, when he looks up and out the window, makes him think of the man he was supposed to be but never will.

A truck double-parks on Jane Street, prompts honks from a line of impatient cabbies. Its mouth yawns open in lazy anticipation of a life's worth of art.

PART SIX

MINUS ANY GOD

If there was such a thing as a mixture of snow and fog, it was what was present on the day of Engales's release from the Rising Sun: the second Tuesday in December. He had been tucked away, in one brightly colored, airless room or another, for almost two months now, which made the air out here feel even denser with moisture, as if the city itself were one giant cloud. He couldn't help wondering, as he emerged into the free, chilled universe, if this could perhaps be a dream. Or if all of it had been, his whole life, maybe.

He stood on the stoop of the Rising Sun with a small sack containing things Darcy had given him as parting gifts—a set of playing cards and a poster, rolled up, of an exotic woman in a bikini drinking a bottle of Jim Beam. He was wearing one of Darcy's suits, which he had won in a breakneck game of Loba de Menos, though Darcy would have given it to him anyway. Darcy had liked Engales from the beginning, and became even more invested in him when he heard the saga of his sister's son; he'd had a son once himself, Darcy explained, though Engales did not dare ask why he no longer did. "Go find that boy," Darcy had said when he handed over the obsessively pressed suit: gray, with white pinstripes. "Go find that boy and look good for that boy and tell that boy he's loved."

That had been Engales's plan, not that he had another option. He couldn't *not* find Franca's boy. He couldn't *not* take care of him. He had spent every moment of the last month thinking about him: while he attempted alphabets with his left hand—he was fairly competent with it now—and while Debbie kissed his neck in the physical-therapy room, and while he played cards with Darcy during social hour. Thoughts of the boy had become the focus of his very limited universe. What would his hair look like? Would he have Franca's teeth? Would he be shy and funny, like Franca was? Or bold and brash, like Engales was? Or worst: Would he be spineless and annoying, like Pascal? Engales had played out whole scenes in his head: Franca showing up in New York and the two of them taking the boy to Central Park, or, more realistically and yet less appealing, the same Central Park excursion with Lucy.

He had thought about this moment, or this series of moments—walking across town to James Bennett's apartment, knocking on the door, meeting the boy—a million times. And yet he was still standing here on the Rising Sun's stoop, a piece of shit with the particles of cold fog seeping into him, the suit practically drenched, unable to move. A church bell from somewhere uptown commemorated his stasis with a melancholy, distant *dong*. Part of him wished he could turn around and go back inside, where at least there were no decisions to be made, no end of any bargain to hold up, no looming responsibility. *Be a fucking man,* he tried to coach himself. But he didn't feel like a man. He was a boy without parents. A drunk without a hand. A goon in a pin-striped suit.

His eyes landed on the squat across the street. There was a prolonged moment where he questioned whether to cross the street and go in, but he also knew himself; he wouldn't be able not to. Finally he took one deep breath and crossed toward it. He shoved open the huge blue door—*Locks are a symbol of proprietary greed*, Toby had once claimed—and entered the big, open front room. The smell overtook him: the lacquer and resin and turpentine mixed with growing mold and old food. Engales kicked a beer bottle over; it rolled jerkily, like a bagged body. In the floor's cracks were the remnants of a party: a green feather, a miniature plastic bag, gold sequins, which distinctly reminded him of Lucy.

Nostalgia swelled within him: these thin walls; this idealistic, bright paint; this house of youth and wonder. The place, of course, had been gutted of the bulk of its furnishings—sidewalk couches, mismatched dishes, wobbly tables, the art—but what was left was enough to make him remember the precise feeling he'd gotten when he walked in here for the first time: *This is it.* The space was the New York he'd come for, and embodied everything it meant to be alive. Even the smell made him ache with a wish he knew would never come true: to go backward. He let himself live inside that wish for a second, imagining Mans and Hans in the corner, taking a blowtorch to a hunk of bronze. Toby coming out from the back room, his arm around Regina, telling everyone: "This is the life, people. We fucking did it." Selma's singing, drifting from the makeshift bathroom with the steam. But this foray into his past life was interrupted by a voice coming from the back, saying what sounded from where Engales stood like: *Failed artist! Failed artist! Failed artist!* The fucking parrots.

Engales went into the back room, which smelled like a thousand rats had died inside of it. He held his breath, kicked through a pile of trash. The bird sounded again, from somewhere in the corner: *Capitalism is for suckers!* When he found it, waddling under an overturned chair, it looked up at him with its creepy bird eyes, shook its matted, filthy feathers. *How had it managed to stay alive in here?* Engales wondered as he stuck his good arm out to pick it up. But then again, how did anyone manage to stay alive these days? They were all hanging on by a fucking feather.

The bird climbed up Engales's arm and onto his shoulder. Engales wanted to hate it, but for some reason the fact of it, this live thing holding on to him with its gross claws, gave him just the ounce of courage he would need for what he knew he had to do next: go back out that blue door, leave this place behind for good, give up any thought of going backward. *Giddyap!* the parrot screamed, which Engales translated to himself as *forward*. Only forward. The messy bird and the one-armed man went out into the world.

Out on Second, the street felt eerily empty. The bars had their neon signs off and their doors locked up. When he passed Binibon, where the windows were usually fogged with the breath and coffee steam of the many regulars, he saw that the grate was down. On the grate someone had taped a note on a piece of binder paper that read: CLOSED TODAY. Then a frowny face and a peace sign. The tiny bookstore on the corner of Fifth Street was locked up, too, and the big beer hall was not crawling with drunks as it usually was. There was no cold-fingered saxophonist on Fourth, where he usually serenaded the street in any weather. There were no sirens. The city seemed to be on pause, like a ghost town after a shoot-out. The only thing open was Telemondo's, and though Engales did not want to see the Telemondo guy, he went in, asked for a pack of cigarettes. He spotted the line of golden flasks on the back wall. "One of those, too," he said. To his relief, the Telemondo guy didn't acknowledge him in any special way, but only slid the cigarettes and whiskey across the counter and said with his flat, accented voice: "That will be five hundred and fifty two pennies."

He could do this. He was armed with booze and a bird and he was cloaked in fog and the Telemondo guy had done his joke. He'd be drunk by the time he got there, and the whole thing would just sink into him like the alcohol did, slowly and warmly. He'd do for his sister what he'd been unable to do before; he'd come through for her. He walked past a vacant lot where a man's dress shirt was hanging on a chain-link fence, sailing in the wind like a ghost. He passed a man in a wheelchair wearing all yellow, with a sign that said something about waterskiing. He passed a woman with very smeared clown makeup. *The beautiful horrors of New York*, he thought as he took a big swig from the bottle. *And I am among them.*

Finally he made it to Greenwich, and turned up toward Jane. He knew this route well because it was how he had walked to the Eagle to visit Lucy on her shifts, to harass her while she worked, kiss her over the bar. The thought of her stung him. He pushed her away, turned left on Jane. He had found James Bennett's address in the Rising Sun's probably very dated phonebook: number 24, a little wooden house crammed between two larger brick apartment buildings. In front of the wooden door, the snow-fog moved in a funny way. The snow-fog moved in a way that said, *You don't know shit.*

Suddenly, when faced with the door that would open onto Franca's big news, he felt paralyzed. What would happen when it opened? What would be waiting behind it? Would he feel anything when he saw Franca's son? Would he see Franca in him? Would the boy see Franca in Engales? Would he remember everything about being a boy himself? How wonderful it was to run through the streets—so much faster than his sister—and feel the wind on his face? Would he know exactly how the boy felt, alone in a strange place, with no parents to speak of? Would the boy be frightened of him? Would the boy be frightened of his hand?

The boy would be frightened of his hand.

No, he couldn't do this. He walked back down the stairs of the stoop, down the block that he and Lucy had once careened down like love-drunk pinballs.

I've never asked you for anything in my whole life.

He turned around. Walked back up.

Rug muncher! the bird spat. The bird. Oh, Jesus, the fucking bird. No way, Engales. No way was he doing this.

Raul, please take care of my son.

Up the stairs again, this time with force and determination and anger, he pressed the golden cat-eye of a doorbell, waited.

No one came to the door. He rang again; still nothing. He peeked through the stained glass window, through a red triangle of glass. The walls of the tiny living room were covered in huge sheets of newsprint, decorated in a child's drawings. James Bennett's hideous white suit jacket was draped over a wicker chair. And there, near the coffee table, was a pair of tiny, ridiculously tiny, shoes.

His heart spun. Franca's son was actually here. Engales felt his chest tighten, and pressure behind his eyes. "God damn it!" he yelled, banging on the glass with the stump of his hand.

He sat on the stoop in the cold for a moment, put his face into his one hand. Now what? Across the street, an old woman peered out at him from her first-floor window. Engales held up the middle finger of his left hand; she shut her purple curtain hastily.

Eventually he got up, teetered down Jane, and rambled down Seventh Avenue, drinking in plain sight from his bottle. The light was fading and the air felt tough on his face. He turned east at some point, and found himself in Washington Square Park, the big arch shining like the inside of a seashell in the dusky light. As he approached he heard a low din: something between a church choir and a static television. A huge crowd of people, congregated in circles and clumps around the fountain and under the big white arch at the north edge. Beyond the arch, the crowd spilled into the street. They wore the merry gear of early winter: patterned scarves and colorful jackets, but their faces, universally, held expressions of pain. Everybody was hugging or had their arms around one another. Some people were sobbing, others singing.

Engales found himself walking into the crowd. No one pushed: they moved to let him through. He saw a man with a giant dog, a dog the size of a horse. The man held his dog around the neck and wept into its silvery fur. A young blond woman, with a short haircut much like Lucy's, was shaking a tambourine slowly, and each time she hit it against her hand, she let out a sad gasp. He came to a large circle opening in the crowd, where he stood next to two short men in plaid coats, who, he realized when they looked up at him with the exact same sad smile, were twins.

There, across the circle on the other side of what looked to be some sort of altar, swaying in her long fish skirt and a coat that was somehow both puffy and flowy, was Arlene. He watched her kneel down and place a bouquet of daisies on top of a large black-and-white picture of John Lennon. As she put them there, the daisies tickling Lennon's neck, a long-haired woman beside her fell to her knees, too, then put her palms on the asphalt as if in prayer. Her hair fell out over her arms and onto the ground like a drawing of a sun.

Arlene looked up and saw Engales. Her face looked older, with more lines around the eyes, and yet also more beautiful than Engales remembered. He suddenly saw her as a woman, not the sailor-mouthed hippie who he shared a studio with, but an actual woman, with feelings and breasts and hair and all the other things a woman came with. She gave a sad smile, not unlike the one the twins had given him. It was the John-Lennon-died smile. The smile you smiled when everybody lost the same thing but still had one another. Arlene crossed the circle to stand next to him. She didn't look up at him, which he was grateful for. But then she did an odd thing—she took her two warm hands and wrapped them around the stump of his forearm, cradled in the fabric of Darcy's suit. He did not pull away. They stood there for a while, suspended in the sadness of everyone around them, her hands on his deformity. She only said, into the wind: *Oh, Raul.*

Engales felt a flood of emotions then, ones he had not brought himself to feel while holed up at the Rising Sun but that out here, in the open air with Arlene's hand on his arm and the entire world mourning, he let enter him. He thought of his father in his battered corduroys, smoking his pipe, his eyes the color of the pipe, his pipe the color of his corduroys, his corduroys the color of the way he made his son and daughter feel: young and brown, safe, like the wooden walls of their childhood home. He heard the record his father had put on: *Little child, little child—I'm so sad and lonely. Baby, take a chance with— If you want someone— Little child, come and dance with me . . .* and he heard his father saying: *Raul, I'm telling you, it's the scratches that make a life.* He thought of *Broken Music Composition, 1979,* of Winona and her hair and the fact that she had saved his life, and what she had said that night they met: *You'll have to lose everything this year in order to make something beautiful.* He thought of the way Franca's face looked in the light of the fire across the street: half-orange, half-shadow black, and of the little boy's shoes in James Bennett's house. He thought of Lucy's sequins, the way they had winked at him, the way they had promised escape. He thought of escape, and how he had attempted it, how he had failed, how he was here now, with his friend Arlene's hands around his arm, mourning the tragedies of the world with the world. He was finally in the pavilion, he thought. Beneath the pavilion, he could finally cry. He had not cried, not once, not when he witnessed his paintings on display without him, not when he saw Lucy betraying him, not when he heard about Franca from James, not when he lay alone and crippled in the stiff bed at the Rising Sun. But now he couldn't stop. Everything poured from him onto Arlene's hair. The parrot, just then, leaped off Engales's shoulder and flew out over the crowd. He looked up, wiped his eyes, watched the bird's dirty wings spread like he hadn't been able to imagine they could.

Arlene turned to him, put a hand on his shoulder. "You look like you're going to fucking church," she said.

"Isn't this sort of like church?" Engales wiped at his face with his floppy sleeve.

"Minus any god," she said. She smiled.

"Minus any god," he said.

"What do we have here?" she said.

Arlene pulled the roll of paper from Engales's bag, unfurled it to reveal the mostly naked woman—a woman who was supposed to be seductive and yet to Engales looked sort of rotten and overly orange. Arlene chuckled, then laid it on the ground with the rest of the make-shift altar, weighting it on its corners with four votive candles. She took the bottle of whiskey from Engales's hand, set that down, too. "John needs it more than you," she said, winking up at him. Engales surprised himself by not protesting. Arlene stood up, her colorful dress trailing out from the bottom of her coat and her red hair aflame against the backdrop of black hats and pale faces. She whispered something.

"Are you going to go tonight?" she said, with an uncharacteristic mischievousness in her eyes. No curse words, no loud squawk, just a little girl who knew something secret. Their eyes locked, the first time they had brought themselves to really look at each other.

"Go where?"

"The *show*," she said. "Didn't you hear about it? James Bennett is selling everything he owns. It's this big deal. Everyone's talking about it, you know, one of those fucking big fusses."

"No, I didn't hear about it."

"You know, I didn't expect him to be a nice guy. I always read those reviews and thought: What does this guy know?"

"You met him?"

"Long story for another time, but yes. I ran into his wife, literally, then followed her home—and I know what you're thinking but try to refrain from judgment, you little shit."

"And?"

"And he's got a black eye and a kid in the house and is selling his whole goddamned collection like an imbecile! He's a fucking mess is what he is!"

"Arlene, where is the show?"

"Fun," she said.

"What?"

"The show's at Fun. Winona's new spot. Not that I give two shits about Winona George, as you know. But you can read all about it yourself in the *Times*."

Engales was quiet, trying to comprehend what this meant to him. The man he had recently punched in the face was selling all his paintings, one of which, he knew, was his own. Did he care? Why should he care? Why was he feeling warm? And also sad? And also . . . *intrigued*?

Arlene leaned in close to his chest, whispered up into his ear.

"Your name's in there," she said. "Go look. Your name is in the *New York Times*, Raul. You're right there. I mean, you're there."

The sun was gone by the time Engales and Arlene parted. As he walked away from her, he heard her shout, in her stupid New York accent, *I love you, Raul!* He smiled to himself, didn't turn around. He made his way toward the edge of the park, then bummed a *New York Times* off a rich-looking woman on a bench, who had tossed him the paper like a shield and scrambled to leave. Nearby, sitting in a circle on the cement, a gaggle of young girls read their horoscopes to one another from a teen magazine. "Aries? You're *all ego*," one was saying. "God, you *so are*," said another. Engales shook the newspaper open with his one hand. When he got to the Arts section and found the piece: a thin article with the headline "Ex-critic Sells Off Coveted Collection."

Engales's chest felt tight. He didn't care, he told himself. He really didn't. He didn't even need to keep reading. He did.

James Bennett, the article read, *longtime contributor to the Arts section of this publication, has officially decided to retire—from writing, at least. The art world's loss may also be its gain, however; Bennett is perhaps better known for his collection of artworks than for his contributions as a critic. Bennett owns pieces by some of the most well-known artists of our time, including*

Eric Fischl, Ruth Kligman, and David Hockney. In addition, the collection includes works by a merry few up-and-comers, including street art collective Avant and painter Raul Engales, whose recent show at the Winona George Gallery made a huge splash among critics and collectors alike. Bennett will show his entire collection this weekend at Fun, George's new sister gallery on East Eleventh Street, where everything will be available for purchase. The show is called, aptly, Selling Out. *It opens tonight.*

The girls next to him were laughing like monkeys. They were onto an article about embarrassing moments: a girl getting a piggyback ride when she had her period, a first kiss gone wrong due to a pesky set of braces. Engales could hardly hear them, though. *A huge splash*, the article had said. *Among critics and collectors alike.* He felt both giddy and repulsed. He, while turning the knobs of an Etch A Sketch in a rehab institution, had made a big splash. He had made a big, one-time splash, that he had been unable to be part of and that he would never be able to make again. He hated himself. He hated the idea of this show, a show that epitomized what James Bennett had always said *he* hated: selling out, commoditizing art, giving in to the market that was destroying the very artists it depended on. And he hated James Bennett. But it didn't matter anymore, did it? What he hated? What he wanted? Because there was Franca's big news. There was Franca's little boy.

FUN

Regina and Toby, from the squat, called Kleindeutschland to invite Lucy to the opening of Fun. It was the second week of December, a Tuesday, and Lucy was very busy doing exactly nothing. "It just popped up," Toby said, referring to the gallery, as if a room full of art was something that propelled itself upward, breaking through the concrete like a jack-in-the-box, greeting the city with a smiling, painted face. "It's supposed to be really fun," Regina said, which had not made Regina or Lucy laugh.

Lucy was not in the mood for Fun, or for seeing all the people who would inevitably be there: all the people from the last disastrous show, Selma and the Swedes and all the artists who had gotten famous by some fluke and who now wore six-hundred-dollar shoes. If you asked them about the shoes, Lucy had found at a party a few weeks ago at Part Deux, they would say it was another of their projects. "I'm literally walking on capitalism," said a woman who was wearing loafers covered in Swarovski crystals. "Isn't it fabulous?" Lucy had nodded and walked away, feeling simultaneous hatred and envy for the woman, at the exact same time: a lady who had found a way to make an intellectual point out of the vain act of wearing glamorous footwear, and who, more importantly, had stolen Lucy's song.

That party was more than two months ago now, the night she'd dropped Julian at James's, and she hadn't gone out since. The night had felt vapid and the Chinese grocery store had smelled of fish and piss and smoke, and she felt too guilty, about too many things, to enjoy herself at all. Then Toby, drunk, had tried to make a pass at her in the bathroom line, which made her feel even more vulnerable and gross and wrong. She had left the party early, thrown her pack of cigarettes into a puddle, and vowed that from now on she'd be good, she'd be nothing but moral and sweet, she'd offend no one, get involved with nothing. In this effort to purify herself, she called Jamie the next morning and asked for her room back.

"Fucking finally," Jamie said in her husky, friendly voice. "I hoped you'd come back before I had to get some other asshole in here."

She moved her things out of Raul's apartment and back to Kleindeutschland. She brought as many Jacob Rey milk cartons as she could fit in a trash bag. She decided she would simply stay in her scotch-yellow room and read all the books she'd never read and think all the pure thoughts she'd never thought before, alone. When she came out again, she reasoned, she'd be cured of all her many vices, stripped of all evil.

But when she got down to it, she knew it wouldn't last, and that *she* wouldn't last, and that when someone, like Regina, called her, she would not only answer but answer hungrily, with the desperation that came from being cooped up for too long in a city where festering was fatal. Plus, Regina was persistent.

"If you don't create an outside self," Regina said on the phone now, "you're never going to create an inside self."

"Are you deconstructing me?" Lucy had said.

"Maybe," Regina said. "Is it working?"

"Not really," Lucy lied. She looked down onto Little Germany, watched a fat man go into the porn shop.

"Too bad," Regina said then. "'Cause we're already here." Lucy looked across the street and saw Regina, at a pay phone with Toby, waving up at Lucy's window.

Lucy smiled. "Fine, I'm in," she said, and she could feel the relief, almost like a sigh, sweep through her. She quickly laced up her combat boots, and stopped to study herself in the mirror.

"You're older," Jamie said suddenly, having once again appeared in the doorway, as was her custom. "You're wondering what's different? You're fucking older, Ida."

"I've been here seventeen months," Lucy said. "I'm hardly older." But she knew what Jamie was talking about. Her profile was the same, her proportions, her pose. Her hair had grown out a few inches, to reveal the darker blond beneath the bleach, but that wasn't it. Something else had changed.

"Seventeen months in New York City?" Jamie said. "You're fucking *ancient*. Not to mention you're *counting*."

"Come with," Lucy said, going to Jamie and tugging on her arm. "There's an opening."

"Not a chance," said Jamie. "You know I hate those things."

"No you don't," Lucy said, not knowing exactly why she felt emboldened to bring this up to Jamie now, after all this time, during which she had never broached the subject of Jamie as an artist. "I know about your projects, Jame," she said.

"Oh, Little Lucy," Jamie said with a laugh. "No you don't. You really don't."

"But I do. I found one of your matchbooks at Binibon. I kept it. I keep them all. And I gave one to this art critic I know, and he said he was going to frame it. They're *art*, Jamie. They are. And so are your videos. Randy showed me some of them. They're *good*, Jamie."

Jamie smiled sadly. "It's just what I do," she said. "It's how I get through the other things I do. It doesn't need to be written about by some critic. It doesn't need to be framed."

"I actually know what you mean," Lucy said.

"Good," Jamie said. "Now let me do your makeup."

Regina and Toby were waiting outside of the bodega on the corner, smoking cigarettes. They were wearing matching ski jackets, of the sort that said: *I am cool because I'm uncool*—part of a thing fashionable people were doing: attempting to look normal as a way to be anything but. They looked like the people who ran the ski lifts at the lodges Lucy had gone to as a kid, only there was an important distinction. They were *not* those people, who spent their winters pulling levers and drinking Coors Light on chairlifts; they were Toby and Regina, artists and philosophers of the East Village, with no connection to the slopes besides the diamond-shaped designs on their chests.

"Got cold again," Regina said, as if to justify the absurdity of their outerwear. She grabbed Lucy around the shoulders and shook her, then kissed her on the cheek.

"Gorgeous woman," Toby said, looking Lucy too sincerely in the eyes. "Gorgeous *women*," he said, coming between Lucy and Regina and wrapping his big conceptual artist arms around them both. "*Andiamo*, gorgeous women! *Andiamo a* Fun!"

When they were only a block down the street, they heard the clip-clopping of high heels and a sexy, breathless voice.

"Wait up," said Jamie, who had thrown an enormous fur coat over her negligee and apparently decided it was an outfit.

"I thought you didn't believe in galleries," Regina said, almost smugly.

"I don't," Jamie said. She winked at Lucy.

"*Women!*" Toby shouted out to the street. "Gorgeous women!"

There was no sign at Fun, and the title of the show wasn't apparent until they were inside, where it was written in pencil on the white wall: *Selling Out*. The first piece of art, just next to the title, stopped both Lucy and Jamie in their tracks: it was two of Jamie's matchbooks, positioned in the center of a huge blank white square in the middle of a frame. The first said: *IS THIS SOME KIND OF ART PROJECT?*

The second: *THIS IS UNHOLY.* The second was the matchbook Lucy had given to James, as a kind of sexy admission of her own regret, a way to acknowledge the wrongness of their affair and also revel in it. Now, the matchbook made her heart stop. How had it gotten here? To this gallery? And why was Jamie, who had so actively negated the idea of presenting her work to an audience, staring almost lovingly at the matchbooks and saying, *"I didn't know it would feel like this."*

"Jamie, I think we've got to get out of here," Lucy said, tugging at her fur-clad roommate.

But Jamie wasn't listening. "You know what? Maybe your milk cartons are something," she was saying. "If this is a project, then maybe your milk cartons are a project."

"Jamie, I'm telling you we need to leave. I think this is—"

But now they were being interrupted by a guy Jamie knew who made working sculptures of trains, who immediately launched into a lecture about pneumatic pressure, and how it was what was used to power the first New York City subways. "So basically a giant fucking fan," he was saying, though Lucy couldn't really hear him. Her heart was bounding like a fast dog in her chest as she scanned the room; she had seen these paintings, all together as they were now, before. They were definitely James Bennett's paintings. The ones in his little house on Jane Street, where she had sat so embarrassingly and cried in front of his wife. And there, on the far wall in a huge cone of white light, was the portrait of her.

Don't move, Engales had said while she sat for him. *Don't move or I'll kiss you till you die.* It seemed so long ago now. A whole lifetime ago.

"So you're the girl in *The American Dream,*" someone said suddenly, putting an arm around her. It was someone she didn't know, wearing a fedora that she decided immediately was ugly.

"No," she said absently, to the hat. "I'm not anything. I don't even know what I want to be."

"Well you're pretty enough," said the hat.

"It isn't enough to be beautiful," Lucy said. She turned away from the hat and saw, on the back wall, the painting of herself, the smooth pink strokes of her skin. In the painting her eyelids were tilted just so, and a spark of white paint hovered just outside her pupil. That's what was different about her, she saw now. It was the sparkle. The sparkle was gone.

She had lost herself. She had completely disappeared. She was no longer the girl in that painting, so hopeful, so new. She was old. She was ancient. She turned to go; she wouldn't be wanted here, at a show put on by the man whose life she'd ruined. She'd leave the gallery and go back to Jamie's, where she'd spend the night with Sartre and a glass of bad wine from Jamie's jug of bad wine. She'd forget about the night, the painting, James, Raul. She would never see or think of Raul Engales again, until he was right there in front of her, standing in the gallery's cold door in an uncharacteristically sharp suit.

"It's him," she said breathlessly to herself, as if Raul Engales were a rock star, or a god, or a man she had admired from afar but never met.

Engales stood in the shadows outside of Fun, dreading his entrance. There was a low drone of dull chatter coming from inside. He could already hear snippets of inevitable conversations: *this new sculptor who was building caves for homeless people to live in; Reynard performing at the Kitchen; this space is amaaaazing, isn't it?; Winona always has her shows on Tuesdays*. He didn't know what people would be saying about James, if they would find the gesture of this show inspiring or crude, worthy of the good or the bad sort of gallery gossip. Either way, all of it sounded awful in his imagination.

Cigarette.

He followed the orange dot of another smoker's ash and lit up one of his own. In the light of the match, he realized the owner of the other glowing butt was Horatio from the squat. He thought of Horatio's pure physical force when he made his paintings, the lack of intellectualism in them, the heart. For some reason Horatio did not feel threatening but comforting, someone he had always trusted, and who smiled at him now without an ounce of pity in his face. Engales smiled back, and that was that. They smoked in silence. Engales looked out onto the street, which was humming with life and taxis and smelling like it did, sewer and trash and smoke and tar. He remembered how much he loved that smell, these sounds, these streets, back when he was new here. The thought made him feel briefly confident in some nostalgic way. He was back out in the world, existing. Horatio had said nothing about his hand. Maybe no one would. He could do this. He could go inside. He blew out the last of the smoke, stabbed the cigarette into the wall, pressed his shoulder and hip into the metal door.

But once inside, he knew he had made the wrong choice to come here. The room's energy focused in on him; eyes flickered up to him and then stuck. He knew everyone, and everyone was looking at him. Selma, probably trying to fix the awkwardness but failing, rushed over and practically fell on top of him. She was more than a little tipsy, and her hair, which had been slicked back into a vicious bun at the very top of her head, was flying out of its knot in ungraceful spurts.

"My Raul!" she practically shouted, petting his chest with her long hands. "We've all been waiting to see you. Impatiently, Raul. So impatiently. And here you are. Back to your friends. We miss you. We do!"

Engales managed a smile. "Thank you, Selma."

"And we're so sorry," Selma went on, trying to give him a meaningful look. "We're so sorry about the accident. We really are. But life has these ways, you know? These ways of presenting us with mountains? And then we just, we just *climb*."

Engales forced his mouth into a scrunched smile, but his eyes refused to follow. "I'm going to find myself a much-needed drink," he said, taking her by the shoulder and physically moving her a pace away.

"Fine," Selma slurred. "But come right back here and be with me. I need to tell you about everything. We moved, you know. The squat? And it's really changed my whole process. I'm in a new space in the new space, you know?"

Engales patted her back before she could finish and walked into the room. He quickly scanned the works on the walls: Diebenkorn, Kligman, Hockney . . . he thought of the binder and the slides, the physical-therapy room with Debbie. And then there was *his* painting, in the most prominent position on the far wall, the painting of Lucy he'd done when they'd first met. The paintings moved into one another fluidly and correctly, he thought, as if the lot of them were one big piece, part of a larger composition. He suddenly remembered the fondness he had had for James when they had talked about Lucian Freud, the way James seemed to have seen the paintings in the exact way he had. He felt oddly guilty, for one second only, about hitting James in the face so many times. But the guilt faded when he saw Lucy—the bright reminder of how he hated James with his whole heart—peering out at him from behind a column in the middle of the room.

Engales quickly averted his gaze. He thought of the white jacket, her chin tilt, James's hand on her shoulder. He wanted desperately to turn and go, but when he looked around he saw all the faces he didn't want to see, all the land mines of all the artists from his past life, and Winona was manning the door now, and suddenly Lucy looked like the most benevolent and welcoming of all of them. And she was moving toward him now, like a little light on a pathway. Like one of those weird orbs of light that float above swamps. Her blondness blinding him. Her eyes hooking him. Her gold sequins, the same ones from the painting, catching all the bits of light in the room, then tossing them back toward him as if she were a human disco ball.

"Not now," Engales said when she arrived to him.

"Then when?" she said. Her voice was her voice. What was it about her voice? Why did it move him so? How could he detest her so much and still be moved by her voice? He thought of the Clemente painting of the woman and her two men. He looked into Lucy's eyes, which were lakes of familiar, easy water, flecked with some dangerous, flesh-eating fish. Suddenly he wanted her so badly he couldn't contain himself.

"Outside," he said gruffly, and grabbed her by the arm.

The show looked perfect, Winona had told James before it opened that evening. Everyone who was anyone was coming, she had promised, and the whole show would sell. Winona had said all of these facts as if they were good things; she had maintained her ecstatic mood, and had told him so in all the ways, including attempting to shove her tongue down his throat in an overindulgent congratulatory kiss just as she swung open the doors to the public. And James had tried hard to believe her. But as soon as people started filing in—and they did, in proud posses and dressed-up duos—and James was forced to begin the requisite kissing of cheeks and kissing of asses, and the explaining of why he was selling the whole lot of his art, he witnessed the slow sinking of his own heart. "It was just *time*," he kept saying over and over to the curious gallery-goers. "Just time to move on."

But it was not time, and it never would be, to be doing the very thing he had vowed never to do: trading art for money. He had told himself it would be worth it, that it would fix everything, that it would smooth the waters with Marge, disperse of their money problems, cleanse him of his obsessions and his misdeeds. He had vowed not to be sentimental, or emotional, or, as he had proved to be over and over, impulsive. He would simply sit back and let this night wash over him, let the smooth promise of a clean, comfortable new life overshadow whatever vision he'd ever thought he'd had.

But as he watched each red dot go up as a painting sold, his heart sank further and further in his body. He thought of the quenching pinks of the Heilmann, the dizzying Germanic gray of his imported

Georg Baselitz, the mirrored lake surface of the painted plate Schnabel had all but forced him to take for free as a sarcastic thank-you for
a very bad review. He could not quite see the colors now—when Raul
had hit him, it was as if he had beaten the colors right out of him—but
he could feel the memories of them, which felt almost as distinct and
powerful as the sensations themselves. Someone pulled out a check-
book and purchased his burnt orange. Someone else put their claim
on his deep-sea ear popping. A woman in a jacket that looked to be
adorned with shards of glass bought his foggy morning, his campfire
smell, and his chartreuse flashes, all in one swoop.

He watched the people's faces as they studied and then abandoned
the paintings. Did they see them as he once had? Alive and bright and
wretched and perfect? Did they see them at all? Did the paintings
move through them and then disappear, put out of their minds for
good? Or would there be a time, years later, when they would remember an image they saw here tonight: a square inch of a painting, even,
that would transport them back in time to the night James Bennett
sold all his art?

He concluded that no, they would not. And yes, this evening was officially depressing. Because even worse than the selling off of the art, the
giving in to the commercial hell of the art world and the contribution to
the thoughtless collections of the city's richest dealers, was the fact that
there was no one here to witness it. Here he was, giving up the things he
had loved so much, without anyone he cared about here to care alongside him, to assuage the blow. Marge had stayed home with Julian, as
they had agreed it would be too late a night for such a little boy. But
James knew that's not why Marge wasn't here. She could hardly play the
role of James's wife at home. How could she do it out here, with people
watching? How could she present herself to a public in a way that didn't
betray her real feelings? Her deep-seated resentment, her despair, her
anger? Not to mention that she didn't support the idea of the show at all,
despite the fact that the point of it was to win her back.

"You're being rash," she'd told James when he'd gotten off the phone with Winona. "You're acting impulsively. Again. This isn't what you want."

"But I'm doing this for us," he had said. "For our family. And I want you to come."

"We're not really a family right now," she had said in the tone she had taken to using with him, which was robust in its bitchiness yet also very normal, as if these cutting snippets were just regular things that people said. He had nodded, as he nodded about everything; she was right about everything now, she had all upper hands. But he had secretly hoped she would show up anyway. She was all he had. Other than her, if he was even allowed to count her, he had no one. He was like a tree in a forest. No one would see or hear him fall.

In an alley called Extra Place, against a wall that read in bulbous yellow letters FOR THE SO-CALLED AVANT GARDE, Engales and Lucy had sex. It was the sort of sex that happened in alleys: hasty and necessary, crude by design. Lucy felt tipsy, and needy, and guilty. She whispered that she missed him. She did. She missed him terribly, the whole thing of him, and his presence was making her drunker than she already was. He did not whisper back but only continued to press her against the wall with his body, her back chafing on the bricks, her face hurting. She could feel a piece of her own hair in her mouth. She could feel the stump of his arm on the side of her stomach, which made her want to cry. He smelled like him: the first good smell of New York City. Cigarette mouth, clean skin, dirty hair. In a way that felt familiar and also crass, he put his mouth on her neck. He tore at the sequins on her shirt until some of them fell, like gold snowflakes, to the ground.

"Call me Spot," Lucy tried.

"No," Engales countered.

When they finished, Lucy pulled down her skirt and wiped her hair out of her face. She tried to smile up at him, but found it was hard to look him in the eyes. What was she supposed to say to him? How was she supposed to tell him about everything that had happened since he'd disappeared from her life two months ago, apparently to some rehab institution on Winona's dime, but how the hell was she supposed to know that? Winona was a bitch for not telling her, not to mention James, and Engales had never called, never thought to tell her he was even *alive*. And too much had happened: the boy, his sister, James. Everything had been upended, and so much of it was her fault. What were her excuses? She bit her lip, as was her custom when she did not know what she should say.

"I like your suit," she said, immediately regretting it.

"Did you meet him?" Engales asked. He was zipping up his pants now, not looking at her.

"What?"

"Did you meet him? The boy?"

Lucy shook her foot. She shook her head. Then she nodded.

"Well?"

Lucy shook her head again. The lip biting was starting to hurt.

"Fucking say something!" Engales screamed. It echoed through the alley and out onto First Street. Two people walking on First Street turned their heads to look down the alley, then scurried away.

"What do you want me to say?" Lucy yelled back. Again, the sound rang off the graffitied walls and was followed by a long, silent moment. Lucy was breathing hard. She felt all her anger rise in her and her body felt hot and tense with adrenaline. "Do you want me to tell you I fucked someone else? Is that what you want me to say? I did, okay? But that's because you threw me out! You told me to go away! That you never wanted to see me again!"

Engales had his hand in his pocket, and his fingers were pushing down on the cloth, digging into his leg. He said nothing as Lucy went on.

"You don't think I feel terrible?" she yelled. "You don't think I wanted to help you? You don't think I cried myself to sleep every single night since you've been gone? But you *didn't tell me where you were, Raul.* You didn't even tell me if you were *okay.* So what was I supposed to do? The last thing you told me was that you *hated* me, remember? You told the nurses to ban me. And then you disappeared!"

"Have you considered for one second that this is not about you?" he said, seething.

She got quiet, looked at her boots, which she was using to scrape at the gravel. Then she looked up at him, straight in the eyes.

"I didn't know you had a sister," she said.

"Well, now you do," he said.

"Why didn't you tell me about her before, though?"

"Because I failed her," Engales said. "I abandoned her just like I abandoned you. That's what I do, Lucy. Don't you see that?"

"But you don't have to!" she pleaded. "I love you, Raul. So much! No matter what!"

"You don't even know what that means," he said coldly.

"Why are you so angry with me?" she said. "What did I do to you? Why do I make you so, so angry?"

"You know what you do to me?" He snarled. "You *need* me."

"Yes, I do need you!"

"But it's not just me. It's everyone. You need everyone because you have no idea how to need yourself. Or even how to *be* yourself."

Lucy looked confused and was shaking her head from side to side slightly. A wind came through the alleyway, and she pulled her jacket tighter.

"Don't you get it, Lucy? That boy is the only member of my entire family. He is the only person who has the same blood as me, the only person on this earth. And what do you do? Drop him off with the *person you're fucking.*"

He began to walk away from her, out of the alley and toward the street. She yelled after him. "That's not true! It's not! I swear that's not true!"

At the end of the alley he turned around. "*Go home, Lucy,*" he said, and it sped toward her like an arrow and brought her, with its sharp point, *down*.

The gravel dug into her knees as she fell to them. She would go home. She wouldn't let the city's lights steal what was left of her innocence, and she would go home and look for it in the grass. She would gather her childhood back out of the branches of the fir trees. She would find her silliness under a pile of old, out-of-style jeans. She would think of Raul Engales while drinking whiskey at a bonfire, and whenever she saw a man with a mole on his face. She'd think of James when she smoked cigarettes in secret on her parents' back porch: the feeling of bad pleasure. She would remember her first and only art project, Jacob Rey, when she saw the many faces of children who disappeared after him, immortalized and then thrown away on the sides of cartons of dairy. She would find Manhattan, often, right before she fell asleep: the honking of a horn, the way it opened and filled her, a blue balloon she'd seen drifting up through the skinny slice of sky between the skyscrapers. She'd hold the Big City to her chest, like a little golden locket that held something only she understood. She and a few others—red-lipped Jamie, loud-mouthed Arlene, maybe, and of course Engales, the original artist, the first one she'd ever loved. All of them were there, right up under her collarbone, lodged and safe.

Later still she would let them all fly away, like that blue balloon. She would untangle herself from the city's gray grip. She would become womanly in the hips and face. Her misdeeds would taper. She would work for Randall the lawyer, not Randy the bartender. She'd smile at a man from across a garden party, where light jazz music played; they'd have a child who couldn't say his R's. If he would have gotten to meet Raul, he would have called him *Owl*. She won't see Raul again, but she'll see his handsome photograph. Printed in a book she pulls from the Ketchum Library, called, simply, *Downtown, Volume II.*

See you soon, girlywog, she said now, through her tears, to the rat that had taken an interest in Jamie's purse. She had never given it back, though surely she had meant to.

At the gallery, the night began to descend in the way that shows do when all the free wine is gone, though there was still a case of it, visibly available under the drink table. Even so, people started tapping one another on the shoulder and listing the names of bars nearby. Four times, James heard the phrase, "I completely forgot to eat dinner," coming from the smarter dressed of the women and, in one case, an extra-short man in a fedora. James wanted to tell each of them that their hungry plight was not nuanced; "forgetting" to eat dinner was an urban norm. Did anyone, anywhere else in the country, even in the world, *forget* to eat dinner? Or was it just the New Yorkers who found themselves, after a night of looking at art, starving?

Sullenly he kissed them all good-bye. He didn't know them or care for them. A few of them he knew, and he didn't care for them still. Winona George, in leather pants that looked to have been applied with glue, announced: "Have to duck out of my own party, sadly, as I was not a good enough hostess to provide more than one olive per guest! But congratulations on an epic show, James. Phenomenal. Just phenomenal."

After Winona left and every painting's tag boasted a red dot and the solitary bowl of chips that Winona had set out was empty, James saw no point in keeping up appearances, and slumped to sitting against the back wall, next to the case of wine. He pulled out an open bottle, drank from it. He wanted only to go home, but his home did not want him. He stared at the painting on the wall in front of him. It was a giant blue square. If only life could be as simple as that, he thought.

Just a big blue square. But when he looked at it for long enough he began to remember all of the things that painting had once conjured for him: molasses, sand dunes, the feeling of holding hands. It was never that simple, he knew. On top of life, there was always more life.

He wanted to cry into the blue square. He wanted to call his mother, whom he had not talked to in close to two years, and tell her about his night. All of them sold, Mom, he would say. Each and every one of them. I've earned millions of dollars, Mom. Are you proud of me? Are you proud of your son? Of course she wouldn't be. Pride wasn't part of her emotional vocabulary. And why was he thinking of his mother? He never thought of his mother; it depressed him. His leg itched with what felt like a fly landing on it, but there was nothing. When he looked up, there were Marge and Julian.

He felt filled with emotion when he saw them walking across the room in their puffy coats, overcome with elation and thankfulness, and for one quick second, he thought he saw Marge's deep red. Or was it the memory of her red? He couldn't tell and it didn't matter. She had come! She had changed her mind and she had come! He didn't care if the red stayed or faded; it didn't matter. He didn't care that he had sold all of his paintings; it didn't matter. She mattered. She was the only thing that mattered.

But when she came closer, James saw the unmistakable signs that she had just been crying. Her gray eyes were glazed over, the lines around her mouth pronounced and shadowed.

He went to her. "You came," he said, putting his hands on her arms.

"Just quickly," she said.

"Why quickly?" he said. "There's wine."

"I see that," she said. "What, the rich people weren't thirsty?"

They both tried to laugh, failed.

"And don't you look like a big kid," James said to Julian. He rustled his hair. No response, of course—Julian had not spoken a single word to them since he arrived—but the fact that he was not crying was enough for the rustling of the hair to feel heart-wrenchingly intimate. He looked back up at Marge.

"What's the matter?" he said.

"I'm tired," she said.

"Me, too," he said.

"But I'm really tired," she said. "Of everything."

"You're tired of me."

"Yes, James. I'm tired of you."

"I know," he said. He looked down at Julian and gave him what he hoped was a kind look. His heart broke.

"I read your book," she said.

James's face tightened; Marge's red flared. *Stay there,* he willed the color, but he couldn't hold on to it, and it smudged away.

"What book?" he said.

"The pages in your study."

"That? Marge. Marge, you read *that?* That's just a bunch of crap I've been writing. Not a book. No, there's no book."

"There is," she said.

James couldn't bring himself to say anything more about what he had written: a document full of ramblings that Marge never should have read in the first place for all the sad, gross, probably poorly written truths it exposed. He remembered his very first review in *Art Forum*: Marge, kissing his white stomach, telling him: *It's ready, James. But are you?* Marge knew. She knew what things were. And her eyes were steady and perfect. And she was tired, and he did not want to tire her more. Instead, he wanted to take care of her. Rock her in safety. Give her things. Give her everything, because she deserved it.

"I sold it all," he said.

"I knew you would," she said.

"Are you proud?" he said.

"Extremely," she said. Then she bent in and hugged him. Into the collar of his shirt, she whispered: *"He's out."*

"Oh," James said. He put his hand on the back of her head. At the very *thought* of Raul Engales, his pupils flooded with blue. The paintings in the gallery sprung toward him: a rap song, the smell of late-spring gardens, the word *caesura*. Marge's red gathered and swelled around her, and his heart chimed and swung.

"He came to the house," Marge said, pulling away slightly, which felt like a window opening, letting in a gust of too-cold air. James wanted to hug her for always. "I saw him at the door," she said. "Through the glass. I couldn't bring myself to open it."

"Okay," said James, nodding.

"I need your help with this one."

"Okay," said James, continuing to nod as if the gesture would somehow bring him confidence, but the colors were swirling around him and Marge, and he wasn't quite sure what he was agreeing to, he just was. He was just agreeing. To Marge. To helping. To the colors. To all of this.

"Good night, James," she said. She blinked, then turned, then began to walk off, her little white triangle heels clacking on the smooth cement floors. The red that had occurred around her followed her like a cloud, and James noted something different about it . . . some multitudinous quality . . . was it . . . pomegranate? Was it, could it possibly be, the same seed-filled red she had embodied when she was pregnant last year? Could Marge possibly be . . . no, she couldn't leave him here now!

"Wait!" said James, uselessly. "Where are you going? Marge, Julian's here!"

"I trust you, James," he heard her say. She did not turn around. James watched his wife tuck out the door and disappear. His heart was somewhere near his ankles, pounding. He grabbed for Julian's hand just as the boy started to cry.

"Gonna close up soon!" yelled a fat security guard at the front entrance. "Everybody's gone!"

Everybody was gone. James's colors gradually faded again: fabric that had been out in the sun too long. The edges on everything blurred, but that was just the water gathering in his eyes.

Engales ran across the street and grabbed the security guard's giant arm. "Are you closing?" he said breathlessly. "I need to get back in." Upon closer inspection, Engales realized it was José, from the arts building at NYU.

"Hey, I know you," said José. "You're that fucker that is always sneaking in over at the school!

"You look different now, though," José was saying, looking Engales up and down. "Something change?"

Engales held up his arm. José said: "Oh, shit."

"That's right, *oh, shit*. Now would you mind letting me in there? It's important."

"Always trying to get into places you don't belong!" José said. "It's closed. No more show."

"José," Engales said, in Spanish now. "I lost my fucking hand. I have one person in my family, and he's inside. Let me in, José."

"Jesus," José said, holding his hands up. "Five minutes, then I'm going out drinking and finding a lady." He wagged his lips.

"Fine," Engales said, unamused. Would there have been a time when he would have given José a high five?

Where the room had been brightly lit and bubbly when he was here last, now many of the tracks of bulbs had been turned off, and there was only one rectangle of light toward the back of the room. In it, sitting against the wall in a row, were James and a little boy. James was petting the boy's hair in a way that was unflattering for both of them: Julian's hair was becoming matted to his forehead; James's face was growing bleak with desperation. Julian cried harder.

Engales went toward them, his nervousness eclipsed by intention.

He knew they couldn't see him; he was in the shadowy dark area. "It's okay, Juli," James was saying in his pandering, desperate James voice. Engales felt a proprietary pull—hearing that name aloud, his grand-father's name, a name that was so like Franca to have chosen—and here was James, uttering it in nickname form. He coughed, announc-ing himself.

"Holy shit, Raul! You scared me."

Engales ignored James now; he could see the little boy's face, splotchy with tears but already so familiar. The boy hiccupped from the last gulps of his crying. Small head, small body, small shoes, huge eyes. Franca's eyes. Franca's everything. James set him down on the floor. With a sudden, awkward movement Engales crouched down to the boy's level. He grabbed him by the arm with his good hand and the stump of his bad one. He searched him. The world stopped when he pulled the boy's small body tightly to his, wrapping his one arm around his tiny body. The world stopped when he smelled the wet crackers and warm milk and the laundry detergent everyone used in Argentina. He let go quickly and the world spun. The boy looked at him with his big Franca eyes. Engales felt stupid, like he shouldn't have hugged him. The boy would have no idea who he was, he would be frightened, probably—Engales flushed with shame. But then the boy said, through his hiccups, with his little mouse's mouth:

"Are you the Brother?"

It was the first thing he had said in weeks, and though Engales couldn't know this, he felt the weight of it, the newness of it: a voice that had been cooped up and preserved, until now. He looked to James for affirmation, or for something, but James just shrugged, his eyes also moist, his mouth pressed into a straight line. Engales realized that James had probably not understood what Julian had said—it was in Spanish—and that *he* was the only one who could. Because *he* was the brother. He was meant to be responsible now.

Suddenly everything became as clear as a freezing night sky. He was the brother. He was the brother who left the egg yolks to fry in the sun. He was the brother who left his sister at the tops of fire escapes, who wouldn't swim out to her if she were caught in the waves at Mar del Plata, who left her to the spineless men and the kidnappers, while he fled toward high ground. *He can't save you*, Engales had said to his sister about Pascal. But hadn't he meant it about himself? He was the brother who couldn't save his sister, and who would surely not be able to save her son.

He was the brother who *left*, just when he was supposed to stay.

His missing hand clenched and stung as he wheeled around to do what he had already done so many times before: beg New York City for an escape. Beg New York City for a chance in hell.

PORTRAIT OF THE MAN IN THE MIRROR

HAND: In the shop windows, you're a blur when you run away. The streaky reflection of the swinging arm: only one. The other, without the pendulum of the hand, stays tighter at the side, its arc narrowed permanently. The shop windows reflect the cadence of your heart. There's a beat missing, a lurching, a missing weight on one side, and you deserve this. You are an uneven man. A man who's leaned so far to one side and then fallen, away from everything that ever loved you.

MOUTH: One, two, three cups of whiskey, four, five, Mexican beers, six, seven in the morning, and you can't go home, oh no, you can't go home yet, because this is as close as you'll get to home in this city: the bar on Second Avenue with the neon clock in the corner that's never told the right time, not ever in its life, not even when you were younger, and you'd just arrived, and time mattered not at all anyway; you were just a boy. Now, there's your face, in the mirror behind the bar. It's heavy, dark, ancient. It's counting: an eyebrow twitch. One, two, three—he must be five or six years old by now, if your own clock is right, five years since you got that letter from your sister with her big news, five years since you'd refused to write back, five years lost and nothing gained, only a body full of alcohol and the sun's coming up already and there's your stupid face, all full of shame and that dumb mole, something you want to pry off with a bottle opener, to distract yourself from the pain with more of it.

ARM: Telemondo's for cigarettes, and there's Jean-Michel in the back of the store, buying the most expensive bottle of whatever he's buying; he's just had his first huge sale. Best to look away from the mirror of Jean-Michel, a mirror that had once reflected your own potential and now reflects your failure, your missing parts. Hold your arm behind you, so Jean-Michel doesn't see. When he does see, try to leave. When he holds you back, *let him*. Let him pull your sleeve up. Let him give you the only gift he's got: his goofy smile, so warm, then a scribble on what's left of your arm. *SAMO is dead*, he writes, blowing a stray dreadlock from his face. *Let him*. Let him tell you with his goofy smile that the world has not ended. That you haven't lost everything. That nothing is everything. That without things there are still more things. There are still the eyes of another human looking at you, seeing you. There is still writing on an arm. There are still things to take care of, things to be done, things to save. "Go get it," he says. And you have to, and you will.

EYES: Because they were just like yours, weren't they? The eyes of that little boy.

EPILOGUE

ONE HUNDRED PICTURES EVERY NIGHT

Julian can't find his pen and therefore cannot fall asleep. It's imaginary, he *knows*, but he also knows that knowing things doesn't always help. For example, his mother knows everything. So why the heck isn't she here?

This is the ceiling: red and blue lights, twisting, like a kaleidoscope he had tried out at the market back home. This is a kaleidoscope: you pick up the skinny pole and look into it and there will be a circle full of colored shapes that shift and spin when you move the pole around. His pen is hiding somewhere in his brain and his heart is clomping like a horse on the loose. His eyes are open as if toothpicks are holding them up.

This is the cat that Julian can hear crying outside: lost. Cats don't sound lost unless they're lost. He wishes there was a certain cry for boys to make when they were lost, but there isn't.

This is who's next to him on the bed: the Brother. It's the Brother from his mother's story, and Julian knows for sure because he did a quiz.

"If you're really the Brother," he had made sure to ask when the Brother came to pick him up that morning at James's house, "what color is our door at home?" "Red," the Brother had answered. Good. "If you're the Brother, what's my mom's favorite food?" "Butter." Good.

"You'll be spending Tuesdays and Thursdays and Sundays with me," the Brother had explained then, while the snow fell sadly behind him and on him, as if he didn't matter. "Mondays and Wednesdays and Fridays and Saturdays here."

"But those are all the days," Julian had said, standing in the doorway, watching one particular snowflake that had made a crash-landing into the Brother's black hair. They'd learned the days in school that year: each day went with a color, until the week made a rainbow.

"Yes they are," the Brother had said.

"What days does my mom have me?" Julian had said, though he feared he already knew the answer.

"No days," the Brother had said. "For now, no days."

Things his mother had not told him about the Brother: that he had a piece of pointy skin at the end of his arm that looked like a sea lion, that he had hairs on his chest, that he had a black spot on his face that might jump out at you, that he smelled like smoke, that he didn't look very magical at all; he had too many hairs on his face.

Things his mother had not told him in general: that she would have him for no days.

Now he doesn't want Tuesdays and Thursdays and Sundays. He doesn't want Mondays and Wednesdays and Fridays and Saturdays, either. If his mother has no days, that's what he wants: *no days*. He doesn't want this whale's back, heaving and black in front of him on the bed. The Brother in the bed with him is scary. He wants the Brother from the story.

This is the story: There were a brother and sister who loved each other as much as was humanly possible. The sister loved her little brother so much that every night, when he was asleep, she baked him a hundred cakes. The little brother thought the cakes just appeared there every morning, as if by magic, and though he loved them at first, he began to take them for granted. He stopped jumping for joy when he saw them. He stopped tasting every single one. He stopped grinning when he woke up to the smell of frosting.

At this part in the story, Julian would be panting with anticipation. He would always say the same thing. *"But it was his sister!"* he'd say. *"It wasn't magic, it was his sister!"*

"Shhhhh," his mother would say. "Let me finish the story. It was only when the little brother saw a fleck of batter on his sister's face one morning that he knew it had been her. His own sister, staying up through the night to make him the most beautiful cakes. He couldn't believe it. Meanwhile, his sister had become terribly sad, thinking her cakes were worthless."

"And so he wanted to give her something back!" Julian would nearly shout.

"Quiet now," his mother would say. "You'll wake your dad. Yes, he wanted to do something for his sister in return, to show her how much he loved her back. So he did what he did best. He began to draw."

"A hundred pictures every night!" Julian would say in a loud whisper, his eyes wide.

"A hundred pictures every night," she would say. "Pictures of all the people they knew. The butcher, the guy who owned Café Crocodile, the man who played the guitar in the park—everybody from around town, all their friends."

"And did the sister like the drawings?"

"Yes, she did, very much. She loved them. She hung them up all over the house."

"So why did the brother leave?"

"How do you know that the brother left? I haven't gotten to that part of the story yet."

"Because you told me the same story last night," Julian would say, grinning and burying his head in the sheets.

"Well tonight is a different night," his mother said. "What if I told you that the brother was still making pictures for his sister? Or that he never left at all?"

"Well, then, that would be a different story," Julian said.

"It would be," his mother said, with a wink.

"How would it end?"

"It wouldn't have to end," she said. "It would still be going. The brother would grow up to be a man, with a big voice. He was a magic man, you see, who could see into people's heads and hearts. And he would find a wife who was also magical, and they'd have a magic child, move into the house next door to his sister, who also had a child. Their two children would learn how to make cakes and make pictures, and they would stay up all night, making things for each other and then calling each other with tin cans from their bedroom windows."

"Tin cans?"

"Tin cans. With a string between them, to carry the vibrations, which turn into sound."

"But that's not the real story."

"How do you know?"

"Because the sister is you!"

His mom would ruffle his hair and smile. "And how do you know so much, little man? How on earth do you know so much?"

"I just *do* know," he would say, nestling his head in the place between her chest and her arm. And always: "If I draw one hundred pictures, can I be like the brother?"

"Sure," his mother would say. "But you'll have to do it in your head, because it's time for sleep. You can use your imaginary pen. Take it to bed with you. Draw up anything you want to dream about, anything you need."

Now: He wants to dream about her. He needs *her*. He needs her tea-kettle voice and her soft hair. He needs her cake smell and her lotion smell. He needs to go to the window and yell for her. But if he moves he might break the spell of the Brother's sleep. Plus, it's snowing out, and if he opened a window, some might get in.

A truck kabooms down the street outside, tossing Julian's heart into the air. He has to find his pen. Should he wake the Brother up? Could he? Or would the Brother yell? Would the Brother have a mean face on?

Julian's eyes land on something scary in the corner of the ceiling: something with wings, as big as a baby bird. It waits like an evil stain with two white eyes.

Wake him up, whispers the creature. Julian plugs his ears. He doesn't want the creature to talk to him.

I said wake him up, pea brain! says the creature. Julian scrunches up his nose, sits up, looks straight at the creature, whispers: *Okay! But be quiet or you'll wake him up yourself!*

With his littlest finger, Julian touches the Brother's shoulder. The Brother doesn't move. With his second littlest finger, he touches the Brother's bicep. Nothing. With his third littlest finger, he touches the very tip of the Brother's arm: the sea lion's nose. Suddenly the Brother jolts up in bed, swings his head from side to side, and lets out a gruff yelp.

Julian scrambles off the bed and onto the floor. He peeks his head just up over the mattress.

"What the hell?" the Brother says, his eyes bobbing with sleep. There is his mother, right there in the lightest parts of the Brother's eyes; what a relief.

"I mean, I'm sorry," says the Brother. Eyes up a little bit, just enough to see the Brother wiping at his forehead with his one hand. His face is lit up from only one side, where the kaleidoscope is coming in, and Julian can see the little hairs coming out of his chin, like a bad cactus.

"What's happening?" the Brother says. "Why are you waking me up?"

Julian stays put and stays silent. He wants to tell the Brother about the creature in the corner, but doesn't think he's allowed.

"Come back up here," the Brother says, patting the mattress and yawning. "Come on. I won't bite."

Slowly, Julian crawls back up to the bed. The Brother tugs on the cord of the lamp and a big circle of light swallows the Brother's side of the bed. Julian sticks his foot out into the light and wiggles his toes. Then he looks up at the creature, who he now sees looks like a brown butterfly.

"That's Max the Moth," the Brother says. "He's harmless."

Julian flashes his gaze away from Max and back to the Brother. He looks at the scary sea lion of the arm, its twisted nose.

"And this," says the Brother, "is my messed-up arm." He lifts the arm into the light and the sea lion's face looks less scary. A cakey line of black blood runs over it. "Do you want to touch it?"

Julian moves closer on the bed, touches the tip of the animal with his little fingertips. He looks at the Brother for confirmation. "It's okay," the Brother says. "It doesn't hurt."

With the boy's little fingers on his arm, Engales suddenly sees it differently. Like the hand is not a part of him but simply an object, something that exists in the world that he can observe and assess. He thinks of the Chinese woman's sagging cheek, of Señor Romano's massive stomach. He thinks of the little wart that poked out of Lucy's armpit, of the constellation of scars she had under her chin, from when she fell into a tree branch as a kid. For the first time since the accident, his own appendage, with its hideous scar, does not frighten him. Suddenly it's like all the other things he's ever found interesting. It's a scratch.

"Pretty ugly, huh?" the Brother says.

"Yeah," says Julian. "Looks like a sea lion face."

Engales laughs a little. "Now tell me," says the brother. "You can't sleep?"

Julian shakes his head.

"I know how you feel," the Brother says. "I couldn't sleep when I was a kid, either. Too much fun stuff to think about."

"And scary stuff," Julian says.

"And scary stuff," the Brother says.

With this, the Brother reaches for a bottle on the floor. Julian watches the arm without a hand as it raises into the air while he turns, like an airplane's wing. The Brother drinks from the bottle and the room smells bad.

"I couldn't find my pen," Julian says, in his smallest voice.

"Your pen?"

"Yes."

"Why do you want a pen in the middle of the night?"

"It's imaginary."

"Why do you want an imaginary pen in the middle of the night?"

"To draw a hundred pictures."

"You're a weird kid, you know that? Did your mother ever tell you you were a weird kid?"

Julian looks down at his hands.

"And why would you do that? Draw a hundred pictures?"

"It's what you do when you want someone to know you love them more than the rest of the things in the world combined."

Engales chuckles. The boy's eyes are so large and intense, and his little voice so serious, that the whole thing seems almost comical. But then there is Franca again, living in the little wrinkle between the boy's eyes: so serious, just like his sister.

"I see," Engales says. He scans the room. Tacked on the wall by the bed are two copies of the Jacob Rey flier, the one he'd gotten from the bearded man on the morning of the accident. Lucy must have tacked them up. But why? And why are there two? Engales pulls one down and flips it over, hands it to Julian. "There's some paper," he says. "Let's see if I have a pen."

While Engales searches for a pen, Julian flips the paper back over, looks at the picture of the little boy. "Who's this guy?" he says.

"It's a boy who's missing," Engales says distractedly, as he rummages unsuccessfully. No pen.

"If you can believe it, I don't have a pen, Julian. You know I'm not that good of a grown-up yet. But I have something else probably."

"But why is he missing?" Julian says.

Engales pushes himself up off the bed and gets to searching beneath it. The light doesn't reach underneath, so there is an expanse of black, probably a few mice, all his painting supplies. He feels the whiskey course through him as he paws the floor with his one hand.

"Because no one can find him. Here. Here are my old paints."

He plops the case that Señor Romano had given him so long ago onto the bed and a smooth wave of nostalgia breaks within him. He sets the case on the bed, opens its little gold lock.

"But is anybody going to find him, though?" asks Julian. His eyebrows scrunch in a pointy state of worry.

"Yes, someone is going to find him. In the meantime, you can draw on his back. Now look, you can use this brush here."

Engales pulls out a skinny red paintbrush and a tube of yellow paint. He sees Señor Romano's big face, his paisley tie, his wide, kind mouth. He is a boy again, sitting on the floor of his dead parents' room, painting the wrinkle in his sister's forehead over and over. *Hey, pea brain*, she'd say. *Do you need to do all the bad parts of my face?*

They're not the bad parts, he wants to say now. He wants to say other things, too. He wants to say everything.

He wants to tell Franca what happened to him at the gallery on the night of James's show: how his body had betrayed him, how he had not meant to leave Julian, but how once he had left he could not undo it, the leaving was part of him, something engrained in his body. He wants to tell her what happened at Telemondo's, how Jean-Michel had made him rethink everything, made him see there were still things to be saved. He wants to tell Franca everything, everything she's missed.

This is him saying everything: he squirts the yellow paint right into the lid of the box. "There you go," he says. "Start your pictures."

"But I don't want to put it on the boy's back because it might camouflage him and then people won't find him and he will still be missing forever."

"Well you sure are a picky one, aren't you? Okay. Hmm." Engales grabs one of the smaller of his old canvases, an unfinished painting of the Telemondo guy, smoking ten cigarettes at once. He sets it down in front of Julian.

Julian looks up at him with those huge Franca eyes. "But it is already full," the boy says.

"If you're going to stay with me," Engales says, "you're going to have to learn to live a little. I don't want this painting anymore, okay? Just go right over the top of it, like this." He holds his hand over the boy's and dips it into the paint. He feels the satisfying goopy grip of it, then the release as it presses into the grain of the canvas. A line emerges.

This is him saying everything: this line. This is him going back to Franca as she crouches over the eggs. This is him telling her: *The world is full of eggs. What do these eggs matter when the world is full of eggs?*

Julian looks up at Engales for approval. "Go on," he tells him, letting go of his hands now. "That's it. Nice. See, you know what you're doing! You don't need my help!"

Julian begins to draw a face over the Telemondo guy's face. He draws long hair and a big mouth. Eyes with dots in them. Circles at the cheeks. While he is drawing, he forgets about everything: the lost cat, the creature in the corner, even the Brother. He could just draw and draw. He could draw for a hundred hours. When he is finished, the Brother hands him another canvas, this time one with a lady in a fish hat on it.

"Who's this lady?" he says.

"Just some lady," the Brother says.

Julian draws his mother's face over the lady's face, and when he is done with that one, there are more. He draws and draws. If he draws enough, she will see them, he knows.

Engales sees her, his sister, coming to life around him. There is Franca in the bathtub when they were small, her tiny hands scooping water. There is Franca riding her bike in a bird-like way, her elbows flapping at her sides. There is Franca making a mud pie in the back-yard and serving it to him on a red plastic plate. There is Franca in her embroidered tunics with the stitches running around like ants on the fabric. Franca standing under their mother like a small version of their mother. Franca getting chased by a bigger girl down an alleyway off Calle Bolívar. Hitting the bigger girl with a stick to protect her and then feeling bad because he had hit a girl. Franca screaming that she hated him because he cut off a chunk of her hair in the middle of the night. Franca learning pastries from their grandfather. Franca not being patient enough for the pastries at first, wanting to run around outside. Franca growing breasts that first came out like little whipped-cream peaks and then became big round cakes that he hated. Knowing what Franca was thinking, even when it was private. Reading Franca's journal, even when it was private. Franca saying *tits*. Franca laughing. Franca moaning with Morales in their parents' room, how hearing her moans was like feeling his parents die again. Franca with a stomach, large and round, coming out of her like a watermelon. Franca in a blue coat, being thrown into the back of a Ford Falcon. Just one whoosh of the car's engine, and she was gone.

She is gone. But she is also here, in the room, smiling atop all of Engales's unfinished paintings. Franca had sent her son *here*. She had chosen *Raul*. She had trusted only the Brother to save her, and to save her son.

Suddenly Julian stands up on the bed in the middle of the pictures, which tilt a little bit when he walks over the mattress to the Brother.

He puts the Brother's head into the place where his arm meets his body. He puts his arms around the Brother's head and rocks the head.

"You're going to have to be quiet for this to work," Julian says.

"For what to work?" the Brother says.

"I'm stirring your head," says Julian.

"Okay . . ."

"And I'm going to tell you the story."

"What story?"

"I said you're going to have to be quiet."

"Lips are sealed."

"There were a brother and a sister who loved each other as much as infinity."

"How do you know such a big word?" the Brother says.

"I just *do* know," Julian says impatiently.

"Quiet," says the Brother. "Being quiet now."

Julian tells the whole thing. The cakes, the ESP, the drawings. The sister pinning the drawings up all over the house, because she loved them so much and she knew her brother had made them just for her.

"So why did the brother leave?" the Brother asks, just at the moment when you are supposed to ask that.

"How did you know the brother left?" Julian says. "I haven't gotten to that part of the story."

"Just a guess," says the Brother. Then the Brother pulls his head from the bowl of Julian's armpit and looks at Julian in the face. Engales wants to tell this boy everything he never told Franca, to make him feel good and safe. "You're a smart kid, Juli. Like your grandpa Braulio. You would have liked him. He had a funny nose. And you're a good artist, too." He pauses, takes the boy's face in his hand. "Did you know that?"

"Yeah. My mom tells me that all the time. And James told me."

The Brother smiles a little bit but still looks sad.

"Did you make these?" Julian asks.

"Yes, I did."

"You're a good artist, too."

The Brother laughs, and when he does the whole year floods through him—Times Square, Lucy on Jane Street, the squat and its demise, Winona's art horoscopes, James Bennett, this boy. Looking back on it, the year felt as distinct and tangible as one of Tehching's years: bound up tightly into one little bundle of time. He wonders how Tehching feels when the years are over, when he can start sleeping inside after being outside for 365 days, when he can stop waking up every hour to punch his time clock. Does he miss the project for what it provided? A structure inside of which to live a life? Does the ending of the project mean the stripping of some kind of shield? The year will end in just a couple days, Engales thinks. Winona will have her party, people will cheer and drink champagne, she'll whisper to each of them their art fortune for the New Year. What will his be? He thinks he has an idea. His chest feels light and his heart swollen and purposeful.

This is him picking up a paintbrush with his left hand. This is him dipping his brush into the paint. This is the sensual suck of the paint's resistance. This is the way it peaks on the brush. This is him painting for Franca.

The canvas in front of him is an unfinished portrait of Lucy. He erases her face with a yellow stroke. He hopes she's okay. He will call her to see if she's okay. He will take her to coffee at Binibon, say he's sorry. He will kiss her on the cheek. He will mix in the tiniest bit of blue.

"This is how you make real skin color," he tells Julian. "You add the tiniest bit of blue."

"No way," says Julian, who is still working diligently on painting out a fishmonger's neck with bright orange.

Engales laughs again. Here is a boy with Franca's big, funny eyes. Here is a boy who is learning how to be in the world, with the whole world in front of him. Here is a boy who wants to make a hundred pictures in one night. It is absurd. It is impossible. It is absurdly, impossibly beautiful. Here is an impossible, beautiful chance.

They spend the whole night finishing the pictures. They don't go to sleep. Engales helps Julian count, to make sure there are one hundred. When they are done, they look out at the room, which has brightened with smooth winter light. There are a hundred Francas. A hundred sisters and a hundred mothers.

They are tired. They have succeeded. Julian lifts up his hand.

"What's that for?" says the Brother.

"You're supposed to high-five me," Julian says. "James does it when I finish a picture. James loves art."

Engales smiles. *James does love art.* He thinks of how James will be here tomorrow at noon to pick up Julian, how James will look around this shitty apartment full of crudely rendered Francas and smile, and understand. Relief overcomes Engales, as if it is only now—when he imagines someone he loves loving it, seeing in it what he sees—that this room full of paintings can become beautiful, or valid, or real.

ACKNOWLEDGMENTS

This book began and ended with a Claudia—Bernardi, whose powerful teachings enlightened me to Argentina's history and sparked Franca's character into being; and Ballard, whose guidance, editorial vision, and belief in this project turned it from a dream into a reality. Thank you for being the strongest and smartest and steeliest of women.

My parents, Nikki Silva and Charles Prentiss, are not only my biggest inspiration but also my unfailing support system. Mom and Dad: your boundless creativity, intelligence, kindness, and love are the reason why this book (and everything else I've ever made or been) exists. I admire you completely.

My brothers and sisters—whole, half, in-law, and commune—are the very best humans I know. I am so grateful for the way you make me feel, think, and laugh.

To the commune and its members: thank you for the way you raised us, the many examples you set for us, the dinners you cooked for us, and for letting me take over the breakfast table when I needed to write. Thank you to my families: Silva, Prentiss, Bennett, Baer, Becker, Bauer, Pruitt, Lewinger, Beckman-Dorr, and Paul. Also: Davia Nelson, Jo Aribas, Bobby Andrus, and Sue Struck.

Thank you to the William Morris team and the Scout Press team, especially Alison Callahan, Jennifer Bergstrom, Louise Burke, Jennifer Robinson, Meagan Harris, and Nina Cordes, and to my publicist Kimberly Burns, for their crazy-hard work, collaboration, and willingness to take a chance on me.

Thank you to the institutions that have guided, educated, and supported me: Children's Alley, Gateway Elementary, Aptos High School, UCSB, the California College of the Arts, the Carville Annex, the Lower Manhattan Cultural Council, the Blue Mountain Center, and the Aspen Writer's Foundation. And special thanks to the teachers who have changed my life: Mary Jo and Jim Marshall, Diana Rothman, Lydia Parker, Mrs. Whitmore, Mr. Baer, Ms. Giroux, Mashey Bernstein, Michael Petracca, Tom Barbash, Daniel Alarcón, Miranda Mellis, Claire Chafee, and Cooley Windsor.

Sarah Fontaine and Melissa Seley: you have read this manuscript too many times to count, in all its iterations, year after year, and for this I am forever indebted to you. Without your two genius brains, this book would not be. And to the other friends who have read or edited all or sections of this book—Elena Schilder, Junior Clemons, Emily Jern-Miller, Dan Lichtenberg, and my many workshop and writing group mates—I appreciate you so much. Jessica Chrastil— thank you for your unflagging friendship, stellar emotional support, wacky mind, and lust for life. Carmen Winant, you were there for the birth of this and through it; you inspire me as an artist and a woman and a being and a friend. And to all my other friends who nurtured me while I trudged through this project, forgave me for missing beach days, and kept me sane with their humor and kindness—I thank the universe for you every day.

To my Bloomingdale's family, thank you for filling my days with bad puns and big laughs.

To the authors and artists whose books and poems and sentences and words and paintings and projects have influenced and guided me, thank you for your generosity.

And last but definitely not least, I would like to thank my soon-to-be-husband, Forrest Lewinger. You are the kindest, most curious man, and by far the best listener I've ever met. Thank you for your patience, your ideas, and your profound love.

He just wanted a decent book to read ...

Not too much to ask, is it? It was in 1935 when Allen Lane, Managing Director of Bodley Head Publishers, stood on a platform at Exeter railway station looking for something good to read on his journey back to London. His choice was limited to popular magazines and poor-quality paperbacks – the same choice faced every day by the vast majority of readers, few of whom could afford hardbacks. Lane's disappointment and subsequent anger at the range of books generally available led him to found a company – and change the world.

'We believed in the existence in this country of a vast reading public for intelligent books at a low price, and staked everything on it'
Sir Allen Lane, 1902–1970, founder of Penguin Books

The quality paperback had arrived – and not just in bookshops. Lane was adamant that his Penguins should appear in chain stores and tobacconists, and should cost no more than a packet of cigarettes.

Reading habits (and cigarette prices) have changed since 1935, but Penguin still believes in publishing the best books for everybody to enjoy. We still believe that good design costs no more than bad design, and we still believe that quality books published passionately and responsibly make the world a better place.

So wherever you see the little bird – whether it's on a piece of prize-winning literary fiction or a celebrity autobiography, political tour de force or historical masterpiece, a serial-killer thriller, reference book, world classic or a piece of pure escapism – you can bet that it represents the very best that the genre has to offer.

Whatever you like to read – trust Penguin.

read more
www.penguin.co.uk